Also by Judith Marks-White

Seducing Harry

Bachelor Degree

Judith Marks-White

Bachelor Degree

—— *a novel* ——

Ballantine Books New York

A Ballantine Books Trade Paperback Original

Published in the United States by Ballantine Books, an imprint of The Random House Publishing Group, a division of Random House, Inc., New York.

BALLANTINE and colophon are registered trademarks of Random House, Inc.

LIBRARY OF CONGRESS CATALOGING-IN-PUBLICATION DATA
Marks-White, Judith.
Bachelor degree : a novel / Judith Marks-White.
p. cm.
"A Ballantine Books trade paperback original"—T.p. verso
ISBN 978-0-345-49239-5 (trade pbk.)
1. Mothers and daughters—Fiction. 2. Rich people—Fiction.
3. Mate selection—Fiction. I. Title
PS3613.A7659B33 2008
813'.6—dc22   2008006179

Printed in the United States of America

www.ballantinebooks.com

2 4 6 8 9 7 5 3 1

Book design by Laurie Jewell

For my grandchildren,
Andrew and Caroline Dent,

the Dynamic Duo

Telling lies is a fault in a boy,
an art in a lover, an accomplishment
in a bachelor . . .

—*Helen Rowland*

ACKNOWLEDGMENTS

To the key players on this grand excursion:

Wendy Sherman, dream literary agent and constant source of my admiration and respect, who weaves her magic in the most extraordinary ways.

My editors at Random House/Ballantine, Charlotte Herscher, with whom I began the journey, and to the wise and wonderful Kate Collins, who joined me in the completion of *Bachelor Degree,* making it a joy ride.

My indispensible publicists: Cindy Murray and Jayne Gottschalk, who help make a book fly.

Signe Pike, who got the job done with quiet efficiency, and who was always cheerfully available whenever I needed her.

My husband, Mark, who shares firsthand the inside woes and wonderment of what writing a novel is all about.

My three special loves: my daughter, Elizabeth, and grandchildren, Andrew and Caroline Dent.

My best friend, the brilliant and intuitive, Ann Chernow, first reader and cracker of the whip.

Dr. Harold J. Goldfarb, cherished friend and expert on all things culinary and intoxicating.

Once again, to Mark Goad and the staff at "V"—my culinary writing refuge where the muse continues to take flight.

Dalma Heyn and Linda Legters, fellow authors and dear friends, with whom I trip the literary light fantastic.

Alan Bearman, my Parisian contact extraordinaire.

My dear friends and family, who, each in their own way, ignite my imagination on so many different levels.

To you all, I offer my deepest thanks.

Bachelor Degree

ONE

Marriage is an institution in
which a man loses his bachelor's degree
and the woman gets her master's.

—Anonymous

I remember the first time she said it. We were in a
taxi hurtling down Park Avenue on a steamy August afternoon.

"Boyfriend," my mother, Madeleine, was saying, not in
a mocking, judgmental tone of voice but matter-of-factly,
as though she could be referring to the weather or an item
on a menu. "Mark Robbins would make a very nice boyfriend, don't you think?"

I was applying mascara at the time. The taxi lurched,
and the brush slipped from my eyelashes onto my eyebrow,
extending my brow line all the way over to my right ear.

"*Boyfriend?* I don't quite picture Mark Robbins as boyfriend material."

"Oh, not for *you*, darling," my mother said, "for *me*."

And then I knew: My mother, Madeleine Krasner-Wolfe, had crossed over to the dark side.

I come from a long line of family members who are crazy, each in his or her own way.

"Not crazy," my mother said (who had begged me to refer to her on a first-name basis since I was three), "eccentric."

"Why can't I have a mother who's normal?" I had implored throughout my adolescence.

"Don't be ridiculous, Samantha. *Anyone* can have a normal mother. Eccentricity is so much more appealing. Someday you'll understand that."

But I could never adjust to the fact that when my friends' mothers were puttering about their kitchens, mine was lying on a table getting a bikini wax or sipping champagne in the middle of the afternoon.

On this particular Tuesday we were on our way to lunch, a pastime my mother considered an occasion, not because she loved to eat but because it allowed her to parade herself in front of the world in her latest fashion ensembles.

"It's so festive dining in restaurants," she said, "eating at home is absolutely dull."

My mother took daily living to new heights and considered Auntie Mame her fictional role model. She watched the film over and over, often quoting Rosalind Russell's famous line: "Life is a banquet, and most poor suckers are starving to death."

Fortunately, my mother could indulge her fancies because she was loaded. My father, her first husband, Henry Krasner, whom she professed to be the love of her life, had croaked at forty-five on the sixteenth hole at the Rock Ridge Country Club, leaving my mother with a gaping hole in her heart, along with a small fortune that Dad had made in disposable diapers for adults, and an art collection worth millions.

As we were leaving the cemetery, my mother told me through a barrage of tears sprinkling down the front of her black veil that she could finally live the life she was meant to lead.

"Your father was a wonderful man," she said, "but frugal was his middle name. He wouldn't part with a cent. Of course," she mused, "in the end that was probably a wise move, because now I won't have to be a bag lady."

That was certainly true. My mother was not one to make do. The only bags she paraded were designed by Gucci, Fendi, and Louis Vuitton. Cutting back was not something she could gracefully handle. And so, before my dad's body was even cold, she went out and bought herself a sporty little Mercedes SLK350 Roadster that she rationalized would help her through the grieving process.

Her accountant, Sheldon Glick, had assured my mother that she would be fine as long as she lived within reason.

"Within reason? What does that mean?" Madeleine had put down her lace-edged monogrammed hankie and stopped crying long enough to inquire.

"You're a rich woman," Sheldon had said. "But like most of us, unless we're Rockefellers, you need to be sensible."

Sensible to Madeleine was having enough dough to keep her in her Upper East Side apartment with Gilda, our housekeeper of thirty years; the summerhouse in Connecticut; and a monthly allowance that guaranteed she could continue living in the style to which she deserved to be accustomed.

"I'm not a woman who takes to change well," she'd said.

"Continue living as you are for now." Sheldon had reached over his desk and took her hand. "We'll revisit this subject in a few months."

"Yes," my mother had agreed. "After the ground settles, I'll be able to think more clearly."

Then she'd taken herself over to Per Se for lunch and drowned her sorrows in a couple of dirty martinis.

That was the one thing about my mother: She had style.

But the relationship I shared with my dad was unique. He was the role model for every man who would eventually come my way. In turn, I was the love of his life. He openly made his affections known, not only through the gifts that he showered upon me but with weekly dinners, just the two of us. From the time I was six, Tuesdays became our night. Although my mother often asked to tag along, Dad refused her entry into our exclusive club. This was our time alone, and no intruders, even my mother, were allowed to trespass on this ritualistic occasion.

Hundreds of such evenings punctuated my future. We began a tradition where these weekly jaunts allowed us to catch up on each other's lives. Not once did I ever remember him canceling our standing appointment. In that way, Tuesdays belonged only to us, and in that way, they became cherished moments.

When he died, that abruptly ended. Dad's death brought with it a sense of longing I had not yet been able to relinquish—a yearning for something that would never be the same again. I had accumulated a wealth of knowledge from our talks. I was privy to personal insights and private thoughts he enjoyed sharing only with me, mainly because my reactions to whatever he told me were spontaneous and deliciously secretive.

There were times I believed my mother was jealous, though she always brushed it aside by asking: "Whatever *do* you two have to talk about?"

"Everything and nothing," I would respond, hoping that would placate her, but it never did.

These dinners, my dad's and mine, provided a setting I could retreat to in ways that I never could with my mother; Tuesdays became some of my happiest times. While my relationship with my mother was close, it was my father who left an indelible imprint on my psyche. Without judgment, he gently guided me through childhood, adolescence, and young adulthood and served as my one-man support system and guardian of my soul. My mother, colorful though she was, exhibited her parenting in more outspoken, symbiotic ways that often put tension between us. As I evolved more into my own, she clung to me with an intensity that often felt smothering.

After my father's death, while my mother lapsed into grieving mode, I mourned his death in a less conspicuous way. In the days that followed, I kept hearing him call my name, which would stop me cold. After that, Tuesdays were never the same again.

Now, at thirty-eight, I lived alone on the opposite side of Central Park in a brownstone on West Eighty-fifth Street. Alone, that is until my first cousin Celeste Bleckner, a sophomore at Sarah Lawrence, decided to invite herself to spend the month of July with me. My mother had a hand in making the arrangements.

"You know I can't stand her," I said.

"Darling, it's the least you can do. Your aunt Elaine is my only sister. When she asked, what could I say?"

"No!" I said emphatically. "The last thing I need is Celeste following me around all summer. I'll have no privacy whatsoever. Why can't she stay at school? Bronxville is only a half hour from the city."

"Celeste wants to experience what city life is all about. It's only for a month," Madeleine said, holding firm. "And you do have that extra bedroom."

"You mean my office?"

"She can sleep on the pullout couch. It will make her happy, and it's good for family relations."

"It might have been nice to have had Celeste check with me first."

"She was afraid you'd say no."

"Well, she's got that right," I said.

"Sweetheart, do it for me." Madeleine played on my guilt. "Celeste looks up to you. You're her role model."

"You're the one with all the space, Mother. Why can't she stay with you? You have all those guest rooms just lying around with no one in them."

The blood drained from my mother's face. "Postmenopausal women don't have roommates," she said. "Anyway, she adores you.

Maybe you can help her get over her shyness with boys. You know, teach her the ropes."

But the only rope I was interested in was a noose to tie around Celeste's chubby neck. Finally, after much prodding, I acquiesced. It was too hard to fight my mother. Celeste moved in on the last day of June with her bunny slippers and five bottles of olive oil she used as both a moisturizer and hair conditioner.

Celeste had an edginess that couldn't be ignored. The elder of two daughters of Elaine and Philip Bleckner from Tenafly, New Jersey, Celeste, at twenty, was the less attractive of the two. Her nineteen-year-old sister, Fern, had no trouble attracting men, but she couldn't care less. Fern was rumored to be a lesbian who was having an affair with a girl she had met at Smith during freshman year. The family tried keeping this hush-hush.

"Even more reason to be compassionate," Madeleine said. "Poor Elaine is beside herself with grief that Fern might never give her grandchildren. At least with Celeste, there's still a chance. That's where you come in. Maybe you can find a suitable man for her."

"The men I know are much older."

"They might have younger brothers. You never know. At any rate, a month with you might be the best thing for her."

"And the worst for me," I said.

"Celeste will be a dream roommate," Madeleine added. "She'll never cramp your style or borrow your clothes. Maybe she can even shed a few pounds."

For years, Aunt Elaine had referred to her daughter as "pleasingly plump." At five-two and 160 pounds she was downright fat. On the plus side: She wouldn't be borrowing my clothes. The negative: She never dated and would be hanging around my apartment every evening. Celeste considered a night at home with a hot novel and a pint of ice cream about as good as it got.

One of the reasons that Madeleine was so adamant about her moving in was that Celeste adored my mother, and with Madeleine, flattery went a long way.

"Aunt Madeleine is the hottest woman I've ever seen. The

woman absolutely rocks. She's more like a girlfriend than a mom," Celeste said.

"Sometimes that can pose a problem," I said.

"I wish my mom were more like her. I mean, at sixty-two, Madeleine is *fab-u-lous*."

"I wouldn't go spreading that around," I said. "Madeleine doesn't exactly advertise her age."

"Her dirty little secret is safe with me," Celeste said.

The year she turned sixty, my mother gave herself a birth-day present of a face-lift, a tummy tuck, and breast implants just so people like Celeste would continue to use words like "hot" and "fab-u-lous" to describe her.

"And those drop-dead clothes. I'd kill for the shoes alone," Celeste said.

And so, on the Fourth of July, while fireworks exploded along the Hudson River, Celeste moved in for what was going to be a month of sheer hell.

When my mother stopped by a few days later to check up on things, she was sporting her latest pair of Manolo Blahniks and a lit-tle Donna Karan purse. I was so accustomed to her beauty, I had stopped being mesmerized years ago. It was only when Celeste raised my consciousness that I had to agree: For "a woman of a cer-tain age" Madeleine was sexy as hell.

I was not the only one who thought so. Grayson Wolfe, widower and one of the most prestigious art dealers in New York, agreed. They had met at an art opening. After only a few months of dating my mom, he asked her to marry him.

That same month I was hired by Alexandra Cole, owner of the Cole Gallery on Madison Avenue, to run her gallery. Alexandra en-trusted me to handle all affairs when she was away in Europe on her frequent "business" trips; really, she was screwing her head off with a Frenchman named Jean-Luc. While Alexandra and Jean-Luc fucked their way through Europe, I was still looking for my Mr. Right. In the meantime, my mother had found hers.

After Grayson proposed, Mom and I went to the Four Seasons,

where, in the Pool Room under a canopy of trees, she told me she was considering accepting his offer. The five-carat yellow diamond from Harry Winston had clinched the deal.

"Granted, he's not your father," she said, "but he's got a lot going for him."

What my mother meant was that Grayson had inherited his family's wealth and wanted nothing more than to lavish it upon her. His two sons, grown and married, were themselves highly successful. Pierce, fifty, owned a thriving orthopedic practice and lived with his wife and two boys in Atlanta. Hillard, fifty-three, a recently divorced real estate attorney from Austin, Texas, specialized in clients with big bucks. Each had become a millionaire by the time he was forty.

"Grayson even agreed to sell his apartment and move into mine," my mother said. "You know how I detest moving."

"The man is a relic. He's as old as Methuselah."

"He's pushing seventy-five, but he's very spry. Don't let his age fool you. He's a tiger in the bedroom."

Grayson Wolfe might have been many things, but an animal between the sheets was hard to imagine.

"And let's not forget his seat on the stock exchange," my mother boasted, "and his board positions at the American Museum of Natural History and Memorial Sloan-Kettering. Grayson is one of the most eligible bachelors in New York."

"For the geriatric set, maybe."

"Not to mention he has season tickets to the opera, first tier."

"You detest opera, Mother."

"That may be true, darling, but I adore dressing up."

That June Madeleine and Grayson tied the knot at a small gathering at the Carlyle. She wore a virginal white Valentino and a Vera Wang veil adhered to her head by a clip of white orchids. Grayson took one look at his blushing bride, and an erection appeared right though his Armani tuxedo pants, helped along by the Viagra he had popped minutes before saying "I do."

* * *

For three years Madeleine and Grayson lived in marital bliss. Between my father's money and Grayson's fortune, my mother was having the time of her life running between the Westport house and Grayson's home in Millbrook, New York, where he kept two polo ponies and his Lamborghini, used only for recreational riding. In between, he and my mother sailed the Atlantic, flew to Paris twice, toured the Greek Islands, and rented a villa in Tuscany for two months.

The night they returned home from Italy, Grayson complained of chest pains, blamed it on the airplane food, and dropped dead three hours later on the new Suri rug for which Madeleine had spent a bundle. Two days later, she gave the rug to Goodwill and buried Grayson Wolfe under a cherry tree at Green Willow Cemetery, where the elite meet in the afterlife.

Madeleine Krasner-Wolfe was a widow once again, only this time the word "filthy" preceded "rich." Between the money of Henry Krasner and Grayson Wolfe, the world was her oyster.

"Life moves in strange and unexpected ways," Sheldon Glick told Madeleine when they were going over Grayson's will. "You're a woman of substance."

Then he tacked another thousand on to her bill.

"I'm a woman alone . . . again," Madeleine sobbed. To cheer herself up, she went over to Tiffany and splurged on a little trinket.

During the weeks after Grayson's death, my mother formed an abnormal attachment to me. She invited me to lunch daily.

On Tuesday morning, she called the gallery at ten.

"Mother, I'm a working woman, remember? I don't have time to go to lunch every day."

"That's completely uncivilized, Samantha, not to mention nutritionally unsound. I'll pick you up in a taxi, and we'll grab a bite at Sarabeth's."

"Not today, Mom, I can't. It's crazy in the gallery. A new artist is coming in, and I have to be here."

"What new artist?" Madeleine switched gears, moving from the culinary to the creative.

"Blake Hamilton, the new rising star. He's one of the exciting neo-expressionists. Very hot on the scene."

Silence on the other end.

"Blake Hamilton? The British artist?" she said.

"You know him?"

"Not personally, but I follow him. That article in *The Observer* sang his praises. I've been admiring his work for several years. Maybe I can pop in. What time is he arriving?"

"That's totally inappropriate, Mother. Anyway, I'll be busy meeting with him. You wouldn't even get to see him."

"I'll just come to browse," Madeleine said. "Another interested party looking to buy some art."

"Absolutely not."

"Don't be absurd. Your gallery isn't off-limits. I'm sure he'd be thrilled to know he has a huge fan who's considering buying one of his pieces."

"His pieces start at thirty thousand."

"As I said, I'm just browsing."

And so it went until I told my mother to leave me alone and let me do my thing.

"Fine, fine, I get the hint, but I had another thought: Maybe you, I, and Blake can all do lunch together."

"That's it, Mother," I said. I slammed down the phone.

Not one to be rebuffed, my mother appeared at eleven-thirty at the gallery, dressed in her latest Barneys acquisition: a beige pant-suit and a straw hat with a brown grosgrain ribbon. I scowled when I saw her. "For God's sake, I told you not to come. I'm expecting Blake any minute."

"I just want to sneak a peek," she said. "I promise I'll behave."

Moments later, a vision of male pulchritude appeared, carrying a burgundy leather artist's portfolio. He was dressed casually in gray pants and a navy blazer. A striped blue and white shirt hung out just enough to make him look hot rather than disheveled. Around his neck was a red silk scarf. A pair of loafers with red socks completed the look. He was drop-dead gorgeous.

Madeleine, pretending to survey the paintings, turned around and smiled. Blake smiled back. Without batting an eye, she walked over to him. "I do believe you're Blake Hamilton," she said.

"In the flesh, although I must admit the flesh is melting as we speak. It's a scorcher out there." Each word was enunciated in a charming English accent.

"Yes, I practically fainted on my way over here. Manhattan in July is brutal."

"Hello," I jumped in, "I'm Samantha Krasner. It's a pleasure to meet you."

"And I'm Madeleine Krasner-Wolfe," Madeleine said, "Samantha's mother."

Blake paused, looking my mother up and down. Next came the predictable response. "Her *mother*? That's quite impossible. You just couldn't be."

My mother blushed. "It's lovely meeting you," she said. "I often come in to peruse the latest work. My late husband, Grayson Wolfe, was a major collector."

"You were married to Grayson Wolfe?"

"Yes, you've heard of him?"

"*Heard* of him. The man was pure genius. I believe he was solely responsible for the success of my friend Ross Duval."

Madeleine swooped in closer. "Yes, of course. We own a Duval. It's hanging in the study. It's one of my favorite paintings."

There was no stopping her now. My mother was charming the pants off Blake, while he, in turn, was undressing her with his eyes. It was a meeting made in hell.

"I hate to interrupt," I said, "but I need to speak with you, Blake. Mother, if you'll excuse us"—I shot her a look—"we have work to do."

"That doesn't mean we can't pick this conversation up later," Blake said, holding her gaze. "I'd love to take you for a drink, Mrs. Wolfe."

"And I would love for you to do that," Madeleine said.

"Let's say five o'clock at the Mark. Is that good for you?" Blake turned back at me as though he had misplaced something and came back to find it. "Oh, and Samantha, I hope you'll be joining us, too."

"Sorry," I said. "I won't be leaving the gallery until late tonight. But thanks anyway."

As far back as I could remember, I had lived in my mother's shadow, and though a high-styled and well-coiffed shadow it was, I never felt I owned my life. Finally, after two years of therapy and becoming a junior partner at the Cole Gallery, I had started to emerge.

Junior, according to Alexandra Cole, was a prerequisite to associate partner. She promised me that come the end of the year, we would "evaluate the situation."

Much in the same way, my mother was the CEO in charge of my life—a position I was no longer willing to accept. Add to that the fact that she thought nothing of insinuating herself in my life socially, much to my chagrin.

"I'm doing it for you, darling," she whispered on her way out. "I'll get the scoop on Blake and let you know if he's as good as he looks."

"I'm quite capable of interviewing my own men," I snapped back.

"Can't you just let me play my motherly role?"

"You're being intrusive, Mother."

"It's just a drink, for God's sake," she said.

• • •

At five o'clock, Blake was tucked away at a small table in the plush Mark bar when Madeleine arrived. He stood up and offered her a seat next to him. "This calls for champagne," he said. "Your lovely daughter took eight of my paintings. I consider it a real coup to be showing at the Cole Gallery."

"The Cole is fortunate to have you," Madeleine countered. "You are, after all, one of the hottest 'artistes' in London."

"I've been lucky."

"Believe me, it takes more than luck." Madeleine helped herself to some nuts from the silver bowl. "You're young and talented. Exactly how old are you?"

"I'll be turning forty in August."

"Oh, the same month as Samantha. You're practically twins. She'll be thirty-nine on August twenty-fourth. If my husband, Grayson, were alive"—she lowered her eyes in a moment of reverie—"he would have snatched you up. Grayson had an eye for the authentic. Today it's all about glitz over substance, and who you know. Your work is won-der-ful-ly expressive."

"I've always had a love of art. Since I was a kid, I've been splashing paint on canvas. Who knew it would amount to anything except some colorful blotches?"

"Obviously *someone* knew," Madeleine said. "That piece in *Art in America* was wonderful. I've been following you for a couple of years."

"You read the magazines and reviews?"

"Never miss them," Madeleine lied. "Grayson, of course, subscribed to every one. The art world was our life—that is, until he passed on only four months ago."

"If I may be so bold"—Blake inched in closer—"you're a very young-looking widow. I'm so sorry for your loss. Your husband was well respected in the industry."

"Twice widowed," Madeleine corrected. "I lost Samantha's father ten years ago." She removed her favorite prop—the monogrammed hankie from her Nancy Gonzalez bag—and dabbed the corner of her eyes, wiping away a nonexistent tear. "It *has* been difficult. If it weren't for my friends and my lovely daughter, I couldn't carry on."

Madeleine, not one for understatement, piled it on while she and Blake sipped champagne, forming an admiration society of two until, two hours later, she looked at her watch. "Oh my God, is it seven o'clock *already*?"

"I never noticed," Blake said. "Do you have dinner plans?"

"Some leftover cold poached salmon that my housekeeper made."

"Well, that just won't do. Would you consider being my guest for dinner this evening?"

Madeleine perked up. "I'd be simply delighted."

"Perhaps Samantha could join us after she leaves the gallery."

"Samantha has other plans," she said without missing a beat, "maybe some other time."

"I'll look forward to that. In the meantime, do you have a favorite restaurant in mind?"

"I'll leave it to you," Madeleine said, adding, "but I never say no to sushi. Let me call Asiate. My husband and I dined there regularly. Chef Noriyuki Sugie adored Grayson. I think we can get in."

"A woman after my own heart," Blake said.

Indeed, Grayson's reputation had preceded him. The finest restaurants in Manhattan had welcomed him with open arms. One mention of his name, and at eight o'clock they were at the Mandarin Oriental Hotel and seated at a table at Asiate by eight forty-five. A view of Central Park added to the ambiance.

"Have you ever dined here before?" Madeleine asked.

"Too rich for my blood," Blake said, laughing, "but tonight's different. As I said, I'm celebrating my entry to the Cole Gallery."

"My treat. After all, it was my suggestion to come here," Madeleine said.

"I won't hear of it," Blake said. "I'm a hot 'artiste,' remember? What else would I be doing tonight except attending those boring parties? You saved me, and now I'm indebted to you."

"Parties?"

"Only two of them tonight, thank God. Last night four. I'm being wooed by two gallery owners."

"I would expect nothing less."

"My first choice was the Cole Gallery. It has more clout than all of the others put together."

Every time Blake opened his mouth, Madeleine practically swooned. His English accent only added to his already handsome face and boyish charm. Madeleine was having too much fun to worry about small incidentals like robbing the cradle. In the middle of her grilled ahi tuna with Thai basil pesto and Blake's lobster sukiyaki with black mussels and clams, Blake suddenly suggested, "After we leave here, let's go down to Chelsea. There's no reason you can't accompany me to one of those 'anyone who's anyone will be there' parties."

"Really? They wouldn't mind?"

"Nobody cares. The loft will be teeming with people. I should make an appearance just to keep my foot in the door. Sometimes reviewers show up. It's a real scene as you know. I'm sure you and Grayson attended many of them. I go just to stay in the groove."

"Yes, I've been to parties," Madeleine said, "but never with the artist of the moment on my arm."

"Then you'll say yes?"

"Love to."

Madeleine picked up her sake while Blake picked up the check. "Here's to life's most enchanting moments," she said.

Back at home, I imagined my mother sitting over drinks and trying to impress Blake. Since Grayson had died, she'd been acting more peculiar than usual, but zeroing in on her latest hot artist was pushing things a bit too far. She was playing her role as the merry widow to the hilt, but when it started to infringe on my territory, some rules needed to be established.

My mother, of course, never considered her behavior inappropriate in any situation. She even went so far as to think that I would be happy she was getting out and having some fun—even if it was with a man who was by all rights more in my league than hers. Then again, there was no stopping Madeleine Krasner-Wolfe. When she wanted something, she went after it without any thought to protocol or propriety.

TWO

Bachelors, like detergents, work fast
and leave no rings.

—*Rich Bossmund*

Madeleine had been to her share of art openings and afterparties, but always with Grayson and never with a handsome young star of the moment who drenched her with compliments and made her feel half her age. She was lapping up every moment as she and Blake taxied down to Chelsea.

The loft on Tenth Avenue belonged to Sonia and Stanley Eberhardt. It was, as Blake had predicted, buzzing with artsy types in fashions that defied imagination. Some familiar faces punctuated the scene, including the poet Marsh

Hopps and his companion, Gordon Starr, whose handbags were legendary and sold in all major department stores from the East to West coasts. Artists of repute paraded about or hovered around the chrome and glass table, dipping into the baked Brie and pouring wine into plastic cups. Stanley Eberhardt, who had acquired his wealth buying art, and whom Grayson had considered a first-class phony, welcomed them with open arms. Sonia, standing by his side, gushed.

"I didn't know you knew *our* Blake?" she said, slurring her words ever so slightly.

"We just met today," Blake jumped in. "I'm showing at her daughter's gallery."

"Well, not exactly my *daughter's* gallery," Madeleine said.

"Samantha is in charge of putting artists like me on the map."

"Nonsense," Stanley said. "You've already gained a reputation in London. I understand that you've caused quite a stir among the Brits."

"How wonderful for us that you've decided to grace New York with your work. Next stop, the Guggenheim," Sonia chirped, not missing an opportunity to reach over and touch Blake.

A blond beauty who looked liked she survived solely on lettuce leaves suddenly appeared, wearing lime lipstick and a long black jersey over black tights. "Tell me I'm not seeing things," the blonde said, staring at Blake. "Is this who I think it is, or are my eyes deceiving me?"

"Darling." Sonia took her arm. "I'd like you to meet our dear, dear friend Blake Hamilton. Blake, this is Geneva Moss, an artist in her own right."

"In her own right" meant that Geneva once had a piece in the Grey Art Gallery at New York University. It hung there for a month and was considered an atrocity by those in the know.

"Very nice to meet you." Blake extended his hand. "And this is Madeleine Krasner-Wolfe."

"Hi," Geneva said, instantly turning away from Madeleine and back to Blake. "I absolutely *worship* your work. You're amazing."

Gloria Reed, owner of the Casey Campbell Gallery, came running over from the other side of the room. "You rat." She kissed Blake on either cheek. "I heard you're not going to be gracing us with your canvases."

"Word travels fast," Blake said. "That's correct. I was lured into the Cole by Samantha Krasner, daughter of Madeleine Krasner-Wolfe here, whom I'd like you to meet."

"We've met before," Gloria said to Madeleine. "I knew your late husband. May I offer my deepest condolences on his recent passing?"

"Thank you," Madeleine said, stuffing a chunk of Gouda in her mouth.

For the next half hour they milled about, shaking hands with the rich and famous and those aspiring to become the rich and famous, until Blake leaned over and whispered to Madeleine: "Have you had enough? Because I certainly have. Let's blow this joint."

"I thought you'd never ask," Madeleine said.

"I'm staying at the Elysee on Fifty-fourth. What do you say we have a nightcap at the Monkey Bar before ending the evening?"

Madeleine's excitement clearly couldn't be contained. Since Grayson's death, her sense of boredom had been palpable, until today—when Blake Hamilton stepped in and she knew he was the perfect man for her daughter. "My dear," she said, "I would love having a nightcap with you, but I'm curious: With all these beauties on your tail, surely you can have your pick of the socialite litter. Why me?"

Blake took her hand and looked deeply into her eyes. "Because, Madeleine Krasner-Wolfe, you're far sexier and more fun than any one of these bimbos. And in case you didn't know, I'm absolutely gaga over older women."

"Old enough to be your mother, I might add, but perfect for my daughter."

"Why can't I have you both?" Blake winked with no sense of impropriety.

"Oh, Blake, you're such a devil," Madeleine said.

• • •

"Mother," I said to Madeleine on her cell phone, "where are you? I've been trying to reach you for hours."

"Can't talk, darling. I'm with Blake. We're on our way to the Monkey Bar."

"You're not serious."

"You bet I am, and might I add, I haven't had this much fun in years."

Blake, seated on her right, and ever the perfect gentleman, gestured. "Have Samantha meet us if she'd like."

Madeleine covered the phone with her hand. "Not on your life," she whispered to Blake. "Samantha, I'll call you in the morning."

"Mother, don't hang up. This is ridiculous. The man is young enough to be your son."

"We already covered that. Look, I've really got to go. What is it you wanted, anyway?"

"I wanted to know what you were up to. How drinks went."

"Beyond your wildest imagination."

"You sound guilty."

"Guilty? Hell, I'm as guilty as sin and loving every minute."

"Tell Samantha she has a most charming mother," Blake broke in.

"I heard that. Are you sober, Mother?"

"I'm flying high, and you're starting to break up."

"I don't believe that for a second," I said.

"Tomorrow, sweetheart, we'll meet for lunch, and I'll fill you in on everything."

"I'm working tomorrow."

"Then I guess you'll never know."

"All right," I conceded. "I'll meet you at one at Jackson Hole."

"Jackson Hole is for the Dalton mothers. Let's have a real lunch. I'm feeling festive. Meet me at Caffe Grazie on Eighty-fourth. Their crab cake salad is divine."

"I think you should go back and see Dr. Milman," I said.

"I don't need a shrink. I have all the therapy I want right here."

After they'd had two B&B's on the rocks apiece, Madeleine said good night to Blake and thanked him for a lovely evening.

I tried brushing my mother's behavior off as bereavement therapy but was furious that she had trespassed where no mother should dare to go. We needed to talk, which was why I agreed to drop everything and meet her for lunch.

I was at Caffe Grazie at exactly one o'clock. Madeleine was already waiting and sipping a glass of white wine.

"You are one piece of work, Mother."

"You look upset. Here, let's get you a glass of wine." Madeleine offered her glass.

"I don't want a drink. I want to talk."

"About what?" Madeleine assumed an innocent stance.

"Are you kidding me or what? I just left Blake Hamilton."

"And?"

"And after we got through with business and planning his show in December, he asked me out."

"How lovely."

"How could a guy who spent an entire evening sucking up to my mother have the gall to ask out her daughter?"

"It was hardly like that. He's completely harmless. We talked about you all night. I am your best spokeswoman, after all."

"You're not running a dating service, Mother. I saw the way he looked at you when you came to the gallery—which, by the way, I asked you not to do. He was practically salivating."

"Stop being so dramatic. He's an artist, for God's sake. Artists are free spirits, and Blake is no exception. So, you were saying he asked you out."

"Yes."

"When?"

"He's in town until Monday night. He wants to have dinner tonight," I said.

"I hope you accepted."

"Of course I accepted. He's a client."

"That's what I told him," Madeleine said.

"Okay, now I need a glass of wine."

"Good, a little wine in the middle of the day is very beneficial to the complexion."

The waiter appeared. I ordered a pinot grigio. "I just want to know one thing, Mother."

"Anything, baby. I have no secrets."

"Tell me that nothing happened between the two of you."

"What are you talking about?"

"You know what I mean."

"Oh, don't be so crude. You don't think I would sleep with a man young enough to be my son, do you?"

"There, you admitted it. He *is* too young for you."

"Of course he's too young. But he's perfect for you."

"I *do* like him."

"Where are you going for dinner?"

"He told me to choose a place with atmosphere, something on the water, if possible. I made a reservation at the Water Club. I thought he'd like that."

"A little commercial, but romantic in a touristy kind of way."

"Don't you think he's great, Mom?"

"Not only that, I think he's smart and surprisingly unassuming. He's not full of himself, like so many of those art hotties are. I had a most lovely time last evening. We went to Asiate."

"So I heard."

"Then he whisked me off to the Eberhardts' loft."

"Grayson hated the Eberhardts. What did they say when they saw you with Blake?"

"Stanley Eberhardt's eyes practically bugged out of his head, and Sonia was too drunk to care."

The menu was presented. Madeleine zeroed in on the crab cakes, while I settled on the goat cheese omelet.

"Sweetheart, an omelet? How boring. Why don't you have some fish or perhaps, the crab. Be adventurous."

"That seems to be *your* job, Mother," I said.

By the end of the meal, which we topped off with a plate of biscotti and some fresh berries, we put the subject to rest and resumed our respective roles of mother and daughter, chatting away about what I should wear to dinner.

"I was thinking maybe my floral Chloé and my red Jil Sander shoes," I said.

"Don't forget the makeup," Madeleine said. "You look as pale as a cadaver."

"Blake seems to like the way I look," I said.

"All I'm saying is that a little blush wouldn't hurt."

"Maybe you'd like to come along and supervise, Mother?"

Madeleine just rolled her eyes and thought how wonderful it would be if Blake Hamilton married her daughter.

THREE

A bachelor is a guy who never makes
the same mistake once.

—*Wentworth Dillon,
Fourth Earl of Roscommon*

"This is like some terrible cliché," I said that same
night at the Water Club.

"Meaning?" Blake asked, sipping his glass of Domaines
Ott, the popular French rosé.

"The up-and-coming London-bred artist comes to New
York, gets assigned to the Cole Gallery, meets the gallery assistant and her mother, and invites them both to dinner . . .
independently."

"You find that a cliché?"

"I find it rather remarkable." And deplorable I wanted
to tell him, but held back.

"I find it perfectly plausible."

"I've been warned about men like you."

"Not from your mother," Blake said, an irresistible smirk on his face. "She really digs me."

"Oh, and conceited, too."

What I really wanted to tell him was that he sounded like a pompous ass.

"When you get to know me better, you won't say that."

"*Will* I be getting to know you better?" Presumptuous, too, I thought.

"We *are* sharing the same gallery. In fact, I'm indebted to you."

"I like that."

"Most women do."

"I'll bet there are lots of them, too," I said.

I was beginning to get fed up with the light banter that was bordering on annoying, yet I couldn't deny that his sex appeal was getting to me.

"Are you usually this direct?" he asked.

"Only with handsome artist types. They keep me on my toes."

"Exactly where you should be," Blake said. "By the way, I really *am* indebted to you. The Cole Gallery isn't the easiest place to break in to."

"You do happen to be talented, in case you haven't noticed. I'll go so far as to say you're about to burst loose on the New York art scene."

"You really think so, and I'm not being coy."

"Of course you're being coy, but I'll let you in on a secret. When Alexandra heard you were coming in this week, she called me from Paris and told me to book you immediately. Alexandra is crazy about your work."

"I spoke with her on the phone months ago," Blake said. "She told me then that she'd be in Europe when I was in New York and that I'd be in very capable hands with you. But she's not half as charming as you."

"You met her, then?"

"A few years ago in London. She came to my show."

"Alexandra is an international beauty. She was married to Harrison Cole before they divorced," I said.

"How old would you say she is?"

"Pushing fifty. That should appeal to you," I said.

"Ah, the sarcasm again. Please have another sip of wine."

"I see: the get-the-girl-slightly-inebriated ruse. I'm onto men like you."

"Men like me?"

"Handsome, suave, predictable."

"Oh, so I'm predictable?"

"Most men are."

I was afraid that Blake might fall into that category of men who wooed their prey, knocked them dead with his charm, and then sucked the lifeblood from them.

"Well, then," Blake said, diverting our banter to a more serious note, "I'll have to do everything in my power to prove you wrong."

"That will be a challenge."

"I adore challenges, especially where attractive women are concerned."

"Are you deliberately flattering me?"

"Just telling the truth. What's wrong with a little flattery? 'It's like chewing gum. Enjoy it, but don't swallow it.' The cartoonist Hank Ketcham said that."

"Oh God, and you quote, too? You see, you *are* predictable."

"And *you're* irresistibly charming," Blake said. "And I'm starved. Let's take a look at the menu."

Blake and I scanned the offerings, each one a culinary treat. Our waiter, the consummate professional, handled us with genuine care, suggesting that at least one of us try the coriander-scented tuna with sautéed watercress. I opted for that, while Blake couldn't pass up the Dover sole.

"We Londoners are suckers for Dover sole," he said. "Even when we're in New York." He poured the last remaining bit of wine into my glass.

"As it is, I'm very tipsy," I said. "Any more might push me over the edge."

"We wouldn't want that to happen, now, would we?" Another bottle of Perrier Jouët was quickly ordered.

There was no denying that Blake Hamilton was dreamy. He was also a one-size-fits-all type, appealing to women from their twenties right into the postmenopausal set. I could understand how my mother had been captivated. Then again, Madeleine Krasner-Wolfe was never known for being a shrinking violet. If she wanted something, she went after it and usually got it. This time my goal was to snag Blake for me, and I was living vicariously on that thought alone.

But I had to admit my protective shell was cracking. At the same time, I didn't want to become another object of Blake's desire that he could manipulate and discard at will.

"European men are different," he said when we touched on the subject. "I never think about age. I'm more interested in a woman's qualities. I was seeing a Swiss woman for about two months. She was a stunning blonde with an even more stunning IQ. The fact that she was pushing fifty-five never bothered me. I never thought about it."

"You would sleep with a fifty-five-year-old woman?"

"My dear, let me tell you something. Some of the best sex I've had has been with older women. They're more experienced, and they don't have as many hang-ups as the adolescent set."

"Are you referring to me as adolescent?"

Blake chuckled. "You're practically an embryo."

Even his laugh was tinged with an English accent. I was falling hard.

After we left the Water Club, sated from our delicious dinner and visually quenched by the view of the East River at dusk, we taxied up to the East Side and back to his usual stomping grounds: the Elysee.

"How do you like this hotel?"

"It's intimate and stylish," he said. "A lot of tradition here. I'll bet you didn't know that Tennessee Williams died here."

"Really? I trust that housekeeping took care of that."

"That's not all. Back in her heyday, Tallulah Bankhead drank here, and it's where many literary legends made their home. It's oozing history. Up on the second floor is a charming lounge where we can have a nightcap."

"Sounds wonderful," I said. "Let's do it." I was filled with trepidation but was too excited and curious to pass up the moment.

"Of course, if you'd prefer, I'd be happy to show you my room," he said.

"I bet you would. I'll opt for the lounge."

We walked up the lobby staircase leading to the second floor, Blake's arm secured around my waist. A part of me wanted to turn back and end the evening now, but I seemed to be guided by some internal force that clutched me in its tight grip.

"You smell delicious," he said.

"L'air du Temps. It's my favorite."

"Subtle though sexy, just like you."

"Thank you," I said, acutely aware that here was a man who could easily get a woman to fall hard if she wasn't careful.

"No, thank *you* for taking that remark seriously, because I meant it. You *are* sexy."

"As sexy as my mother?" My biggest fear was suddenly verbalized.

"You just can't resist plying me with questions, can you?"

"No." I giggled, and with that, Blake stopped halfway up the stairs and kissed me passionately. It was without question the best kiss I ever had.

"I've wanted to do that all night," he said.

After two White Russians apiece, Blake reluctantly took me home. It was almost one o'clock when I opened the door of my apartment. Much to my chagrin, Celeste had waited up to catch a glimpse at "the artist," as she referred to him. She was in her terry-cloth bathrobe, holding a copy of *Jane Eyre* and eating a Ring Ding.

"Oh, hi, Sam, I was just about to go to bed."

"Right," I said. "This is Blake Hamilton. Blake, my cousin Celeste Bleckner."

As Blake extended his arm to shake Celeste's chocolate-stained hand, her eyes seemed glazed over by the sudden appearance of this male answer to all her dreams. Subtlety was not one of Celeste's strong suits. I was infuriated to find her there.

"Oh my God, *the* Blake Hamilton," she said.

"Nice to meet you," he said.

"I am sooo in love with your work. Your painting *Woman in the Glass House* absolutely blew me away."

"Thank you. Where did you see it?"

"In *Smithsonian,* when they ran that piece on you back in March."

Shut up, I wanted to tell her.

"So you didn't see the real thing?" Blake asked.

"I wish. No, but it was a great print."

I rolled my eyes, wishing their little dialogue would end.

"If I had thirty thousand dollars at my disposal, I would have bought it," Celeste went on.

"Lucky for you, it's already sold."

"Wow," Celeste said. "Double wow. Imagine paying thirty thousand dollars for a painting. Maybe someday I'll be able to afford that. When I do, yours will be the first piece I'll buy."

I could hardly stand it. "See you in the morning, Celeste," I hinted. "Blake and I were just saying good night."

The top of Celeste's robe fell open ever so slightly, allowing her left breast to escape. Blake looked and then drew his eyes away. I gestured to her to pull herself together. It was a moment so awkward that I found myself wondering how I had ever agreed to allow Celeste into my life, and what Blake must be thinking.

"I should be going, then," he said, pulling me into the outside hall, shutting the door behind us.

"I am *so* sorry," I said. "Celeste is a real piece of work."

"I was afraid she was going to disrobe right there in front of us," Blake said.

"Given the chance, she would. Celeste never dates. Even worse, she's as horny as hell and doesn't know it. Food is her outlet."

"Hence the Ring Dings." Blake pushed me against the wall, kissing me again. "How long have you two been living in cohabitual bliss?" he asked between kisses.

"Too long," I said, kissing him back. "She's here for a month."

"If you'll pardon the expression, that girl needs to be fabulously fucked."

"And you're just the one to do it, eh?"

"Not if she were the last living female left in the world, but I will tell you something—"

"Shh," I said, placing my hand over Blake's full and luscious lips, "don't say it."

There was enough talk between us. What I wanted was more kisses.

"Don't say what?" he asked.

"You know what."

"I think you have a fantastically dirty mind."

"I do."

"Just the way I like you."

With that, Blake moved his hands along the top of my dress, lightly brushing my breasts. I nearly gasped at his touch.

"Sorry," I said, "Celeste already gave you your thrill of the evening. Only one breast a night."

"Well, there's always next time," he said.

"When will that be?"

"You tell me. I'm still here for a few days. How about dinner tomorrow?"

"Should I play hard to get and tell you I'm busy?"

The rational part of me knew I should do exactly that.

"Definitely not, and if you *are* busy, I demand that you cancel your date."

"Happy to oblige, sir," I said, which, under normal circumstances, I would never consider. But Blake was hard to resist.

"I'll call you in the morning, and we'll set up a time and place. And Samantha . . ."

"Yes?"

"I think I need to kiss you again."

There in the dark hallway, he gave me a kiss that radiated through my entire body, all the way down to my toes.

When I walked back inside, Celeste was sitting on the couch, waiting.

"I can't believe you just spent the night with Blake Hamilton," she said. "That man is totally movie-star material."

"And I can't believe you were waiting up with your boobs hanging out."

"Was I? It wasn't intentional."

"Don't hand me that crap. You were coming on to *my* date. I think it's time you started dating your own guys, Celeste."

"God knows I try. I just never meet any eligible men."

"Try harder, and if you don't mind, please keep your bathrobe closed when I bring my dates home. Better yet, stay in your room. I deserve some privacy."

"I was just grabbing a quick glance. I wanted to see for myself what *the* Blake Hamilton was all about."

"You're worse than Madeleine," I said. "And all that talk about his paintings. What was that about?"

"If I had the moolla, I *would* buy one of his paintings. God! Blake Hamilton was standing here in our apartment. I mean, can you stand it?"

"I think we need to lay some ground rules," I said.

"Such as?"

"Such as, eavesdropping is off-limits."

"I wasn't eavesdropping, Sam. But come on, it isn't every day we have famous people hanging around our pad."

"I'm going to bed. And Celeste . . ."

"What?"

"You need to get laid."

"That's what my vibrator is for," she said.

FOUR

Bachelor: A person who believes in life, liberty,
and the happiness of pursuit.

—*Anonymous*

Bright and much too early the next morning, my
mother called. I picked up in a sleepy stupor.

"Tell me everything, and don't spare a word," she
said.

"Mother, it's not even nine o'clock. I went to bed after
two A.M."

"Does that mean what I think it means?"

"What would that be?" I detested her bluntness.

"Samantha, be honest: Did you sleep with Blake Hamilton, and if so, how was it?"

I shuddered. "Why can't you *ever* be normal, Mother?"

"And why can't *you* ever call me Madeleine? It would make me feel so much younger."

"I'm the daughter, you're the mother, remember, Mom?"

"Now tell me everything."

I tried brushing her off: "We ate. We talked. I had fun."

"That's it? Are you seeing him again?"

"I am. Tonight." I felt like the good little girl who was doing exactly what was expected.

"I knew it. Was I right or was I right when I said he'd find you appealing?"

"You were right." I continued the charade, wishing my mother would leave me alone. Every time she opened her mouth, I regressed another year.

"I'm absolutely walking on air—for *you,* I mean."

"Can't you find your own man? You're worse than Celeste."

"I'm still in mourning," my mother said. "I'm not out in the world yet."

"What do you call the other evening with Blake?"

"A woman occasionally needs a male companion to get her over the hump."

"Now that you had your brief 'hump,' maybe you can let me have mine."

"Samantha, you might want to keep in mind that it was I who suggested Blake call you for a date."

"Thank you, but I'm quite capable of handling my own social life. I don't need any favors from you in the men department."

"You should be glad you have a mother who cares."

"I'm most appreciative. Now, if you don't mind, I want to go back to sleep for a few more hours. I'm exhausted."

"Sounds like you had a very busy night, Samantha."

"You'll never know, Mother."

"Madeleine," she barked back.

• • •

Just as I fell back asleep, Blake called.

"I didn't stop thinking about you all night. Are you awake?"

"I am," I said.

"No, you're not. I can hear that silky, sleepy voice, but I don't care. I needed to hear you."

"Apparently, my mother did, too. She just called to check in."

"To see if I passed the test? How did you tell her I rated?"

"B-plus," I said, smiling.

"What? Not A?"

"A connotes perfection. Are you perfect?"

"Absolutely."

"B-plus," I reiterated.

"We'll have to work on upgrading me. How does One if by Land sound?"

"That's an upgrade right there. I adore that place."

"I knew you would, and wear something sexy. You were too covered up last night. A bit of décolleté is definitely called for."

"I have just the dress in mind."

"I can't wait. I've been thinking about painting you."

"In my dress?"

"In the buff, or don't nice girls like you go in for that sort of thing?"

"Could happen," I egged him on. "But I'll turn into an abstract painting no matter what I wear. That's your thing."

"I would love doing a portrait of you. How does eight o'clock sound?"

"For a portrait?"

"For dinner. Do you know that I even dreamed about you last night? I take that as a very good sign."

"Sign of what?"

"That you've worked your way into my head . . . and heart."

"Hold that thought," I said. "I'll see you later."

"I'm getting hard just thinking about it," Blake said.

"Too much information," I chanted back.

As much as I wanted to nip it in the bud and not become embroiled in a love affair with my client, I had invested an entire evening with him and wanted more. I had never dated any of my artists before, but Blake drew me in, and I found him irresistible. Up until now, men like Blake had been exactly the types I shied away from, for fear of getting hurt, but his smoothness and easygoing manner were reassuring and comforting. In some strange way that I didn't fully understand myself, I was willing to take a chance and let myself go.

Things were looking up. Fortunately for me, Celeste was leaving town this afternoon to join a college friend in East Hampton for a few days. I would have the entire apartment to myself. That alone was cause for celebration. I tried going back to sleep, but I was too excited by Blake's phone call to even close my eyes.

I thought about Blake kissing me in the hallway last evening. I imagined him making love to me, his hands exploring every inch of my body. I made myself come. I must have gasped loudly because a few minutes later, Celeste knocked on my bedroom door.

"Everything all right in there?"

"Yes," I shouted back. "I just bumped into a chair by accident. I knocked my knee."

"Ouch," she said. "That can hurt. Are you sure you're okay? You were moaning."

"The pain is exquisite," I said.

I called my best friend, Lily Ann, to see if we could have lunch together. She had just returned from California, where she was visiting her bicoastal boyfriend. We needed to catch up after not talking for a week.

"Oh my God, Sam. I was just this second thinking about you. How *are* you? Have you gotten into any trouble while I was away?"

"Loads. You'll never guess who I went out with last night."

"I knew it. One week away, and the whole world changes. Fill me in."

"How about brunch at Popover Café?"

"Give me forty-five minutes."

"You got it."

"And Sam, you'd better not leave out a single word."

"You sound just like my mother," I said.

L ily Ann Kahn and I had been friends for what seemed like for-ever. We'd gone to Brearley together and, later, to Bennington, where she majored in English and I in visual arts. Lily Ann had a cushy job as editor of Buttercup Press, a small boutique publishing company that had an elite clientele of children's book illustrators and writers, among them Bennett Verlaine. Lily Ann and Bennett had lived together since they met three years ago. Recently, he'd moved to Los Angeles, where he was offered an even better job as managing editor of a new kids' magazine. That didn't stop them. Twice a month Lily Ann boarded a plane for California, and every other weekend Bennett came to New York. He had given her an en-gagement ring just before he moved, although any mention of set-ting a date never came up.

"I'll give him until Christmas," Lily Ann said. "If he doesn't set the date by then, that's it. In the meantime, it's kind of fun. Bi-coastal has its perks. When we're together, we spend every minute in bed."

"Why ruin it by getting married?" I asked her.

"I don't know. I love him. It seems like the thing to do."

"Don't let conventionality get in the way of good sex," I said.

Lily Ann was tall, wiry, and gorgeous, a natural redhead with a to-die-for figure.

"Now, that's what I call a girl with the perfect body," my mother once said. "Lily Ann Kahn never experienced a homely day in her life. And that hair. Women would kill for hair like that." A pause en route to her next remark. "You know, Samantha, you would look stunning as a redhead. You might want to think about it. Mousy brown doesn't exactly win you points."

"Thank you, Mother, but I like my hair. My hair is one of my main attributes."

"Your hair is fine, darling. I'm just saying—"

"Please—don't say."

"I'm just saying that hair like Lily Ann's can stop traffic. She never had trouble getting men. She knows how to make the most out of what she's got."

If murdering mothers were legal, mine would have croaked years ago.

Popover Café, a New York institution on Amsterdam Avenue, was bustling with brunchgoers. Lily Ann, lucky to get seated so quickly, was sipping a glass of freshly squeezed orange juice when I arrived.

"You look great," I said.

"That's what happens when you don't get out of bed for seventy-two hours. And you, I might add, look exceptionally agreeable."

"That's what happens," I parroted, "when you go out with men like Blake Hamilton."

"Blake Hamilton, the artist who has every woman in London lusting after him?"

"His sex appeal now extends beyond the Atlantic. Even my mother is getting into the act."

"Madeleine is a pistol. Tell me everything."

While I sat there downing a Popover Flopover, the café's famous egg-baked pancake, Lily Ann nibbled away on a Mad Russian sandwich. I regaled her with the events.

"Only *your* mother," Lily Ann said. "Just don't tell me they slept together."

"Of course not. Madeleine's outrageous, but I doubt she'd go that far. She's grooming him for me."

"Yeah, that sounds like Madeleine. She's been doing that for years."

"All I know is that the next day, when Blake came back to discuss the nitty-gritty details of his show in December, he asked me out, too. The rest is history."

"You like him?"

"Like him? I'm completely unglued. After the first kiss, I was ready to move to London, get married, and have his children. And the worst part? He seems to be into me, too."

"Worst part?"

"Blake Hamilton is out of my league."

"How so?"

"I'm supposed to hire artists, not *date* them. This guy can have all the women he wants."

"Obviously. So?"

"So why me?"

"He likes your big brown eyes?"

"He also likes the Cole Gallery. Let's face it: It's a big deal to show there."

"You think he's using you to get ahead?"

"The thought crossed my mind."

"Or could it be that the guy has excellent taste?"

"In galleries?"

"In women, you dope," Lily Ann said.

"I'm seeing him again tonight. He's taking me to One if by Land."

"Excellent choice. Must mean he wants to get into your panties."

"I certainly hope so. The guy is amazing: brains and beauty. But I usually spend the first three dates playing hard to get."

"Don't wait too long, sweetie, he might not be in town much longer."

"Who's waiting? I plan on losing my virginity tonight."

We clicked coffee cups. "To becoming deflowered . . . yet again," Lily Ann said.

FIVE

New York is all about sex.
People getting it, people trying to get it, people who
can't get it. No wonder the city never sleeps.
It's too busy trying to get laid.

—Carrie Bradshaw, *Sex and the City*

The dress I chose to wear to dinner was a low-cut, short, and sassy Marchesa in varying shades of black, white, and gray. It hugged my body in all the right places. My legs were accentuated by a pair of Prada metallic sandals with a hint-of-sequins strap winding around my ankles and up to my calves. I looked hot, if I do say so myself, so much so that when Blake arrived to pick me up, he actually whistled.

"That's a dangerous dress. I didn't know they allowed women like you on the streets of New York. You might cause an accident."

"That's why you're here: to protect me."

"Oh, baby, I'd like to do more than protect you," he said.

On the taxi ride over to the restaurant, Blake could hardly keep his hands off me. "Maybe we should have skipped dinner," he whispered in my ear.

"I'm a sucker for romance," I said, "followed by loads of foreplay."

One if by Land, Two if by Sea on Barrow Street was the Disneyland of foreplay. The ambience alone was orgasmic. Once Aaron Burr's carriage house, it now had the reputation of being one of the most sumptuous dining establishments in New York. Here, among bouquets of flowers dripping from all corners, candlelight, and a piano that tinkled throughout the night, couples professed their undying love.

Blake and I were seated at a cozy corner table under a canopy of bulbous cabbage roses. The martinis, considered the best in the city, arrived minutes after Blake's request. I took one sip and felt a rush.

"You look dazzling in the candlelight." Blake took my hand and brought it to his lips.

"You certainly have perfected the right facade for an artist of acclaim."

"My dear, underneath that so-called facade is just another regular guy, as you American types call us."

"Trust me," I said, "there's nothing regular guy about you—thank God. That's reserved for American men."

"You don't like American men?"

"Sure, they're fine, a bit full of themselves. At least the ones I met."

"Don't let the English accent fool you. I'm full of myself, too. But what I'd really like, Sam, is to be full of you."

"Why, Blake," I said coyly, "we haven't even had dinner."

And so it went. We bantered our way through the appetizer—the trio of caviar for two—preparing the way for what and whom were yet to come.

"You do know that I am starting to fall for you, don't you?" Blake asked.

"And you do know that you have black fish eggs between your teeth?" I retorted.

Blake grabbed a napkin, brushing it along his teeth and removing all traces of the caviar. "Better?"

"I would have preferred licking it off."

"Do you usually talk like that? Are you always this sexy?" he asked.

"I don't know. Am I?"

"I sure would love to find out."

I took his hand and drew it beneath the table, rubbing it gently along my leg. He took my lead, moving his hand higher. Just as he reached my inner thigh, I pulled his hand away.

"Was that you being a tease?" he asked.

"Just a prelude of things to come."

"I'm a sucker for preludes," he said.

"And I'm a sucker for sexy men with black caviar on their teeth," I said.

Being with Blake was better than any romance novel. It was one of the best dates I'd had in years. He was easygoing, funny, and sexy as hell. No wonder Madeleine was smitten. He took his recent success in stride, seeming almost surprised at his rising stardom. However, having him as a client was one thing, but falling hard was something else. My emotions were being yanked in several directions. I wanted nothing more than to let go and be in the moment. Yet in only three more days, he would be back in London with an ocean separating us. I thought of Lily Ann and Bennett. If they could make long-distance work, maybe Blake and I could, too. But I was jumping the gun. This was only our second date, and I was already envisioning us a couple. Too fast, too soon, I thought. I need to calm down—pace myself. I also knew that once I slept with Blake, any hope of playing it cool would fly out the window.

The waiter interrupted my reverie. The appetizer plates were cleared to make way for our entrees. I had chosen the spice-rubbed yellowfin tuna with fresh corn fondue. Blake had chosen the Australian rack of lamb accompanied by a fricassee of spring vegetables and fava-bean puree. A bottle of Beaujolais was a lovely accompaniment to both the meat and fish. We were off to a good start.

There is nothing like a leisurely, romantic dinner that spreads out into the evening to entice a woman into bed. By the time we left the restaurant, I was ready to experience the very best of Blake Hamilton and his repertoire of artistic achievements.

While he was trying to lure me back to his hotel, a voice message from my mother kicked in to my cell.

"It can wait," I said. "It's my mother."

"Maybe it's important."

Not as important as having you inside me, I wanted to say.

"Damn! She knows it's Saturday night and that I'm out for the evening."

"Just check in," Blake said. "Maybe there's a problem."

"Undoubtedly."

Blake's concern was annoyingly appealing, but to appease him I called my mother back.

She picked up on the first ring. "I've fallen. I'm on the floor."

"A bad fall?"

"Is there any other kind?"

"Did you break anything?"

"Yes, my Steuben swan."

"I mean your body, Mother. Any broken bones?"

"How should I know? I'm not an orthopedist. I twisted my ankle when I tripped."

"Tripped on what?"

"The needlepoint footstool. The one I made for your father years ago. I knew I should have taken up knitting instead."

"Can you move your ankle, Mother?"

"I don't even want to try. I might jiggle something."

Then came the obligatory question. "Would you like me to come over?" I asked.

"Would you, darling?" Her voice perked up.

"If you think it's necessary, I will. I'm with Blake."

"Wonderful. It's always good to have a man aboard in such situations."

"Blake isn't a doctor."

"No, but he's a good morale booster. Yes, come over, and we'll have a nightcap together."

"I thought you were on the floor."

"I am, but Gilda is here. She can serve drinks."

"Why can't Gilda stay with you while you call the doctor?"

"*Doctor?* It's Saturday night. The only doctors on Saturday night are emergency room interns. Anyway, it's probably just a mild sprain."

"Can you get up?"

"I could probably hobble over to a chair."

"Tell her not to move," Blake interjected. "It might cause more of a problem."

"Stay right where you are," I said. "We're on our way."

"Where are you?"

"We're just leaving One if by Land."

"I *adore* their chocolate soufflé."

"I'm not bringing you a chocolate soufflé, Mother."

"Who's asking?" she said.

By the time we reached my mother's apartment on Park and Seventy-sixth she was sitting up in a chair wrapped in her favorite silk flowered Ferragamo shawl she had bought in Italy. She was sipping a glass of port, served to her on a small silver tray by Gilda, who by now was practically hysterical.

"Your mother," Gilda said between gasps, "could have been killed."

"Fortunately, she seems very much alive," I said.

"And that beautiful glass piece." Gilda clapped her hands together. "Mr. Krasner bought it for her, and now it's gone. Beyond repair."

"It's only an art object," I consoled. "Nothing that can't be replaced."

"Steuben doesn't make glass swans anymore," Madeleine chimed in.

"How do you feel?"

"Like a broken woman."

"Let me take a look at that ankle," Blake said. "I'll be gentle."

Willingly, my mother extended her leg, allowing her robe to ride up just a tad more than necessary, exposing her still-gorgeous gams.

Blake held her foot in his hand. "It's a little swollen, but not too bad. Can you move the ankle at all?"

"I can try."

"Very carefully. Just enough to give it some slight tension. Nothing too vehement."

"Will you keep holding my leg?" Even in her compromised state, my mother never missed an opportunity to flirt.

"I won't let go, I promise. Good," Blake said. "It doesn't appear to be broken."

"Maybe a doctor should look at it," I said.

"Let's see how it is tomorrow. I can always call Grayson's son, Pierce Wolfe, and see what he says."

"Pierce lives in Atlanta, Mother. I can take you over to Lenox Hill."

"More port, Gilda," my mother yelled out. "That's what I need. A little libation should cure my ills." She relaxed. "It's so nice to see you again, Blake." She smiled at him widely, lowering her voice. "I didn't want you to leave town without saying good-bye."

"I wouldn't have, but I would have preferred more salubrious circumstances."

"I'm feeling better already. You obviously have a marvelous effect on ankles."

"Especially ones as graceful as yours," he said right on cue.

. . .

Blake stayed until my mother was safely in bed. I walked him to the door.

"I didn't expect the evening to turn out like this," I said.

"It looks like the only woman I'm bedding down tonight is your mother." Then he got serious. "You probably should stay over. I'm sure she'll feel more comfortable with you here."

"Are you always this good a son?"

"Mothers and animals love me. I'll call you tomorrow, and we'll take it from there," he said, giving me a good-night kiss I would keep with me until morning.

I kissed him back. "I'm starting to find it hard to let you go."

"It's only for a few hours," he said. "Then, if you'll allow me, I'm going to make mad, passionate love to you."

"Oh, Blake." I batted my lashes. "You do say the nicest things."

The next morning, with both Gilda and me assisting her, my mother shuffled into the Lenox Hill emergency room. After an hour's wait due to emergencies of a more serious nature, X-ray findings were confirmed: My mother had done more damage to her Steuben swan than to her ankle.

"I could have broken my neck," she squawked.

"Luckily, you didn't," I said. "The doctor said it was only a minor sprain."

"You mean that infant in the green scrubs? That was no doctor. That was an intern passing himself off as an orthopedist."

"He's a third-year resident, Mom. He told you to rest for a few days and you'll be as good as new."

"Fine. I'll rest at brunch. Let's go to Café des Artistes. I adore their Bloody Marys."

"I think the doctor wanted you to go straight home and get into bed."

"What? And stare at four walls all day? That's not my style. No, thank you. I can recuperate just as easily over a couple of drinks."

The fact was that Madeleine's four walls had the same wrap-around view of Central Park for which most hotels charged obscene amounts of money. Yet, she took her slivers of scenery for granted. Not wanting to argue after putting Gilda in a taxi and popping two Advils (for my headache, not my mother's ankle), I called the restaurant and was told there might be a wait.

"It's for Madeleine Krasner-Wolfe," I said. "She turned her ankle and must be seated immediately."

The maître d' gushed into the phone. "Ah, a table for Mrs. Krasner-Wolfe, of course. Come right over."

I had to hand it to my mother: When it came to reservations, she was never turned away.

"I make it a practice to tip well and give little Christmas presents to the maître d's all over the city," she said. "Remember that, Samantha: 'Grease the palms of others, and you'll always have a table at any restaurant you want.' That was Grayson's motto."

Madeleine often quoted Grayson's little bons mots.

"Now, darling, you'll tell me all about your evening with Blake."

"Nothing to tell. We spent most of it with you."

"Don't be ridiculous. What about One if by Land?"

"Divine, as always."

As was her usual style, my mother proceeded to question me about every nuance of the menu choices. Her claim to fame was that she was up on which restaurants served what and could talk menus ad infinitum. Because dining out had been a hobby of hers and Grayson's, she could rattle off chefs' names and the dishes for which they were famous.

And so, with food on Madeleine's mind, we taxied over to Café des Artistes and slid into a banquette under a mural of a tree nymph in the buff, while the maître d' scurried over with a pillow for my mother's sprained ankle, an injury she was going to milk for all it was worth.

∙ ∙ ∙

Madeleine was obsessed with her favorite subject: Madeleine Krasner-Wolfe. She adored talking about herself.

"It's so refreshing being with a younger man," she told me over her second Bloody Mary. "That's because they live in the now. They're not preoccupied with their impending demise. I'm sick and tired of discussing Medicare and trusses. I adore men who are in their prime. The geriatric crowd even smells different."

"Whatever are you saying, Mother?"

"Take Blake," she said, biting into her waffle. "He has an aroma of peppermint and soap."

"Must be his aftershave."

"What I'm saying, Samantha, is that after one dinner with Blake, I came alive. He did more for me than my daily dose of Wellbutrin ever could."

"I was kind of hoping to have Blake all to myself. Not to share him with, of all people, my mother."

"Maybe Blake has a friend," Madeleine mused. "The next time he's in town, we can double-date."

"That's just what he needs: supplying eligible bachelors for my mother."

"Oh, don't go getting all pissy, darling. I'm only teasing. For your information, I think for a woman of a certain age, I'm holding my own quite nicely, thank you. Why wouldn't I attract a younger man?"

"You're stunning, Mother," I agreed. "But why can't you stick with men your own age? My God, you were attracted to Grayson . . . remember?"

"That was then. This is now. Between you and me, I'm tired of looking at men whose asses jiggle. Every time Grayson emerged from the shower and dropped his towel, my libido took a nosedive. I had to close my eyes so as not to vomit. I'm turning over a new leaf: From here on out, it's single men with baby faces and tight tushes who don't have sexual meltdowns when their penile prescriptions fail them."

"So, Samantha Krasner knows how to cook."

"Not just how to cook—how to create a meal fit for the gods. You'll be so knocked out by my culinary efforts that you just might find me totally irresistible. One taste of my pasta puttanesca, and I can't be responsible for what might happen."

"I'll come prepared," he said, tossing out one of his seductive double entendres.

"Prepared?"

"I'll bring the wine. Whatever were you thinking?"

Promptly at eight o'clock, Blake stood at the door of my apartment, laden with a bouquet of flowers and two bottles of Barolo, which I accepted graciously as he kissed me lightly on the lips.

While we stood in my small kitchen with barely enough room for the two of us, he uncorked one of the bottles.

"The Italians call Barolo 'the king of wines, the wine of kings.' I read somewhere that, 'like a woman, it needs time to express itself—to mellow and soften so its flavor and aroma can expand and be fully savored.' I didn't tell you that I study wines."

"And women," I added.

While I tore romaine leaves into a salad bowl, Blake stood behind me. He pressed his body deeply into mine. I could feel him harden. Suddenly, he turned me around. My stance automatically widened as he reached down, placing his hand between my legs, simultaneously lifting my cotton skirt and letting his fingers roam free. I gasped slightly when his mouth was on mine with kisses that spilled over our lips, tongues that traveled every inch of our mouths.

Then, in Gothic-romance-novel style, he scooped me up in his arms and carried me from the kitchen to the hall. Between kisses, I directed him to my bedroom, where we collapsed onto my ivory-colored comforter.

"I've been waiting all week for this," he said. "I need to hold you in my arms."

The waiting had made the moment even more intense, for within seconds we were straining to release ourselves from the confines of our clothes, leaving nothing between us except our own naked bodies and all the time in the world to explore them. I was caught between insatiable desire and the trepidation that always accompanied those first moments of lovemaking with someone new.

Yet in the arms of Blake Hamilton, artist extraordinaire, it was different. I was with a man who knew exactly what he was doing. The fear that he might find my gestures awkward flashed through my mind.

A seasoned lover guides rather than leads, and Blake knew exactly how to release the passion within me while simultaneously making me feel comfortable. Instead of taking over, he encouraged me to express myself, and in doing so, my inhibitions fell away so that I was taking charge and loving every moment. With Blake, it all seemed so natural, as though I had been making love to men all my life. Unlike the others, who had viewed sex as a competition, I found myself caught up in the nuances—the hidden areas that longed to be awakened. Unknowingly, my body took over, as though it had a mind of its own, acting on its own impulses.

Blake moved from above me to a more passive position below, where, under my spell, he was receptive to my every whim and desire. Slowly, I moved my tongue up his muscular thighs until I reached his cock. There I paused to look, to admire his luscious specimen of manhood. As I caressed him with my hand, he began to rise and grow hard. His deep moans inspired me further.

"Where*ever* did you learn how to do that?" he said in between staccato breaths.

I was at once elated and surprised. Encouraged by Blake's responses, I proceeded uninhibitedly. He had bestowed upon me the greatest gift of all: sexual confidence, allowing me to move freely and proficiently, unleashing my most ardent passions and in turn arousing in him his own fervent desires.

"I've never known a woman to manage me so exquisitely," he said between deep kisses. "I'm totally within your control. Keep doing what you're doing. I love it."

Horny as hell after a string of disappointing lovers, now in my twilight-lit bedroom with the sun melting down over Manhattan and the most magnificent man I had ever met, I was aroused to such a point that I didn't know what part of him to savor first. My tongue flitted along his shaft, then to his scrotum, which I circled with wet kisses. Then back to his cock, where my mouth opened as I gently accepted his penis until it fit perfectly between my lips.

"Oh, baby, you're absolutely marvelous." Each sexual accolade aroused me further. My mouth moved up and down on him until, without warning, he parted my legs, grazing my clitoris with his tongue as I writhed in pleasure.

"Tell me you love this," he said, "tell me how much."

Unabashedly, I cried out words I had never used before. Words dripping sex—love-tinged words that I called up from places I never even knew existed. A plethora of love sounds reverberated through the room until I screamed out, begging for Blake to be inside me.

"Not yet, darling. I can't stop ravishing you."

He continued pleasuring me as I moaned beneath him until we could stand it no longer. Then, in one intense and penetrating thrust, we climaxed together, Blake's body pressed into mine. We lay there entwined in each other's arms for what must have been a half hour until we broke away. Our bodies meshed together as we fell into a deep and glorious sleep.

For much of my late-adolescent life, I had toyed with sex built mostly on gropes and feels with private school boys who didn't know what the hell they were doing. There had been a series of necking sessions when, high on beer, my first real boyfriend, Andy Weill, had expressed his sexual prowess in less than satisfactory ways.

When I entered Bennington, I began dating a Princeton boy: Evan H. Trumbull III, who, in the grass behind the Tower eating club, managed to clumsily deflower me. His penis was hardly inside me when he came, leaving me burrowed into the damp ground with grass stains all over the Victoria's Secret panties I had bought for just this occasion. If this is what it's all about, I thought while Evan H. secured his trousers, forget it. After that, I viewed sex as an unnecessary evil, a letdown to be endured rather than enjoyed. Following a string of unsophisticated lovers, I began relying more on masturbation than the real McCoy.

Then, at twenty-nine, for a brief two-year period I would later come to refer to as "the blip," I met and moved in with Ira Alan Goldfein, with whom I had been fixed up on a blind date. This move was based mostly on pleasing Madeleine, who, in desperation, kept reminding me that my biological clock was running on overtime. With that in mind and the fact that Ira possessed all the right qualities, including being a whiz at cosmetic dentistry, I was giving marriage serious thought. The time was ripe, and so was I.

Ira's parents, Dr. and Mrs. Neil Goldfein, lived in Woodmere, Long Island, where Neil practiced dentistry and his wife, Nancy, perfected gossiping. Ira, an Amherst grad with his Phi Beta Kappa key prominently displayed on a chain around his neck, thought he was God's gift to women. After dental school, he joined his father's practice. Madeleine thought that the sun rose and set with Ira and considered him the catch of the century.

"Men like Ira Goldfein don't come around very often." My mother continually echoed this refrain. In time she wore me down. On an early-June morning, I accepted a three-carat Tiffany diamond that Ira slipped on my finger on the sixteenth hole at the Woodmere Club.

My entire life flashed before me as I envisioned life with Ira: a house in the 'burbs, three kids, a golden retriever, tennis, golf, successful friends, and the best perk of all: good teeth, the latter of which made me finally say, "Yes, Ira, I will marry you."

We sat under a protective weeping willow, where we kissed amid the spray of flying golf balls. There Ira removed his horn-rimmed glasses and wiped away tears of happiness that had accumulated on each lens. We moved in together that week and set the date. Six months to the day later, Ira was moving out, and I was giving back the ring. This was because while Ira Goldfein, D.D.S., might have been a real catch, he also had a roving penis, which, on a regular basis, had been introduced to the vaginas of numerous young and attractive New York ladies.

My mother was shocked. "Who would have thought it? Ira seemed so perfect. He was a real whiz with a drill."

"Yes," I agreed, "he drilled his prick into every woman in the tristate area."

Madeleine cringed. "I hate when you get crude, Samantha." Then she took me to Saks to buy a little black dress.

"I'm not in mourning, Mother. It's just a breakup. I don't need to wear black."

"Black is for all occasions. Now that you're single again," she whispered, stumbling on the word "single," "you'll need the proper wardrobe for meeting men." She added: "And the sooner the better, Samantha. Tick-tock. Tick-tock."

"Mother, I'm only thirty-one. I still have time."

"That's exactly the age when the vagina starts getting dry," she said. "Sperm lie down and die in dry terrain."

With that in mind, we made a pit stop at Duane Reade for a little "gift" of K-Y jelly.

"Take it from me, sweetheart," she said, "you never know when a little dab'll do you."

And so I dabbed away, using up numerous tubes of K-Y on men who made getting into my pants their raison d'être. But none of them interested me until Blake Hamilton walked into the Cole Gallery and took my breath away.

The next morning, right on cue, while Blake and I were locked in coital bliss, Madeleine called.

"Aunt Elaine and I have tickets to the ballet, but she has the stomach flu. Can you join me?"

"May I call you back? I'm still in bed."

"It's ten thirty."

"It's also Sunday. I like sleeping late on weekends."

She poured on the sarcasm: "My ankle is fine, thank you."

"Oh, sorry, how's your ankle?"

"It's very painful."

Blake stirred and stretched. He leaned over and kissed my neck. I cooed slightly.

"Are you alone?"

"Mother, I'll call you back."

"What about the ballet?"

"Call a friend. I'm tied up."

"Sounds like fun. Tell Blake I said good morning."

I hung up and turned to Blake, who, even in a sleepy haze, looked deliciously disheveled.

"The big, bad *Wolfe*, I presume."

"You guessed it."

"Let's not worry about sweet Madeleine, shall we?" Blake said. "Come here, you." He grabbed me, pulling me over to him. "I haven't had my good-morning kiss."

"And I haven't brushed my teeth."

"I'll brush them for you," he said, running his tongue over them. "My God, you taste good."

"You're a liar."

"You taste like Sunday morning," he said, "after a perfect night of lovemaking."

"It *was* perfect."

"Damn straight it was. And you seemed to be enjoying every minute of it. You're insatiable."

"Is that all right?"

"All right? My good woman, it's more than all right. It's a goddamn turn on. I do believe you came at least three times."

"Three fabulous times."

"How about making it a fourth?"

"Are you up for it?"

"Darling." Blake placed my hand on his crotch. "I'd say I'm up for just about anything you want."

With that, we were back in action, making love for the next hour and a half, with two more orgasms apiece to top off the morning. We lay there for another hour, intermittently nuzzling and sleeping until Blake stretched and said, "All this coupling has made me hungry."

"What are you in the mood for?" I asked.

"That's a dangerous question. Honestly, I could eat you up again, but that would defeat the whole purpose. I was thinking something brunchy: a cheese omelet, perhaps, a steamy café au lait, croissants."

"I'm afraid the cupboard is bare."

"Well, then, Mother Hubbard, it's off to brunch we go."

I started to rise from the bed. "Stop right there," Blake ordered, "and hand me that pad of paper and a pencil." He sat down in the chair next to the bed.

I reached over to my night table and retrieved the blank legal-size pad I kept there for jotting down gallery notes when Alexandra Cole called.

"Perfect. Now stand there just as you are while I turn you into the most magnificent creature you've ever seen."

"You're sketching me? In the nude?"

"You bet I am. That's it. Hold that pose. My God, you have the absolute perfect breasts, so high and round, and those nipples—pure rosebuds. I could devour them right here and now."

"Keep drawing." I giggled.

"Turn a little to the left, darling. That's it. The sun is hitting you in all the right places. You're beautiful."

"Stop it."

"I'm serious, Samantha. Your body is sensational. Now wet your lips slightly."

"I'm starting to get turned on again."

"And your legs . . . move them apart . . . just a little. Yes, that's it, now turn toward me. Oh yes, lovely."

As Blake kept drawing, I felt so aroused it was hard to stand still. I placed a hand between my legs, moving it toward my labia. Blake stopped and stared as I moved my finger between my vaginal lips and rubbed myself.

"Oh my God, Blake, look what you're doing to me."

"Keep stroking yourself," he said. "Yes, baby, that's it. Move your finger over your clit . . . faster . . . faster. Look at me, I'm getting hard."

"Let's get back into bed."

"No, I want to watch you come, and I'll come with you . . . separately . . . together."

"Oh, Blake." I swung my head back, and moved my finger wildly. "I'm coming."

"I'm coming with you, darling." His hand was on his cock. "Oh yes, this is wild, crazy." And within seconds, Blake let out a guttural moan as he ejaculated and fell back into the chair, completely spent.

Thoroughly sated, we crept back to bed and slept until close to four P.M. So much for brunch. Without disturbing Blake, who was still half asleep, I got up, making my way to the bathroom, nearly stumbling over the drawing pad. I picked it up from the floor and studied it in the late-afternoon light streaming through the window. There I was; all five feet five inches of me, my thick, wavy hair cascading gently over my bare shoulders, my body firm, my breasts small though rounded, my hard nipples standing pertly erect and proud. Moving down to my belly button and the curve of my tummy, my hands came to rest just above my pubis, with tufts of hair peeking through between my opened fingers. My hips undulated down to meet my slightly parted, long legs accentuated by strong calf muscles and slim ankles. My feet stood firm on the little round rug I had found in a thrift shop one rainy autumn afternoon. Moving up to my face, my nose looked sharp and sculpted. My cheekbones, high and haughty, were well defined. My eyes, wide and deep, peered out as though fixed on something in the far distance. But most revealing was my mouth and the faint hint of a smile that rested there. It was the smile of a woman who seemed at peace—a happy woman whose life, unknowingly, was about to change drastically.

Blake stirred, wiping sleep away from the corners of his eyes. "Do you like it?"

I held the drawing in my hands. "Like it? It's fantastic. Is that really how you see me?"

"It hardly does you justice."

"And I'm not even in the abstract."

"I wanted to capture the real Samantha. It's my gift to you for a night of countless pleasures."

"Thank you. It's beautiful."

"And now, my lovely girl, I am completely famished. How about that pasta puttanesca you were promising me last night?"

"Seems we had better things to do with our time."

"I'll say. But now's your chance to show off your attributes."

"I thought I already had."

"And quite well, I might add, but if we don't eat something soon, Celeste might find two skeletons lying here."

"Oh my God . . . Celeste. She's arriving back tonight. I've completely lost track of time."

"In that case, let's do what all savvy New Yawkers do," he said. "Make reservations."

An hour later, we were seated at a table at Café Lalo on West Eighty-third. Blake, with pasta puttanesca on his mind, ordered a bowl.

"This is delicious," he said. "But I'll bet it doesn't touch yours."

"I'm going to prove that fact to be true," I said. "When you return from London, I'm cooking you the best meal you've ever tasted."

"I'm holding you to it," he said, filling our glasses with more Chianti.

It couldn't be going better. A week before, I hadn't even known Blake Hamilton, and now, the day before he was to leave, we were inseparable, having spent the last four evenings together. It would have been a perfect farewell dinner had not Madeleine called my cell during dessert, asking that the two of us see her before Blake left for the airport.

"A little bon-voyage lunch will be so festive," she chirped.

I placed my hand over the phone. "Do you want to join my mother for lunch tomorrow?"

"Why not? My plane doesn't take off until ten. She'll enjoy that."

"All right, Mother," I said begrudgingly, "Blake says it's fine."

"I'm reserving a table at Le Bernardin for one o'clock."

Who could argue with that? One taste of their fish delicacies and Blake would be swooning.

"Between you and your mother," Blake said, "I'm being spoiled rotten."

"My mother is a royal pain in the ass."

"Yes," he said, "but it's so hard to resist me."

"Your arrogance is absolutely reaching offensive proportions." I reached over and tweaked his perfect nose.

"What can I do? I'm irresistible."

"Shut up and drink your wine," I said.

The thought of leaving Blake was difficult, made even more so since I would be facing Celeste once again. Her absence had been like a breath of fresh air, giving me two of the best days of my life. After dinner, we taxied back to my apartment, where we parted reluctantly at the curb while Blake stayed in the cab; he would go on to his hotel.

"Tomorrow. One o'clock. Le Bernardin. West Fifty-first, between Sixth and Seventh."

"I'll be waiting." He leaned his head through the taxi window. "Thank you, my darling, for the grandest time. It was spectacular. *You're* spectacular."

"Oh, you're so bloody British," I said, kissing him on the lips. "Until tomorrow, and come with a huge appetite. Le Bernardin is the cat's meow."

"I'm purring already," he said.

As predicted, Celeste waltzed through the door at exactly eleven o'clock P.M., speaking in superlatives of her weekend in Bermuda.

"The Elbow Beach Hotel is absolutely over-the-top, Sam. I could have stayed a week."

I wish you had, I wanted to say.

"And the food. I must have gained five pounds."

"I can't tell," I said.

"I went completely off my diet."

"Oh, you're dieting?"

"You *know* I've been watching what I eat. I'm trying so hard to shed some of my thigh muscle."

Celeste never admitted to having body fat. Instead, she complained that her muscles were too pronounced from her fitness workouts. For the month of July, she had joined my health club where, daily, she put three miles on the treadmill, hoping that would help to slim her down. Clearly, her fat (not muscle) had accumulated in all the wrong places.

"God, I wish I had your figure," she told me ad infinitum. "You have perfect proportions. I'd kill for your butt."

Celeste studied me constantly to the point where it was starting to make me self-conscious.

"So, tell me about your weekend, Celeste," I said, more to change the subject than out of genuine interest.

"We sat by the pool every afternoon and didn't budge. It was divine."

"That's it?"

"We ate. We shopped. We stared at the hunky men."

"Any dates?"

"Sam," Celeste said, her voice becoming slightly uppity, "it wasn't like that. It was a girls' weekend. We weren't going there to meet guys."

"Right," I said.

"But I did finish reading *Madame Bovary*. You probably noticed that I'm into the classics."

"Wow, Celeste," I said, "I'm impressed."

SEVEN

A bachelor is a man who
comes to work each morning
from a different direction.

—*Sholom Aleichem*

To say that Madeleine Krasner-Wolfe was a piece of work was putting it mildly. The woman was unabashedly provocative, and yet, although I hated admitting it, she had taught me well. She was vastly more intelligent than she often let on but seemed most comfortable being a character, a role she played to the hilt. At first glance, what registered in the minds of those who met her was a woman who was no stranger to the glitz and glamour afforded to only a privileged few. She lived high, dressed impeccably, had money to spend and spent it well. But beneath that outer layer of opulence, she also had the best gut instincts of anyone I knew.

Through the years I had come to rely on her smarts and referred to them as Madeleine Krasner-Wolfe's "Words of Wisdom." As far back as I could remember, Madeleine had been tossing out her witticisms with wild abandon.

Lily Ann was equally impressed.

I reflected back to when I was prepubescent, a time when sleepovers were popular. I recalled a night when Lily Ann was over.

"Madeleine is a one-woman operation," she said after my mother had burst into my room. It was almost one A.M. on a Sunday morning in December. My parents had just returned from another one of their holiday fetes, and Madeleine was eager to chat.

"My darlings." She sat down on the bed, her ruby and diamond necklace aglow in the dark. "You'll never believe it. Gladys Berman served Ritz crackers with the baked Brie."

While to us, at age twelve, this was not of monumental relevance, Madeleine loved sharing all the nuances of her nights on the town.

"Ritz crackers? Is that bad?" Lily Ann asked.

"Bad?" Madeleine's eyes widened. " 'Bad' doesn't even begin to explain it. If it weren't so late, I'd tell you girls just *how* bad."

Our ears perked up.

"Girls, you're too young to care about such matters, but one day you'll appreciate these tidbits."

And so it came to pass that these "tidbits" would become the measuring rod for all that I would come to know as the Gospel According to Madeleine Krasner-Wolfe.

One evening when I was fourteen and watching my mother dress for a benefit at the Rainbow Room, she suddenly blurted out: "Samantha, never, and I mean never, wear faux."

"Faux?"

"Fake. Imitation. I'm talking mostly about leather bags and shoes. I can smell a faux alligator the minute it enters a room. When Daddy and I were at the Pierre the other night, in walked my friend Allegra Marks-Stein, carrying the most hideous faux reptile I've ever seen."

"What kind of reptile?" I was intrigued. I envisioned a large boa constrictor winding its way around Allegra Marks-Stein's neck.

"Something in the lizard family. I couldn't quite tell. But it reeked knockoff, which, if it's kitschy, like costume jewelry, it's fine, but when it comes to leather, that's a no-no. Trust me, Samantha, if you can't afford the real thing, forget it, but never go faux."

Over the years I took it all in as my mother regaled me with these snippets of information, which on the surface, seemed relatively harmless though often questionable. Her friends found her amusing, while I, her daughter, considered her undeniably outrageous to her core. As I grew older, it became even worse. When I least expected it, another sage remark would issue from her mouth. Such was the case when, on the rim of sixteen, I stood in the dressing room at Saks with Madeleine slumped in a chair, commenting on every garment I tried on.

"It's ghastly, simply ghastly," she said, watching me zip up a blue taffeta dress that flowed to the floor.

"I love it," I said. The dress had a huge tulle crinoline resembling a ballet dancer's tutu. I pirouetted around, filled with anticipation of my upcoming sweet-sixteen party.

"Samantha, unless you're willing to give up those hot-fudge sundaes and after-school snacks, you'll never be able to do justice to a dress like this. It won't work unless you suck in your tummy, and you can't walk around all night doing that."

The pain was palpable. I could feel my exuberance fade. My mother's words had diminished me in a flash.

"Trust me, sweetheart." She was relentless. "That dress doesn't do a thing for you."

And I who had thought I was a vision of loveliness watched my fantasy being swept away.

How much emotional damage took place in those dressing rooms was hard to surmise. But it came up endless times in therapy and left an indelible mark on my psyche. They were more than shopping sprees; they were to become the baggage I would carry with me into adulthood. As I watched that blue taffeta dress being carried back to the racks by Miss Minton, my mother's favorite salesgirl, my hopes were dashed. It wasn't that my mother consciously meant harm. She only (as she put it) "had my own interests at heart," and wearing a dress that "played down my attributes" (her phrase, not mine) would not serve me well. Instead, to quell my disappointment, we stopped at the perfume counter for a bottle of L'air du Temps so I wouldn't go home empty-handed.

I learned a lot about my mother on those Saturday afternoons spent under her watchful eye. She could be unknowingly cruel and misguided yet well intentioned. But when I was sixteen, her good intentions didn't matter. I wanted a mother who was empathic and kind—a mother who was on my side, applauding me and making me feel I was the most beautiful girl in the world in a dress that would guarantee magical moments in the making.

Back then the dressing rooms at Saks were spacious, carpeted chambers appointed with small puffed-velvet cushioned chairs. A silver bowl of hard candies was offered as a genteel expression to revive tired shoppers from the strenuous task of trying on clothes. There was also the obligatory ashtray, as smoking was never prohibited and even encouraged as a form of relaxation.

But then came a day when, at age eighteen, home from Bennington just before Christmas, I was back at Saks with Madeleine for another shopping spree. I had slimmed down considerably and was contemplating a dress for a holiday party at the Harmonie Club, the social event of the season. There was no doubt that my body had changed. Clothes previously rejected now fit more smoothly over new curves that had materialized in the space of two years. My pleasingly plump adolescent awkwardness had been replaced by a body I now admired. Conversely, as I felt more comfortable in my own skin, changes in Madeleine became notably apparent. Tiny wrinkles that hadn't been there yesterday seemed to appear around her eyes and mouth. Her skin seemed less taut, and a slight weight gain of only a few pounds, but enough to make a difference, had added a slight extra fold of skin under her chin.

In typical Bette Davis fashion, she sat there, flicking her cigarette ashes and simultaneously watching me pour myself into a form-fitting black sheath. Without warning, she looked up and, as though from nowhere, asked, "Darling, do you think I still look attractive?"

The question was startling.

"You look beautiful, Mother," I said.

And there it was: the moment I had spent my childhood waiting for—the moment when I acknowledged that first tug of separation between us. I stared out the large picture window overlooking Rockefeller Center and the Christmas tree off in the distance. It had just begun to snow, that first December snow covering Manhattan in a sleek white glaze. The sounds of the season were in full bloom. Taxicabs and buses on the street below drove by, honking their horns. People moved along Fifth Avenue as though in slow motion. And there I stood on the carpeted floor at Saks, tossing my long hair into the air, occasionally pausing to check myself in the full-length mirror. I didn't need Miss Minton or my mother's approving smile to validate what I already knew: I looked good.

This recognition, subtle though it was, was profound as I kept my eyes fixed on the window, watching snowflakes dance in the glow of the cars' headlights. My mother's voice faded away as I was encircled in a haze of cigarette smoke, feeling simultaneously grown-up and sad, as though the passage of years had all taken place within these dressing rooms of my youth, where today I would finally emerge triumphant.

We bought the black dress, which my mother agreed "looked stunning."

"All my nagging obviously paid off. Since you've shed your baby fat, sweetheart," she said, not letting an opportunity escape her, "see how much better the clothes fit."

By the time we reached the sidewalk, the snow was several inches high. Darting through the crowds, we headed up Fifth Avenue. I led the way, my mother's hand held tightly in mine as we crossed over the curb, shopping bags in tow, on toward home and my hard-earned victory so dearly won.

· · ·

But she never stopped trying. Not then. Not now. Twenty years later, I was still privy to her whims and caprice. Such was the case on Monday, when Madeleine took our perfectly lovely lunch at Le Bernardin and turned it into hell.

"You did *what*?" I screamed into my cell right in the middle of Fekkai at Bendel's where I was having a trim at eleven that morning.

"I invited Celeste to join us for lunch."

"Have you gone absolutely mad, Mother?"

"Celeste doesn't get to meet artists very often. I thought it would be culturally inspiring. And anyway, we really couldn't leave her out, now, could we?"

"Of course you could. Just because she's staying with me doesn't mean she needs to be part of my daily activities. I wanted this to be a lunch, just for the three of us. She already made a fool of herself in front of Blake when he picked me up at my apartment."

"You need to learn tolerance, Samantha. It's a trait that will hold you in good stead. I'll see you at one. Celeste will meet us there."

I slammed down the phone, fuming.

Two hours later, perfectly coiffed with two inches off my hair, I walked over to Le Bernardin. It was a bright and sunny day, hotter than it had been in weeks. I was the first to arrive, with Blake following five minutes later.

"Brace yourself," I said. "We're going to be blessed with the presence of my cousin Celeste. My mother invited her to join us. There goes lunch."

"Did anyone ever tell you that you look even more alluring when you're angry?" Blake said, slipping in next to me.

"You won't be too happy when Celeste completely monopolizes the conversation."

"That can't possibly happen with Madeleine present."

"I'm just warning you. This wasn't part of the plan."

Blake picked up my hand and kissed it gently. "You look absolutely marvelous. I like your hair a bit shorter. Quite fetching."

"And you're so damn complimentary," I said, kissing him on the mouth.

The waiter appeared. We ordered a large bottle of mineral water to quench our thirst, which was made even more intense by the oppressive outside heat.

My concerns were correct. The minute Madeleine and Celeste arrived together as they had planned, I inwardly cringed. Celeste had chosen the most inappropriate dress, with a neckline that plunged so low, her breasts made their debut before she did. Shades of the other night flashed through my mind.

"My God, but it's an oven out there." Madeleine took out another of her monogrammed hankies and dabbed her upper lip, taking care not to muss her lipstick. "Oh, good, pour me some of that fizzy water immediately."

"Me, too," Celeste said, taking her napkin and wiping her cleavage, "I'm dripping all over."

The waiter filled their glasses while Blake grabbed my hand under the table, giving it a knowing tweak.

Le Bernardin ran the gamut from the simple to the imaginative, with Chef Eric Ripert at the helm, making for a spectacular experience. Despite the hefty prices, its patrons seemed grateful to be there. We settled in to lunch with a menu presentation that had us salivating.

"Their cold foie gras is the best I ever tasted," Madeleine said. "Nothing less than exquisite." She rated jewelry, clothes, and food with equal superlatives.

"Are you sorry to be leaving New York?" Celeste asked Blake.

"I need to get back to London. I've much to do before my show next month, not to mention getting my work in order for the Cole Gallery in December."

"Ooh," Celeste practically tweeted, "so you'll be back here in a few months?"

"Even better than that." Blake shot me a look. "Just this morning

I arranged for a flat on the Upper East Side. Seems my old chum Charlie Bjornstad is going to be away all winter. He and his family are spending several months with his wife's folks in Switzerland. He asked if I would mind staying in his Ninety-third Street pad and keep my eye on things, including his sheepdog, Muriel. What could I say?"

"What *did* you say?" Madeleine was practically vibrating.

"The only thing I could say: emphatically yes."

God bless Charlie Bjornstadt, I thought.

"So you'll be spending the winter in Manhattan, then?" Madeleine said.

"Afraid so," Blake acknowledged. "The Big Apple is going to have to contend with yet another artist on its island. But, what really clinched it for me was that old Charlie has a guest room with northern light that can serve as a studio. I'll be able to paint to my heart's content. I'll have the entire brownstone to myself until mid-April, when Charlie returns."

I tried to conceal my excitement, to remain as cool as ever, but I was about to burst at the thought of having Blake in New York for several months.

"This is great news," I said. "In fact, I'd say it warrants a celebration."

"I'll second that," Blake said. "You ladies have made my stay here sheer perfection. And with all that's happening at the Cole Gallery, I should be here in New York instead of red-eyeing it back and forth across the pond."

"Well, I for one am absolutely thrilled," Madeleine broke in. "But what about your London flat?"

"I suppose it will be lying dormant for a spell, unless you'd like to come over and keep the home fires burning."

"Is that an invitation?" Madeleine perked up. "I just might take you up on it."

I had to hand it to my mother. She never let an opportunity escape her.

Celeste was practically gushing as well. "Then we'll get to see a lot more of you. Maybe you can even give me private art lessons. I've always wanted to try my hand at painting."

"Why not?" Blake squirmed uncomfortably.

As we settled in to our lunch of stunning fish presentations, I noticed that Celeste was shifting slightly in her chair. As Blake regaled us with stories of the London art scene, he sat up, noticeably startled. He glanced over at me. I returned his gaze. Then his eyes shifted over to Celeste, who was cutting into her Peking duck–green papaya salad and didn't even look up. Madeleine was too busy spewing forth accolades over her appetizer of wild Alaskan salmon to register any other emotion.

"I've never tasted scallops quite like this," Blake said as he wiped his forehead, where beads of perspiration had appeared.

It was obvious that something had gone amok—something having to do with Celeste, who had hardly taken her gaze off Blake since she arrived. I studied her in between my bites of food as she wet her lips and adjusted the neckline of her dress, leaning over ever so slightly to get to the bread, her cleavage exposed just enough to grab Blake's attention. But it didn't stop there. I sensed further undercurrents. I casually dropped my napkin on the floor and bent down to retrieve it. I saw Celeste quickly pull her foot away from Blake's crotch.

Goddamn that bitch. While the four of us were making small talk, Cousin Celeste Bleckner was nonchalantly playing footsie with "our" Blake. I was nonplussed. These were definite grounds for eviction. As soon as July was over, Celeste and her disgusting bunny slippers would finally be out of my hair. Her departure, though three weeks away, couldn't come soon enough.

Two and a half hours later, after one of the most culinary satisfying lunches I'd had in months (for which Madeleine shelled out a couple of hundred bucks), she, with Celeste by her side, stood outside, chatting.

"Darling"—Madeleine had now moved into her terms-of-endearment phase and was directing her talk to Blake—"getting to know you has been sheer perfection. You've lifted my spirits more than you'll ever know."

I expected that at any moment she was going to whisk the mono-grammed hankie from her purse and dab the corners of her eyes.

"The pleasure has been all mine, Madeleine," Blake said, "and I am so pleased that your ankle has healed so well."

"By the time you're back here in December," she reiterated, lest he forgot, "I'll be as good as new."

She slipped her calling card into his ivory linen jacket pocket and patted it closed. Then, with both hands on either side of Blake's face, she kissed him on each cheek. Celeste followed suit, emitting a little "hmmm" in the process.

"Wait until I tell my college roommate I had lunch with *the* Blake Hamilton," she said, high on a winey-lunch glow.

And toe-fucked him to boot, I thought.

Madeleine and Celeste shared a cab as we watched them drive away. Blake wasn't leaving for the airport until seven, which gave us little time for a proper good-bye.

I couldn't wait to bring up the subject. "Nice toe job that Celeste gave you. I can't believe she crammed her foot into your crotch. The girl is beyond presumptuous."

"Okay, I'll admit it. I'm secretly in love with your cousin Celeste and I'm using you to get to her."

"I knew it." I laughed. "You have such impeccable taste in women."

"Indeed I do," Blake said giving me a knock-your-socks-off kiss right in front of Le Bernardin. "Now, what would you like to do in these last remaining moments?" he teased.

"Surprise me," I said.

"That will be my supreme pleasure," he said, hailing a cab. Within minutes we were on our way to the Elysee and in his room, where, under a painting of a sixteenth-century courtesan, we made mad, passionate love until the concierge called promptly at six P.M. Blake showered, dressed, and grabbed his suitcases and whisked us into the elevator, where we said our bon voyages.

"Well, my darling, I guess it's off with you, then," he said, holding me in his arms.

"Yes, back to Cousin Celeste the hussy."

"I'll call you. E-mail you. Better yet, would you consider a visit to London before December?"

That was the first time the subject had come up, and I was reeling.

With that, Blake was in a taxi heading toward JFK, leaving me standing there blowing kisses as I walked slowly up Fifty-fifth Street and reentered my life.

Back at my apartment, I never let on to Celeste that I was aware of her flagrant shenanigans, nor did she acknowledge that I had caught her in the act. The subject of Blake never came up again except that night, when we were watching reruns of *Sex and the City*. Out of the blue, she blurted out: "I wonder what it would be like sleeping with Blake Hamilton."

There was an awkward silence during which I said nothing.

"You can't tell me you don't know, Sam." Celeste wouldn't let up.

"I don't think that's any of your business."

"I'm just saying . . . he must be the world's greatest lover. I imagine he has women all over the place clamoring to get into his pants."

"I think Blake is more discriminating than that."

A sharp jab of uneasiness cut through me. Since we met, I hadn't allowed myself to even contemplate such a notion. Then along came Celeste, who had flagrantly and, most likely, deliberately put it out there. I became immediately defensive.

"Blake is much too busy working on his art. He doesn't have much time left over for the ladies."

"Are you delusional? Celebs like Blake have little black books regurgitating women's names. I read somewhere that he dates super models."

"Maybe you should stop reading those garbage magazines," I said.

"Maybe you should stop being so naive."

"Oh, like you're an authority on guys like Blake."

"I just might be," Celeste said. "Just because I don't date much doesn't mean I don't observe what's going on around me. And I'll bet anything that you and Blake fucked your heads off while I was in Bermuda."

"Okay, that's it," I said. "I'm going to bed."

"But *Sex and the City* isn't even over. Don't you want to see Carrie and Mr. Big get it on?"

"I've had all the sex I can handle for one night," I said, leaving Celeste curled up on the couch with her pissy attitude and a half-eaten Snickers bar.

I lay awake for hours thinking about Blake: our week together in New York and our hours of endless lovemaking. And then the thought I didn't want to entertain: When Blake got off the plane on the other side of the ocean, was there another woman waiting? I had been so caught up in the glow of the moment that I had pushed all else aside. At three A.M., I sat up with a start and was knocked silly by the realization that despite the undivided attention he had thrust upon me until I was half crazed, I might not be the only one in Blake's life. Such thoughts kept sleep at bay and had me shifting fitfully for the rest of the night. Worst of all, I hated Celeste for opening up her big mouth and tarnishing my fantasies.

I awakened at seven A.M., sleep-deprived and feeling terrible, along with an achy longing for Blake, who was now three thousand miles away. Celeste was still asleep, and I tiptoed about the apartment so I could make a clean getaway. I showered and dressed, grabbed a bagel and coffee on the run and was at the gallery by eight. My schedule was filled to the brim with wannabe artists who were begging me to look at their slides. My boss, Alexandra Cole, was expected to phone at noon from Paris, where she was spending the month of July. No sooner had I settled into my paperwork than the phone rang. I picked up on the first ring, my mouth stuffed with bagel and cream cheese.

"Alexandra Cole Gallery," I said.

"Oh, is it?" the voice on the other end inquired, sounding particularly seductive. "I'd like to speak to the sexiest woman in Manhattan."

I could feel my heart racing right through my navy blue Chanel sweater set. I toyed with my Frank Ghery pendant, hardly able to breathe.

"I haven't stopped thinking about you all the way from JFK to Heathrow," Blake said.

"Me, either." I tried to conceal my excitement and sound cool.

"You do know, Samantha, that you've completely upset my equilibrium."

"Have I?"

"Let's just say, my dear, that hearing your voice is causing quite an uprising, if you catch my drift?"

All my doubts and insecurities vanished as Blake and I, at thirty-five cents a minute, engaged in a delicious and seductive phone-sex moment all the way from London to New York.

Blake's unexpected call put me on a high for the rest of the day as I sailed through work, feeling unusually gay. Even Alexandra, who called promptly at noon, commented on the je ne sais quoi quality in my voice.

"Sounds like *you're* having a good day," she said. "Anything special to put you in such a good mood?"

I dared not tell her that her favorite up-and-coming star and I had shared more than a passing acquaintance.

"So, have you firmed things up with Blake Hamilton?" she asked.

"Absolutely, very firm," I said, the mere sound of his name sending a charge right through me. "We're all set to go with his opening on December twenty-third."

"I have a really good feeling about Blake," Alexandra said. "I think he'll hit the town with a bang."

She could not have said it better.

"He seemed pretty excited. He told me several times how much showing at the Cole means to him."

"I hope you treated him well. After all, he *is* the hottest thing to come along in years."

"I gave him the royal treatment," I assured her.

"Attagirl. That's what I'm paying you big bucks to do: woo our clients while simultaneously making them feel grateful."

She should only know how much wooing I did.

"I think Blake and the Cole Gallery are the perfect fit," I said.

"Blake will take New York by storm. What better time to show him than right before Christmas, when the city is abuzz with people who are high on egg nog, ready to spend their money. We'll have an opening to beat all openings. I want you to start planning early, Sam. Call our favorite caterer, and let's make this the splashiest do in the city. We'll want champagne. We'll want top-of-the-line hors d'oeuvres. We're going all out on this one," she bubbled over. "Did Blake happen to mention where he'll be staying and for how long? I'd like to keep him here as long as possible."

When I shared the news of Blake spending the winter in New York, she squealed into the phone.

"It just can't get much better than this," she said. "He'll be the toast of the town. The fact that we'll have easy access to him opens up all sorts of possibilities. Who knows? If the reviews are what I think they'll be, we might be looking at museum material. I'm telling you, Sam, I have very good vibes about Blake Hamilton. He's our leading man, the new hot-boy artist, and we're going to push him for all he's worth. Together, Sam, we'll put on a show that will rival all others. People will be swarming in. Did he agree on eight paintings?"

"Yes, he said that's not a problem."

"Good, I don't want more than eight. His canvases are large enough to take up all our wall space. God, Sam, I can't wait to get back to New York and get started. Oh, and good work," she tossed this in as an afterthought. "I see compensation for you in the not too distant future."

"Compensation," in her language, meant a hefty raise.

"You've got the stuff, Samantha," Alexandra said. "Keep it up."

After getting off the phone, I found myself reminiscing. I thought about the "stuff' to which Alexandra had referred, and how I had evolved to where I was today.

I might have been as nondescript and ordinary as many of the late-thirties overachieving, desperate to meet Mr. Right New York women had I not possessed that one necessary ingredient to get by: a sense of humor. It was mostly that humor which allowed me to get through the business of daily living despite a mother who was constantly on my back, reminding me that with a face like mine, I could go anywhere.

But pretty though my face was, what it got me was pinched regularly by well-meaning family members who couldn't control themselves. This lasted well into my childhood.

"What a gorgeous punim," Grandma Tessa told my mother, taking a chunk of cheek and kneading it so hard it left welts that often lasted for a couple of days.

Such was my plight: a roster of relatives who pinched, aunts who hovered, and uncles who hugged too hard, a couple of them even bypassing my cheek altogether and landing their lox-smelling breath and creamed-herring kisses on my mouth.

My most illuminating attribute was that I was a keen observer, and I put it to good use. I went to the right bars for my drinks, the hottest restaurants for my meals, and had the smarts and sophistication to know how to play the game—whatever the game of the day was. Most of the time it was about meeting men: how to meet them, where to meet them, what to do once they were met, and most important, how to snag one and get him to walk down the aisle without appearing as though he had been pussy-whipped and married against his will.

As for my most stunning and startling personal physical state-ment, I'd have to say it was my hair. It was a deep, rich chestnut brown and was so soft it felt like satin, aptly described by an early boyfriend, Aaron Feldman, who told me the first time we kissed that he would like to come in my hair. Upon hearing this, Lily Ann dubbed me as having "orgasmic hair."

As qualities went, my favorites—subtle though they were—were my gut instincts and my ability to size up most situations even before they unfolded. I knew the score, and in the end, this would hold me in good stead, both personally and professionally. Even though my mother tried governing my every move, I learned how to play her to my advantage, never succumbing to her antics but giving her just enough room to think she had control. In my attempt to break free, I learned how to navigate my way around my mother, and in doing so, holding on to my most precious gift: my autonomy.

Lily Ann said I had my own brand of beauty—more interesting-looking than traditionally pretty. My lips were full, my green eyes soft and sensual and framed by long lashes. My complexion was helped along by good genes and the most expensive facial products. But according to all, my most engaging feature was my smile, which I offered openly, as though sending out a message that life had not yet hit me hard below the belt. It was for this reason that Blake had found me extremely sexy and approachable, which both surprised and delighted me.

My thoughts turned to Alexandra, who paraded around Manhat-tan as though she were ready to be fucked at a moment's notice. After she interviewed me, she hired me for my knowledge about art, but more because of my connection to the art world, namely a stepfather who was, before his death, a leading art collector, aficionado, and patron.

Alexandra had her own style, which was a far cry from mine. She was aggressive and could be bitchy as hell. She knew what she wanted and went after it with a vengeance. And, despite being al-most fifty, she was gorgeous, an attribute she played up by appearing understatedly savvy and sexy—quite a winning combination. Best of all, she had a reputation of owning one of the most sought-after galleries in New York. The entire art world (Europe included) flocked to her feet and sucked up to her every chance they could. Alexandra, moneyed from family wealth and a tony divorce, took it all in stride. She paraded herself like a grand peacock, which, on the surface, was all glamour, but dare to rub her the wrong way, and like a cobra, she was known to attack.

The first time we met, she cross-examined me for two hours.

"I see something in you, Samantha. You have smarts. Best of all, you've grown up in an art family. Grayson Wolfe was a man of integrity and taste, not incidental qualities. Obviously, it's rubbed off on you. You know the score, and I'd like to take you in as an associate. In a few years, if you do as well as I expect you will, we could be talking partner."

Doing as well as she expected meant following Alexandra's lead. I learned how to meet and greet and discreetly handle pushy hopefuls who were dying to show their work but would never make it. I dressed well, had a flair for turning on the small talk when necessary, and was able to spot a diamond in the rough. More important, I knew enough not to crowd Alexandra or outshine her. I kept my distance yet resurfaced when she invited me in. In short, I knew how to play that game, too.

"I'm away a lot," she told me during that interview, "my two passions are travel and work. I try combining the two whenever possible."

That was how she had discovered Blake Hamilton. He was at a boutique gallery in London where he was first showing two of his large paintings. I remembered that day well. Alexandra called me in the middle of the night, gushing incoherently and sounding slightly drunk.

"I found us a winner, Sam," she had said. "They're singing Blake's praises all over London, and I'm bringing him to New York. Even if it means bumping my other artists' shows, I don't care. We'll squeeze him in. And he's adorable, which doesn't hurt. He'll have all the rich dowagers fawning over him in no time."

My mother was one of them.

"I'm bringing back a dozen or so of his slides. I think we need to book him straightaway."

Alexandra sounded very British, with an accent picked up on her frequent travels to London. She incorporated the accent of each country she was visiting at the time. When in Paris, she tossed out a barrage of French phrases, to be followed weeks later by a stream of Italian ones. Three summers ago she had taken up with Giorgio, a lesser member of the Borghese family. She later shared a secret with me.

"When I have orgasms with Giorgio," she whispered, "I come in Italian."

"Really?" I was impressed. I imagined her belting out an aria as Giorgio royally fucked her in his villa under a Venetian moon.

"Yes, in the heat of passion, I always use the appropriate tongue. I think it's the polite thing to do."

I wasn't sure what tongue she was referring to, dialect or sexual technique. With Alexandra, nothing shocked me. Even Blake had told me when we talked business over dinner the other night: "Alexandra Cole is a wild and crazy woman."

"How wild? How crazy?"

"It's only an assumption, but I can assure you that she's very high-maintenance. Women like Alexandra might be a great fuck, but it stops there."

"And did you fuck her?"

"Never. She's hardly my type, but don't think she didn't try. I told her I don't mix art with lust. She's unaccustomed to being rejected. I'm surprised she was willing to accept me into her gallery after I rebuffed her advances."

"She obviously knows talent when she sees it."

"I think I pose a challenge to her. She's the kind of woman who never stops until she gets what she wants."

"And she wants you?"

"She wants what she can't have," Blake said.

"I'm starting to get jealous."

"She'll never get even a piece of me," he said, leaning over the table and kissing me. "In case you haven't noticed, I'm absolutely loopy over her assistant."

After that, I knew I could never trust Alexandra alone with Blake.

Alexandra held her five feet nine inches well. Her long jet-black hair and a straight and narrow figure made her seem hard at first glance. Upon closer scrutiny, one realized how truly gorgeous she was. Conversely, her mouth, though full and sensuous, was slightly crooked and always covered in bright red lipstick. Her eyes were too close together and her nose a tad too long. Her Jackie O sunglasses sat on the top of her head at all times, as though they were a permanent appendage. She could be both warm and intimidating, depending on her mood. Her most alluring trait was her enthusiasm, which overflowed, especially with men with whom she enjoyed taking charge.

"I prefer being on top during sex," she confessed to me over a two-martini lunch. "That way I have full control."

That said it all. I knew I had to be careful, lest Alexandra turn on me when I least expected it. So far we had managed a successful working relationship.

"You can learn a lot from a woman like Alexandra Cole," my mother told me after they first met. "She speaks her mind and knows how to flaunt her stuff."

"Stuff?"

"She has a persona, darling, and she makes the most of it. It takes more than looks, Samantha—it takes charisma. And Alexandra Cole has charisma up the kazoo."

Alexandra was equally taken with Madeleine. "Your mother is a real broad, Sam. My God, the woman is absolutely electrifying. No wonder Grayson Wolfe fell for her. I'd say she's one of your best accessories."

I didn't tell Alexandra that I found this one of the most offensive remarks anyone had ever made to me.

"Not that you don't possess your own sterling qualities, Sam, but

Madeleine is undeniably chic and smart, and I don't mind telling you, she reminds me a lot of me."

"That's so Narcissus of you." I actually uttered those words. That was also about as confrontationally brazen as I would ever get with Alexandra.

"Only people who appreciate themselves can understand others. I'll take that as a compliment, Sam."

She even sounded like my mother.

"As it was meant to be," I lied through my teeth. "Everyone finds my mother a regular showstopper."

"I'll look forward to getting to know you better," Alexandra had told my mother the first time they met.

"Yes, dear, I'm sure we'll find we have so much in common," Madeleine replied.

It was all I could do to keep from screaming.

EIGHT

Wedding rings:
the world's smallest handcuffs.

—*Anonymous*

During the next two weeks, I managed to tolerate Celeste, knowing that on the last day of July, she would be gone. I would have my apartment and my life to myself again.

Occasionally, when Blake called me at home, Celeste picked up and, with her hand over the receiver shouted: "It's your boyfriend, the artist." Then she'd hand over the phone with a smirk on her face—the same face I wanted to smack.

"Maybe it's best to call me on my cell," I told him. "At least until Celeste moves out."

On other occasions, Celeste would chat with Blake before she even told me who it was. I could hear her giggling quietly, the telltale sign that there was a man on the other end.

"I hope I'll be invited to your show in December," she said once. Silence.

"Yes, I know that Samantha handles the invitations, but I want to hear it from you."

More giggles until I grabbed the phone from her, giving her a look to kill.

"You *were* planning on inviting me to the show, right?" Celeste asked after I hung up.

"I'll be sending invitations to the entire family," I said. "That includes you."

"Well, Blake just told me he hopes I can be there."

"Good," I said, "then I'm sure you will be."

"Since he asked, how could I possibly refuse?"

I looked over at the kitchen calendar. July twenty-fifth. Six more days, and she would be gone. The question was: Could I hold out and not kill her before then?

To make my day even worse, my mother had invited herself to join me for dinner and a movie. Of course, Celeste was part of the plans.

"I adore nights out with you and Madeleine," Celeste said. "It's so girly and fun."

If I'd had the choice, I would have preferred that the two of them spend the evening together, but not wanting to go through an explanation as to why I was being so hostile, I succumbed. We grabbed La Scala salads at Joe Allen to be followed by two hours of silence as we sat together in the movie theater, Celeste between us feeling all cozy and warm.

"So, how is Fern doing?" I had deliberately asked over dinner, just to provoke, knowing the two hated each other's guts.

"Fern has her sexual preferences all screwed up," Celeste said. "She's an embarrassment to our entire family. My mother said she brought her girlfriend home for the weekend, and they slept together in Fern's bed. It's absolutely disgusting."

"As I always tell Samantha," Madeleine said, "being open-minded is what makes life more interesting. College girls like to experiment. It's probably just a phase that Fern will outgrow. At least that's what your parents told me."

"Fern has been a dyke since she was born," Celeste said. "She used to fantasize about having sex with her Barbie dolls."

"Well," Madeleine continued, ignoring that remark, "at least *you* like men. In fact, I was hoping that Samantha might have found you some eligible ones during your visit with her."

"The only one I like is Blake Hamilton," she said. "He's my kind of man."

"Darling," Madeleine said, "Blake Hamilton is *every* woman's kind of man."

Yes, and he's all mine, I wanted to tell her, though I kept quiet, knowing that I didn't quite believe that myself.

"Tell me, Celeste, you do date, don't you? Surely there must be men at Sarah Lawrence."

"Sarah Lawrence is filled with dorks. Honestly, I want to date, but the opportunity never presents itself."

"That's because *you* need to make it happen, dear. You can't sit back and wait. Do something. I tell Samantha all the time: You need to be proactive. Only then will you become a man magnet."

The fact that my mother lumped me into the advice category with Celeste made me temporarily lose the edge that I'd had on her, but once Madeleine got started, there was no stopping her.

"Take me, for instance, girls. I'm considered one of New York's most eligible widows. I intend to milk that for all it's worth . . . as soon as I come out of my mourning period, that is."

"Oh, Mother, stop it. You finished mourning as soon as Grayson was in the ground."

"I'm only saying that I'm biding my time before I get out there. I have a few matters to tend to before then."

"What matters?" I asked.

"Between us girls"—Madeleine rested her elbows on the table

and moved in—"I've always thought my labia were too large. The last thing I need is a turkey wattle between my legs."

"Mother!"

"Oh, Samantha, if I can't tell you, who can I tell? Yes, I could use a little repair down there. I have an appointment to see *the* labia expert. After that, I'll be ready to take on all the bachelors in the city."

Celeste's mouth was hanging open as she hung on Madeleine's every word.

"It's very important to tend to your personal gardening. The genitals play a very important part in the dating game. Men don't like women with weeds or excess flesh, and of course, there's the issue of safe sex." She looked at Celeste. "You do practice safe sex, don't you, sweetheart?"

"Actually, I'm a virgin," Celeste admitted.

"Out of *choice*?" I asked, slightly dumbfounded.

"As I told you, the opportunity hasn't presented itself."

"Does my sister, Elaine, know this?" my mother asked.

"Are you kidding? My mother and I never discuss sex."

"Knowing Elaine, that doesn't surprise me," Madeleine said. "I'm going to make a suggestion. I think it's time for you to have a complete gynecological exam. When was your last Pap smear?"

"For Christ's sake, Mother, leave Celeste alone." Surprisingly, I came to her defense.

"Celeste is family. It's perfectly fine . . . necessary, in fact, for me, her aunt, to be concerned. I happen to know that there's a new gynecologist on the scene who is supposed to be the hottest act in New York. You can't even get an appointment."

"In that case, we might as well forget it."

"I mean *most* people can't get appointments, but with my connections, I can get Celeste in. His name is Spencer Gould. He just joined the practice of his father, Alden Gould, and he's already being touted as one of the best in the city. Also," she whispered, "I understand he's very single, and his father, Dr. Alden Gould, is a recent widower. What could be more perfect? It's the ideal combo."

"Just what Celeste needs," I said.

"Not only Celeste, precious, all of us. I say we make appointments and go and check ourselves out while checking them out in the process. Frankly, I've always had a passing interest in Alden Gould."

"How do you know him?" Celeste asked.

"He collects art. In fact, Grayson and he often lunched together."

"But you already have a gyno," I said.

"Dr. Mendelson? For God's sake, Samantha. The man is the walking wounded. He has a bad hip, terrible breath, and his hands tremble. Early Parkinson's, I believe."

"The best kind," I quipped.

"I've been with Dr. Mendelson for so many years, it's time for a change. I'll set up appointments for all of us. Imagine, all our vaginas together. It will be so festive, and we can do lunch afterward."

Nobody else but my mother, Madeleine Krasner-Wolfe, could turn a gyn visit into a barrel of laughs.

My mother successfully pulled a few strings, dropped names, and put on the charm. She wrangled us appointments with the Doctors Gould, MD, FACS, PC, for the following Tuesday at eleven o'clock. The three of us sat in the waiting room, ready to be examined and cross-examined by Madeleine. Celeste and I would be seeing the younger Dr. Spencer while my mother preferred to check out the elder, Dr. Alden Gould, a man in his late sixties who had lost his wife a year ago in an automobile accident. The Upper East Seventies office was in pristine condition, designed elegantly, and appointed with fine antiques and art.

Two receptionists sat at a long desk with a glass partition separating them from the long line of women who passed through daily. The waiting room was filled to capacity with women of all ages there to see their beloved, Alden; the younger ones were patients of the up-and-coming star Spencer. The chrome and glass table was brimming over with the latest fashion magazines. Interspersed among those were a few on sailing.

"Grayson told me that Alden Gould is an avid sailor," Madeleine said. "If he's as good with your vaginas as he is with a rudder, we're in excellent hands."

"Dammit, Mother," I said. "Can you *please* keep your voice down?"

"Oh, Samantha, stop being so uptight. You have got to learn to relax."

"Please, I beg of you. Just act normal."

"Celeste, tell her: Isn't it fun having a mother with a gregarious personality?"

"I wish my mother were more like you," Celeste responded right on cue.

"I know what you mean," Madeleine said. "Elaine was never much in the humor department."

I buried my nose in the latest *Elle* and didn't look up until my name was called. I followed the pretty, young nurse into a consultation room where, a few minutes later, I was greeted by a man just over six feet, with sandy-colored hair and a smile that put me immediately at ease.

"Hello, Samantha," he said, extending his hand. "I'm Dr. Spencer Gould. It's a pleasure to meet you."

He sat down behind a long teak desk that took up half the room. His walls were adorned with degrees and awards from Princeton, Yale School of Medicine, New York Presbyterian Hospital, and more. In fact, the room was regurgitating medical recognition from the most prestigious institutions in the country.

"I like to first sit and chat with my new patients—get a sense of who they are, which is as important to me as their medical histories. Tell me about yourself."

For the next twenty minutes, as though he had all the time in the world, I chatted with Dr. Gould, with whom I felt an immediate rapport. Here was a man, probably in his early forties, with a bedside manner bar none and a sense of humor to go along with it. For a moment I forgot why I was here as he continued to inquire about my life. Then came the question that snapped me to attention: "Ever been pregnant?"

"Never," I said, with a modicum of guilt, as though I were out of sync with most women my age.

"No abortions?"

"No."

"Ever been married?"

"Almost."

He smiled. "Any problems I need to know about? Any surgeries?"

"Tonsils, age eight. No others."

"You sound like a healthy young woman."

I hung on the word "young."

"What kind of birth control are you using?"

"I tried the pill for a while but hated it. Next came the IUD—even worse. I'm an old-fashioned girl, I guess. I've been using a diaphragm."

"The diaphragm is still considered a viable form of birth control. Are you sexually active?"

As I stared across the desk at this Adonis, a sudden sense of modesty took hold. I felt awkward sharing this information. How stupid, I thought. He's a doctor. He's not here to pass judgment on my dating regime.

"Sporadically," I said.

"When the mood strikes?"

"When the right man comes along," I retorted. "And that doesn't happen too often. The last sexual encounter I've had in months was just last week."

"And, of course, you practice safe sex."

"I'm not stupid."

"I can see that."

Did I detect a slight bit of flirting oozing into our conversation? I couldn't be sure. But one fact was evident: Dr. Spencer Gould had a professional charm and appeal that I found extremely attractive, his long white coat adding the perfect touch to the entire package.

"All right, then, Samantha, I'll have you go down the hall to the examining room and get settled. I'll be with you in a few minutes. My nurse will accompany you."

We shook hands again. "It's been a pleasure getting to know you," he said.

I stepped outside the door, where Nurse Gorgeous was waiting to escort me to the inner sanctum of white sheets, cold stirrups, and speculums. My first instinct was to turn and run.

"You can change in here," she instructed. "Everything off, and I'll meet you inside the room on your left."

And so began my first encounter with Dr. Spencer Gould.

Twenty-five minutes later, I was back in the waiting room after being pronounced fit as a fiddle. Celeste, who had followed soon after me, was still inside with Dr. Spencer G. when my mother appeared, all brightness and smiles.

"Dr. Alden Gould is a sheer delight," she said. "It's such a shame I won't be using him, but I've decided to stay with Dr. Mendelson."

"What are you talking about?"

"The minute I walked into his office, I knew he was marriage material. I certainly can't use him as my doctor if I'm going to date him."

"He asked you out?"

"I'm getting to that. We had a lovely chat. We discussed art, our respective marriages, and the untimely death of our spouses. Then we moved on to our favorite restaurants and how he had heard so much about me when he and Grayson lunched together over the years. He absolutely worshipped Grayson and often consulted with him before buying art. Apparently, he's a major collector. Then he suggested I see another gynecologist."

"I thought you said Dr. Alden Gould was the be-all and end-all."

"Precisely, darling. That's why I accepted a dinner date with him for Friday night. After which he wants to show me his art. I'm absolutely smitten. And, I might add, so is he."

"Mother, I can't believe what I'm hearing."

"Why not? Turns out we have lots in common, but he obviously can't be my doctor and see me socially. It goes against the Hippocratic Oath or something. But whatever the case, I'd much rather be in his bed than on his examining table. In a few weeks I'll have my labia surgery and be as good as new. He'll never even know."

"Of course he'll know. He's a gynecologist."

"I'm not going to think about that right now. So, tell me about Spencer Gould. Did you like him? How are you?"

"He's great. I'm fine. I liked him."

"Of course you did. I'm sure the apple doesn't fall far from the tree. And according to Alden, Spencer just broke his engagement a few months ago with a girl from Sands Point."

"Meaning?"

"Meaning, lovie, that he's about as eligible as he can get."

"Sorry, Mother," I said, "but I'm taking on Dr. G. as my new gynecologist. So that ends that fantasy."

"I'd love to meet him."

"Why?"

"Alden couldn't say enough about him. Their practice roster tripled the minute Spencer joined the practice."

Ten minutes later, Celeste appeared, looking like she had just been through the most horrific ordeal of her life.

"My goodness, Celeste, sweetheart, sit down. Are you all right?"

"I've never been to a gynecologist before. If that's what it's like, I'm never setting foot in this office again."

"You didn't like Dr. Gould?"

"Are you kidding? He's divine. That made the whole experience even worse. When I told him I was a virgin, he raised an eyebrow. Right there in his office, he looked at me as though I were some sort of an anomaly."

"That's because most women your age have already . . . uh . . . sampled the goodies."

"Well, I haven't, and you know what Dr. Gould did?"

"What?" we asked in unison.

"He fitted me for a diaphragm."

"And?" I asked.

"I'd say that's very presumptuous of him. I mean, I never asked for one. The man is promoting sex."

"I don't think he meant it that way, dear," Madeleine said. "It's just that we're living in a time when sex beckons to us at every turn. It's epidemic. He simply wants you to be safe should an unforeseen opportunity come along. Think of it as an insurance policy."

"And to make it even worse," Celeste said, "they make you cough up the loot at the time of your visit."

"Of course," Madeleine said. "It's not a department store, where they send you a bill for minimum payment."

"Dr. Gould should be paying *me,*" Celeste said. "After all, he got his jollies."

"A test of endurance is more like it, Celeste," I said. "The man deals with women all day long, and it's not always easy listening to their complaints, real or imagined."

"Jesus," Celeste said, "Jesus. Let's blow off this little Chamber of Horrors. I've had it."

Madeleine jumped at the idea. "I know a darling spot just a few blocks away," she said.

Ten minutes later, we were seated at Vivolo, ordering glasses of wine. Celeste accepted hers eagerly. She slugged it down with gusto and, within a few minutes, had calmed down enough to be barely tolerable.

NINE

Bachelor: the only man who has
never told his wife a lie.

—*Anonymous*

Despite the fact that Madeleine claimed she was still
in mourning, she made it a point of shopping for "just a little something to throw on my back" Friday night.

"Alden Gould called this morning," she told me the next
day. "He's made reservations for Friday at Esca at eight. It's
his favorite Italian restaurant in the city. I feel like a
teenager about to go out on her first date."

"I see Alden didn't waste a moment calling you," I said.
I sat at my desk at the gallery, sorting through a list of cater-
ers for Blake's opening.

"I'm going in for my 'work' in two weeks," she added. "Until then I'm going to simply have to play hard to get in the sex department."

"Good God, Mother, sixty-two-year-old widows don't need to play hard to get. We all know you've been around the block."

"That may be true, Samantha, but until I recover from my tweaking, I prefer to keep sex out of the picture. When Alden Gould takes his first look at my nether region, I want it to be as tight as my face. So," she changed the subject, "have you heard from Blake?"

"He's called several times since he's been back in London."

"I think that's very good news. The prognosis is most encouraging."

"This isn't a biopsy, Mother."

"Obviously, the man can't get you out of his mind."

"That's a bit of an overstatement."

"My advice is—"

"I don't want advice."

"My advice is to sit tight until December, do some harmless dating, and use this time for a self-improvement regimen."

"What are you saying?"

"You know, exercise regularly, tighten up the loose ends, have a makeover, and most important, keep up with your Brazilian waxing. You are waxing regularly, aren't you, dear?"

"Mother, I'm really busy at the gallery. In fact, as we speak, I'm deciding on who is going to cater Blake's opening reception."

"Look no further," Madeleine said, "there's only one caterer in the city who you must use: Garden of Earthly Delights. I know Sebastian personally. He did the fashion show that I hosted last year, remember? He drove all the way to Westport, and let me say: They're still talking about it at the club."

"Thanks, I'll look into it." Once again, my mother was insinuating herself in my life as though I were a child who couldn't handle things on my own.

"Make sure you have him do the tornadoes and pesto on toast

points. They were the hit of the afternoon. Speak only to Sebastian, and mention that I'm your mother. The man is absolutely in love with me after I introduced him to his new lover, Pepe."

"Who's Pepe?"

"Only Ralph Lauren's best salesman. The man could sell a tie to an aardvark."

"You're a regular matchmaker, Mother."

"Don't kid yourself, Samantha. When it comes to affairs of the heart, I weave magic."

"And Sebastian is under your spell."

"Okay, be fresh, but you don't give me credit. Someday you'll come to appreciate me."

Perhaps someday you'll learn to treat me as the adult I am.

"Got to go," I said. "We'll talk later."

"I suppose you're not free for lunch?" Madeleine put in a parting shot.

"You guessed right." That was all I needed: a two-hour lunch where Madeleine could really work me over.

"Why do I even bother asking?" Madeleine sighed so audibly that I could hear her through the phone.

"Maybe later this week," I said, "don't give up hope."

"My dance card is already full," she said, hanging up on me.

I could always rely on my mother for all the small incidentals. I jotted down "tornadoes" on my notepad, surrounded by the tiny red hearts I had scribbled above Blake's name. I continued writing over and over again until the entire pad was filled.

As the days went on, I found myself preoccupied with only one thought: Blake Hamilton, who consumed most of my waking hours. If I wasn't rewinding the mental tapes of our lovemaking, I was busy planning his debut party. In between, I pushed aside all thoughts of other women who were probably bombarding him daily. Yet with each phone call and e-mail, one more sensual than the other, my insecurities were laid to rest. Blake's return to London had not diminished his ardor. In fact, the distance between us had added even more fuel to the sexual inferno raging within us. This morning's flowery e-mail was a perfect example:

> *My darling Samantha,*
>
> *It is early morning in London, with you still asleep after a day of running about the city, enjoying client lunches or perhaps an evening at the theater. Now, as I picture you in your bed—our bed—I can't seem to erase the smell of you. It is one thirty A.M. New York time and I am just rising. Only hours ago, you were probably immersed in a warm tub, luxuriating among the bubbles. Later, perhaps, sipping a glass of port before bed and thinking of me as I now think of you. I wonder what you are wearing: your little silk nightie with the florets on the straps I once lovingly removed? Or are you naked beneath your sheets, your body stretched out, fully exposed? Oh, Samantha, think of where I would like to be kissing you now.*
>
> *My love,*
> *Blake*

As if by rote, I had run to my desk first thing to read his e-mail. I'd laughed at how excessively mawkish sentimental lovers can become when faced with the blank page. I'd sat back and stared at my laptop, expecting that at any moment it would go up in a molten-lava-type eruption from the sheer heat generated by Blake's letter. I'd been delirious and overtaken with a frenzy so intense, nothing else could remove me from my task at hand: to respond. So it is with lovers. They exist in a world known only to them, and for that moment all outside stimuli are nonexistent. "Ah, e-mails," Lily Ann once said. "They can rouse people to unattainable heights. Bennett and I once had simultaneous orgasms on the Internet after two hours of back-and-forth e-mail foreplay."

My hair was sleep-disheveled. I had slipped into a pair of old sweatpants and had on a Bennington T-shirt. I pushed the reply button and began composing an equally sentimental letter.

Dear Blake,

I just woke up and am off to the gallery, but I just read your beautiful letter. Darling, I am filled with such longing for you that supersedes all else.

I ache for your touch. I think of your hands, your mouth roaming free, my body opening to you. Make love to me, Blake—all the way from London to New York. Hold that thought, my darling.

Yours,

Samantha

And there we were, two lovers separated by an ocean and united by our mutual overheated fantasies, or how Madeleine once described a love letter: the petit mal of literary fulfillment.

I would not be able to last until December.

Bright and early Saturday morning, before I left for work, Madeleine was on the phone: "I'm delirious. I'm beside myself."

No tempering of emotions where she was concerned.

"I take this to mean you had a good time with Dr. Alden Gould."

"Good time? That hardly describes it. The man is masterpiece quality in a most substantial frame."

Madeleine's analogies to art were the highest form of compliment.

"And darling, that's not all. We spoke at length about Spencer and what fun it is having him join his father's practice. Samantha, he sounds absolutely dreamy."

"I already know that."

"Darling, you need to do what I did: step away from your doctor/patient relationship immediately and let him know you're available."

"Are you serious, Mother?"

"There are plenty of other fine clinicians in the city. The sooner you leave the practice of Drs. Gould and Gould, you'll be open game."

"You've reached the absolute height of your craziness, Mother."

"Alden said that Spencer dates only the finest people in New York. After his latest romantic fiasco, he's become very picky."

"You seem to know a lot."

"That's what made it all so perfect: By the end of the evening, I felt that Alden and I were close friends."

"You're unstoppable, Mother. So tell me everything." I tried moving the conversation away from me.

"Alden picked me up at my apartment. Even Gilda agreed he was divine."

"Well, now that you have your housekeeper's approval . . ."

"We had drinks and then went on to dinner. He thought the apartment was a regular art museum. He swooned over the Jasper Johns in the foyer."

"As well he should."

"Samantha, we have so much in common, it's unbelievable. There wasn't a lull in the conversation all night. I'm seeing him again on Sunday. We're going to the ballet. Brunch first. I was even thinking we could double-date sometime: Alden and me, you and Spencer."

"Don't you dare entertain such an idea." My mother had now pushed the envelope.

"Oh, stop it. If it comes up naturally, I will. Timing is everything."

"I'm perfectly capable of meeting my own men."

"Not men like Dr. Spencer Gould."

"What about Blake? Have you dismissed him already?"

"Blake is lovely. He's also in London. You're not going to sit around waiting for him, are you? Why can't you have some fun in the meantime?"

"You're so fickle, Mother. I thought you adored Blake."

"Of course, but there are many other good eggs in the carton. Play the field, Samantha. Tick-tock, tick-tock. You're not getting any younger."

"Neither are you, Mother," I zinged back. I was finally gaining some control, and I enjoyed giving her the occasional tweak as I retaliated defiantly.

"My point precisely. That's why I intend to make every day count, and so should you. But I'm not in my childbearing years, and you are. Don't forget that. The more men we date, the better our chances."

"Chances for what?"

"Husbands, of course, Samantha. I'm not planning on entering my golden years without a man by my side. And I would like a couple of grandchildren to leave my art to."

She was off on a tangent. There was no stopping her where her fictional grandchildren were concerned.

"That's it, Mother. I'm hanging up."

"If I don't enlighten you, who will? Someday you'll realize that I'm your best friend. So what are your plans for this evening?"

"Lily Ann and I are doing dinner and a movie."

"How's her Bennett?"

"Fine. Their bicoastal relationship is alive and well."

"Do you think they'll ever get married?"

"That seems to be part of her plans. They haven't set a date yet. But she would like to stay in New York."

"I would hope so. L.A. is so otherworldly. I don't know how she does it. All those plane trips—all those airborne germs. Personally, I prefer sea travel."

"I might be going over to London myself."

"Really? When?"

"Nothing definite. Blake simply tossed out the idea."

"Well, that sounds serious."

"Don't get all excited, Mother."

"In the meantime, why not try Spencer Gould on for size? I can arrange it."

"I'm getting off the phone, Mother. I'm going to the gym."

"Good idea. I'd concentrate on your upper arms if I were you. They're the first to go. The other day on Madison Avenue, I saw a young woman in a sleeveless dress whose arms looked like slabs of raw veal."

"Thanks. I'll keep that vivid image in mind."

"Kiss, kiss, and huggie love," Madeleine said, her usual closing remark.

"You have *got* to love that woman," Lily Ann said over dinner at Sushi Hana on Amsterdam and Eighty-second Street. "She's always looking out for you."

"Give me a break," I said. "Imagine the four of us double-dating."

"Anyone else's mother, no, but Madeleine is in a class by herself. So what's wrong with dating the gyno? He sounds edible."

"He is, but we already established a medical rapport. I mean, the man has already looked up my wazoo."

"Even better," Lily Ann said, "he knows what to expect."

"You're as bad as my mother."

"In case you haven't noticed, there's a shortage of men in New York. If there's an eligible bachelor on the loose, why the hell shouldn't you date him? This seems like a natural move."

"You're saying that my mother should fix me up?"

"It's not as though he hasn't already met you. He might go for the idea."

"He knows my entire sexual history, which, I might add, is painfully limited."

"Men prefer women who don't sleep around."

"He's also aware that I just slept with a man only a week ago."

"He does?"

"Yes, he takes a very detailed patient history. He asks all the right questions. He even knows that I still use a diaphragm."

"I think the whole thing sounds incredibly charming."

"I'm his patient, you dope."

"That can easily be fixed. Madeleine can explain to Alden Gould that you'd rather see his son socially than professionally and let Alden take it from there. He might like the idea of Madeleine's daughter dating his son. It's all so *Brady Bunch*."

"I can't believe what I'm hearing. Are you and my mother in cahoots?"

"Sometimes, Sam, mothers come in handy. You have nothing to lose. My God, I'm waiting every day for Bennett to set the date. I swear, if some great guy came along, I just might test the waters."

"Are you and Bennett okay?"

"Yes, we're fine, but he has cold feet, and I'm getting impatient. That's why I'm saying: If there's a bachelor out there, carpe diem. You've got it made: With Blake in London, you have the entire island of Manhattan to explore. Could it get any better?"

Lily Ann had a way of putting life into perspective, even if it was my life and not hers. Just this morning I had written another passionate love letter to Blake, and now I was already thinking of dating another man. The dichotomy was almost too much to handle. But she had a point. I was thirty-eight, single, and unencumbered. Yet in some inexplicable way, my tie to Blake was growing stronger by the day through our constant barrage of e-mails. If I did go out with Dr. Spencer Gould, would I be cheating on Blake? Neither of us had laid claims on the other. Who knew what was happening on his end of the world? For all I knew, he could be dating every night. I was confused as hell.

I remembered a psychic my mother had seen after Grayson's death who'd helped her through the grieving process while mapping out the rest of her life.

"Samantha," my mother had told me, "my psychic, Aurora, accomplished more in one session than all my years with Dr. Milman. That's when I decided to give up psychoanalysis and spend my money on couture instead of lying on a couch rehashing my childhood. Aurora has an entirely different approach. She says my future looks rosy and bright. Dr. Milman never told me that. He said unless

I come to terms with my out-of-control ego, I'm headed for trouble. I've had it with these mental-health bores. It's so tedious talking about myself. Who needs to travel back in time? It's all about what's happening tomorrow."

"A psychic, Mother?" I said. "I don't think so."

"Why not? Dr. Milman accused me of being in a state of denial just because I refused to discuss my sex life. So I picked myself off his couch and taxied over to Bergdorf's, where I dropped a bundle on a Dolce and Gabbana bag. For the amount of money I spent supporting Milman, I could have an exciting new wardrobe. Shopping, now, that's real therapy. Trust me, Aurora is a godsend."

Now, recalling that conversation and feeling somewhat desperate, I called my mother about consulting her psychic.

"Aurora? *Now* you're making sense," she said.

"Tell me what to expect."

"She's as smart as a whip, and she doesn't waste time. Shrinks want to keep you in their clutches forever. With Aurora, it's a quick summation of your life in one fell swoop."

"I never even considered this before."

"Don't knock it until you've tried it. All my friends swear by Aurora. Nina Tuttle told me about her."

A recommendation from Nina Tuttle? Not a comforting thought. Nina was about the ditziest woman I had ever met, though one of my mother's closest friends.

"Nina has pizzazz," my mother said. "Underneath all that flightiness lies a very bright woman.

"Aurora will set you straight," she went on. "Her card is in my drawer. Hold on." She came back and read it to me: " 'Aurora. Spiritual guide and healer. Put your future in my hands—212-555-5551.' Don't forget to tell her I'm your mother."

"Will that make a difference?"

"You never know, but it certainly can't hurt. It might even be helpful."

That, I suspected, was a matter of opinion. I kept Aurora's number by my bed, wrestling all night about whether to call her. As long as I didn't take it too seriously, it would be fine. In fact, there was an air of frivolity to it—a harmless diversion that might inadvertently shed light on my present dating dilemma. With that in mind, I phoned her on Sunday morning.

"Aurora speaking. How may I guide you?" She sounded friendly enough to alleviate any slight trepidation.

"I'd like to make an appointment."

"I have an opening at five this afternoon."

"Perfect. I'll take it," I said.

It was as simple as that. No idle chitchat, no flowery greetings. Basic and to the point. I could handle that.

Aurora operated out of her fifth-floor walk-up in SoHo. She had wild black hair, three cats with even wilder hair, and was into bandanas. When she shook my hand, I was nicked by one of her stiletto fingernails. She reminded me of a gypsy but had enough contemporary art on her walls and some fine antique furniture to be considered a woman with a modicum of taste. She greeted me in bare feet, holding two of her cats.

"Shoes interfere with my aura," she said. "All my sensory perceptions come through my feet. Sit down on the sofa, take off your shoes, and show me your hands."

I dared not argue with Aurora, who, despite her petite stature, had a commanding presence. She sat back on her frayed green velvet chair and peered into a crystal ball. I couldn't decide if she actually believed this crap or if the ball was simply there to create the right mystic effect.

"I see interference. I see static. I see two men."

"That's amazing," I said.

"There's a woman who's creating chaos in your life—a woman who is controlling you, trying to push you in several different directions." She took a deep breath. "Does any of this ring true?"

"It's my mother to a T," I said, without mentioning Madeleine's name. "Please continue."

Aurora dipped her fingers into a bowl filled with colored crystals and lit some incense. She closed her eyes. "I'm sensing confusion. Have you been experiencing carnal cravings?"

"Yes, I have," I admitted.

"As I suspected." She looked down at her feet. "These feelings I'm having are emanating from my feet."

"I'm new to this. Are your feet always correct?" I asked.

"Always. The answers to everything lie at the earth's surface, not in the stars, as some psychics believe. My big toe is starting to tingle—a telltale sign."

"What kind of a sign?"

"Something, but I can't say for sure. I'm receiving some interference."

She picked up a glass filled with a muddy-looking substance and drank. She closed her eyes again and crossed her arms, rubbing her hands across both breasts. "I see water—a large stretch of water."

"Yes, yes . . . keep going." I was becoming intrigued.

"You recently met someone."

"I did."

"A man who lives far away. Across an ocean, perhaps."

I was astounded. How could she possibly know this? Maybe there was some validity to all this voodoo about which I had been suspicious for years.

"Can you tell more about this man?" I asked.

"I can tell you that he possesses a great talent. Is he in the arts?"

"Yes, he's an artist."

"And you have been intimate with this man."

"We have."

"But he's gone from your life, at least for a while."

"He's back at his home in London."

"You still correspond."

"Yes, we send letters back and forth. Passionate letters. Should I be telling you this?"

"Of course you should," Aurora said. "A psychic is analogous to seeing a shrink, except I provide snacks."

"You do?"

"Yes, are you hungry?"

"I'm starving."

"Wait here. I'll go and get some ginger snaps. Would you like some herbal tea?"

"Do you possibly have a can of Diet Coke?"

"Sure," she said. "I'm a Coca-Cola addict. That's all I drink."

"What about the tea?"

"Purely for effect. Some of my clients like me to read their tea leaves. It creates the right ethereal ambience."

While we nibbled our cookies and drank Coke, Aurora grew more interested in my life.

"Have you been single for long?" she asked.

"Most of my life. I had one long-term relationship years ago."

"I might have told you that if we had talked longer," she said. "So, you're playing the field?"

"Not really. Most men I meet are colossal jerks. The rest are strictly platonic. All the good ones seem to be married or in relationships."

"Let me see those hands again." She ran her fingers along my lifeline and then went back to her crystal ball. "Aha, I see another possible romance brewing."

"You do?" I hung on her every word.

"It's a cloudy image, but yes, I definitely feel my toe tingling again."

"Can you tell me more?"

"As I said, it's a bit vague, but I see the color white."

"Yes, there is a man I met, a professional."

"A medical professional?"

"Oh my God, yes."

"Instinct, honey. ESP. Even as a kid, I could predict things before they happened. I once told my mother that her brother, my uncle Leo, wasn't long for this world. Leo croaked a week later. My mom wouldn't talk to me for a month. I used to scare everyone. Nobody wants to hear the truth, especially when it's ugly."

"What's your advice, Aurora?"

"Call me Estelle," she said. "I grew up in Brooklyn. My real name is Estelle Goldstein, but let's keep that between us. Aurora works better in my circles. My advice is to keep yourself open and available. I can't say in which direction you're headed, but maybe we can talk again in a month or so, when your aura is more pronounced."

"What about the man in white?"

"Too soon to tell. But it might complicate things, especially with that other woman around."

"My mother?"

"I'm not sure about that. I see a woman, that's all I can tell you."

I paid Aurora her three hundred bucks and thanked her. Then I went home and called Lily Ann.

"You don't really believe that crap, do you?" Lily Ann said.

"I'm telling you, the woman was a witch. She picked up all kinds of nuances, including a man in white. I paid her three hundred bucks."

"Are you going bonkers on me? Please, I need you sane. You're the only really normal friend I have," Lily Ann pleaded.

"You had to be there. She was so right-on scary."

"You're not going back, are you?"

"Honestly, I don't know. She suggested I see her again in a month, when my aura is more pronounced and she can tell me more."

"Jesus, Sam, you *are* crazy."

"Oh, stop it, it was just a whim. I always wanted to see what it would be like to consult a psychic, that's all."

"Well, now you know. It's a lot of empty assumptions without any validity."

"I'm not so sure. She had a real handle on my life and the key players in it. She even knew I had a romantic involvement with someone far away."

"Everyone has an involvement with someone far away."

"Do you?"

"Yes, my dentist in New Jersey. I've been going to him since I was twenty-one."

"That's hardly the same thing. And let me just say this: She said there was another woman in my life."

"That's easy. It's Madeleine."

"Maybe yes and maybe no. Aurora said it was too soon to tell."

"Of course she said that. She wants you to come back and drop another three hundred smackers."

"You're such a goddamn cynic," I said.

"I know," Lily Ann said affectionately, "that's what separates me from nuts like you."

When my mother asked how it had gone with Aurora, I placated her by saying it had gone well and left it at that.

"Any revelations?" Madeleine asked.

"Nothing cosmic," I said.

"Well, you sound better. Anything you want to tell me?"

"Not really."

"Someday, Samantha, you won't need to be so secretive. But I won't probe."

After that, we dropped the subject. I never brought it up with her again.

I tried pushing Aurora's predictions from my mind. I told myself that what she'd said about another woman and a man in a white coat could apply to anyone. Then again, she had hit close to home and gotten me thinking, especially about who the other woman was. If she had accomplished one thing, it was to completely unnerve me.

Blake and I continued to exchange passionate letters. One night after a particularly hot e-mail, on the pretense of seeming playful and light, I dared to slip in a question that bordered on the intrusive:

Dearest Blake,
  You have turned me into a pile of protoplasmic mush. Your last letter pushed my temperature up to the searing point. I'm completely spent on your words alone. And yet I feel a tinge of

uncertainty gnawing at me. I imagine you leaving a trail of
women all over London prostrated at your feet. Am I being silly?

Love,

Samantha

I pushed the send button and immediately regretted this impulsive move. Rereading my letter, I realized I had gone a step too far, sounding needy and clingy, a major turnoff to a man like Blake. What was I thinking? My God, we had only met a few weeks ago, and already I was behaving as though we were a couple. Bad move—one I would probably come to regret. Then again, why couldn't I be myself and share a revealing moment with the man I had slept with? Perhaps he would find my "silliness" engaging and sweet?

I wouldn't know, at least not tonight. There was no reply from Blake, nor was there any e-mail waiting for me the next morning. I felt ridiculous for even allowing myself to be so uncool. I left for work feeling out of sorts, with a knot in the pit of my stomach. Finally, at lunchtime I called Lily Ann.

"Okay, so you let your hair down a bit. Big deal," she said. "As you said, you were being playful."

" 'Presumptuous' is a better word. What gives me the right to probe into Blake's love life? What he does is his own damn business."

"Hold on, babe," Lily Ann said. "You don't exactly have a nodding relationship with the man. You've had hot sex, and along with that comes some sort of emotional license. Since you two met, you've spent every night together. I would say that entitles you to say what you want."

"I don't think I needed to bring other women into the equation. After all, we're not exclusive. Frankly, I think I scared him."

"Time will tell," Lily Ann said.

"You're starting to sound like Aurora," I said.

"Best to leave that name out of our conversations," she said.

I got through the day checking for e-mails, but nothing. By five I was becoming slightly unglued. It was unlike Blake not to have written back with a parting e-kiss or a good-morning hug, as we referred to these letters. My recourse was to do nothing but wait, and that alone was enough to infuriate me. I hated playing a passive role and toyed with the idea of writing a friendly e-mail, then decided that being pushy on top of everything else would be the kiss of death. I had lumped myself into that category of women who'd lost leverage in a relationship and found themselves at the mercy of the man. Goddammit, I admonished myself every time my mailbox ran on empty. It had been only a day and a half, though it felt like an eternity. Maybe my mother had a point. Why concentrate on one man when the city was filled with eligible bachelors? I called her that night, never mentioning Blake's sudden disappearing act.

"All right," I said, "if it comes up naturally in conversation, go ahead and tell Alden that I'd be happy to date his son. But please do it gracefully."

"Darling," Madeleine said, "I'm an expert at social innuendo. Leave it to me."

"But not the double-dating part. I'm not quite sure I could handle that."

"I wasn't serious," Madeleine said quite seriously. "Just a fleeting thought that had passed through on its way to my mouth. I'm seeing Alden this evening."

"This is getting to be a regular habit."

"And not one I'm soon to break. I think I'm falling for the man."

"You don't waste any time."

"I told you, Samantha, I'm en route to earning my bachelor degree. And sweetheart, I've only just begun."

TEN

A bachelor is a guy who
leans toward women—but not far
enough to lose his balance.

—*Earl Wilson*

Madeleine wasn't kidding. Talk about man magnets. She was like honey to a bee, and the bee of the moment was Dr. Alden Gould. Often I marveled at the way she put herself out there. It wasn't just her good looks, quick wit, and smart clothes that appealed to men, but her genuine interest in the male sex that charmed the pants off them. Even her doorman was smitten, in his way. He made sure she never had to wait for a cab or open a door herself. Of course, the big tips and fat Christmas envelope didn't hurt, either. Madeleine knew exactly how to win over a man, from the minor players in her life to the most significant. Grayson once said about her: "Put your mother in a room, and all the men will be hovering about her in minutes. She gives off a scent."

Madeleine dismissed the remark humorously: "It must be my Clinique body lotion."

But truth be told, Madeleine possessed one giant attribute that was her secret to success: moxie. Coupled with that was the fact that she liked men, and sensing that, they were flattered and responded in kind.

"There's no such thing as a dull man," she once told me. "Every man can be made interesting with the right woman to bring him out of his shell. It's all in the technique, Samantha, and I have my technique down pat. Study me, darling. Learn from me."

Whether I wanted to or not, it was hard to ignore Madeleine at work, since she wasn't exactly subtle. Once, years ago, when my father was buying ties at Paul Stuart, me at his side, a stranger walked up and asked my mother for her opinion on which tie looked best.

"There's no question, it's this one," she said, reaching out to touch the strand of silk paisley wound around his neck. "It brings out the man in you, and the colors go so well with your brown eyes. You'll have every woman sighing."

The man was grateful, thanked my mother, and immediately purchased the tie, giving her a parting wink. It had nothing to do with ties but everything to do with making him feel handsome and powerful.

"That's your mother," my father said with slight resignation. "She was put on this earth to keep the male population happy."

"Oh, what's the harm?" she scoffed it off. "The poor man was completely helpless. I made his day. It was just a silly tie we were talking about."

But "harmless" was hardly a word that one associated with Madeleine.

I grew up watching her in action, picking up her "tidbits" and trying to apply them to me. But our styles were completely different. My mother had an in-your-face effect that she carried off with aplomb, while for me, the low-key approach seemed to work best. If

Blake had rebuffed her, she would have quickly blown him off and said: "Next!" She didn't brood; she didn't sulk. I was a master of both. She wore her air of insouciance well, while I, in the throes of rejection, practically fell over myself and didn't quite know what to do next. If I had shared my humiliating e-mail to Blake, she would have looked at me askance and said, as only she could, "Big mistake." Rather than subject myself to my mother's ridicule, I said nothing about it and sat back and gloated. When it came to men, I was often reduced to a tortured soul, whereas Madeleine wouldn't waste a minute of her time on self-recrimination. In that way, she was the perfect role model. Another daughter might have benefited greatly. But I, her only child, was rebellious to the core, having spent most of my childhood and adult life trying to preserve my autonomy. Any intervention from my mother was considered interference rather than a legacy to admire and rely on.

Those were the thoughts I hashed over while waiting for Blake to write, to call. Still no word, until two days later, on Thursday afternoon, when the phone rang at the gallery.

"I suppose you were wondering what happened to me," came Blake's voice on the other end.

I nearly jumped. "I did give it a passing thought." I could feel my entire body stiffen.

"I had places to go, people to see."

"Oh, really?" I felt secretly elated while equally peeved. "What places, what people?"

"New York . . . and you."

"What are you talking about?"

The phone suddenly went dead.

A minute later, the door of the Cole Gallery opened. There was Blake, a bouquet of roses in hand and a look on his face that instantly pushed all negative feelings aside. I was speechless.

"Did you know," he asked, "that you look mighty odd with your mouth hanging open?"

"I do?"

"Absolutely. Stop gaping at me as if you've just seen a ghost. I expect a proper greeting. After all, I did travel all the way from London to see you."

"You have?" I could speak only in short, cropped phrases.

"Yes, a lot better than an e-mail, don't you think?"

"I do."

"Although I will admit: I am rather fond of our correspondences. In fact, I can't remember ever having a sexier pen pal."

"Me, too." I was grinning from ear to ear.

"Even so, there's nothing quite like an up-close-and-personal encounter."

"My sentiments exactly."

"Well, I can't stand here all day holding these blooming buds in my hands."

I took the flowers and tossed them on my desk. Then I threw my arms around Blake. We kissed long and passionately.

"I don't know what to say. When did you arrive?" I asked.

"Early this morning. I'm in for a long weekend, and I'm beat. By any chance can you be naughty and take the rest of the day off?"

I can take the rest of my life off, I could have said.

"You *know* how naughty I can be. But what would Alexandra say?" I said.

"Alexandra is tucked neatly away in Paris. We won't bother telling her, if that's all right with you?"

"You're completely incorrigible."

"Just the way you like me."

"You know me so well."

"Yes, I do. And I want to keep knowing you—every inch of you."

"When do we start?" I asked. The flirting had morphed into aphrodisiac proportions.

"I say as soon as possible. Close up shop, and as soon as you can, meet me at the Elysee."

"Even better, why not stay with me?"

"You don't have other plans? I'm not barging in on anything? A hot new lover, perhaps?"

"Shut up."

"Celeste wouldn't mind?"

"You couldn't have timed it better. Celeste is supposed to leave this morning. She's probably packing her suitcases as we speak."

"That's it, then. I'll call the hotel and cancel my room."

"Why didn't you tell me you were coming?"

"What? And miss that priceless look on your face? Never. It was worth the entire trip just to shock you. And Samantha, about all those London birds who are falling at my feet? My heart is in New York. Your e-mail sounded somewhat weird."

"Oh, that. Let's pretend I never sent it. I don't even know why I did. I've been regretting it ever since."

"Contrary to popular belief, I'm not dating half the UK. The paparazzi and gossip columnists like creating that image. It's called celebrity-fucking. They love getting their hands on the so-called hotties and running with them. They never let the truth get in the way of a good story. As for your e-mail: You sent it because you were feeling insecure, the side effect of long-distance relationships. It goes with the territory."

"You're not mad?"

"I'm experiencing lots of feelings, but anger isn't one of them."

"I think you just might be the most fantastic man I've ever met."

"You *think*? I damn well bloody am, and that's a fact." He kissed me again. "Okay, my love, I'm outta here," he said. "I need a nap. Stick these flowers in some water, do what you need to do, and then come home and do me."

"At your service, sir." I rummaged through my bag and handed Blake my apartment keys. "I'll be home in a couple of hours," I said, still nonplussed. "I have some phone calls to make, and then I'm all yours. My God, Blake, you've practically given me a heart attack."

"I brought along the nitro, just in case."

Another kiss and he was out the door. I stood motionless, watching him through the large gallery window as he hailed a cab. Then, because I couldn't keep this to myself, I phoned Lily Ann at work.

"Hey kiddo, what's up?" she asked.

"I think I stopped breathing."

"That would solve everything."

"You'll never in a million years guess what just happened."

"I love it already."

I filled Lily Ann in.

"This is the most romantic story I've ever heard. Better than any movie, for God's sake. Geez, Sam, the man is a regular Cary Grant."

"I know. I'm still vibrating."

"I would have had my way with him right on the floor of the gallery."

"Yes, that way everyone on Madison Avenue could have seen us."

"Where is he now?"

"On the way to my apartment. I hope to hell Celeste is gone. She was supposed to leave a few hours ago."

"My advice, honey, is to get the hell out of there and take your hot bod home. There's a man in your bed waiting to do all sorts of obscene things to you."

And hurry home I did within the hour, canceling my two afternoon appointments and locking up. If Alexandra had known, she might have fired me. Then again, she wasn't one to let anything stand in the way of a good fuck. When I reached my apartment, much to my chagrin, Blake was sitting in the living room chatting with Celeste. The two of them were eating peanut butter and jelly sandwiches.

"You never told me Blake was in New York," Celeste said coyly.

"Blake is a man of many surprises. I thought you'd be gone by now," I said, hoping she would grab the hint.

"What's the rush? I'm only going back to my parents' house. Personally, I prefer staying here. It's been a ball."

A ball for her, maybe. For me: my worst nightmare.

I tried being gracious, but every time I looked over at Blake, all I could think of was jumping on his gorgeous bones. Instead, here we sat, the three of us, making small talk.

"It was very nice of your cousin to make me a sandwich," said Blake, ever the perfect gentleman. "I was famished."

"Airplane food sucks," Celeste said. "I took pity on him."

"Admittedly, I haven't had a good peanut butter sandwich since my old school days. Then I ate them like they were going out of style."

"I used our new English jam, too," she said. "After all, it seemed only fitting."

You mean *my* new English jam, you little wench.

"So, Celeste," I mustered up my courage, trying not to be obnoxiously blunt, "when *are* you planning on leaving?"

"I'm trying to make the most of my last day here. Why, is there a checkout time?"

Blake sat back, amused by our verbal combat, of which he was clearly and subliminally the center of attention.

I threw all formality aside. "I—we—would prefer a little privacy."

Celeste shot Blake a knowing look. "I definitely get what you're saying. If I had a man who traveled all the way across the Atlantic to see me, I'd want my privacy, too. Look, you two have fun. I'm almost packed and out of here."

I thought she was going to cry right there on her peanut butter and jelly sandwich. Blake, clearly feeling a sudden empathic rush, came to her rescue: "Celeste, please, no hurry on our account. I'll be perfectly fine taking a much needed nap while you enjoy your time here in the apartment. I'm sure that would be okay with Samantha." He nodded at me in acknowledgment.

I acquiesced. "Good idea all around. You take your nap, and Celeste, whenever you leave is fine," I said, putting the bitch in me temporarily on hold.

"Thank you so much, Sam. I hate being rushed. Always have. It makes me nervous when someone is breathing down my neck."

"I can relate to that," I said.

"Well, then, ladies, I'm off to slumberland for an hour. Celeste"—Blake extended his hand—"nice seeing you again, and thanks for the PB and J. One of the best, and I'm an expert."

Celeste bypassed his hand and, emitting one of her little

squeaks, kissed him on either cheek. "I do hope we'll meet again . . . and soon," she said.

"I'm certain we will." He turned to me. "Darling, feel free to join me for a nap, too, if you want."

This was the first time Blake had used an endearment in public, and I loved it. It was the best form of validation.

Celeste pretended not to hear. "Mind if I borrow a suitcase from you, Sam? I'm leaving town with more than I came with. I did too much shopping."

"No problem. There's an extra one in the back of my bedroom closet."

"Should I get it now before Blake gets into bed?" she asked. Every word was smothered in innuendo.

"*I'll* get it," I said.

Blake followed me down the hall, his hand pulling the waist of my skirt so that I fell back into him. "Come here, you." He cornered me between bedrooms. "As soon as your cousin has what she wants, come to bed."

"My cousin obviously wants *you.*"

"And I want *you,*" he said. "Feel me. I'm as hard as a rock."

He placed my hand between the creases of his trousers. If Celeste weren't a few feet away, I would have unzipped his pants and taken him right there. Instead, regaining my composure, I left him sitting on the bed and grabbed a suitcase for Celeste. I returned to the living room and handed it to her.

"I *know* what *you two* are going to do," she sang out. "Don't let me stop you."

"Celeste." I finally could stand it no longer. "I think you're starting to outstay your welcome."

"Fine, Sam," she said soberly. "While you're humping away, I'll be finishing up my packing. So sorry I've been such a drain on you."

I softened. "Let's not get dramatic. It's just that Blake's surprise visit has gotten me a bit unraveled. I'm sure you can understand that."

"Actually, I can't," she said. "I don't have some handsome dude camping out in *my* bedroom."

"You could if you wanted to. Perhaps it's time for you to seriously consider dating."

For a moment Celeste dropped all pretenses. Her anger dissipated. "Believe me, I'd like to, Sam, but I just don't know how to attract men. It is pathetic, but that's the God-awful truth."

And there in my living room, Celeste all vulnerable and gooey, purged her woes while we sat on the couch, my arm around her shoulder. Even though I didn't want to, I suddenly felt terribly sorry for her.

"When you go back to Sarah Lawrence next month, you'll have a chance to change all that," I said. "A new school year, a new beginning. Just let yourself go, and you'll see: The guys will be chasing after you. You have so much potential."

Whether I meant it or not, it needed to be said.

"But I'm not all that sexy, Sam, really."

"Celeste, sex appeal is all in the head. Trust me on that."

"But you're so pretty, and you have an amazing body."

"There are lots of pretty girls out there. It takes more than that, believe me."

"What *does* it take? I sure would like to know."

Reaching down as far as I could, I conjured up my mother's secret ingredient—the secret to her success.

"It takes *moxie,* Celeste," I said. "That's pretty much all you need."

"And a diaphragm, too, of course."

"Yes, Celeste: moxie and a diaphragm, and you're pretty much set."

ELEVEN

Men who have a pierced ear
are better prepared for marriage—they've
experienced pain and bought jewelry.

—*Rita Rudner*

Our little heart-to-heart had been enough to smooth over Celeste's ruffled feathers. She was packed and gone within the hour. I was heading to my bed the minute she closed the door behind her.

"Free at last, free at last," I sang, ripping off my clothes and sliding in next to the half-asleep Blake. "I *could* let you nap, or we could have sex. Your call," I teased.

"I'll need a minute to think about that." He got on top of me while I lay beneath him, my arms raised, his hands holding my wrists, rendering me completely immobile and passive.

"The question," he said, between a series of sweet mini-kisses, "is what part of you to ravish first?" He kissed my right breast and moved over to the left one. "Oh, yes, very tasty indeed."

I lay back, enjoying every step along the way.

"And those nipples . . . we can't neglect them, now, can we?"

Gently, lovingly, his tongue rolled around each one, causing them to harden and redden. I was becoming more aroused by the minute, my body undulating to his touch.

"I do sense the lady is enjoying this," he said.

All I could muster up was a series of moans, sighs, and little cries of delight as he made love to every part of me. Hardly able to endure another moment, I reached out to him. "Now I want to make love to you."

Willingly, Blake allowed me to take the lead and, relinquishing control, lay down next to me. My hands moved in all directions, my tongue exploring every inch of his body until we were caught in a cross fire of lovemaking so intense we weren't certain who was doing what and to whom.

"My beautiful Samantha," he whispered. "I need to be inside you."

"Yes, baby, yes." I positioned myself above him, sliding down slowly onto his fully erect cock until we were completely connected. We moved in perfect rhythm like a lovely, well-timed, melodic piece of music.

"I don't want us to come," I burst out. "Let's keep going like this for hours. It's all too perfect. Let's not end it now."

But Blake couldn't speak. He was lost in the heat of the moment, straining to hold himself back. I lifted myself above him again until only the tip of his shaft was inside me, holding that position until he begged for more. Then, lowering myself all the way until there was no space between us, I called out his name, and moved up and down faster as we simultaneously exploded into a most glorious orgasm.

"Am I dead?" he asked a few minutes later. "Because I'm quite sure I died some exquisite death."

"Yes, and we've gone directly to heaven," I said, "where we can make love day and night without any interruptions."

"Oh, so this is what heaven is all about?"

"You didn't know?"

"Now, that's a thought I'd like to wrap my mind around," he said. "My darling, you are simply the most extraordinary woman I have ever known."

"I take that to mean I was worth the six-hour flight?"

"I would fly circles around the world for you, Samantha."

We fell into a long and rapturous sleep until we were awakened by the phone ringing at eight-fifteen that night. I fumbled for it on my night table.

"Oh goodie, you're there," my mother's voice broke my sleepy stupor.

"Just barely," I said.

"Is this a bad time?"

"What is it, Mother?"

"I have the best news, sweetheart. Alden Gould said that Spencer would *love* to join us for brunch on Sunday."

"What 'us'? I sat up, barely awake. Blake was playing with a strand of my hair that had cascaded down my back.

"You heard me. Spencer jumped at the chance. What do you have to say to that?"

"May I call you back?"

"I thought you'd be thrilled."

"This is really not a good time." I tried hard not to react.

"Samantha, are you alone?"

"No." I could no longer contain myself. I actually yelled out loud. I hoped she would take the hint and leave it at that. But with Madeleine, there was no end to conversations until she decided they were over.

"Does that mean there's a man in your apartment?"

"Later, Mother." I hung up.

"Ah, sweet Madeleine, I assume?" Blake said. "How is she?"

"The same as usual: totally infuriating."

"Be kind, Samantha. Madeleine is probably the savviest woman in New York. Next to you, of course."

I hated when Blake tried to be so damn conciliatory at my expense. "Yes, we do make quite the dynamic duo, wouldn't you say?"

"I *would* say. What did she want, and should we pay her a surprise visit?"

"Haven't you already reached your surprise quota for the day?"

"You mean you're not even going to tell her I'm in town?"

"You want me to?" I glared at him, daring him to continue.

"You *know* that I have a slight crush on your mother."

"I thought it was the other way around." I couldn't resist.

Picking up on my discomfort, he quickly changed the subject. "Here's an even better idea," he said. "We can stay right here until it's time for me to leave on Sunday and make nonstop love all weekend."

"Now you're talking. But all right, out of the goodness of my heart, I'm going to call my mother back, and you can say hello. That will put her over the moon."

Now that he was on my side, I no longer needed to self-protect but could allow some sweetness to seep in between the cracks. Blake seemed almost grateful not to have to deal with any mother/daughter confrontation.

"Did I put *you* over the moon, my love?"

"I believe I actually reached Mars," I said.

A half hour later, Blake phoned my mother while I sat back, amused, watching him luxuriate in what he did best: flirt.

"This is Blake Hamilton calling. Am I speaking with *the* Madeleine Krasner-Wolfe, New York socialite, mother of Samantha Krasner of the Cole Gallery?"

My mother's delighted scream could be heard all the way from the other end. "Blake? Darling? Where are you?"

She was speaking so loudly that I could hear every word clearly enunciated.

"I'm in your daughter's apartment. She's holding me captive and won't let me go."

"Neither would I," came the quick response. "*Now* I understand why Samantha refused to talk with me. She never said a word about you coming to New York."

"That's why they invented surprises," he said.

"How long will you be in town?"

"I leave Sunday night."

"Perfect. Then by all means you and Samantha *must* come to brunch on Sunday. I want you to meet my new man of the hour and his charming son."

I listened closely, my ear glued to the phone, and gestured "no," but Blake was caught up in the conversation and ignored me. He said, "I'm sure we can arrange that."

"I can't wait to show you my latest painting. It's an Andrew Dent. Say around one?"

"Perfect. Sounds like a plan."

"I just can't believe you're here, Blake. I adore a man with spontaneity, and in that department, you take the cake."

"As you can tell, I'm just a little bit crazy about your daughter. See you on Sunday."

And that was that. In the space of only a few hours, Blake had managed to turn me into a blob of protoplasm.

Blake and I stayed in for the rest of the night. We watched two old black-and-white movies, gorged on defrosted waffles, and made love again before falling asleep at three A.M. We didn't awaken until close to lunchtime the next day.

I looked at the clock. "Oh my God, we completely missed Friday morning. I was supposed to be at the gallery hours ago."

"It's all my fault," Blake said, only half seriously. "I'm *so* bad for you."

"You are very, very bad for me," I said. "I just pray that Alexandra hasn't phoned the gallery and found the machine on."

"And if she did, you can simply tell her that you spent the night in the arms of her favorite new artiste."

"Good idea. She'll really go for that." I jumped out of bed and scurried into the bathroom, Blake following behind me. I turned on the shower, where, under the spray of hot water, we had a quickie lovefest that lasted close to twenty minutes.

I dressed quickly and made it to the gallery by one o'clock, grabbing a sandwich on the way. Blake decided to spend the afternoon at MoMA. Once I was settled in at work, I phoned my mother.

"I can't believe that you invited us to brunch. Really, Mother, that's just about the worst idea you've ever had."

"Don't be ridiculous. I think it's very civilized."

"Blake Hamilton and Spencer Gould together? I don't think so."

"When you simmer down, Samantha, you'll realize there's a method to my madness."

"I'd like to hear you explain this one."

"It's simple. And it's shrewd. It will show Spencer that you have other men in your life, and it will put Blake just enough off center not to take you for granted. Let him have something to think about when he returns to London."

"This is an extreme form of game playing that I detest."

"Samantha, you have so much to learn. When it comes to the ways of love, a little game playing is in order. The beauty of it is, you simply have to show up and do nothing. The rest will take care of itself. Just make sure you look fantastic, and you'll have two men who won't be able to stay away."

"Why do I need two men? Frankly, Mother, I'm wild about Blake. He flew over here just to see me, and things couldn't be going better. Why would I want to give all that up?"

"You wouldn't, and you won't. But I do think you owe it to yourself to give a man like Spencer a look-see. You might find there's a spark."

"A spark? The last time he saw me, I was completely naked, and not in a good way. As far as sparks, there are fireworks with Blake."

"This is your year, Samantha. I can feel it. You might never have a chance like this again. Be adventurous, darling, and see what happens."

"I smell disaster."

"Oh, pooh, how did you ever become so *you* with a mother like *me*? If I allowed myself to be this cautious, I never would have met Alden. You need to grab the opportunity and run with it. Trust me on this, you won't regret it."

"I regret it already," I said.

After another long diatribe, I agreed to brunch just to get her to stop.

"I'm looking forward to Sunday," Blake said that night at dinner at Union Square Café. "Your mother's new painting sounds interesting. Andrew Dent's work is good—really good. Maybe one day she'll add a Blake Hamilton to her collection."

"You never know, she just might, especially if you keep pouring on the charm."

"I'd even knock a little off the price," he said, "if I could convince my gallery to go along with that."

"You'd have to ask Alexandra," I said. "She makes all the big decisions."

Lily Ann called that same afternoon. "So when do I get to meet The Man? Bennett's in town. Any possibility we can all do dinner together tomorrow night?"

I jumped at the chance. "Sounds great," I said.

"There's this great Turkish place: Zeytin, over on Columbus and Eighty-fifth. Cozy, intimate, Bennett adores it. Are you game?"

"Why not?" I said. "And we won't even have to drop Madeleine's name to get in."

Later, I told Blake, "You'll like Bennett. He's very avant-garde and has your brand of humor."

"Oh, so the guy's funny as hell?"

"And smart. I think you two will hit it off."

I couldn't have been more correct. The minute we sat down, Blake and Bennett began discussing the literary and art worlds of which they were respectively familiar.

"Who's worse?" Lily Ann asked as we piled our pita with fresh eggplant dip. "Artists or writers?"

"Worse in what way?" Blake asked.

"I'm speaking competitively," she said.

"The art world is filled with piranhas. They'll eat you alive, and you won't even feel it. That's how fast it happens. It's all quite political: who you know and all that bullshit."

"Doesn't talent even enter into it?" Lily Ann hung on Blake's every word.

"It's *all* about talent," Blake confirmed, "but as we all know, talent is an easy commodity. In fact, it's running rampant. It's epidemic. But once you separate the potentially talented from the truly gifted, then the madness begins. It's a three-ring circus and a race to the top."

"Is that your story?" Bennett asked. "Were you one of the groupies who had to kiss ass?"

I had never asked Blake that question for fear of sounding crass, but I loved that Bennett had the nerve to do it.

"Ah, the big question so delicately put," he ribbed Bennett. "Frankly, I thought it was required, but I wanted no part of it."

"Meaning?" Lily Ann asked.

"Meaning that I stayed in my studio, painted my butt off, and approached a few galleries. Then, as was my good fortune, I met a guy named Stripley Hughes at one of those god-awful London dinner parties, and old Stripley—and he *was* old, pushing late eighties—had a thing for young artists."

"You mean had a thing for your work," I said.

"No, darling. Stripley, as it turned out, liked boys."

"Now it's getting interesting," Bennett said.

"Please, Blake, tell me you didn't." I laughed.

"What do you think? No, I'm happy to report that while I did find Stripley Hughes a most colorful character, bedding down with him just wasn't part of my MO. I rejected him on the spot, which Stripley found even more challenging. In fact, he was relentless and wooed me by bringing me along to all the biggest and best parties and openings."

"And?" we asked in unison.

"And I caught the eye of a collector, Chilton Patch, who drooled all over me. Stripley, of course, took full credit and expected me to fall at his feet."

"And be eternally grateful," Lily Ann said.

"That's what he was counting on. Anyway, Chilton dug my work. He spread me around London like marmalade on a scone. By attending strings of weekly parties, and doing nothing else, I was pretty much an overnight sensation and even more attractive in Stripley's eyes. A few years later, Stripley Hughes left this world, tired and horny, leaving me to fend for myself. But he did pave the way for my future success. He even lent me his flat in Notting Hill, where I paid him a monthly stipend just to keep watch over the art and other valuable possessions. When he died, he willed the flat over to me to live in for as long as I want— rent-free."

"You see, Lily Ann, baby?" Bennett said. "I told you, the art world is much sexier than hanging around with a bunch of writers."

"But you're in kiddie lit," Blake said. "It's got to be a gentler, kinder lifestyle."

"Don't fool yourself: Children's writers are as bad as the rest. We all despise each other equally."

"Oh, Bennett, that's not true," Lily Ann snapped. "I think Blake is right: All our artist friends are crazy, each in his own way. But the writers and editors we know aren't so ready to stab each other in the back."

"That's because we need all the friends we can get. And as a group, we live a more solitary life. We hole up for days without coming up for air. But artists are out there, attending openings, screwing the right people, and getting drunk on cheap wine. There's merriment attached to being an artist. Writers are definitely more sullen and depressed."

"Yes, just like you, Bennett sweetie," Lily Ann said.

"Van Gogh wasn't exactly a laugh riot," I said. "That whole ear thing and all."

"I'm just a lowly editor," Bennett said, "in a class of my own. My job is to chop writers to bits and gobble them up. Don't get me started on that."

"You may not know this," Lily Ann said, "but Bennett is also writing a book—an adult novel."

"Yeah, sex and everything," he said. "My secret is now officially out." He threw up his hands.

"That's wonderful news." I lifted my wineglass. "When did this happen?"

"I've been working on it for about six months but haven't talked about it until my lovely Lily Ann here opened her gorgeous mouth and spilled the beans. Now you all know."

"Well. This calls for a toast," Blake said.

We clicked glasses. "To insufferable artists and writers, of which Bennett is now a member," Blake said.

"And to his future best seller," I added.

The evening couldn't have gone better, lasting for hours, with no desire on anyone's part to leave. As we lingered over dessert, Blake and Bennett were practically new best friends and played off each other as though they had been pals forever.

"Lily Ann's some sensational broad," Blake said on the walk

home. "I can see why you two are best friends, and she's very easy on the eyes. That mass of red hair is smashing. What a great couple."

"I wouldn't sic you on just anyone who wasn't."

"I'm sure tomorrow's brunch with Madeleine will be equally entertaining."

I was jolted back to that unpleasant thought: tomorrow. Not knowing what to expect, I wanted to cancel, but my mother never would have forgiven me. Neither would Blake, who was always up for meeting new people, another one of his sterling attributes.

After awakening early the next morning to a band of light streaming through the window, I kissed Blake gently, leaving him to lounge around in bed. Once again, as was our pattern, lovemaking had superseded sleep, but being on an adrenaline high, I didn't even feel tired. I showered, washed my hair, and quietly rummaged through the closet to find a suitable brunch outfit. My choice was a simple pair of beige linen pants and a buttery-cream-colored silk shirt to give me that "adorable yet seductive look" that Madeleine encouraged me to aim for. There was no way to know how the day would play out.

We arrived at my mother's apartment before the others. She opened the door and kissed Blake, bypassing me altogether.

"Come, dear." She took his hand, leading him into her study. I followed after them like an obedient pet. "Feast your eyes on *this*," she said. Andrew Dent's painting *Peace and War* hung over her desk. "Isn't it exquisite?"

Blake and I studied the piece. A child, standing in a field of grass, held a bouquet of wildflowers. The scene was mesmerizing, the panoramic nighttime view of the Manhattan skyline in the background even more so.

Blake put on his horn-rimmed glasses to examine it. "That's what's so interesting," he said. "The way he married simplicity with chaos—it's haunting."

SIX

By persistently remaining single,
a man converts himself into a permanent
public temptation.

—*Oscar Wilde*

My mother limped around for a week. On the eighth day, she discarded her crutches, claiming they detracted from her fashionista look. It was during the same week that Blake and I were to share a farewell dinner before he flew back to London the next day.

"I have an idea," I told him over the phone. "Let me cook dinner for you."

"What about Celeste? Will she be joining us, too?"

"Celeste is taking a much needed vacation. She and two of her work buddies are hopping a plane down to Bermuda as we speak. The coast is clear."

"So you're going after the young, eligible bachelor set?" I asked, somewhat awed by my mother's bravado.

"Honey"—she leaned over and looked at me through her azure-blue contact lenses—"luckily for me, I adore men of all ages. By the time I'm through, I will have dated so many fascinating men that I will have earned my bachelor's degree."

Then, with a satisfied look on her face, Madeleine ordered another drink and sat back, basking in her mimosa glow.

"I knew you'd see what the artist was after," Madeleine said. "It's really two paintings in one."

"There's a definite story behind this," Blake added. "The artist is making a statement."

"A *profound* statement," Madeleine acknowledged.

"Consider the child for a moment"—Blake pointed—"and the juxtaposition between peace and war and how the painting evolves into chaos. It has a most contemporary theme—a sign of the times, yet the thread of innocence runs rampant throughout."

All this artsy-fartsy mumbo-jumbo was starting to annoy me. I didn't know if Blake was for real or simply sucking up to my mother.

"Yet there's a tremendous feeling of tranquillity when you look at this painting," Madeleine pressed on.

"Yes, but once you move past the child, concentrating only on the skyline, you're immediately brought to another level—another place."

"It's gripping," Madeleine concurred.

"Post-nine-eleven, that's why," Blake waxed eloquent. "And the obvious omission of the World Trade Center."

"Yes, we're offered a glimpse of life before the tragedy as depicted by his daughter, the grassy glen, and the flowers. But dispersed among them are the fiery red splashes of color in the rear of the canvas where the Trade Center once stood—when life as we once knew it still existed. It's incredibly humbling." My mother took Blake's arm, practically salivating over the artistic bond growing deeper by the minute. "I just couldn't resist buying it, even though, as well you know, Blake, an Andrew Dent can run in to obscene amounts of money."

"But well worth it. The man is pure genius."

"Not that you're exactly chopped liver," I interjected.

"My work is completely different, Samantha."

"Dramatically different," Madeleine said. "I mean that literally. There's high drama in your paintings. Grayson predicted you were headed toward greatness."

"*Only* greatness?" Blake gently mocked.

"Yes, that was the exact word he used. 'That new London artist has a quality I haven't seen in anyone for ages. It exudes greatness,' that's what he said."

"I'm flattered. A comment like that from Grayson Wolfe is not to be taken lightly."

"You *should* be flattered. Grayson was a man of few words, but those words were chosen carefully. It's an absolute shame he isn't here now. He'd love knowing you were having brunch with us."

The conversation was aborted by the arrival of Alden and Spencer Gould, who were directed to the study by Gilda.

"Well, well," Alden said, "I hope we're not interrupting."

"Alden, dear . . . hello," Madeleine gushed, breaking away to greet the two men and kissing Alden on the cheek. "And Spencer—how lovely to meet you. Alden told me so much about you. Please join us. Allow me to introduce you to Blake Hamilton."

The men shook hands.

"And my darling daughter, Samantha, whom *you've* never met, Alden."

More hand-shaking.

"Of course, *you've* met Samantha." She directed me toward Spencer. "Under different circumstances, of course." She giggled.

Spencer blushed slightly while I stood there cringing.

"We're just discussing my newly acquired painting. It's been up only a couple of days," Madeleine added.

"Ah, yes, an Andrew Dent," Alden said. "I know his work well."

"I wouldn't have thought otherwise," Madeleine said, "being the patron of the fine arts that you are."

"I'm partial to his work," Alden said. "In fact, after meeting the artist last year in Santa Fe, I bought one of his paintings."

"*Really?*" Madeleine sounded effusively impressed. "My goodness, Alden, we seem to share common tastes."

"Mine is a much smaller piece, but equally significant."

They then went off on a tangent that included Blake, who seemed eager to add his opinion on the painter's technique. I moved over to the window overlooking Central Park, Spencer following behind me.

"This has been the hottest summer on record, hasn't it?" he said.

"Sizzling hot." I nodded as though we were two meteorologists about to analyze the latest weather conditions.

But the thought that kept running through my mind was that only a few days before, I'd been spread-eagled on Dr. Spencer Gould's examining table. I couldn't help but wonder what he considered more appealing: the painting or the view between my legs.

Madeleine had decided that a buffet would lend a more casual feeling to the day. She had put place cards around the table so she could control the seating; Spencer and Blake were next to each other. This allowed for easy conversation between them, plus a perfect full-frontal view of me: I was directly across from them, between Alden and my mother.

"That way they can admire you from afar," she said. "If you were seated between them, it would ruin the entire effect. They would only get to see your face. This is so much sexier. You are, after all, the star of the show. You need to be in prime position."

As usual, Madeleine had orchestrated every detail.

Gilda had laid out a spread of culinary delights on the sideboard that included a smoked Scottish salmon with dill and rosemary, platters of mild to offensively smelly cheeses, and a large basket filled with rolls, mini-bagels, and croissants. There were two pates, a vegetable quiche, and a sliced ham. Several varieties of mustard: honey-flavored, Dijon, and basil with tarragon. ("A good mustard covers up a multitude of sins": another Madeleine tidbit.) A plate of thinly sliced vine-ripened tomatoes completed the menu.

"Let's take our conversation into the other room," Madeleine said. "Samantha, darling, please ask Gilda to bring in the bubbly."

I was grateful for small gifts. The champagne would provide the much needed high to get me through the afternoon. As soon as the bottles were chilled, Blake asked if he could begin uncorking.

"By all means." Madeleine picked up her glass. "Pop away."

We stood in a small semicircle in the dining room and toasted to "Happy Times."

"And may I add," Alden said, "to the two most beautiful women in the room: Long may we bask in their glow."

Please, God, I reiterated silently, just let me get through this day.

I couldn't tell if Blake suspected anything strange, or if he thought it perfectly natural that Spencer had been invited to brunch. After our second glass of champagne, we all became looser and more relaxed.

"Best damn smoked salmon *I* ever tasted," Alden complimented Madeleine. "In fact, I've done some salmon fishing myself in Scotland."

"Best to stick to your golf game," Spencer chimed in. "Dad's fishing will never rival his putting acumen. But speaking of Scotland, we've both done some of the best courses over there."

Blake perked up. "I've hit a few balls I'm proud of."

"At St. Andrews?" Alden asked.

"Even better, in my opinion, is the Kingsbarns course," Blake said. "The sea views alone are worth everything. The fairways roll over the dunes and hollows right through the heather. Magnificent."

"Ah, yes, but St. Andrews is smothered in history," Alden protested. "Golf was first played there in the fifteenth century. It's reputed to be the best."

Spencer joined in. "Maybe so, gentlemen, but my favorite course is the Royal Dornoch. I'll tell you why."

And there they were, gobbling up their food and talking golf as though they were members of the good old boys' club.

Madeleine rescued the moment. "I, too, have played a few holes. My first husband, Henry, was an avid golfer. I still keep my membership at the club. Alden, we *must* play there sometime."

I stared at my mother. A few holes? According to my father, she was the absolute worst golfer in history. But there was that moxie again. When one least expected it, out it came.

"I'm holding you to it," Alden said.

"It's a date. I'd love you all to visit our Westport home. It has the most delightful water views and plenty of spare bedrooms."

My mother captivated the men by describing in minute detail the merits of the town. She could have been a real estate broker.

"When do we go?" Alden asked.

"I'm thinking Labor Day weekend could be fun. You and Spencer *must* come up, and Blake, of course you'll join us, too."

"Love to," he said, "but I'll be in London."

"Then, you'll just have to fly back here for the weekend. I'd love having you see my house."

Brunch was bad enough. An entire weekend would put me over the top.

"Mother," I interrupted, sensing the worst was yet to come and wanting to nip it in the bud, "Blake can't simply hop on a plane every time you extend an invitation. He's a working man, you know."

"It's Labor Day, darling. Nobody works on Labor Day."

"Our Labor Day is the first of May," Blake said.

"I've been over there on May Day," Alden said. "In fact, my late wife, Marcella, and I spent a lovely time with friends over in London one May Day. Hyde Park was in full bloom."

"Nevertheless"—Madeleine wouldn't quit—"you have an open invitation. But Alden, please say that you and Spencer will absolutely come."

"It's a date," Alden said.

Spencer fumbled, nervously, feeling pressured.

"Well, you two boys think about it," my mother said.

I sat back, sipping my champagne, watching in awe as my mother, in the space of a few minutes, pulled off an invitation to three men. Then again, she had always been able to manipulate and cajole to get her way. I shot Blake a look and he smiled back. Two out of three isn't bad, Mother, I wanted to say.

. . .

Brunch lasted well into the afternoon. After the sixth bottle of champagne was opened, the three men were feeling no pain and seemed to be enjoying one another. Celeste was right: Spencer was definitely movie-star material and bore a faint resemblance to George Clooney in both looks and demeanor. Blake, on the other hand, was more the sweet and sexy Jude Law type, with a smattering of James Bond. Either way you couldn't go wrong.

For years Lily Ann and I had narrowed men and women down to current film stars and writers. She likened herself to the sultry Rita Hayworth, while I attested to being a Susan Sarandon look-alike.

"You can't go out with that dork," she had once said back at Brearley when I was fixed up with David Hoffman, a Collegiate boy. "He's the spitting image of Woody Allen."

That said, "Woody" and I dated for six weeks until I decided he was indeed a dork, but not only because of his physical resemblance to the film magnet.

There had been a series of others: Todd Michaels, who was Brad Pitt incarnate; Andy Minotti, an Al Pacino look-alike; Harry Engler, who had a rugged Philip Roth look; and Sam Wheaton, who couldn't walk down the street without being asked if he was or was related to Charlie Sheen.

So here I was, having brunch with both "George" and "Jude." Alden, striking in his own way, might have been labeled an older Richard Gere. Not a bad way to spend a Sunday afternoon.

By the time brunch was over, Blake and I had only a few hours before he left for the airport. The interrogation began on the taxi ride home.

"Okay, what's the story with Spencer?" he asked.

"There is no story."

"Obviously, your mother invited him for a reason."

"Was it *that* transparent?"

"Are you kidding? She's obviously quite fond of him."

"I think it's the elder Gould she prefers."

"I wouldn't put it past her, Samantha. I suspect she has her eye on Spencer."

"For *whom?*"

"For *her,* of course. Madeleine likes men—all men—and age is never a factor."

"Really?"

"Really. I've got her number. You're not surprised, are you?"

"But Alden is much more appropriate."

"As if that mattered. Alden is quite smitten with your mother, but darling, she defies the norm. And that's a good thing, but please, don't be naive: Madeleine has a definite agenda, whatever it may be."

"You really think so?"

"Absolutely, otherwise why would Spencer be at brunch? After all, Madeleine knows I'm with you. I say she's cornered the market on both men."

"Don't be absurd. That would be crazy, even for Madeleine."

"Mark my words," Blake said. "I could feel the vibes all afternoon. Those Gould men don't know who they're messing with."

"Blake Hamilton, you have my mother down pat."

I sat back and closed my eyes. Spencer Gould and my mother? I didn't think so. Then again, anything was possible.

In the space of four days, Blake and I made love eight times. His brief surprise visit had clinched it: Any doubts I had entertained fell away. While Dr. Spencer Gould was handsome, smart, and had showered me with as much attention as was possible with Blake present, I didn't for a moment think he would ever call me for a date. Now Blake had put a bug in my ear that maybe, just maybe, my mother had designs on him herself. It was a preposterous thought, but preposterous personified Madeleine. I called her on Monday morning.

"Mother, thanks for a lovely brunch. You outdid yourself."

"Did Blake make his plane on time?"

"He left JFK on a champagne glow. Wasn't it lovely of him to fly over for the weekend?"

"Blake is about as good as it gets," she said.

"About?"

"He's divine, but Spencer Gould is running a close second. I did notice him flirting with you."

"He most certainly was not."

"He was checking you out every chance he got. I noticed he kept filling your champagne glass. What do you call that?"

"Being polite."

"The man has designs on you," Madeleine said. "His je ne sais quoi was running rampant. I know you adore Blake, but do you have any interest at all in dating Spencer Gould?"

"Why? Should I?"

"I'm simply inquiring."

"I'm a one-man woman all the way, and that man happens to be Blake."

"Might I remind you again that Blake lives in London?"

"We seem to be managing quite well despite that, as indicated by his weekend jaunt to New York."

"So, what you're saying is that if Spencer called you, you wouldn't accept a date?" Madeleine asked.

"Why, *will* he be calling?"

"Alden says his son was very taken with you. It can't hurt to be friends, have dinner perhaps. What harm can come from that?"

"I don't think Blake would go for that idea," I said.

"Why must he know?"

"You are so devious. And what was that about inviting us all to Westport for Labor Day weekend?"

"I was being gracious and hospitable. I thought it would be fun. Samantha, why do you need to complicate everything? Can't you relax and let the chips fall where they may? Now I'm late for my Pilates class, sweetheart. Kiss, kiss, and huggie love. We'll talk later."

I stood there holding the phone and staring into space. Why couldn't I have a mother like my aunt Elaine, whose biggest concern of the day was what she should cook for dinner? Madeleine would have done best with a daughter like Celeste, who hung on her every word and thought the sun rose and set with her. A girl like Celeste would have considered Madeleine's antics the be-all and end-all, while I believed that underneath it all—designer clothes and moxie aside—my mother was more than any daughter should ever have to handle.

TWELVE

The only good husbands stay bachelors:
They're too considerate to get married.

—*Finley Peter Dunne*

The first few weeks of August flew by at breakneck speed. My mother went in for her labiaplasty, or what she referred to as her mini-touch-up "down there." Blake and I were back on track with e-mails and frequent phone calls, and the Doctors Gould were off to Italy. Two weeks every August they closed their offices and escaped to Europe for a father/son vacation. This brief respite couldn't have been timed more perfectly, as it gave Madeleine a chance to heal before Alden returned home. She had also taken to wearing sunglasses indoors.

"You didn't have a face-lift, Mother," I reminded her. "Do you really need the shades?"

"Nonetheless, until my hoo-hoo heals, I'm going incognito," she said. "Alden wanted to make love to me the first night we met. This is all entre nous, of course. Even though I haven't had sex since Grayson's death, Alden awakened in me carnal stirrings. This renovation has given me a new lease on loving."

"Mother, please."

"The mature vagina needs to be occasionally pruned," she said, "and mine has never looked better."

"What's gotten into you?"

"Nothing yet, sweetheart, but that's about to change. Alden, I discovered, has a very active libido, and since he's a connoisseur of the genitalia, I don't think he'll be disappointed. I feel like a vestal virgin who has been deprived for too long."

"This entire conversation isn't normal."

"That's because you think of me as your mother and not a friend. If you started calling me Madeleine, you'd find our relationship would improve dramatically."

With Celeste gone and my apartment all mine once more, I felt liberated. This brief interlude was exactly what I needed. The time was my own to savor, and savor it I did. I made dinner plans with friends, caught up on films, and went to bed early to make up for the late hours Blake and I had kept when he was in town. With the end of summer approaching, and with Alexandra on my back almost daily about Blake's show, we were ready to rock.

"Booking events early is key," Alexandra called from her room at the Ritz in Paris, "we need to take care of the caterer and the flowers now."

"We" meant that I was in charge of everything while all she did was check with me, making sure I had followed through.

At my mother's prodding, I called Garden of Earthly Delights and reserved the evening. From there I rang up the flower guru of Manhattan and spoke with Duncan, a flaming homosexual with a flair for the most imaginative arrangements in the city. I invited him over to the gallery to see Blake's slides.

"Leave it to me," Duncan said, "I'll do a banquet of blooms that will blend in beautifully with Blake Hamilton's paintings. It will be an extravaganza; the place will ooze gaiety."

He pirouetted around, his bracelets jangling as he inspected each corner, every angle, of the gallery. "A vase of anemones here, some stephanotis there, and at the entrance I envision a terra-cotta pot spilling over with the most divine array of seasonal floral splashes of color. Trust me, darling, the place will resemble the Botanical Garden. And I'll tie it all in with the food. I need the caterer's number."

Next: the invitations to be sent out after Thanksgiving. Blake and I exchanged lengthy e-mails, discussing what painting should be displayed on the announcement.

"I was thinking that *Panoramania* would knock them dead," I said, "especially at holiday time. That painting exudes New York and will light up the gallery more than a Christmas tree."

"That could work," Blake agreed. "In fact, I like it."

"Good. I'll let Alexandra know. Can you do a mock-up for us?"

"I love when you talk business," Blake said. "It's so damn sexy."

"Happy to oblige," I said.

"But do you know what's *really* sexy?"

"Tell me," I said.

"You—on top of me."

"I thought we were talking about *Panoramania*," I said.

"Where do you think I get my inspiration?"

I could imagine him getting hard all the way from his London flat.

By the time Labor Day arrived, we began planning Blake's show. Alexandra was due back in late October. Her arrival would lessen the burden that now fell exclusively on me.

Spencer, back from Italy, decided to take Madeleine up on her offer and join us in Westport for the long weekend. When I told Blake, he went ballistic.

I said, "I didn't have to tell you, but I thought you'd want to know. Anyway, blame it on my mother. It's all her doing. Once she gets an idea in her head, nothing can stop her."

"You and Spencer alone in Westport? I just don't like it."

This was someting new: Suddenly, Blake showed a side of himself I hadn't seen before. He apparently thought that Spencer had designs on me as well as my mother.

"We'll be with Madeleine and Alden the entire time," I said.

"Except for those long walks on the beach and all those in-between times when the two of you sneak off."

"There will be no sneaking off, I promise."

I had fallen into the role of caregiver, whose job it was to placate the ever anxious Blake.

"I see it all clearly and hate it."

"So fly in and join us," I said, not really meaning it.

"Would that I could," he said. "I'm expected at the Pugg Gallery this weekend. They're showing three of my pieces. It's kind of a big deal."

"All right, then, but don't say I haven't begged."

"I'm trying to be a cool cat," Blake said, "but I don't trust Spencer. He has 'devious' written all over him."

"You mean: You don't trust *me* with Spencer."

"I mean any way you slice it, I smell trouble. What's an eligible bachelor doing in Westport over a long weekend unless he has ulterior motives?"

"And you're suggesting that *I'm* his ulterior motive?"

"Exactly."

Blake was starting to sound whiny, which in a man is most unattractive. I couldn't wait to get off the phone.

"My cell phone will be on twenty-four/seven. Don't give it another thought."

"That's all I *am* thinking about. Don't you adore a man who isn't afraid to humiliate himself by being utterly and completely jealous?"

No, I thought. Actually, it turns me off. Instead I said: "I adore you," hoping we could put this conversation to rest.

"I suppose that's going to have to hold me for a while—but if the guy so much as looks at you the wrong way, my intercontinental radar detector will go off."

"Oh, really?"

"Absolutely, my love."

On that note, we hung up. What Blake didn't know was my uneasiness about the weekend was greater than I would ever let on, because no matter how much I protested, I knew Blake might be right. Added to that equation was Spencer Gould, MD, a most attractive man who could definitely give Blake Hamilton a run for his money.

The plan was: My mother and I would drive up to Westport on Thursday morning, with Alden and Spencer arriving early evening and staying through late Monday afternoon. Gilda would be tagging along to tend to our needs, as Madeleine wanted time to play hostess and not, as she put it, "have to putter."

My mother's phone call roused me from sleep. "Are you packed and ready?"

"It's six-thirty in the morning, for God's sake."

"The Labor Day traffic can be brutal."

"I just have to jump into my jeans."

"You *are* bringing some *nice* clothes."

"Mother, I'm almost forty. I think I know how to dress myself."

"I'm just saying, you have so many stunning outfits."

"It's a holiday weekend. We're supposed to relax. I don't need to do stunning."

"I simply meant casual—nice casual."

"I'll see you in an hour, Mother."

We decided to take my Honda, used mostly for weekend jaunts, and leave my mother's Mercedes sitting in her garage eating up gobs of monthly rent. She and Gilda were in the lobby when I arrived. Madeleine had packed three suitcases, while I had managed to squeeze everything into one large tote bag. Gilda had one small, scratched, and peeling overnight case. She carried food supplies for the weekend, including a pan of rump roast that had been marinating for a few days. It was covered with a cloth and looked like a shrouded head.

"Dexter, be a dear," Madeleine addressed her doorman, "and toss our grips into the trunk of Samantha's car. My ankle and all, you know."

"Don't lift a thing, Mrs. Krasner-Wolfe," Dexter obliged. He escorted her to the passenger seat while my mother slipped him a ten. Dexter waited for such moments knowing he would be rewarded handsomely, if just for hailing a taxi. He helped Gilda into the backseat.

"Ooh, I am so excited," my mother said as we drove away. "A weekend in Westport with two handsome men. I feel so utterly wicked."

Gilda stirred slightly, then fell into a deep sleep. Through the years, she had been privy to all of our conversations but was viewed by us as an invisible force who heard nothing or pretended she couldn't care less. Whether or not that was true was another matter. "Gilda is like a shrink," my mother once said, "she knows all, but her lips are sealed."

Gilda Kruell had been with our family since I first began walking. To my mother, she was more than a housekeeper; rather, she was the voice of reason in an unsteady world.

"Gilda smoothes out the rough edges," she told me, "she's like a well-oiled machine."

When we were ill, Gilda soothed our feverish brows and made German chicken soup. When Madeleine entertained, Gilda was her backup, making sure that everything was carried off to perfection. She knew more about gourmet cooking than the most seasoned chefs. Gilda was in on everything: family squabbles, money discussions, our mother/daughter fights, and Madeleine's whims and mood swings. Through the years, Gilda was the one to whom I un-burdened my latest angst and who applied endless amounts of TLC to get me through my adolescence. She was Madeleine's fashion consultant, my confidante, and my father's "right-hand gal," as he called her. He had trained Gilda to handle his phone clients with alacrity and aplomb. "Gilda does more for my business than any professional ever could," he said. She in turn adored my father and pampered him by cooking his favorite meal or whipping up a crème brûlée at a moment's notice.

In our world, Gilda reigned supreme. Most important, she was the guardian of all our secrets, the protector of our neuroses, hear-ing all while pretending to know nothing. We treated her as a cher-ished and loyal family member who kept the home fires burning brightly. When she was privy to arguments that were none of her business,we simply pretended she wasn't there, like the pink ele-phant in the room.

"Gilda's best attribute is she knows when to keep her mouth shut," I told Lily Ann when Gilda had caught us at sixteen both smoking a joint in my bedroom. "Girls," she said, "those cigarettes are going to do you in."

"They're not cigarettes," I said, full of piss and vinegar. "It's pot."

We begged her not to say a word.

"I see nothing. I know nothing," Gilda said, raising her hands and closing her eyes.

"Want a drag?" we asked her, convulsed in giggles. "You'll like it."

"You girls will be the death of me yet," she said, opening my bedroom window to obliterate any traces of the illegal substance. "Praise the Lord, praise the Lord."

That was the other thing about Gilda: She believed that religion could save the world.

Now, with Gilda asleep in the backseat, I purged my latest con-cerns.

"Mother, we need to talk—seriously talk. I'm worried."

"Why, what's wrong?"

"This entire weekend is wrong. I probably shouldn't even be coming. For starters, I *am* kind of seeing Blake. Inviting Spencer to join us gives off mixed messages."

"There you go again, overreacting. Why can't we just enjoy ourselves and not make this a cause célèbre?"

"Why did Spencer even accept your invitation unless he's interested in me?"

"Of course he's interested—interested in getting away from the city and unwinding a little."

"He and Alden just got back from Italy, where I'm sure they did as much unwinding as they needed. This is an entirely different matter, and Blake isn't exactly thrilled."

"We asked Blake to come."

"You know he can't do that. He has a show in London this weekend, and besides, he's not going to get on a plane every time an invitation is extended."

"That's the problem with long-distance relationships: They're so unreliable."

"Still, I was up half the night feeling guilty."

Madeleine brushed it off. "A little guilt never hurt anyone. Look, darling, we're already in the car and on our way. I'm sure you can handle yourself under these circumstances."

"I feel badly for Spencer," I said. "I don't want to give him any wrong ideas."

"Maybe his coming to Westport has nothing to do with you. Did you ever think of that? Maybe he just assumes we're all friends away for some R and R. Not to worry, I'll make sure Spencer is well taken care of. We'll be one big happy family."

"How can you be so laissez-faire about this, Mother? What am I supposed to do with Spencer while you're off cavorting with Alden?"

"Cavorting? I cavort?"

"You know what I mean. You'll be so caught up in flirting with Alden."

"So I'll flirt with Spencer, too."

"I'm sure you will."

"You see? Problem solved."

"You're serious."

"Oh, don't be ridiculous, darling. Everything will be fine. You'll see. But one word of caution: It might be better *not* to give Blake a blow-by-blow about everything you do. Men love women to be mysterious. The less he knows, the better."

"That's not how we operate."

My mother shot me her first big zinger of the day: "Maybe that's why you're still single."

The ensemble my mother chose to wear was all yellow: yellow pants, a yellow cashmere sweater set, and Jack Roger sandals in white with yellow leather trim. She looked like a tall glass of chilled lemonade.

I had tossed on an old pair of faded jeans and a white T-shirt. I had flip-flops on my feet, and my hair was pulled back in a ponytail.

"I thought you were doing casual chic," she said.

"I'll change later. I don't need to be chic in the car.".

"Gilda," Madeleine awakened her when we were on the Merritt Parkway, "as soon as we get to Westport, I'd like you to air out the house and put fresh linens on the guest beds."

"Not to worry, Ms. Krasner-Wolfe. I'll take care of everything." Gilda emitted a soft sigh, closed her eyes, and didn't awaken until we pulled into the driveway of our house.

Our contemporary Westport house was situated on five acres along the water on Beachside Commons, just at the beginning of the long stretch of a residential area known as the Gold Coast. It wasn't unusual on early mornings to bump into a famous film star or a CEO of a large conglomerate out for a morning constitutional or walking the dog.

What attracted my parents to Westport years ago was its reputation as an artists' colony. Even now residents from the arts—theater, publishing, fine arts, and media—resided here. My father often entertained members of the New York art world, inviting them on weekends to Westport where, over long, leisurely dinners overlooking Long Island Sound, many a deal was cemented and pieces of art accepted or declined.

After Henry's death, Madeleine kept the house for weekend romps—a place to retreat to when life in the big city zapped her of all her physical and mental energy.

"Westport is my lifeline to sanity," she told Sheldon Glick when they were designing Madeleine's financial future. "Now that Grayson's Millbrook home was divvied up between his sons, I simply can't give up my little Westport oasis."

Some oasis: six thousand square feet of glass and redwood, including six bedrooms with water views, a fully equipped Poggenpohl kitchen, entertainment center, dining room, and rock garden pool that wound around a granite patio overlooking the Sound.

Beating the traffic, we reached Westport in under an hour. Gilda, refreshed from her catnap, was raring to go. "Don't do a thing, Mrs. Krasner-Wolfe," she demanded. "Just go inside and I'll take care of the bags."

Gilda was as strong as a bull. She wielded three suitcases at once with a hanging garment bag flung over her shoulder. I carried in the roast. My mother tossed open the French doors of the living room, leading out to the deck, allowing the fresh smell of sea air to waft through.

"Ah, what a glorious morning. I hope the boys won't be arriving too late so they can enjoy some of this beautiful day."

"The boys" were planning to be in Westport in time for cocktails. I offered to go to Balducci's to pick up hors d'oeuvres and wine for dinner and make a stop at the nursery for fresh flowers. Gilda was making her famous sauerbraten with raisins and gingerbread, a dish I despised but which my mother said would delight the men.

"And for you, Samantha, I'm going to make my raspberry soufflé," Gilda promised. "I'll need some eggs."

Gilda's soufflés were legendary.

Driving around the familiar roads of Westport was a welcome change from the cacophonous roar of the city, where the air hung heavy over mountains of skyscraper and people walked around enveloped in the end-of-summer heat. It was several degrees cooler here, and I could actually breathe easier as I shed my city persona and embraced the serenity of the country.

I found myself missing Blake and wishing he were going to be here instead of Spencer, who would soon become my weekend responsibility. I began mentally planning an itinerary of events that would take us right through Labor Day. For starters, Gilda and my mother had painstakingly planned an extensive six-course meal. That would take care of tonight.

"Dining under the stars provides the perfect ambience," my mother said. "It sets the stage for romance."

Tee-off times had been reserved at the club for Friday, and tickets to the Westport Playhouse took care of Saturday evening. Sunday, my mother had invited some of her chums over for brunch. In between, there would be quiet time to sit by the pool and read or stroll along the water's edge.

Even so, I smelled trouble. In retrospect, I should have stayed in the city for the long weekend and eliminated all the fuss and bother of having to play runner-up to my mother, the hostess with the mostest.

"Sweetheart," my mother called out when I returned from my errands. "Alden just phoned. They're on their way. Let's have our cocktails on the patio, and Gilda can set the table beneath the willow tree with a perfect view of the Sol LeWitt sculpture."

I feigned enthusiasm. "Sounds dreamy. I'm going to grab a bath and change for dinner."

"What are you wearing?"

"I haven't decided. Why do you care?"

"Who cares? I'm just interested."

"What are *you* wearing?" I countered.

"My new Cynthia Rowley. It's darling and ever so sexy, but in a refined way. Come into my bedroom and I'll show it to you."

"I'd rather be surprised," I said.

Leaving my mother alone to handle the flower arranging, I went to my room and tossed some bubbles into the tub. I luxuriated there for a half hour and then, feeling tired, lay down on my bed for a short nap.

"Wake up, lazybones," Gilda roused me an hour and a half later, "the guests just arrived."

I jumped up with a start. "Why didn't anyone wake me?"

"I came in once, but you were sleeping so soundly. I figured you needed your beauty sleep."

"Thanks, Gilda. I'll be dressed in fifteen minutes," I said, rubbing sleep from my eyes.

I had brought along a simple Norma Kamali dress that was guaranteed to win the Madeleine Krasner-Wolfe stamp of approval. It was teal blue with a celadon-green sash around the waist and neckline, short enough to show off my legs. I slipped into a pair of Jimmy Choo strappy sandals, brushed my hair into a shiny mass of curls, and applied a light coating of Laura Mercier moisturizing makeup to my face with a hint of Berry-Crush lip gloss and some cream blush to my cheeks. After checking myself in the mirror, I was ready to make my grand entrance.

Everyone was on the patio drinking strawberry daiquiris when I appeared. The men immediately snapped to attention, giving me the once-over. My mother nodded approvingly, handing me a drink. "We thought you'd never show up," she said. "Here, try this. They're fresh from the blender."

"Might I say that you look absolutely ravishing?" Alden said.

"I'd like to second that," Spencer joined in.

Talk about ravishing. Spencer looked like a golden god standing there in his white linen pants and navy jacket and a yellow cotton T-shirt. He could have just stepped off the pages of *GQ* magazine. Not a strand of black hair was out of place. His teeth seemed extra white against his tan, and his Cole Haan tasseled loafers were perfectly shined. "Hot" immediately came to mind. Blake Hamilton would not be a happy camper.

Gilda's sauerbraten served with spaetzle and a cucumber salad was a huge hit. Accolades spewed forth from the boys, who couldn't stop raving. Preceding the main course was a chilled berry-cabbage soup garnished with fresh mint, the only part of the meal I could tolerate.

"Why is Gilda serving sauerbraten in the summer?" I had asked my mother that morning. "It's so heavy."

"Gilda's specialty is German cooking. Men love sauerbraten any time of the year. It's a very masculine dish."

"And *of course* we need to please the men," I retorted.

They had driven all this way. Why not cater to their culinary desires? I was still convinced the reason that Grayson had proposed marriage was because Gilda was part of the package. She was better than a dowry.

The conversation flowed smoothly as the meal lengthened into twilight, the sky casting a tangerine-pink glow over the horizon. Candles were lit, and the gentle sound of the incoming tide made for a picture-postcard setting. While we were being regaled with tales of their recent trip to Italy, I observed Spencer sitting there, handsome and suave, holding his own and looking totally cool despite the high humidity. He was the epitome of a fairy-tale prince who slew dragons and made entrances just in the nick of time to save the damsels in distress. Yet while that was a most appealing image, it was also Spencer's one glaring flaw: He seemed almost too perfect. The fact that he had just given me a pelvic exam only weeks before didn't exactly add a touch of romance to the night. My mind began wandering to thoughts of Blake.

"Well, I for one am stuffed to the gills," Alden said.

"Let's take a short break before dessert," Madeleine said. "Let me show you to your room. It's the one with the Jacuzzi. Then we'll meet back here in a half hour for Gilda's famous raspberry soufflé." She scurried off with Alden on her arm, leaving me alone with Spencer.

"Would you like to see *your* room?" I asked.

"Does mine have a Jacuzzi, too?"

"Only one Jacuzzi to a customer," I said. "But you have a fabulous water view. Sunrises are complimentary. Or if you'd prefer, we can stay here and talk."

"You seem a bit anxious." Spencer had picked up on my edginess. "Does it have anything to do with our professional relationship?"

"You mean am I feeling odd because the last time you saw me, my legs were in stirrups?"

"Something like that."

"Yes, I am a little uncomfortable."

"Please don't be. I have a marvelous ability to separate business from pleasure."

"As long as business *isn't* pleasure," I said.

"You *are* nervous. I have an idea—why don't you show me around the grounds? I'd love to walk down by the water and watch that sunset."

Obligingly, I led Spencer past the house and down the long stretch of lawn toward the beach.

"Your home is lovely," he said. "Do you get to Westport often?"

"I came here all the time when I was a kid, but less so lately. I've been so busy with the gallery. My mother loves coming out. She and my father spent all their summers here, and Grayson enjoyed it, too."

"I can see why. It's a piece of paradise only fifty miles from New York."

"So the Realtors tell us. It's one of their best selling points—that and the great school system and the beaches."

"My dad said you also have a home in Millbrook."

"We did. It was Grayson's house for thirty years. When he died, it went to his sons, who sold it a few months ago, along with the two polo ponies. Apparently, the new owners are both equestrians."

"I hope *this* house isn't up for sale."

"My mother would never hear of it. Westport is as important to her as Manhattan. She has lots of friends here, some of whom you'll meet at Sunday brunch."

"Madeleine seems like a real social butterfly."

"Nothing stops her. She's on a zillion committees and goes to most of the major New York City charitable events. You might say she's out there."

"One of her big attractions," Spencer said. "Since Mom's death, Dad hasn't been getting out much. His entire life is medicine. Most men his age are talking about retiring, but he keeps on going, even though he's exhausted. Bringing me on board has lightened his load a bit. I handle much of the obstetrical side of the practice."

"Did you always know this was going to be your specialty?"

"The first time I brought a new life into the world, I was hooked. There's nothing like a newborn's first glimpse of the world."

"Spencer, that's downright touching," I said.

"Yeah, sappy but true. I'm a sucker for babies."

"Really? With that attitude, I'd think you'd already be married with a slew of kids."

"You'd think," he said.

Spencer was becoming more real by the minute. Behind the classy duds and stellar looks was a man with a soul. I liked what I was hearing.

"So you just haven't met the right woman, I guess," I said, probing further.

Spencer stopped walking and looked at me. "You mean haven't met the right guy. Samantha, I'm gay."

"Oh."

"Yes, oh. Are you shocked?"

"Uh . . . not exactly shocked."

"Surprised, then. That's okay. Most people are."

"But I could have sworn you were flirting with me at my mother's brunch."

"And why not? I can be a very big flirt. I enjoy beautiful women even if I don't sleep with them."

" 'Oh' again. But I heard you recently broke an engagement to a woman from Sands Point."

"Yes. Charlotte Mosley's family and mine were friends for years. Charlotte and I have been thrown together since we were kids. It was our parents' unspoken wish that we would end up together—you know, keep the old family ties intact."

"That must have been a terrible pressure."

"It was. Charlotte, beautiful and strong-willed, was accustomed to getting her way. She came on to me like gangbusters and wouldn't let up. I decided to give it a shot, and after several months of dating, I gave her a ring. It was such a sham, but I was in major denial and wanted to please my folks. After a few months of the most unsatisfactory sex I've ever had, I broke it off."

"What then?"

"Charlotte blamed herself, which was the worst part of all."

"How awful . . . for both of you. What did you finally do?"

"What I should have done all along: I told her the truth."

"That must have been difficult."

"It was the first time I had publically acknowledged I was gay. It was awkward but honest and, in that way, a huge relief."

"Good for you." I was offering short but supportive responses. "What was Charlotte's reaction?"

"At first she called me a liar, thought I was making it up. Then she hated me. Finally, she felt sorry for me, which really got me mad. She wouldn't talk to me for months and moved to San Francisco, where she met a stockbroker and got married. The last time I heard from her was when she sent me a birth announcement."

"So her family knows the truth, too?"

"Oddly enough, Charlotte decided to keep this news between us. I told her I didn't care, but it was as though she was too embarrassed to tell her folks. I realized what a lamebrain she was, shallow and unsophisticated. But in the end, it released me from the confines of my own insecurities, and I was able to accept myself fully. There. You now have the whole gory story."

Suddenly, the heaviness fell away and the pressure was off. All guilt associated with Blake and the weekend vanished. I felt as light as air.

"Are you usually this open about it?"

"I haven't exactly posted it on a billboard, if that's what you mean, but my father certainly knows, and my close friends."

"You father never mentioned it to my mother. She would have told me."

"Why would he? It's not his place to do that."

We were walking along the water's edge, stopping to pick up a few random shells, when I laughed out loud.

"What's so funny?"

"Nothing. Everything," I said. "I'm just thinking of my poor mom. Her hopes will be dashed. She was counting on you finding me interesting."

"I do. You seem like a *most* interesting person."

"You know what I'm saying."

"I suppose what you mean is that we won't be walking off into the sunset together—at least not in a Madeleine Krasner-Wolfe kind of way. But that doesn't stop us from becoming friends, does it?"

"I'd like that," I said.

Spencer bent down, snapping a dandelion from a cranny of beach wall. He handed it to me. "To friendship," he said.

"To surprises," I added.

"You know," he said as we moved along, "you don't *have* to tell Madeleine. I wouldn't want to ruin her weekend."

"What fun would that be?" I asked. "But you know what? I like the way you think."

"Anyway, your Englishman will be happy."

"I don't need to tell him, either. We can play this to the hilt."

"So you want me to impersonate a straight guy for the sake of all involved?"

"It does have an air of frivolity about it," I said. "My mother has been dying to marry me off for years. Since my divorce, she just won't let it go. The biological-clock thing and all."

"I can tell you, my dear, that your childbearing years are hardly over. Women well into their forties are having babies."

"I'll be thirty-nine in August."

"A mere maiden," he said.

"Not according to Madeleine. She's constantly tick-tocking me to death."

"Sounds horrible." He chuckled. "And like typical Jewish mother behavior."

"You have no idea. She's a real Jewish mother."

"Oh, but I do. WASP mothers are exactly the same. And don't forget, I'm the confidant to many of my patients. I pride myself on being sensitive to women's concerns and needs."

"I find this all so wonderfully refreshing."

"You're saying that you're happy I'm gay?"

"I'm happy that you're so forthcoming about it. It does relieve a lot of emotional tension."

"Tell me about Blake Hamilton," Spencer said.

For the rest of the walk, I filled him in: how Blake and I'd met and what had progressed so far in our relationship.

"Sounds serious."

"It is, but the transatlantic maneuvering is a bit rough."

"Which is why dear Madeleine is so intent on arranging a match made in heaven?"

"You got it. The woman is impossible. All she talks about is New York's eligible bachelors, and you're high up there at the top of her list."

"How about her? Do you think Madeleine would marry again?"

"I think she's open to the idea. She told me she's out to earn her bachelor degree, and I don't think she was referring to a diploma."

"I only ask because I think my dad is quite smitten."

"I adore men who use words like 'smitten,' " I said.

"Oh, Samantha Krasner," Spencer said, "I have a feeling that you and I are going to be very good friends."

"Maybe even relatives," I said.

• • •

By the time we got back to the house, the dinner dishes had been cleared, making way for dessert. My mother and Alden were already seated at the table.

"Well, you two must have had quite the walk," Madeleine said. "You've been gone forty-five minutes."

"We found we had lots to say," Spencer said.

"How lovely." Madeleine beamed, looking as though she had been presented with a shiny new gift. "Sit down. Gilda has been waiting to serve us her signature soufflés."

Out came four perfectly formed mini-ramekins, foamy-brown crusts rising above the rims with candied violets perched on top. Gilda placed one in front of each of us, then carried out a three-tiered cake plate on which sat an assortment of cookies and petits fours.

"Much too beautiful to eat," Alden said.

"I agree," Spencer said. "I think we should sit here and stare at them as though they were perfect little object d'art sculptures."

"I prefer the lawn sculpture," Alden said. "I couldn't stop noticing it all evening. A Sol LeWitt, of course."

"Yes," Madeleine said casually. "It was one of Grayson's favorites, although he was also a big fan of Henry Moore. And don't get me started on Calder. Wait till you see his twelve-inch sculpture in the library."

"Grayson Wolfe was a man I held in the highest esteem," Alden said. "He knew art better than most of the dealers I've known. He never steered me wrong."

"After dessert, I'll give you a house tour. You'll see just what a genius Grayson was, although his tastes were more classical, while mine are much more eclectic."

"I could tell that," Alden said, turning to me. "Your mother wears many different hats. Nothing ordinary about her. Not that Grayson was ordinary, either, but I can tell, Madeleine—you're an adventurer, willing to take chances in life and especially with art."

"Oh, Alden dear, you're such a flatterer," Madeleine said.

"What can I say? I speak the truth."

Watching the two of them play off each other, while slightly revolting, had its charm. Alden and my mother were getting on famously. I had no intention of ruining her fun by telling her that Dr. Spencer Gould, gynecologist extraordinaire and man about town, enjoyed a lifestyle that was, as they say, of another persuasion.

THIRTEEN

My husband and I divorced over
religious differences. He thought he
was God, and I didn't.

—*Anonymous*

The rest of the weekend went beautifully. Now that Spencer's closet door was ajar, the pressure was off. I sat back and relaxed, enjoying every moment of our time together. Blake called me from London several times, asking me pointed questions as to how everyone was getting along.

"My mother and Alden Gould make quite the team," I said.

"I was referring to the other Gould. Is he boring you to tears, I hope?"

"I think you'd find him very interesting."

"The question is: How interesting?"

"If you're asking if he's interested in me, he and I have lots to talk about."

"Has he made a pass yet?"

"He's a perfect gentleman, just like you."

"Oh God, now I'm really worried."

I managed to keep it light, but I could feel Blake's uneasiness right over the phone. His attempt at humor seemed anything but droll. In fact, I found it intrusive and dull.

"If he tries anything funny, you'd better tell him he'll have me to contend with."

"I do love it when I make you jealous," I played along.

"Not jealous. Just restless."

"You'll be back in New York before you know it," I said. "That should relieve some of the restlessness." The reminder of Blake's arrival washed over me like a giant wave that weighed me down. I just wasn't ready to see him.

"I'm not sure I can wait that long, darling. I might have to invite you over to London."

"Alexandra would never agree to that. Autumn in New York is when the entire art scene explodes. She'll be back in town in a month."

"She won't miss you for a few days—a long weekend, perhaps."

"She's absolutely obsessing over your show. Nothing will be spared in marketing you. As soon as Alexandra gets back from Paris, she's concentrating exclusively on you. In case you forgot, your name holds some clout around here. You'll be more of an attraction than the Statue of Liberty."

"Highly overrated." Blake laughed. "But you, my dear, have officially managed to unnerve me."

"I have?"

"You know it. Spencer Gould isn't exactly chopped liver."

"I agree. He's more of a pâté de foie gras."

"Do you like pate?"

"Love it," I replied as a direct blow, trying to prove to Blake he wasn't the only man of my dreams and that he shouldn't take me for granted. As his arrival date came closer, I felt more intent on hitting this point home.

"You're mean."

"You asked for it," I said.

"I'll remember that. Good-bye, my love. I'll call you back tonight. In fact, maybe I should keep you on the phone for the rest of the weekend."

"Now, there's an idea," I said. "Good-bye, sweetheart."

"Oh, and Samantha, just in case you might have forgotten, I think I may be falling in love."

"Anyone I know?" I asked, hanging up.

There is nothing in the world that makes a woman feel more adored than two men simultaneously vying for her attention. Except in my case, there was only one man, and the illusion of another in the first one's mind. That was enough to not only amuse me but to validate Blake's feelings for me. "Falling in love" was not a phrase he had used before. The question was: Was he really in love or simply afraid of the competition? I couldn't be sure, and I didn't care. For the first time in my life, I was exactly where I wanted to be. I was playing Blake exquisitely without having to even work at it. Spencer, unknowingly, was taking care of that for me.

On Saturday, Spencer and I relaxed, reading and enjoying a leisurely lunch, taking naps and even grabbing a late-afternoon movie. We ended the evening at Bogey's, the local Westport pub.

Sunday's brunch was equally entertaining. The guests fawned over Spencer and Alden, asking Alden questions about art and hanging on his every word, some of them gushing to the point of excess. One woman had bought a new dress in honor of the occasion.

Hattie Mills, a local icon in her own right, having screwed half the men in Westport, was married to Roddy Mills, a bridge champion who got his jollies by entering countrywide tournaments and leaving Hattie to fend for herself. This gave Hattie all the time in the world for frivolous pursuits, namely flirting with any man who was willing to notice her. Today her target was Spencer, who managed to escape her clutches after Hattie got so drunk she had to be sent home in a taxi.

Monday morning, rain clouds rolled in. Westport was awash in a deluge of showers.

"I was so hoping we'd have sunshine right through the weekend," Madeleine whined over our breakfast of pancakes and fresh fruit.

"Mother, even *you* can't control the weather."

"Don't be disappointed," Alden said. "We've had a grand time. You planned so much for Spencer and me that it'll be nice to sit back and relax before the drive back to the city. In fact, a rainy morning is exactly what we needed. It will keep all those flowers in bloom. Did I mention that you have the most sumptuous gardens? Like a Monet painting."

Alden poured it on as thickly as the maple syrup he doused his pancakes with. Occasionally, Spencer looked over at me and smiled while I rolled my eyes in acknowledgment.

"Dad, I think you're making Madeleine blush," Spencer said.

"Rest assured," I said, "my mother never blushes. She's eating it up."

"And so I am," she acknowledged. "Alden, I give you permission to shower me with your flowery words anytime."

"I'm going to take you up on your offer," he said.

"Yuck!" I wanted to say, but instead, I bit into a ripe strawberry and snickered.

By three, we were in our cars and on our way back to Manhattan, hoping to miss the Labor Day traffic. As soon as were settled in, with Gilda once again in the backseat snoring away, Madeleine began her cross-examination.

"Don't spare a word. I want all the details."

"What details? You were with us the entire time."

"You and Spencer managed to cram in quite a bit of alone time. That's what I'm talking about."

"Mother, you're impossible."

"It's obvious to me that the man is wild about you. He hung on your every word all weekend. How do *you* feel?"

"About what?" knowing full well where she was headed.

"About Spencer."

"I'm delirious."

"So tell me everything. You know how I thrive on the juicy details."

"Nothing to tell. Spencer is a great guy."

"And will you be seeing him again?"

"Yes, we already have a lunch date for next week."

"Lunch? Why not dinner?"

"We're working our way up. Cocktails are next." God, but she could be exasperating.

"I knew it. I could tell the man was head over heels."

"It's just lunch. He hasn't proposed."

"Not yet, he hasn't."

"What about you and Alden?" I changed the subject.

"I'm floating on air, can't you tell?"

"Spencer asked me if you would ever consider marriage again."

"He did?"

"He said his father is smitten."

" 'Smitten'? That was his exact word?"

"Verbatim."

"Samantha, can you imagine? The two Krasner women and the two Gould men?"

"I find it depraved."

"I find it adorable." My mother's mind wandered further. "And you won't believe where that thought has taken me."

"Don't tell me."

"It's taken me to Vera Wang."

"Mother—"

"It's taken me to Tiffany."

"You don't need another diamond ring."

"You can't be too thin or too bejeweled. So, is Spencer a good kisser?"

"That's none of your business."

"You can tell a lot by how a man kisses. In case you're wondering, Alden is a marvelous kisser."

"I wasn't wondering."

"And that's not all."

"Stop," I said so loudly that I awakened Gilda. "I don't need to hear another word."

"What I was going to say is that Alden invited me to Nantucket next weekend. He said early September is the most beautiful time of the year on the island."

"And of course you accepted."

"Wouldn't you?"

"That depends."

"On what?"

"On how seriously I felt about him."

"Darling, I felt seriously about Alden the minute I stepped into his office. Aren't you happy for me?"

"I am, but I'm also cautious, and you should be, too. He's the first man you've been with since Grayson's death. Not counting Blake, of course." I finally had the chance to zing her back.

"Don't be ridiculous. I haven't 'been with' Blake. By the way, how many times did he call you over the weekend?"

"A few times."

"Don't you just love it? You have a man pining for you across an ocean and a doctor in New York who obviously thinks you're the living end."

"You really eat this up, don't you, Mother?"

"It's an ideal situation. I know how much you adore Blake, but you can't deny that Spencer is divine."

"What are you saying?"

"You have the best of both worlds. Enjoy it."

"I am."

"Good. I'm glad to see you're being sensible. By this time next year, we might be planning a wedding."

"For whom?"

"For one of us—both of us. Who knows? Love is in the air. I see blue skies ahead with no precipitation."

"Ain't life grand?" I said.

"I think I'll pay a visit to Aurora," Madeleine said. "You might, too."

"I prefer surprise endings," I said.

I tried assimilating it all. A part of me was greatly disappointed by the news that Spencer was gay. As a result, the scenario had radically changed. As much as I adored Blake, I found Spencer most appealing. The downside: Now that he was sexually unobtainable, we had no future together except as friends. At the same time, he was the perfect foil—the beard who, if used properly, could get my mother off my back and keep Blake nervously off kilter and completely under my spell.

I had known and dated men who, by all outward appearances, were bordering on metrosexual. Spencer Gould didn't even come close. He was the epitome of masculinity, proving that you couldn't always judge a man by his cover. Long after the weekend was over, I found myself thinking about him and eagerly awaiting our lunch on Saturday at A Voce, the hot, trendy restaurant that Spencer had raved about. I arrived there at one o'clock. Spencer had taken the liberty of ordering champagne, his beverage of choice, which sat chilled and ready for my arrival.

He wore a hunter-green jacket and striped tie with tan pants that blended perfectly with the green leather tabletops. He swiveled his Eames chair around and greeted me with a warm kiss on my cheek. "You're looking wonderful," he said. "Absolutely radiant on this early-fall afternoon."

The weather still reminiscent of late summer, allowed me to get my last mileage out of one of my favorite outfits: a black Celine pantsuit accented with touches of red. Chanel on my feet and a canvas and red leather Kate Spade tote rounded out the look.

"Have you been to A Voce before?" he asked.

"No, but I've heard great things."

"Wait till you try the duck meatballs. We can start with those."

Chef Andrew Carmellini, who had honed his skills at Café Boulud and, before that, Lespinasse and Le Cirque, had come to A Voce and turned it into one of the best culinary acts in town. His praises were being sung by many, with Spencer heading his list of fans. His duck meatballs had become legendary.

"He mixes the glazed duck with foie gras and pork, turning them into little jewels," Spencer said.

One taste and I had to agree: They were, to borrow one of Madeleine's phrases: beyond fabulissimo. While we drank and ate well into the afternoon, I swooned over a salad of gorgeous asparagus with Parmesan and truffles and Spencer's homemade pappardelle (lamb Bolognese with mint and sheep's milk ricotta). We exchanged stories of our lives.

"I feel like we've been friends forever," I said.

"You're so easy to talk to," Spencer complied.

Our mutual admiration society ran rampant right through dessert: A Voce's famous bombolini, consisting of Tuscan doughnuts with chocolate sauce. The subject of homosexuality never came up, but there it was again: the pink elephant, this time languishing at our table, being politely ignored.

As I worked my way toward a third glass of champagne while Spencer ordered a Jacopo Poli Lamponi grappa, without forethought, I asked Spencer the question that had been on my mind since we met: "Are you involved with anyone?"

He paused and put down his drink. "Before Charlotte, I was in a relationship with a man for a few years. It didn't work from the get-go. He was closer to my father's age than mine. In fact, he was an old friend of Dad's."

I sat silently, waiting for his next revelation.

Spencer did not hold back. "Bruno Wilding. He's a top New York criminal attorney and very much out there in the social circles. You may have heard of him."

I nodded. Bruno Wilding had handled some of the biggest legal cases that had made the front page of all the major newspapers. Grayson had once remarked: "If I needed anyone to get me off the hook, the first person I'd call is Bruno Wilding."

"Bruno and my dad grew up together," Spencer said. "I've known him since I was a kid. One night at a chic dinner party my parents threw, I drove down from Yale and popped in to say hello. He cornered me later and made his intentions known. I was in the library poring through one of Dad's medical tomes when he put his arms around me."

"That was your first time with a man?"

"The first overt move, but there were subtle rumblings I chose to ignore: furtive looks, the occasional hand on my arm, that sort of thing, but I never suspected. Other than that, Bruno never gave any indication that he was interested in me, let alone that he was gay. I was pretty shocked. But what surprised me even more was that he assumed I was gay, too. When I questioned him, he smiled knowingly and told me it was more than obvious."

"How?" I asked him.

" 'My darling boy,' Bruno said, 'I've been watching you for years.' Whatever that means, I thought. I suppose I must have surreptitiously been giving off vibes."

"How long have your parents known you were gay?" I asked.

"My dad always suspected. After I broke the engagement with Charlotte, the barrage of questioning began. I told him that Charlotte and I were not going to make it for a variety of reasons. Pops was most understanding. His response was: 'Well, I guess the fact that you and she knew each other all these years made it seem incestuous.'

" 'It's a bit more complicated than that,' I told him. "That's when he asked me straight out if I preferred men to women. I stopped talking. My face went beet red, as though I had been slapped. But I didn't deny it. Dad put his arms around me and held me for what seemed like an eternity. I believe he even cried. I know I did. In a way, it drew us closer. Then he was jolted back to reality and said, 'It might be best not to tell your mother.' I knew then he still hadn't fully accepted me."

"What did you do?"

"I never told my mother, though I eventually would, had she not had her accident. By then Bruno and I considered us a couple, though we were discreet. I had many friends of both genders, and he dabbled with a few men here and there. To the outside world, we were very much in the closet."

"How long were you and Bruno together?"

"On and off for three years. I'd meet him on the sly. Never told anyone. It wasn't that Bruno wasn't fantastic, because he is, but truthfully, I'm looking for someone more age-appropriate. Bruno was pushing sixty, and I was a senior at Yale."

"So no one ever knew? Not even your dad?"

"No. That would have killed him. Or, even worse, he might have killed Bruno."

"I suppose all of us have the same issues," I said, smiling. "It's hard to find suitable men. No one special since then?"

"No, not really. I don't go to gay bars, and I'm very careful about the men I see. I've dabbled in a few brief relationships, but nothing lasting. My reputation as a gynecologist is building all the time. In my profession, we like to keep things neat and tidy. Despite the gay movement, many people still shun homosexuality. I'm not denying who I am, but I choose to be discreet."

"For fear of being judged?"

"For fear of being labeled. That's different. I've always been a private person, and I'd like to keep it that way."

"I can understand that," I said.

"Samantha, I'm truly glad that we met. I'd like to see you again—as friends, of course. But I would ask that you keep this conversation between us."

"Let's make a pact," I said. "Whatever we discuss goes no further. But what should I tell my mother? She's practically salivating over the fact that we're having lunch together."

"Tell her that I'm crazy about her daughter."

"Are you?"

"Samantha"—Spencer took my hand—"if ever the tides were to turn and I start to dig women, I can promise you: You'll be the first on my list."

"So you're saying you're attracted to me?"

"As much as a gay man can possibly be, yes. I find you thoroughly adorable. What do you have to say to that?"

"I say wow."

"And I say let's have dinner next week. In the meantime, if I meet any hot heterosexual guys, I'll send them your way."

"And if I can reciprocate with an equally fabulous fellow, I will."

We clicked glasses. "To fabulous fellows," Spencer said.

I was now involved in what I despised most: elaborate game playing. Yet it wasn't altogether deliberate. The situation had evolved on its own. I had no intention of giving up my friendship with Spencer and was titillated by the fact the Blake was so distracted by him. The same went for my mother, who pressed me for information every chance she got.

"Just tell me this," she said after our lunch at A Voce. "*Could* you be interested in Spencer?"

"I am interested in Spencer."

"I mean in *that* way."

"I'm taking things slowly, just the way I like them."

"Tick-tock, tick-tock" came her worn-out response. "And how is the foreigner?" That was the term Madeleine now used when referring to Blake.

"Peachy keen. Couldn't be better. He asked me to fly over to London."

"And?"

"Alexandra is returning from Paris in a month. I'm working on Blake's show. This is the worst time to get away."

"I can tell you this," my mother said, her voice slightly reminiscent of Kate Hepburn's. "Once Alexandra gets her hands on Blake Hamilton, your problems will just begin."

"For your information, Mother, Blake has already had his little go-round with Alexandra. She put the moves on him months ago, and he rejected her on the spot."

"How come?"

"He said that Alexandra isn't his type."

"Alexandra Cole is every man's type," Madeleine corrected.

"She's too pushy for Blake. When Alexandra gets going, she can be borderline scary."

"Nevertheless, I'd be very careful if I were you."

"Careful about what?"

"That she doesn't swoop down and grab Blake up by her well-manicured talons."

"You're impossible, Mother."

"Alexandra is a bird of prey. I know her type. Such women go after exactly what they want and don't stop until they get it."

"Blake isn't that gettable."

"Darling," Madeleine said, "every man can be reeled in by a beautiful and conniving woman."

"You've been reading too many bad romance novels, Mother."

"Cast not your eyes away lest trouble befall you."

"Are you quoting Shakespeare again?"

"Shakespeare? I'm quoting Madeleine Krasner-Wolfe, who knows more about love and sex than Shakespeare ever did."

I continued seeing Spencer for lunches, dinners, theater, and movies. Because there were no hidden agendas, our friendship flourished. Alden Gould and my mother began discussing us.

"I told Alden last night that you and Spencer seem to be quite the duo," my mother said.

"Personally, I'm delighted," Alden said.

Blake asked me daily how my "friendship" with Spencer was progressing.

"He keeps me entertained," I said.

"The faster I get to New York, the better. Really, Samantha, can't you pop over to London for a long weekend? I miss you."

Popping in for a drink with Lily Ann was one thing. Popping over to the cleaners to pick up my clothes, another. Popping off to the UK was not exactly part of my daily itinerary.

"I can show you all around London," he went on.

"Oh, a sightseeing trip? Why didn't you say so?"

"Yes, we'll start with my flat and move on from there."

"I'm warming to the idea," I said.

"Warming? Baby, you ain't seen nothin' yet. I guarantee that by the time you hit Heathrow, you'll be sizzling hot after the kind of tour that I have in store."

"I'm weakening. Tell me more."

And so for the next half hour, Blake and I had the most delicious phone sex. That was the clincher. I decided to leave New York on Thursday night and return home just in time to open the gallery on Monday morning.

"Travel lightly, darling," Blake said. "A toothbrush and your diaphragm will suffice."

FOURTEEN

A man without a wife is like a
vase without flowers.

—*African proverb*

In the hour after I'd agreed to come to London, Blake
had arranged for a round-trip ticket on British Airways.

"I pulled strings to get you on the red-eye," he said.

"Guilt will get you everywhere," I teased. "I can't wait to
see London."

"First stop, my flat," he said. "We can take it from there.
In fact, we might never leave."

"As long as you promise to feed me," I countered. "I
wouldn't want to starve to death and have my corpse hanging around your flat."

"That's risky. I might very well devour you," he said.

"I do want to see your show at the Pugg Gallery, so we will occasionally have to come up for air."

"I wouldn't let you leave without seeing my show. In fact, I sold another painting today."

"Congratulations. Wait until you hit the Cole Gallery. There will be no stopping you."

"November can't come soon enough. I can't wait to settle into New York life and have you at my beck and call."

"My, aren't we presumptuous. But you're right, it will make things a lot easier. No ocean to contend with." As soon as the words fell from my mouth, that nagging feeling took hold again, reminding me how ambivalent I was about Blake's move to *my* city.

"I think it's the ocean that's making me more attractive. You'll probably tire of me in a week."

"Oh, you do, huh?"

"Absolutely. Once I'm living in Manhattan, you'll start taking me for granted. I'll be yesterday's fish and chips."

We continued in this vein until we were both sufficiently heated up. I could hardly wait for Thursday to arrive. I packed lightly, as Blake had suggested, not worrying about looking chic, but concentrating more on being in his arms and making love all weekend. I even bought a new bottle of the seemingly aphrodisiac L'air du Temps for the occasion. Added to that was a little Victoria's Secret teddy with just the right hint of seduction.

"So, a weekend in Merry Ole," Spencer said when I told him I'd be away. "Make sure to pass on my best regards to your squire."

"Squire, yet. Aren't we veddy British?"

"Should be fun."

"I'll send you a postcard."

"Please do. Everyone needs a photo of Big Ben on their fridge. It's been a while since I've been to London."

"I'll be back in town late Sunday night."

"Just in time for dinner on Monday. Are you free?"

"As a bird."

"Good. And Samantha, I have some news."

"Tell me."

"Over dinner at Balthazar."

"Playing coy, I see. Is it big news or the usual garden variety?"

"Knock-your-socks-off news," Spencer said.

"You can't let me hang all weekend. I need a hint."

"His name is Roger, and that's all I'm saying."

"I have an uncle Roger. He's a podiatrist—lives in Syracuse and operates on people's corns and bunions."

"No resemblance to Uncle Roger, I promise you," Spencer said.

"Sounds intriguing."

"That's putting it mildly," Spencer said.

I got off the phone, not entirely thrilled by this news. If Spencer had indeed met Mr. Right, I, Ms. In-between might be taking a backseat. I hated myself for even entertaining the thought. Spencer deserved to be happy, and if his true love wore pants and a tie, so be it. After all, I had Blake. So why the sudden tug of mixed emotions?

On Thursday the plane took off with no delays and hardly any turbulence from JFK to Heathrow. I was too excited to sleep. Six hours later, with red eyes and an overheated libido, I made it through customs smoothly. Blake was waiting, a bottle of Dom Pérignon and two glasses in his hands.

"You're a sight for sore eyes," he said, kissing me.

"I'm the red-eyed one."

"You look gorgeous to me." Blake took my bag. "Follow me. I conned the concierge to keep a watch on my illegally parked car. I tipped him handsomely, so he couldn't refuse."

"Now, that's service," I said.

Within the hour, we were driving toward Notting Hill and Blake's flat. The morning sun shone high over London as people, looking crisp and well groomed, poured from doorways onto the streets en route to work. I expected at any moment for Mary Poppins to ascend the sidewalk and fly over the rooftops. It was all so deliciously British, and though there wasn't a cloud in the sky, men in black suits carried their "bumbershoots," looking like identical Charlie Chaplin windup toys, moving mechanically into their day.

Notting Hill had always been one of London's most fashionable areas. Its reputation for shopping and Victorian town houses attracted a wide variety of cultures living among the upper crust. Blake, young and upwardly mobile, was the darling of the glitterati, who made a career of sucking up to artists and other hot celebs of the moment.

The taxi pulled into a street overlooking Holland Park, stopping in front of a flat with a portico and window boxes filled with red geraniums. Blake helped me out and paid the driver, escorting me to the door and into his flat. It was oozing more storybook charm than I ever could have imagined.

"This is absolutely breathtaking," I said.

"I know. Stripley Hughes was a man of excellent taste. When he left me this place in his will, I was stunned. It didn't sink in for weeks that it was really mine."

"I'd say this is about as extravagant a gift as I've ever seen. Are you sure you and he weren't more than just friends?"

"I hope you're not serious," Blake said.

"Can't you tell when I'm joking?" I said. "But I am rather stupefied."

"As was I. Now make yourself at home while I show you around." He tossed the *Times* of London on a chair.

The high living room ceilings seemed to reach the sky. French doors led out onto a private balcony overlooking the park. The sun poured in casting a glow on the entire room. A sixteenth-century Spanish painting by some obscure artist to whom Blake had taken a liking hung over the marble Victorian fireplace in the corner.

Next, we walked into the open kitchen with a large picture window above the sink. All the newest modern appliances were integrated into the walls. Copper pots and pans swung overhead like a bronze chandelier.

"I didn't know you were into cooking," I said.

"There's a lot you don't know about me. That's the fun part: finding out more about each other as we go along.

"Now for the rest of the tour." Blake directed me toward his bedroom. A king-size bed covered by a Swedish duvet and pillows greeted me. The nightstand was filled with art books and magazines. A couple of English landscape paintings hung on the walls, adding a most romantic touch. There was an old skylight over the bed. A large bay window overlooked a backyard garden bursting in bloom, too beautiful to be real. Off the bedroom was a bathroom that Blake had totally renovated with gold faucets and a marble shower, rare for typical London flats. A footed antique porcelain tub added to the charm. He had even tossed in a heated towel rack with bath sheets and face cloths in muted shades of buttery cream and taupe.

"This is so Jane Austen," I said.

"No, darling, this is so Blake Hamilton," he said.

The pièce de résistance: The studio was in a loft above the flat. Up the winding staircase was a huge room with windows on all sides and a view of the park below. Paintings were scattered on the floor or rolled and stashed in corners. One large piece on which Blake was presently working rested on a large wooden easel.

"I found this easel in an old warehouse in Paris," Blake said, "and of course, I had to have it."

The studio smelled faintly of oil paint and turpentine, mingling with the fresh air that wafted through the open windows.

"So, this is where the genius creates," I said. "It's perfect. Is this where the magic happens?"

"I can think of a better place where the magic happens," Blake said, taking my hand and leading me back downstairs and into his bedroom.

• • •

For the rest of the morning, with no lunch break, we made love, drifting in and out of sleep and finally resurfacing in the late afternoon.

"Ready for a little sightseeing?" Blake asked.

"I prefer the sights right here in this bed," I said as I stretched and yawned.

"Aren't you hungry?"

"I'm sated on love," I sang out, throwing a body pillow over me.

"Well, I for one am absolutely famished. I've made a reservation at one of London's hottest spots. And tomorrow, without fail, I'm taking you to the Pugg Gallery as the first order of the day."

"Aye-aye, sir."

"But now, while you luxuriate beneath the sheets, I'm going to heat up the best cranberry scones you've ever tasted. They should hold us until dinner. Just lie back and think happy thoughts. I'm here to serve you."

I blew a kiss, observing Blake's naked and perfectly sculpted body as he exited the room on his way to the kitchen.

The fabulous dinner spot was Sally Clark's. The food was nothing short of exquisite and prepared in such a way that the flavors seemed to dance on our tongues. The superb wine list and the sommelier steered us in the right direction, with a lovely light pinot noir to accompany Blake's lamb and my poached organic Irish salmon with dill flatbread, fennel, pea leaves, and dill crème fraîche dressing.

We dined slowly, tasting each other's food and interlocking fingers like the two lovers that we were. Blake frequented Clark's and knew the owner personally.

"Sally's seasonal greens and her vegetables and herbs are from small organic growers in the south of England," Blake said. "Her Buffalo mozzarella is flown in from Naples twice a week. Sally prides herself on using only the freshest ingredients. She offers a small menu, but everything is picked to perfection and kept simple. Wait till you taste her bitter-chocolate truffles and the oatmeal biscuits that accompany the cheese selection."

"I'll hardly have room for that."

"Darling, you *can't* come to Sally's and not sample the cheeses," Blake said. "It's forbidden."

"Actually, I have my eye on the dark-chocolate pudding with hazelnuts," I admitted.

"Good, we'll have both."

I marveled at the ease with which Blake played at dining. Each course, every bite, was a culinary adventure, and I was caught up in it all. Dinner lasted for several hours, with a walk back to the flat to work off the calories.

"That was probably the best meal I've had in years," I said.

"Sally's never disappoints. Every food lover knows that. She makes it a moveable feast, as Hemingway would say."

"And I have the tummy to prove it," I said.

The evening air was fresh with the smell of lilacs mixed with honeysuckle as we walked through Westbourne Grove past a row of Victorian town houses.

"Notting Hill's steeped in history," Blake said. "The name is very old and derives from the Saxon personal name Cnotta, as in Cnotta's Hill. In early times it was entirely rural and part of the northern district of the parish of Kensington, once called Notting Barns. The name Notting Hill came about when a turnpike gate was constructed at the foot of the hill on the main road from London to Uxbridge. The actual gate was removed in the nineteenth century. The neighborhood is now one of London's trendiest spots."

"The stucco pillars and porched houses are amazing," I said.

"You should see some of the private gardens. They're outstanding. And Holland Park across from my flat and Kensington Gardens make living here an absolute paradise. All the parks of central London are right at your doorstep where you can bike, skate, ride horses, row boats, or simply walk around Kensington Palace, the home of the late Princess Diana. And right around there is Hyde Park. We can walk to Buckingham Palace and Trafalger Square."

I was becoming more excited by the moment.

We'll take a walk through Portobello Market on Saturday when the antiques buyers pour out into the street. This jacket I'm wearing was sold to me by an old English woman who made her living from selling her wares at the market. It's a shopper's paradise. You'll love it all, Samantha."

What I really loved was how relaxed I felt as we strolled along holding hands. We were right out of the film *Notting Hill*. I was imitating Julia Roberts with Blake, my very own version of Hugh Grant.

As Blake had promised, on Saturday afternoon after lunch at Babylon, with its to-die-for views of London and flamingo-studded roof garden, we went on to the Pugg Gallery in Mayfair. It was small and intimate and represented some of the best contemporary artists in London. Blake's large piece *Abracadabra* took up the entire rear wall and was the first painting one saw upon entering.

"Nothing subtle about you," I said.

"I know. It gives one quite a start, doesn't it?"

"It's utterly fantastic." I walked closer.

"Stay right here," Blake instructed. "It's meant to be viewed from several feet away."

I stared and was immediately struck by how the light played off the different shapes and images, all very abstract but striking in tones and colors.

"Care to define this for me?" I asked.

"Definition is in the eye of the beholder," Blake said. "That's how I get myself off the hook every time."

"The title exudes a sense of magic," I said.

"Ah, yes, but keep looking. You'll see lots of illusions taking shape if you stay with it."

I sat down on a mahogany bench and held my gaze steady. What had seemed only moments ago to be a large black blob became a magician's hat. The line of gold materialized into what was conceivably his wand. Loosely painted forms in the background were the audience, who sat transfixed as silver birds in flight spilled onto the canvas.

"I see a dove," I said.

"Where?" Blake questioned.

"Right there"—I pointed—"that splash of white next to that crimson blotch of paint."

"Stay fixed on that. Don't turn away, and now tell me what you see."

I felt as though I were being subjected to a fancy Rorschach test where my mental diagnosis depended on what the images meant.

"It's a large wavy mass of red. It seems to be attached to a figure: the magician and his red cape."

"Excellent. Exactly what I hoped you'd say." Blake joined me on the bench. "This painting is all about magic and illusion. Nothing can be defined exactly. Forms change as you continue to observe. In that way, the magic lingers for a while, and when you turn away or blink, it's simply an abstraction of colors that interact with each other purely for art's sake, with no metaphoric intention."

My art lesson was interrupted by a tall woman in a Burberry poncho. "Darling, is that *you*?" She tapped Blake on the shoulder.

"Amelia Stanton." Blake jumped up. "However the hell are you? Meet Samantha Krasner, flown in fresh from New York."

We shook hands.

"Amelia is the owner of the Pugg. And Samantha runs the Cole Gallery in New York."

"Your next stop. Nice to meet you, Samantha," she said with a slight edge. "Our Blake is quite something, wouldn't you say? You're lucky to have a piece of him."

"How about six pieces?" Blake shot back.

"My goodness, the Cole must be humongous to be able to accommodate so much of Blake Hamilton."

"I'm easy to spread around. Just like butter." Blake smiled.

My first and negative impression of Amelia was growing stronger by the minute.

"We're devoting our entire show to Blake's work," I said.

"As well you should. A Blake Hamilton doesn't come along every day. I'd grab him while you can."

"That's exactly what I'm doing."

"I won't interrupt. Blake, we're doing marvelously well with you. Just sold another one of your smaller paintings. You're a hot commodity, my dear." Turning to me, she reached for my hand again. "Very lovely meeting you, Samantha. Take care of our man. I understand he'll be with you in New York for the next several months."

"I'm heading out in November." Blake put his arm around my waist. "I have a flat waiting for me where I expect to paint away during that time, among other things." He gave me a knowing smile.

"Let's have drinks before you leave for New York." Amelia kissed each of his cheeks. "So we can discuss your next show."

"Will there be a next show? I'm flattered," Blake said.

"I'm booking you for early 2010," she said. "By then you should have a new body of work with which to dazzle us."

"I'll see what I can do."

With a swing of her poncho, she walked away, leaving a whiff of perfume in the air.

"That's the infamous Amelia," Blake said. "She gobbles up artists for lunch."

"Or seduces them. She looks lethal."

"You can tell that in a few minutes?"

"Alexandra Cole taught me well," I said.

"Amelia Stanton knows the biz. She comes on strong, but she has a great eye."

"You've slept with her, haven't you?" I wished I could have retrieved those words as they fell from my mouth.

"Wow, you do get right to it, don't you?"

"It seems obvious."

"Would you believe me if I said I haven't so much as kissed her?"

"No," I said emphatically. "She looks too kissable to resist."

"Well, I haven't. Amelia flirts the same way Alexandra does."

"Must be something about gallery owners."

"Yes, they're a horny bunch. But don't blame me. I plead innocent."

"All right then, Mr. Innocence, let's see the rest of the show," I said, changing the subject, a stab of insecurity overtaking me as I watched Amelia work the room and lure unsuspecting visitors, mostly men, into her lair.

The subject of Amelia Stanton didn't come up again, but I sensed that Blake had a bevy of beauties all waiting to pounce on him if ever he gave the signal. The question was: Was he as oblivious as he pretended to be, or was he in fact the bon vivant of London who slipped in and out of women's beds at will? He seemed more discreet than that, but I knew I was fooling myself if I thought he wasn't many women's fantasy.

Later, over afternoon tea at Fortnum & Mason, the sinking feeling that had washed over me at the Pugg Gallery dissipated.

"I'll bet you didn't know that afternoon tea was invented by Anna, the seventh duchess of Bedford?" Blake said.

"I'll bet you're correct," I said.

"Anna was one of Queen Victoria's ladies-in-waiting. In their day, the upper crust ate huge breakfasts, a light lunch, and a late dinner. The duchess, obviously suffering from low blood sugar, instructed her servants to fortify her with little cakes in order to keep her going. The idea caught on, and taking tea became a daily ritual."

"My, but aren't you the trivia maven."

"We Brits pride ourselves on such facts." Blake leaned over and placed a scone and some clotted cream and jam on my plate. "Fortnum and Mason still serves the best high tea around. While you Americans are slugging down your Starbucks macchiatos," he said with a slight jocular sneer, "we, who are obviously more civilized, are following the duchess's lead and biting into little cucumber sandwiches and growing stout on petit fours."

"Makes coming to London all the more worthwhile," I said.

We laughed and loved our way into the weekend with more restaurants, art galleries, Portobello Market, the Tate Modern, and a stop at Harrods, where Blake bought me a burgundy leather Filofax.

"This is to replace that goddamn ugly black notebook you carry around. A Filofax is so much more in keeping with the Cole Gallery image."

"I like my ugly black notebook. It's compact."

"It's awful. I need to break you in to the ways of the world. You're terribly chic, and then you ruin it all by dragging out that abysmal-looking monstrosity that you probably purchased at CVS."

"I did buy it at CVS. How did you know that?"

"Darling, it has CVS written all over it. Now here, let's get this monogrammed, and you're on your way. I refuse to be written inside anything but a Filofax from Harrods."

"You're such a snob."

"Yes, I know. I'm an insufferable snob. What else do you need? A Coach bag, some lacy knickers, whatever your fancy, tell me and it's yours."

"How about a long and lingering kiss?" I said.

And right there in the middle of Harrods, Blake Hamilton, artist and lover extraordinaire, gave me one of his state-of-the art kisses that nearly caused me to swoon.

"That's my special Harrods-variety kiss," he said.

With that, he whisked me off in a taxi and back to his flat, where we made love for the rest of the afternoon and into the night, waking up on Sunday morning in time for brunch at Giraffe on Blandford Street. By six I was back at Heathrow, Filofax in hand, as we stood at the gate, kissing until the last boarding call was announced.

Still full from our late English breakfast, I declined the in-flight meal and sank into a deep sleep. It had been a whirlwind weekend, and I was thoroughly exhausted and completely pleased with the way it had all gone. Blake couldn't have been more gracious, making my stay lovely and memorable. There was no denying that I had fallen hard. He seemed equally enamored. Yet, despite the fact I had shaken my ambivalence, there was something telling me to be careful lest my lover prove too good to be true.

FIFTEEN

> It gives me a headache to think
> about that stuff. I'm just a kid. I don't
> need that kind of trouble.
>
> *—Kenny, age seven,*
> *when asked if it's better*
> *to be single or married*

Although I was somewhat jet-lagged, I knew with the Cole closed on Tuesdays, I could catch up on my sleep then.

From JFK, I headed straight to the gallery instead of going home. I had just settled in to read the mail when my cell phone rang. It was Spencer.

"Aha, so you *are* there. When did you get back?"

"About a half hour ago."

"I didn't wake you, did I?"

"No, I'm at work. So much to catch up on that couldn't wait."

"We're still on for tonight, I hope."

With all the excitement of the past few days, I had completely forgotten about my dinner date with Spencer. But I said, "Yes, of course. Looking forward."

"Balthazar at eight. Shall I pick you up?"

"I'll meet you there," I said.

"How's the Brit? Was it a glorious weekend?"

"Five stars. We'll talk all about it tonight. But first you're going to tell me everything about you and the man of the hour."

"You bet I will. I can hardly contain myself. See you then."

Not five minutes later, my cell rang again, this time Blake.

"So, are you still in love?"

"Nah. That was just a passing fancy. As soon as I hit New York, it was all over. How about you?" I asked.

"I'll have to give that a think. Oh yes, now I remember. I'm quite mad over a certain woman."

"Anyone I know?"

"She's from the States."

"So you prefer American women over all those British birds hovering about?"

"I wouldn't have believed it, but yes, it's true."

"Sounds serious."

"It is. So serious that November can't come quickly enough. In the meantime, how was the flight?" Blake asked.

"I never even had to use my flotation device."

"Those British Airways pilots sure are something, aren't they?"

"The Brits do have a flair, I'm discovering."

"Darling, I miss you," he said.

"No more than I." My mind wandered as I inspected my nails, thinking I needed a manicure badly.

"I won't keep you. I just wanted to see that you made it back in one piece. We'll talk tonight."

"Great. I'm having dinner with Spencer, and I'll be home early."

"I should have known." Blake's voice shifted. "Spencer Gould doesn't waste a minute."

He was becoming tedious. "We had this date set up before I left. What could I do?" I tried sustaining a normal tone despite the fact that he was irking me big-time.

"Break the date. Tell him you're accounted for. Erase him from your mind?"

"It's just dinner and then home to bed."

"Ouch, that did it. Alone, I presume."

"I'm much too tired for anything else. You wore me out."

"Good."

And you're wearing me out right now, too, I thought.

"Before you hang up, there's something I need to tell you," Blake said.

"What?"

"You left your panties in my bed."

"Really? Now, how did that happen?"

"Shall I remind you—in detail?"

"No need. Just make sure you put them to good use." I knew exactly how to maneuver him.

"Let me count the ways," Blake said.

At one, I picked up a turkey sandwich at the corner coffee shop on Madison Avenue and brought it back to the gallery. I gobbled it down and, feeling tired, decided to take a short nap. Alexandra kept a cot in the back room for such purposes, often using it after a hectic day on the "front lines" with potential suck-up clients. An unbrushed sage-colored mohair throw from Simon Pearce lay over the top of the cot, a purchase Alexandra had made when she and one of her up-and-coming artists had run off to Vermont together for a weekend. Even though the artist's talents left something to be desired, in the up-and-coming department, he excelled.

Just as I closed my eyes, my cell phone bleated its familiar ring.

"Darling, I didn't want to wake you, so I didn't call until now. I assumed you went straight home from the airport to get some sleep."

"Mother, I'm at the gallery. I've been here since early this morning. In fact, I was just about to take a nap."

"Why didn't you call me?"

"I've been swamped."

"So . . . tell me everything. Was it devastatingly boring or extraordinarily fabulous?"

With Madeleine, life was either one or the other, with no in-betweens.

"What about you and Alden?" I changed the subject.

"We did it."

"As in . . . *did* it?"

"Yes, and let me just say: The man is a tiger in the bedroom. Unfortunately, he has the body of a shar-pei: wrinkled all over with an ass that gave me instant nausea. I kept my eyes closed the entire time. But I will say this: He's great with his hands, as well he should be, considering his profession."

It was hard to listen, and I squirmed as my mother gave me a blow-by-blow of her and Alden's romp beneath the sheets.

"On the plus side, he performed magnificently. He admitted to me that he doesn't use Viagra. I was impressed."

I managed to eke out a weak "congratulations."

"Not only that, he said I have the most perfect body he's ever seen for a woman my age. Obviously, my little tweaking paid off. My wa-wa never looked better. It should be on display in Tiffany's window."

"Now, there's an image I'd rather forget. How was Nantucket?"

"We didn't have much time to explore the island. We were too busy exploring each other."

"I really *do* need a nap," I said.

"Oh, posh. Don't you want to hear more of the sexy parts?"

"Definitely not."

"Let me just say that aside from the fact that his flesh hangs in all the wrong places, I did manage to have an orgasm."

"That's it, Mother, and I mean it."

Knowing Madeleine, it would be only a matter of time before her shar-pei would be taking a backseat to a sleeker breed of animal.

"So," Madeleine wisely changed the subject, "when will you be seeing Spencer?"

"Actually, we're having dinner tonight," I said, offering more information than was necessary.

"*Now* you're making sense. Keep all your options open. While Blake might be a rich and frothy dessert, Spencer is meat and potatoes all the way."

"Meaning?"

"Spencer is solid and substantial. Not a fleeting indulgence whose appeal eventually fades."

"Blake is fleeting?"

"He's an artist. That's part of the attraction."

"Just so you know, I'm falling in love with Blake."

"Of course you are. He's very lovable. But as marriage material, I just don't know."

"It's not *for* you to know, Mother."

"Of course it is. I was put on this earth to know."

"I need to grab a nap, Mother. I'm exhausted."

"You're sitting in the catbird seat, and you don't even realize it."

"Talk to you later."

"Time waits for no one, Samantha."

"What is *that* supposed to mean?"

"Keep your eye on the clock, darling, that's all I'm saying."

By eight o'clock, Balthazar was bustling as usual as I inched my way past tables filled with beautiful people and a few celebrity faces punctuating the scene. Spencer was already seated in a red banquette, working on a mango martini, when I joined him.

"I was lucky to get a table," he said. "They're really packing them in tonight."

Balthazar, one of the best and most authentic French brasseries in town—with its tiled floors, retro ceiling and lighting, and large brass mirrors—exuded an image of another era. The decor was as pleasing to the eye as its menu selections.

"I'll have the same," I said, knowing that just one sip of a mango martini would put me on an immediate high.

"Well, Ms. Jet-setter," Spencer said, "London certainly agrees with you. You look gorgeous."

"Why, thank you, Doctor. It was lovely getting away."

"How is the man?"

"Oh, no," I said, "no wangling of information until I hear yours. You've kept me on pins and needles all weekend. What's up?"

"Roger Sutton is up, or should I say I'm up because of Roger Sutton? I've been on a high ever since we met."

"And where did that memorable meeting take place?"

"If you promise not to laugh, I'll tell you."

"I'll try."

"Between two Degas at the Met. Could it get any more clichéd?"

"It's perfect. Keep going."

"It was last Wednesday. I had just finished a slew of paperwork and had the afternoon free. I was badly in need of fresh air and decided to walk over to the museum for an hour. While I was checking out the Degas, the man next to me was doing the same. We turned to each other at the exact moment and locked eyes. The next thing I knew, we were having cappuccinos in the café and dinner later that night."

"Does Roger live in town?"

"Roger keeps a two-bedroom apartment in the East Sixties. He's here when he's not at his B and B in Lenox, Massachusetts."

"A B and B? Now, *that* is a cliché."

"I know, but Roger is anything but. He's amazing and brilliant and strikingly handsome."

"Sounds like someone has fallen deeply in lust."

"I still haven't touched the ground. You might have heard of his father, the Boston economist Hartley Sutton. He died a few years ago, but his books are still on the required reading list at the Harvard Business School and the Kennedy School of Government. He's a legend."

"What does Roger do?"

"For many years he was a curator at the Museum of Fine Arts in Boston. He's pretty well known in his field. And he sculpts. He probably knows as much about art as good old Blake. He was educated at Exeter and Princeton and gave up his job at the museum four years ago, when he discovered an empty old Victorian house smack in the middle of Lenox. He bought it and turned it into a B and B. He's also on the board of the Lenox Arts Council."

"And the apartment in the city?"

"It's family-owned. His parents used it when they were in New York, and now Roger and his younger sister split their time there. His eighty-three-year-old mother still maintains her town house in Boston's Beacon Hill. His sister lives in Boston, too, with her family."

"I guess that qualifies Roger as borderline geographically desirable."

"He's here a lot. His B and B is fully staffed, so he can spend as much time in New York as he wants. His business partner lives there year-round."

"Seems neither of us can get away from the art scene, can we? Now for the big question: How old is this fabulous man?"

"Again, I ask that you don't react."

"I promise."

"Pick a number between thirty and forty."

"Uh-oh, he's an adolescent."

"No, he's thirty-five. That makes him a definite toddler."

"Spencer Gould, I didn't know you preferred younger men."

"My dear, a few weeks ago you didn't know I was even gay. Nothing should shock you."

My martini arrived while Spencer ordered another. He talked about Roger. I rattled on about Blake, all the while noting what a truly handsome man Spencer was, and what a waste for the female population that he was "gender-challenged," as Lily Ann liked to say.

"Have you heard that Madeleine and Alden's big Nantucket adventure sounded quite cozy, indeed?"

"So I discovered this morning when Dad came into the office grinning from ear to ear."

"Isn't this all so insanely bizarre?" I asked.

"Probably the weirdest thing I've heard, although I am finding it rather amusing."

The waiter arrived with menus and a basket of freshly baked breads and pastries. The martini had given me a slight buzz, and I needed to eat.

"Let's share a plate of the raw oysters," Spencer suggested. "They have three varieties."

"The warm goat cheese and caramelized onion tart sounds equally delicious. So does the roasted pumpkin ravioli with sage and walnut butter."

"Great. Let's order them all and move on from there if we decide we want more."

As was always the case with Spencer, the time flew. As tired as I was from the time change, I could have stayed at Balthazar and talked all night. After devouring our appetizers with gusto, we decided to forgo entrées and share a decadent dessert.

"So, when do I get to meet Mr. Heartthrob?" I asked.

"My, aren't we pushy?"

"Not pushy, curious. Describe his looks. What movie star resembles him?"

"Lassie."

"I thought Lassie was a girl," I said.

"They have the same hair."

"Wow, I can see why you were attracted."

"What are you telling Madeleine about us these days?"

"That you're divine as ever?"

"Am I divine?" he fished.

"Spencer," I said, taking his hand in mine, "if you weren't seeing another man, I just might have to kiss you."

"Whew," he said, "close call."

· · ·

By the time I got home, there were already two messages waiting from Blake.

"Hi, it's your jealous lover calling. It's also eleven o'clock your time, when all jet-lagged ladies should be in bed asleep."

The second message had come an hour later.

"Where the hell are you, anyway?"

It was now five A.M. in London. That message had been left an hour ago, meaning that my dinner with Spencer had turned Blake into a raving insomniac. Dare I call him back at this ungodly hour? I decided to put him out of his misery.

"Darling, did I wake you?" I asked, knowing otherwise.

"Yes, you have. I've been sleeping soundly for hours," he quipped. "You have some nerve calling me. I hope it's for a damn good reason."

"How about I adore and miss you?"

"In that case, all right. I forgive you," Blake said.

"Thank you."

"How's our boy Spencer?"

"Funny, he asked the same about you."

"I hope you set him straight."

"Meaning?"

"Meaning that as soon as I get to New York, Spencer's history."

"But he's *such* a good friend."

"Good, then he can be my friend, too, and we'll all hang out together."

It actually sounded perfect.

"You do realize that you're starting to sound possessive," I said.

"Does that bother you?"

"I find it endearing," which was only partially true. The tables had turned. It was now Blake who was playing the desperate lover. Needy guys were even worse than needy chicks, and Blake, with all his pizzazz and sex appeal, was bordering on irritating. I chalked it up to long-distance paranoia, a feeling with which I was not entirely unfamiliar.

"I am going out on a limb here: Are you alone?"

"You'll never know," I said.

"Have a heart."

"Yes, I'm alone."

"Good, I can finally get some sleep."

"I could be lying," I shot again, realizing that I was bordering on cruel.

"I'm hanging up. I've reached my pain threshold for one night."

"Sleep well, darling," I said.

"Ya talkin' to me?" he asked in his best De Niro imitation.

"Oh, are you still on the phone?" I continued to tease.

"Samantha Krasner, I do love you."

"Shut up and go to bed," I said. "And being that the gallery is closed tomorrow, I'm going to sleep in."

"Don't worry, I won't call before noon your time. God, but these long-distance relationships are the pits."

"I'll second that," I said, thinking they could actually be divine interventions when one had reached her bullshit quota.

I didn't awaken until eleven o'clock on Tuesday morning. My cell phone was turned off, my land phone picking up all messages, one of them from Blake. I would call him back later. The day stretched out before me like a large, lazy yawn. My first thought was a leisurely late lunch followed by a movie, with time to indulge myself any way I chose. My plans were squelched as soon as Lily Ann called.

"Great. You're back. I can't wait to hear all the sexy details," she said.

"And there are many."

"I'm taking a personal day," she said. "By any chance are you free for lunch?"

Lunch with Lily Ann was always a high priority. "Meet me at the Boathouse in an hour," I said.

· · ·

The Boathouse in Central Park was especially lovely in early fall, when summer was waning and the leaves were just turning. I showered, threw on a pair of jeans and a long-sleeved button-down shirt, slipped into a pair of Marc Jacobs flats, and was out the door.

Lily Ann was prompt, as always, a trait I admired, and since it was close to two o'clock, most of the lunch crowd had already left or were on dessert. We were seated immediately at a table overlooking Central Park's lake.

Lily Ann was all aglow as she presented her left hand to me. On her finger was a thick sterling silver wedding band.

"Oh my God, how fantastic," I said. "And you were worried."

"I have to admit, the guy is as corny as hell, but lovable. We took a Circle Line cruise around Manhattan, and as we sailed toward the Statue of liberty, the tour guide announced over the loudspeaker: 'Ladies and gentlemen, we are coming up on one of Manhattan's most famous landmarks: The Statue of Liberty, where Bennett Verlaine is about to propose marriage to Lily Ann Kahn.' I nearly died. Bennett got down on his knee, and in front of all those midwestern tourists, he asked me to marry him."

"And you said yes."

"I was too embarrassed not to. It was kind of romantic, in its way, except for this big, burly Texan who felt compelled to kiss the bride and planted one right on my lips. We decided to keep our marriage a secret. The next day Bennett and I went down to city hall and made it official. You're looking at Mrs. Lily Ann Verlaine."

Lily Ann, with whom I had shared all of our most intimate moments—first boyfriends, first periods, and the loss of our virginities—had decided to play it cool this time. My genuine excitement for her was interspersed with the slightest sting of disappointment that she hadn't called me with the news.

"Madeleine will never let me live this down," I said. "I'm surprised your mother didn't kill you. She's been talking about your fairy-tale wedding since you were six. You've also deprived me of one of the most humiliating moments in my life: being a bridesmaid and wearing one of those ghastly sorbet-colored dresses."

"I did it for you," Lily Ann said. "Now you're indebted to me forever."

"And where is Bennett now?"

"Back in L.A. He was here for five days and had to get back."

"So what's the plan, and if you tell me you're moving to L.A., I'll shoot you on the spot."

"Moi? Move? I don't think so. No, Bennett is working on trying to get transferred back here. A couple of publishing houses seem more than interested. L.A. is great, but he says that his IQ diminishes every day he's there. New York is surging through his veins. He can't wait to get back."

"Sounds like Blake."

"Speaking of which: Tell me about the weekend."

"Nonstop sex interrupted by a few dinners and a trip to his London gallery. I even met the owner, who is the second coming of Alexandra Cole."

"When *is* the bitch returning?"

"She'll be back in a month. In the meantime, I'm getting all the plans laid out for Blake's show. The flowers alone will cost us a bloody fortune. Alexandra is pulling out all the stops."

"That's because she has the hots for Blake."

"So I hear, but he made it clear he's not interested."

"I never trusted that woman. Hasn't she slept with every eligible bachelor in the city?"

"And those who aren't so eligible, plus half of Europe."

"Only half?" Lily Ann asked.

The next few weeks flew by. Blake and I spoke morning, afternoon, and night, he professing his love, while I was unable to verbally reciprocate. The tides were turning—the more attentive he was, the more I retreated. Ambivalent about his arrival to New York,

I decided to once again seek out the help of my psychic, Aurora, aka Estelle Goldstein.

"It's quite simple," Aurora said on a Saturday afternoon as we were nearing October. "You're not in love with the guy."

"Of course I am," I said.

"There's a difference between wanting to be and really being." She handed me a Diet Coke.

"But he's fantastic and wonderful."

"Something's getting in the way. Let's take a look."

Out came the props: the incense, the muddy drink, the crystal ball. And we couldn't forget Aurora's tingling toe.

"I'm definitely getting that strange toe sensation again."

"Maybe it's a plantar wart," I said.

"I see interference—that same body of water I saw the last time you were here."

"Yes, I told you: Blake and I are separated by an ocean."

"But he's trying to break through."

"Break through?"

"I see chaos. I see high waves." She stared further. "I see dense fog."

Perhaps the crystal ball needed dusting, I thought. For the next half hour, I hung on Aurora's every word, and while I wanted to buy into the mumbo-jumbo, a part of me thought that Aurora and her speculations were all crap. Yet she was right: There was interference.

"Blake is coming to New York to live for a while," I said.

Aurora toyed with the crystals around her neck. "And that makes you less than happy?"

"On the contrary, I'm looking forward to it. Long-distance relationships are difficult."

"And safe."

"What do you mean?"

"Having an ocean between you is both a blessing and a curse, especially when there's another man on the scene."

"There is no other man."

Aurora put her face so close to the ball that her nose was practically touching it. "There's that fog again. A tall male figure is moving closer."

"You can see all that in a crystal ball?"

"My big toe," she said. "It's killing me."

Tight shoes, perhaps. Except she was barefoot.

"When the toe tingles, it's a sign. When it starts to pain me, that's all the proof I need."

"Proof of what?"

"I dabble in the stars, and your moon is in the wrong house."

"What can I do? Move?"

"You need to address the confusion. Remove the clutter so you can see your way clear. The man in the ball is not your present lover."

"He's not? Who is he?"

"Samantha." Aurora stopped ball-gazing. "Are you sure you're not seeing another man?"

"Just a friend. Not a sexual relationship."

"But you like him. You're attracted to him."

"I am, but he's unavailable."

Aurora began rubbing her toe. "He's not married."

"That's right."

"He's already in a relationship."

"Yes," I said, becoming more absorbed.

"I see another figure emerging . . . a man. By any chance is your friend gay?"

"That about sums it up," I said. "Can you elaborate further?"

Aurora further examined the ball. "I'll say only this: The fog that keeps appearing is changing over to static. Where there's static, there's instability. The next few months are most precarious. You'll need to be careful. Be aware."

"I will."

"And Samantha . . ."

"Yes?"

"If you meet any eligible men who don't interest you, you can send them my way."

"Of course, Aurora, I will."

"Please call me Estelle," Aurora said.

I left feeling slightly off balance. If what Aurora/Estelle had said was true, I had some issues to address. I loved Blake, but I couldn't deny the ambivalence that was creeping through at the thought of his arrival to New York. Even worse, I didn't understand why. I had been waiting for Mr. Right for years, and here he was: tall, handsome, smart, and creative, with a British accent, no less. So why was I less than thrilled? I decided to share all with Lily Ann.

"Change," Lily Ann said. "You're accustomed to brief, passionate interludes with Blake. You go at it hot and heavy, and then he gets back on a plane and you've got your breathing room again, time to absorb it all. That's why Bennett's and my relationship has never been better."

"But you got married. He's coming back to New York."

"And don't think that doesn't scare me. I've become accustomed to my alone time and rely on it. Sure, I love Bennett, but I cherish my autonomy. Marriage is an adjustment, a full-time commitment. Men know that. Why do you think there are so many bachelors on the loose?"

"So you're saying we have bachelor mentalities?"

"I'm saying that underneath all that programming we've been subjected to by our mothers are women who want it all: love, commitment, passion, and independence—or space, as the guys like to call it. But we make concessions. Something's got to go, and we reach the point where we either move forward or stagnate. It's what I call the Grand Fizzle. And that's the most frightening of all. Stagnation entertains the idea of being alone forever. That's when we decide to go for it."

"Aurora questioned my feelings for Blake. She said there's a difference between wanting to be in love and really loving someone."

"*Do* you love Blake?"

"I think I do. But now that he's all over me with his undying devotion, I find myself pulling away."

"My God, you *are* a guy," Lily Ann said.

"My mother thinks that Blake isn't marriage material."

"Madeleine wants you to marry a man with a solid profession, not an artist whose career could suddenly go down the toilet."

"You mean marry someone like Spencer," I said.

"Exactly. How are you and Spencer doing, anyway?"

I bit into my Boathouse burger and said nothing.

"Samantha, are you there?"

"I'm here, but there's something I've been meaning to tell you."

"I knew it. You seem a little weird. Let me guess. There's a Mrs. Spencer Gould in the picture."

"No."

"He's seeing someone?"

"Sort of, but that's not exactly it."

Lily Ann put down her sandwich. "You *have* to tell me."

"You can't say a word or let on in any way."

"Come on, Sam, we share everything."

"We do? You didn't tell me you had gotten married," I blurted out.

"Oh, so you're punishing me now?"

"No, but we've never kept big news to ourselves."

"Apparently, we do. As for Bennett and me tying the knot, we wanted it to be our secret for a few hours. You can understand that."

"I guess. All right, but you have to promise—"

"Shut up!"

"Spencer is gay."

There was a brief moment of silence during which Lily Ann chugalugged her iced tea and stared.

"You're not serious?"

"It's true," I said.

"My God, who would have believed it?"

"Certainly not I."

"I'm nonplussed . . . but." With Lily Ann there was always a "but"—two sides to every situation, no matter how challenging. "The way I see it, you can milk this one for all it's worth."

"Care to comment on that?"

"Spencer just might turn out to be the best thing that's ever happened to you—the most fun you've had in years, as long as he's willing to play it straight. Gay men are a woman's best accessory. They're like girlfriends with penises."

"What's in it for Spencer?"

"Are you kidding? He'll have the entire New York art scene falling at his feet. He can have his pick of the most eligible gay men in town, as long as he does it discreetly. But he's got to promise to keep the charade going, as far as Madeleine and Blake are concerned."

"Spencer: my partner in crime. Sounds interesting. And guess what: He's willing to play along."

As long as I kept Spencer a central player in my life, my mother would be happy, and Blake might stop taking me for granted.

"Good old Spencer. He's a gem—and your best weapon. Just think of the possibilities. That is, until he turns up with some gorgeous guy and blows your cover."

"Actually, he does have a gorgeous guy," I said. "His name is Roger Sutton, and they just met a week ago."

"You see, you don't tell me anything."

"Now we're even," I said.

I felt a sense of relief at having brought Lily Ann onto the scene: I could vent to my heart's content instead of bearing my burden alone.

"There's just one small problem," I said. "I really like Spencer. Maybe more than like."

"You mean you could fall in love with Spencer?"

"Maybe, but that's out of the question. My mother is obsessed with the idea. She and Alden Gould have become an item, and she'd like us to follow right behind them. She's even talking double weddings."

"That's one way of keeping the mother/daughter relationship symbiotically intact," Lily Ann said. She laughed out loud.

"What?"

"I'm just thinking. Can you imagine the look on Madeleine's face if she knew Spencer was gay?"

"She'd go into immediate cardiac arrest," I said.

"Sam, this is about as salacious a situation as you could be in. I think it's great."

"I think it sucks."

"You've got it made."

"Good. All you need to do now is redirect your thinking so we can devise a game plan. When did you become so devious?"

"Years of practice," Lily Ann said.

SIXTEEN

*Summer bachelors, like summer breezes,
are never as cool as they pretend to be.*

—Nora Ephron

Lily Ann took life's situations and ran with them, turning doom and gloom into an adventure to be experienced and savored. According to her, Spencer was the perfect foil—the beard who, if used properly, could get my mother off my back and keep Blake off kilter and completely under my spell until which time I decided if he was the man for me. I had taken game playing to a new art form.

As we moved into October with Alexandra returning at the end of the month, I solidified plans for Blake's December show. The days melted into one another as life continued at its usual pace. Spencer and Roger were going strong, as were Blake and I with phone calls that were fraught with excitement over his imminent arrival to New York. And yet something gnawed at me.

There was no denying that I loved Blake, but I was also feeling ill at ease. I chalked up any apprehension to what Lily Ann had said was change. Once Blake was here, we could settle into a more normal routine and find a consistency in our relationship that up until now had been nonexistent. That thought both frightened and delighted me. I decided to stop analyzing and let life happen. My daily schedule was a constant helter-skelter barrage of appointments and interviews.

One morning, looking up at the calendar, I realized that in just three days, Alexandra Cole was due to return.

I spent the time cleaning the gallery, discarding the clutter that had accumulated in her absence and making sure the place shined.

"It's about time that woman came home and took over some of the responsibilities," my mother said. "She can't expect you to do everything. You don't get paid enough for that. She's taking advantage."

True, but I had enjoyed my solitude and freedom. With Alexandra back in action, breathing down my neck, I would have to tread more carefully and could no longer enjoy the occasional two-hour lunch or come in after nine. I would now take a backseat to her daily dramas and try placating the artists she was known to handle with less than diplomacy. In short, I would once again be her lackey who catered to her every whim and desire.

When I told Blake of my concerns, he was empathic and supportive. "There's no doubt Alexandra is a tough broad, but she relies on you more than you think. If she didn't trust you, she wouldn't have stayed away so long and left you in charge of the gallery. You don't have to put up with any of her crap."

"That's easy for you to say. You're a guy. Alexandra basically despises women and sees them all as her personal competition."

"She adores you."

"No, she's afraid I'll quit, so she sucks up."

"Sucking up is good. I like sucking up. That means she needs you."

"I suppose, but I've gotten so used to her not being around."

Blake brought the subject back to us. "So you *do* prefer long-distance relationships."

"Only with Alexandra," I lied.

Blake's bouts of insecurity always seeped into our conversations. I preferred him to be self-possessed, not whiny. Whenever he sought reassurance, my tendency was to become quiet and non-responsive.

"Samantha? Are you still on the phone?"

"Interference," I said. "Lots of static," I quoted Aurora. "I can't hear you clearly."

We would then get off and wait until I could get a better signal, both electronically and emotionally.

I despised the fact that I felt so unsure. Wasn't I supposed to be reveling in the fact that Blake would be here in a matter of days? Yet every time I let that thought in, my stomach churned, and I felt a tension headache develop over my right eye—a telltale sign that trouble was brewing.

The morning of Alexandra's return, I woke early, dressed impeccably, and was at the gallery by eight A.M. At ten thirty, Alexandra waltzed in, looking as though she had spent the last month at a spa. She was tanned, and her hair had been styled into a shorter bob. She wore a silk shirt unbuttoned to her navel, so that when she turned sideways, her perky breasts were visible. Her tight-fitting beige pants hugged her body, accentuating every curve. A thick brown leather belt made her waistline look twenty inches. Her heels were so high that any normal woman would have suffered altitude sickness.

"Darling," she burst forth, "I've missed you."

I was sitting at my antique desk toward the rear of the room, facing out on the street, when she walked over and hugged me.

"You look *fabulous*," I said, a word I detested and had perfected where Alexandra was concerned.

"And you—you look divine as well. Let me grab my caffeine fix, and then we'll catch up."

"Catch up" meant that Alexandra would scrutinize everything with a fine-tooth comb, making sure I hadn't neglected any of my duties in her absence. She filled her mug to the brim and pulled up a chair next to mine. The smell of her Chanel No. 5 filled the air. A large wall calendar of the year's events was scribbled in with names of various artists highlighted in red, Blake heading the list for December. It was that to which Alexandra turned her attention.

"Let's go over the fine details," she said. "Blake Hamilton is our main attraction, and that's where we need to focus. He has six paintings arriving, all of which must be perfectly placed. I've asked Wesley to come over and do the hanging. He was the first one I called this morning."

Wesley Whyte was considered one of the finest experts around, and worked with many of the galleries. Blake's works were mammoth, requiring not only a good eye but careful hands as well.

"The look we're after is startling," Alexandra said, meaning her opinion alone. "As soon as people walk in, we want to stop them dead in their tracks. You know: gaping mouths and all. The beauty of Blake's work is its sensationalism. You can't ignore it. It's not just the size of his paintings, but the way his colors play off each other. He brings the canvas to life. I know one dealer in particular, Gladys Pringle, who is already talking about purchasing one. I'm telling you, Samantha, this will be *the* hottest show in town. I expect hordes of critics. When was the last time you and Blake were in touch?"

She took a sip of her coffee, giving us both a moment to catch our breath in between the Q&A.

"Blake and I spoke last night," I said.

"And is he ready with everything?"

"He'll be arriving in just a month. He's seems pretty excited."

"He damn well should. He's got the best fucking space in the city." Alexandra used "fuck" as a natural part of her daily vocabulary. "Did he say when the paintings are being shipped?"

"I believe he's taking care of that now."

"Believe? No room for *believe*. We need to *know*. We'll want to get on the phone today and solidify those plans."

"By 'we,' I assume you mean me?" I asked.

"Of course. I have too much minutiae to deal with today. Be a puss and handle that, will you? God, but I'm starving. I didn't have time to eat a thing. Would you be a dear and run over to the coffee shop and get me a bagel? Toasted ever so slightly, light on the cream cheese."

My subservient position had officially kicked in.

When I returned ten minutes later, Alexandra was on the phone, laughing flirtatiously and gesturing to me to leave her bagel on her desk, which was directly across from mine. She put her hand over the receiver. "It's Blake," she whispered. "He called while you were out."

I pretended not to eavesdrop but kept my ears peeled.

"And yes, we'll have drinks as soon as you arrive. Wonderful." More laughter. "Yes, Wesley Whyte will do the hanging, with you overseeing everything. I know. I know. You have the final word as far as placement is concerned. Wesley is simply the maintenance man, if you will. He knows better than to ruffle the feathers of my artists. Yes, darling, you know best. Kiss kiss and talk later."

"How *is* the artist?" I said nonchalantly.

"A pain in the ass, like all of them. Except Blake Hamilton is oozing sex appeal, which makes him easier to take."

"You should only know," I wanted to say.

"The fact that he'll be here for six months is a dream come true."

"Why is that?" I played dumb.

"I prefer having my artists in close proximity. Makes life so much easier. It's not easy working with an ocean between us."

"That's true," I said.

I wanted to blurt out that Blake and I had become lovers. That I had traveled to London and spent practically all last weekend in his bed. That his body was so exquisite, I'd had multiple orgasms each time we made love. That the man was absolutely crazy about me and I, him. Knowing that Blake and I shared this sweet secret made it all the more delicious, even better than the Spencer charade.

Alexandra spent the rest of the day on the phone, schmoozing with her friends. While she was away, the bills had been sent directly to me so I could write checks for heat, electricity, and rent without her having to worry her head with the petty "incidentals" she so despised.

At four o'clock she looked up. "Samantha, we need to rethink these walls. They look depressingly drab."

The gallery had been painted from head to toe only a year ago, in an unobtrusive café au lait that allowed the paintings to pop. Already she was tiring of the color.

"I see a soft green. Perhaps salmon. I don't know, what's your opinion?"

The thought of moving all the furniture and rehanging the art was about the worst ever.

"I like the color," I said. "It's the perfect backdrop for the work. You want the art to be the main focus. The walls are merely an afterthought; they don't jump out at you."

"Maybe. We'll see. Just a thought. I'll ask Wesley about it when he comes in to hang Blake."

Alexandra's whims were easily dismissed. At least three times a week, she became dissatisfied with something and needed to address it. It drove me crazy.

By five, she had started yawning. "I'm calling it a day," she said. "I'm jet-lagged, and I need to go home and get some sleep. Tomorrow is another day. You can stay on and finish up. Oh, and Samantha?"

"Yes?" I feared she was going to shoot another errand at me.

"You've been great, organizationally speaking. We'll talk about a little raise when I get back tomorrow. Does that sound good to you?"

Would wonders never cease? "A raise sounds perfect," I said, hoping she would replace "a little" with a more appropriate sum of money, which I felt I richly deserved for endurance alone.

"Did Alexandra completely unnerve you?" Blake asked when he called that evening.

"The woman could drive anyone to drink. She had me waiting on her, as usual. But she intimated there would be a little raise in my future."

"How little?"

"She didn't say. Said we'd talk about it tomorrow."

But the next day Alexandra had completely forgotten the subject, and it never came up. Before she left for Paris, she had promised the same, then dropped it like a hot potato. If I were going to wangle a raise out of her, I would have to be assertive and blunt. I decided to give her a few days to unwind before broaching the subject of money, which, according to my mother, was never supposed to be alluded to, as it reeked of bad taste.

Instead, I went about my business while Alexandra barked orders to do this, take care of that, and make sure everything was running on schedule.

Thursday night, Spencer and I had dinner. I begged him to introduce me to Roger. "This mystery man is just too much of a mystery. I want to meet him."

"He's up in Lenox for a few days. After he returns, we'll meet for drinks."

"We'd better. In the meantime, the latest news is that my mother wants us all to have dinner together. I don't think I can get off the hook."

"A harmless dinner can't hurt, and it will make Madeleine happy."

"No wonder the woman is crazy about you," I said.

· · ·

Autumn in New York was in full swing, the Algonquin bar packed to the gills when I walked in to meet Spencer and "the man" the following Thursday.

Tucked away in the rear of the room, his back toward me, was Roger Sutton. I could hardly contain my curiosity. Spencer stood up and waved me over.

"Samantha Krasner, I am so happy to finally introduce you to Roger Sutton."

I was greeted by a pair of searing-blue eyes and a warm smile as Roger stood up and offered a hand. "Spencer has been talking non-stop about you. I'm thrilled to meet you," he said.

I was immediately captivated by Roger's friendly demeanor, which was evident at his first hello. After only five minutes, I felt as though we were old friends. He was elegantly dressed in gray flannel pants with a black cashmere blazer, a crisp white shirt, and a paisley tie. He bordered on preppy, with just enough sophistication to make for a winning combination.

"Spencer tells me you own a B and B," I said.

"Yes, and I hope you'll get to see it firsthand. Do you know Lenox?"

"Know it and love it," I said. "My family has spent many summer weekends there. Tanglewood, Jacob's Pillow, the Berkshire Theatre, how can you not fall in love?"

"Which is exactly what I did," Roger said.

Drinks had lasted for nearly two hours when Spencer suggested we go on to dinner. "I've been telling Roger about Tasca. It's got the best tapas bar in town. You haven't lived until you've tried their chorizo with sweet sticky figs."

"Let the feast begin," Roger said.

The interaction between the two men was as warm and loving as that of any two friends could be. Their reserved affection gave no indication to the outside world that they were lovers, but after I'd spent several more intimate hours in their company, the sexual energy was apparent, subtle though it was: a sudden look where their eyes locked for an instant, the brush of a hand when Roger reached over to taste Spencer's snails, the knowing glance when a thought was expressed by one and acknowledged by the other. The sweet allure of affection that bounced back and forth between them were all indicators of a relationship in the making.

Not once did I feel like an intruder but, more, a welcomed guest who had been graciously invited to share in their happiness and savor their mutual attraction. Spencer came alive in Roger's presence in a way that was different than I had ever seen him before.

By the time dessert arrived and we were still sipping our velvety Rioja wine, Spencer lifted his glass.

"To Degas," he toasted.

SEVENTEEN

All marriages are happy.
It's the living together afterwards
that causes all the trouble.

—*Raymond Hull*

The following weeks flew by. Alexandra became more frenetic every day. Blake was due to arrive in New York in a week, and with that came a sense of anticipatory dread, as Alexandra felt she and the gallery weren't prepared.

"The paintings are *still* not here," she wailed. "Wesley Whyte is chomping at the bit and wants to start hanging before he takes off for Provincetown with his new lay of the moment."

"It's much too early to hang Blake," I said. "We shouldn't get him up until after Thanksgiving."

"Tell me about it," Alexandra went off. "I told Wesley

we're squeezing in a smaller show before Blake's, but being the prima donna that he is, he reminded me his schedule is getting tight. Blake's canvases are enormous, not to mention that Wesley's hernia is starting to bother him and I had better have proper machinery around to assist him." She took a breath. "I called The Home Depot and asked if we could rent a dolly from them, only to be told they weren't in the furniture rental business. I'm at my wits' end, Samantha."

I tried smoothing Alexandra's ruffled feathers and went so far as to suggest she up her Prozac.

"This is bigger than Prozac. Blake Hamilton will be the death of me yet. When exactly will he be here?" she asked for the fifth time that week.

"He's flying over and moving into his friend's apartment on Sunday. He's already shipped his clothes and I'm going to pick him up at the airport."

Alexandra suddenly warmed. "*That's* very nice of you."

"It's the least I can do," I said.

As anxious as Alexandra was, I was equally jumpy. Blake was becoming increasingly amorous on the phone, announcing that he couldn't wait to bed me in New York.

"I get hard just thinking of the ways I want to ravish you," he said. "Now, when the mood strikes, your vagina will be only a cab ride away."

"Perhaps I can send it over to your apartment and you can start without me," I said.

"Samantha, I'm not sure what I love more: your sense of humor or your incomparable sex appeal. You keep me so amused."

But I wasn't laughing.

On Sunday, as promised, I was at JFK to meet Blake's plane. He was one of the first ones off and greeted me with a broad smile and one carry-on bag. The rest of his clothes were already waiting in his apartment.

"You travel light," I said.

"I detest excess baggage. This way, no waiting. We can go directly to the apartment and make mad, passionate love."

But I was in no mood. I had just gotten my period, and the cramps had still not subsided. I was also not emotionally ready for an intimate encounter. I needed time to transition.

"Bad timing," I explained.

"Darling, you're never off-limits to me. You know that."

"I was hoping we could go over to your apartment, get you settled and unpacked, and then grab a bite."

"I'll give you a bite," he said, nibbling on my neck as we got into my car. He was hardly able to keep his hands off me.

"Try and contain yourself," I said, "we don't want to have an accident on your first evening in town."

I could detect the chill in my voice as I disengaged from Blake, trying to maintain enough distance to keep myself in control.

All the way into the city, Blake rambled on while I drove silently, listening to him jump from one subject to the other. "So, is Alexandra ready for me?" he asked.

She's ready, I wanted to say. The person who isn't so ready is I. Instead, I said, "Alexandra is her usual crazy self. She's obsessing over the fact that your paintings are never going to get hung. Wesley Whyte is throwing a hissy fit, too. You're causing absolute mayhem."

But Blake was cool as ever. "It will all get done, even if I have to hang them myself."

"I told Alexandra that it's too early to get you up. There's a small show before yours."

"Never too early to get *me* up, darling." The sexual innuendos were flying. "Whose show?"

"Some obscure artist. Norbert Ashe, whose prints Alexandra flipped over."

"Norbert Ashe happens to be from Sussex," Blake said. "His work is terrific. I didn't know he was showing at the Cole."

"Yes, he's there simply as an aperitif, to whet the appetites of the masses before you arrive on the scene."

"Great. I'll get to see him. It's been a while."

"Have you and Norbert been friends for long?"

"Acquaintances, really. We've shared a few ales together and discussed art."

"Well, that will be fun."

"I'll tell you what will be fun." Blake lowered his voice to a deep, sexy pitch. "Getting to Charlie's pad and devouring you."

"I told you: I have my period."

"Even better," Blake said. "No holds barred."

Making love when the mood is right knows no boundaries. But I was feeling out of sorts and wasn't physically or mentally up to any grand sexual display of affection.

"Samantha, this is so unlike you. We're usually so free and easy with each other."

"You're not listening: I'm not feeling well."

"Darling, I'm sensing distance."

"I'm fine," I said. "Let's get you unpacked, and we'll go on to dinner."

"The hell with my unpacking. Aren't you happy I'm here?"

Blake had dared to ask the big question, which caught me off guard. For weeks I had been trying to adjust to his arrival, asking myself why the thought of it filled me with such dismay. Now, sitting on the bed with the late-afternoon light shining on us, I couldn't ignore the fact that I was pulling away. Any way I sliced it, something was wrong.

"I'm a little nervous."

"*I'm* supposed to be the nervous one," he said. "After all, I'm the intruder in this big city. But having you in my life makes it all worthwhile."

"You're here for your show and to paint." My aloofness was bordering on downright unfriendliness.

He took my hand. "Samantha, is all this happening too fast? Is that it?"

His words jolted me. "No . . . maybe . . . a little, I guess."

"I knew it. I've been coming on a bit strong lately. But I'm excited because you're so exciting."

His directness was sweet and reassuring. My icy demeanor began to thaw. As we talked, I became more complacent and relaxed.

"It's not that I'm not happy to see you, because I am," I said. My defenses were receding. "It's that I'm unaccustomed to all this attention."

"Get used to it, because during the next six months, I'm going to shower you with attention and affection."

That was the last thing I needed to hear.

"I feel suffocated," I admitted, finally able to release the tension that had been building up inside me for months.

"Funny, it makes some women feel loved."

"I know, I know. I'm an anomaly. It's silly," though I didn't really believe that to be true.

"You can't deny your feelings," Blake said. "I wouldn't want you to."

"This isn't the way I wanted to greet you." I felt extremely guilty.

"Better to get this out of the way now, so we know the ground rules," Blake said.

And with that, the floodgates opened. I purged every feeling without regard to how Blake might react. "I'm afraid now that you're on my turf, our relationship will change."

"New York is your turf?"

"Yes, just as London is yours."

"That's impressive. I never knew I ruled an entire city."

The notion, preposterous and grandiose though it was, rang true. Even more: I equated an entire country with Blake, while the U.S.A. was all about me.

"Are you concerned that I'll get in your way and interfere in your life?"

"The *idea* of that happening makes me a basket case," I said.

"You sound like long distance *does* work best for you."

"In many ways, it's been awful."

"Well. Now you won't have to miss me," Blake said. "I'm here."

That's what had scared me the most: the not missing him.

We continued on for another hour until I started feeling hungry and light-headed.

"I need to eat," I said. "There's a charming place on Madison and Ninety-third: Bistro du Nord."

"Let's do it," Blake said. "We can pick up the conversation over a bottle of wine."

One of Blake's more endearing qualities, I had begun to discover, was allowing me room to vent. As we walked toward Madison Avenue, I tucked my arm through his. Then I stopped walking and kissed him.

"Thanks for getting me," I said.

"I don't just get you, Samantha. I also accept you. I'll tell you what: We'll take it one day at a time. I'm going to be busy with work and getting ready for the exhibit; I just might not have time for any frivolity. You'll be begging to see me."

"I'm not sure I like that, either," I said, squeezing his arm tighter.

"You can't have it both ways, now, can you?"

"You'd be surprised," I teased, sounding more like an arrogant bitch.

Bistro du Nord resembled a tiny gift box that, once unwrapped and opened, equally delighted the eye and taste buds. The menu boasted bistro classics, with an onion soup that melted in the mouth; add to that a green peppercorn pâté, an enticing start to any meal.

We were promptly seated in a burgundy banquette, looking out at the beige walls with black-and-white portraits and a staircase leading to an open dining loft over the main room below. The cozy ambience immediately relaxed us. Blake was offered a wine list. Starved as we were, we ordered some steamed mussels in a most delectable, perfumed sauce.

"These can calm the most savage beast," Blake said, tasting one.

"And you are definitely *my* savage beast," I said, starting to feel a warm glow penetrate my body.

He chose a hearty burgundy that we could hardly wait to let breathe. We asked the waiter to pour us two glasses and toasted to new beginnings.

"Wherever they will lead us," I added.

The talk became lighter as our stomachs filled. More wine was poured. We shared an arugula salad, sautéed with shitake mushrooms, roasted peppers, and slices of ripe Parmesan cheese.

"Feeling better, sweetheart?" he asked.

"If I keep drinking wine, I'll be fine," I said.

"Aha: vino, the magic ingredient. I had better order several more bottles."

"There's something to be said about being in a constant state of inebriation," I said. "And wine is proved to have health benefits."

"We'll keep it pumping through our veins at all times," Blake said, pouring the last remaining drops into my glass.

Over Blake's penne pasta with eggplant, tomatoes, black olives, and fresh mozzarella, the conversation turned to his upcoming exhibition and Alexandra.

"I'll stop by the gallery tomorrow," he said. "So I can smooth out Alexandra's rough edges. Tell me, what does she know about us?"

"Only that I'm in charge of every move you make—artistically speaking, of course."

"I like that. Does she also know you're in charge of my orgasms?"

"I decided to spare her the details."

"Probably a wise move. I'll pretend I hardly notice you exist. I'll give Alexandra my undivided attention."

"As well you should. She is your keeper, after all."

"She wishes."

My duck a l'orange gave off a citrus aroma as I passed over a forkful to Blake.

"I've died and gone to heaven. More. I want more. Feed me, darling. Ply me with duck. Quack, quack."

For the next two hours, we dined, laughed, drank, and made verbal love. By the time we were back in Blake's apartment, I was feeling no pain and fell onto his bed, where, period or no period, we made mad, passionate love well into the night, not awakening until six A.M.

"Oh my God, I've got to go home and change," I said, scampering about, retrieving pieces of clothing that lay haphazardly around the bedroom. I kissed the half-sleeping Blake and left quietly, making it to the gallery before Alexandra arrived at nine-thirty.

"Well, *you* look a bit green around the gills," she said. "Rough night?"

"I stayed up watching an old movie, after I delivered Blake to his apartment."

"Oh, that's right. Our artist is in town. I almost forgot."

Yeah, right, who was she kidding? I chuckled to myself, noticing that Alexandra had carefully chosen the perfect outfit and was dressed to the nines just in case the artiste did show up.

"Did he by any chance say he might be coming in today?" she casually asked.

I played it to the hilt. "He said he might stop by."

"Did he happen to mention what time he might be here—*if* he comes in, that is? I have a pedicure at three."

"No, not really," I said in my most who-gives-a-damn voice.

But at exactly eleven, while Alexandra kept looking out the front window every chance she could, in walked Blake, looking drop-dead handsome.

"Blake, darling, my goodness, what a surprise. I had no idea you'd be here so soon after your arrival to New York," Alexandra gushed.

"Oh, Samantha didn't tell you?"

"She said you might stop by, but since you're jet-lagged and all, I never expected to see you looking so fresh and dapper. Please, sit down, let me get you some coffee. You must be bushed."

"Actually, I had a splendid night's sleep. New York agrees with me."

He looked over at me while I lowered my eyes into my appointment pad.

"Samantha picked me up right on time. She made sure all my needs were taken care of."

"Yes, that was so dear of her," Alexandra said. "Do you take your coffee black?"

"Cream and sugar. Yes, Samantha made my transition first-rate." He wouldn't let up. "You've got some fantastic girl here, in case you didn't know."

"Ah, shucks," I said, wishing he would shut up.

"Of course, I know," Alexandra acknowledged, emitting a little laugh. "Sam is a treasure. Worth her weight in gold. Speaking of which, I keep forgetting: Sam, we *must* discuss that little fiscal matter."

Blake picked right up. "You two make quite a team. How fortunate to have an associate who keeps this place running so smoothly in your absence. So, how was Paris?"

"Very French," Alexandra said, sounding as though she had swallowed something she couldn't quite digest. Then, catching herself, "It was absolutely divine, as Paris always is. Blake, please, sit down. Can I offer you something to eat? Sam wouldn't mind fetching you a bagel or even a scone, perhaps. They make the most fabulous blueberry scones at the corner café."

Café? Since when had the Madison Avenue coffee shop morphed into a café.

"Samantha fetches food?" Blake asked.

"We both chip in and help each other out," she said. "If I'm busy, Sam always offers to lend a hand. If she needs anything, she knows I'm here to oblige as well."

"A perfect marriage," Blake said.

By his second cup of coffee, the two of them were on the business at hand, namely Blake's paintings and Wesley Whyte.

"Because of the scope of your work," Alexandra said, "Wesley is a bit unnerved."

"The canvases *are* large," Blake agreed, "but two able-bodied men should be able to handle them."

"Wesley works alone."

"I'd be happy to assist. I know exactly where these paintings should go." Blake scoped out the gallery. "Samantha and I agreed that *Panoramania* should be the first one people see. The far wall would be perfect. It's meant to be viewed at a distance. In fact, I'd like to be here when Wesley hangs."

"Wesley is, shall we say, a tad temperamental. He hates when the artists hover."

"I don't hover, dear. I direct."

"Oh no, even worse. Wesley Whyte does not take direction well. He's a one-man operation—a frustrated painter who considers his job as important as the artist's. We wouldn't want to interfere with his creative intuition."

Blake grew more assertive. "This isn't about intuition, Alexandra. It's about getting the job done, and as far as I'm concerned, he's a laborer."

"Of course," Alexandra acquiesced. "But I can tell you, Wesley won't be happy."

"His job isn't to be happy. His job is to hang paintings."

"Whatever you say. And speaking of paintings, when do you think they'll be arriving?" she inquired meekly, treading ever so carefully so as not to arouse his ire.

"I had them shipped a week ago. Any day now."

"Oh, goodie." Alexandra clapped her hands. All right, then, I'll ring Wesley up, and we'll plan a meeting."

I had never seen Blake so take-charge—to the point where he was bordering on obnoxious. I had also never seen Alexandra cave in to the point of cowering. It was the best entertainment I had had in years.

"Samantha," Alexandra snapped, gaining her equilibrium, "would you get Blake's slides?"

I responded on cue, going into Blake's file and pulling out slides of the paintings he would be exhibiting plus a few more.

Blake caught my eye and winked. It was all I could do to keep from laughing.

The pecking order had been established.

Blake left an hour later, just in time for my lunch break. I met him around the corner, where we grabbed a sandwich.

"You were magnificent," I said.

"I despise the way she talks to you."

"That's Alexandra," I said. "All sweetness and light."

"I'd let her have it."

"I do, in my way. She goes just so far, and then I zap her."

"Her problem is she looks so damn good, she gets away with this crap."

I perked up. "You think so? *That* good?"

"She's got the stuff. A great ass. Tits, legs. Yeah, she's a looker."

"A looker?"

Blake sat back and laughed. "I'm diddling you, darling. Alexandra is a walking block of ice. She's got the equipment, but hell, once she opens her mouth, she turns into a piranha who could scare anyone."

"You don't seem scared."

"Of course not. I'm on to her. She knows that and backs off. I'm her hottie of the moment, and she lets me run the show. Otherwise, she risks losing me."

"Aren't *you* cocky."

"Not cocky. Realistic. And I'm all set with Wesley Whyte next week."

"That should be interesting. I'm sure the fur will fly."

"All I have to do is stroke his ego and pinch his behind, and Wesley Whyte will be putty in my hands."

"Especially if you pinch his behind," I said.

The paintings arrived a few days later, just as Blake had promised. Not only did he and Wesley hit it off, but as soon as Wesley laid eyes on Blake, a slight bulge appeared right through his tight-assed jeans.

"You obviously have a great eye," Blake said, "and I bow to your creativity, but I know which paintings I want to go where."

And Wesley, so enamored that he was practically salivating, agreed for the first time in his life to allow an artist to assist him in the placement of the canvases.

"As soon as Norbert Ashe's work comes down," Alexandra said, "up goes Blake's. In the meantime, we'll store the paintings upstairs, ready to be hung in time for the December fifteenth opening."

It couldn't have gone better. Placement of the work was finally decided, and Wesley Whyte was eating out of Blake's hands. Once he went so far as to make a pass, which Blake brushed off as a minor slip of the hand on Wesley's part.

"Hands off," Blake told him. "In case you haven't noticed, I don't do boys."

"Not *boys*, darling, men," Wesley whispered. "I can promise you the come of a lifetime."

"One more crack like that, and I'll hang you along with the paintings."

"Don't say I didn't ask," Wesley lisped, skulking off, thus ending his fantasy love affair, placated only slightly by furtive looks and longing whenever Blake passed by.

"The man has the hots for you," I told Blake over dinner. "You're admired by all. What can you do?"

"Punch him in the gonads," Blake said. "Alexandra is enough to deal with. I don't need some sleazy queen trying to get into my pants."

"Occupational hazard," I said. "But it's so reassuring knowing you're straight."

"Straight and hard," he said, "and I'd like to show you just *how* hard."

A half hour later, I was inside Blake's pad, in his bed, and in his arms. And five minutes later, he was inside me.

· · ·

November came and with it a Thanksgiving feast the likes of which I had never seen. We all gathered at Madeleine's apartment to witness, as big birds go, the Rolls-Royce of turkeys. The guest list included the Doctors Gould, Blake and me, Lily Ann and Bennett (her parents were in Spain), and Seena and Martin Tobin, longtime friends of my parents. Alden, surgeon extraordinaire, had brought along a pair of rubber gloves befitting the occasion and carved the turkey as he would a patient. A few hours before the meal, just as Gilda was about to stuff the fowl with her famous mushroom pâté dressing, Alden stood by, poised and ready, placing his hand inside the cavity and giving the turkey a pelvic exam.

"I'm surprised he didn't do a Pap smear," I whispered to Lily Ann.

During dinner, Blake kept his eyes on Spencer the entire time, still unsure what his motives were regarding me.

Spencer, amused by the entire facade, took it all and flirted unmercifully with me. All the while I observed Alden, the lovesick puppy that he had become, lower his hand beneath the table to give my mother a quick feel. She in turn giggled and pulled away, gently slapping Alden on his wrist.

The Tobins, stuffy to their multimillion-dollar core and oblivious to everything, oohed and aahed over Gilda's cooking. Despite the fact that Seena Tobin ingested a cranberry and had to be Heimliched by her husband, Martin, a man who knew more about mergers and acquisitions than he did about saving lives, we made it through another Thanksgiving.

My earlier apprehension about Blake's arrival to New York vanished. The past weeks had gone better than I had expected. As promised, he was so involved with his show and a new painting he was working on that he kept a low profile and made few demands on my time. We saw each other two times a week. I stayed at his apartment one night, and the other, he was at mine. We had settled into a routine that seemed to work for both of us, at least for now.

My mother inquired every chance she could about how Spencer and I were getting along. I assured her that all was fine until she cornered me in her bedroom after Thanksgiving dinner and asked if Spencer and I had had sex.

"I can tell there's something between you," she said. "I can feel it all the way across the table. Don't be coy, Samantha. How is it?"

"Leave me alone, Mother," I hissed. "Some things are private."

"I knew it," she said. "You can never fool me. Is he as great in bed as his father is?"

"I'm so glad you're having fun, Mother."

"Fun? Who said anything about fun? I'm getting laid, that's it. Between you and me, he could use a little liposuction. But who's complaining? I still manage to cough up an orgasm."

I left the room with Madeleine following after me, her Olivia Morris sling-backs clicking down the hall. "Orgasms, Samantha, are crucial to your vaginal health. Alden tells me all the time: Use it or lose it, so who am I to argue?"

"Sounds like you're living in debaucherous bliss, Mother."

"For now, sweetheart," Madeleine said. "Until my restlessness kicks in or I throw up looking at Alden's swinging scrotum, whichever comes first."

EIGHTEEN

"I am" is reportedly the shortest
sentence in the English language. Could it
be that "I do" is the longest?

—*Anonymous*

I t snowed from Thanksgiving into the first few days
of December. Alexandra tried holding it together. "Art
openings and snowstorms don't mesh," she said. "The entire city slows down the minute a flake appears."

As we neared the third week, the mercury rose, the snow
melted, and early Christmas shoppers lined the streets.
Merriment abounded, and Alexandra relaxed. The show
would go on.

Wesley Whyte, still secretly lusting over Blake, gave him
carte blanche to hang his paintings at will. Occasionally, he
balked, but when Blake told him to back off, Wesley turned

on his elevator shoes, shook his tight, little ass, and shimmied off to quietly sulk.

By Wednesday, the gallery began taking shape as passersby peered through the windows to catch a glimpse of the preshow preparations. The big night was only hours away. Alexandra was psyched and looking exceptionally shiny after her mini-peel, a few shots of Restylane, and several seaweed scrubs. The day before the show, she and I went over to Barneys for some recreational shopping and reserved a table at Fred's for lunch and were seated directly next to Bruce Springsteen.

"Samantha, tomorrow night will be the biggest coming-out party in the city. Duncan assures me the flowers will arrive by four. I'll want you there all day, and don't plan on leaving until every detail is accounted for."

"I'll need to go home to shower and change," I said.

"Not before the flowers are perfectly arranged. If you take your eyes off Duncan for a minute, he's liable to sneak away. I happen to know he's doing another party all the way over on the West Side. He's not to leave, no matter what, and neither are you. You understand me?"

"Where will you be?" I dared to ask.

"Getting ready, of course. I took a room at the Carlyle, where I'm planning to stay the night. I have a hair appointment with Rudy at one, my yoga class at three, a manicure, hand plumping, a full-body massage, and I'm seeing my shrink at five. I begged him for an additional session. As you can tell, I'm a total wreck. I need to look perfect. You never know who I might be going home with, if you get what I'm saying?"

"Anyone special in mind?" I prodded.

"Darling, I won't know that until the evening is in full swing. Everyone will be there, and if I'm lucky or drunk enough, I might even leave with our Blake."

A cold sweat washed over me, leaving little droplets on my face and forehead. "Blake? Really?"

"Haven't you noticed the way he flirts with me? It's obvious the man can't wait to get inside my Victoria's Secret thong. Don't look so shocked, Samantha. He's wanted to fuck me forever. Tomorrow could be the night."

It took every ounce of strength for me not to smack Alexandra across her perfectly made-up face. I entertained the idea of picking up my water glass and splashing it all over her Hermès scarf. I wanted to smear her face with butter, strike her in the chest with my knife, and deflate her breast implants. Instead, I sipped my Pellegrino, listening to her go off on a tangent of all the ways she and Blake would make love. Poking her in the eye was another option that delighted me. A swift kick in the shins could raise a huge welt and placate me for a while. Grabbing her neck and strangling her brought a smile to my face, as did the idea of cutting off all her hair and screaming out loud for all of Barneys to hear: "Alexandra Cole is a fucking whore cunt."

"You look like the cat that swallowed the canary," Alexandra interrupted my reverie. "Whatever are you thinking?"

"That it's going to be a night to remember," I said.

Alexandra picked up her chardonnay. "A night to remember." She clicked my glass.

Like the sinking of the *Titanic,* I thought.

It *was* a night to remember. Duncan kept his word and arrived on time, looking particularly fetching and très gay in a chocolate brown velvet suit and silk paisley bow tie.

Instead of attracting the usual rush-from-work crowd, the opening was called for eight o'clock. People had a chance to go home and dress for the occasion. And an occasion it was.

The Garden of Earthly Delights didn't disappoint. Mavis York, headed by her staff of six, bustled about, making sure the canapés, platters of cheeses, and hors d'oeuvres were properly positioned. Mavis ruled with an iron hand and, by doing so, gained her reputation of being the best caterer in the tristate area. She had won awards on her desserts alone. My mother was particularly pleased that Mavis was her personal contribution, having used her for many events and dinner parties.

"Mavis York can take a sprig of parsley and turn it into art," Madeleine said. "Her asparagus creations alone were all the buzz at the American Museum of Natural History's last charity benefit. Yes, *my* Mavis leaves a trail of culinary splendor wherever she goes. Alexandra Cole should be kissing my feet that I was able to get her to do Blake's show."

"She'll be indebted to you forever," I said.

"As well she should," my mother clucked. "I do hope that Mavis will be serving sushi. Word has it, she flies it in fresh from Japan."

"I hardly think so," I said.

"Why not? If Nobu does it, Mavis York can. At any rate, and don't quote me, but I hear Mavis is catering the Clintons' next party."

"How do you know these things, Mother?"

"Darling," she said, "I told you: I know everything."

Part of Madeleine's outrageous charm was that she actually believed this to be true.

I had only an hour to get ready. As soon as Duncan arrived and swore on his life he wouldn't leave, I grabbed a cab to my apartment, washed my hair, showered, and dressed in twenty minutes. My makeup was quickly though painstakingly applied. I jumped into my new and obscenely expensive Jean Paul Gaultier dress, slipped on my Michael Perry shoes, attached my Piaget evening watch and, swinging my Francisco Costa crystal-encrusted bag over my shoulder, dabbed on some Sean Jean Unforgivable Woman perfume, a far cry from my old standby: L'air du Temps. My look exuded sexy elegance with just enough glitzy sparkle to cause a mild volcanic eruption. Even I had to admit I looked hot—hot enough to give Alexandra a run for her money.

When I got back to the gallery, I was stunned by what I saw. The room was ablaze in floral excess. Duncan, as promised, had turned it into his version of the Botanical Garden. His approach to flower arranging combined his improvisational techniques with a sense of flair and good taste. Tossing conventionality aside, he had let his imagination run amok.

Those entering were immediately struck by the blend of old-world elegance with the freshness of the outdoors. Bulbous cabbage roses mingled with wildflowers; baby's breath lay in between cut flowers, draping them like a lacy shawl. The floral palettes coincided with the colors in Blake's paintings. Anemones spilled over bouquets of blue delphinium. Rare Asian violets, the color of jade, dripped over dozens of bright red dahlias. As I made my way farther into the room, the real drama began. Using Mavis York's incredible edibles, Duncan had borrowed the best from Mother Nature's garden, arranging his flowers among the food so that tiny cherry tomatoes filled with Gruyère mousse or kiwi and prosciutto were surrounded by a spray of Malaysian orchids.

Yellow, green, and red peppers were stuffed with crudités and studded with white daisies. Scooped-out zucchinis filled with green peas as bright as emeralds merged with white tulips. Wire egg baskets housing lemons and limes were intertwined with ivy and sweet pansy faces peeking through. Blood oranges studded with cloves overflowed from wicker baskets, ready for the plucking, scenting the room with a spicy aroma.

Salad greens and fruit varietals—purple radicchio and baby eggplant, cranberries, black cherries, crabapples, and brown chestnuts—nestled among eucalyptus leaves. Geraniums, coleus leaves, and sweet William rested on the edge of the settee or were tied to arms of chairs with strips of grosgrain. Birds of paradise were hidden among these, looked shockingly authentic, ready to take flight, but were restrained by thin wires, clustered among an array of peonies.

Wherever I turned, the scene was mesmerizing. Oriental poppies in rich pinks and oranges and white camellias were strewn across hors d'oeuvre trays and platters of imported cheeses. Add to that blue cornflowers, foxtail lilies, spider chrysanthemums, and sunflowers the color of marmalade, all there for only one purpose: to enhance the paintings. But they were as much a part of the main attraction as Blake Hamilton himself.

Not wanting to miss an opportunity, Duncan had left his business cards scattered about. The crowd fawned over him as he cooed, announcing to his ardent fans that his glorious floral mélange was a mere afterthought—an accoutrement that blended in with Blake's masterpieces. He then plucked a tea rose, handing it to a blue-haired lady with teeth too white to be real. She oohed and she aahed as Duncan kissed her hand. She was now under his spell, and he grabbed the moment to hand her a card.

"Keep me in mind for your next soiree," he told her.

"My dear boy, the only soirees I have are with my cats. But perhaps you'll drop by for tea sometime." She, in turn, handed him her calling card.

"I'll come bearing plump strawberries and Queen Anne's lace," Duncan said.

Her smile widened, her pearly whites sparkling like large Chiclets against her pink Chanel suit, circa 1965.

Blake was somewhere, but I couldn't find him amid the throngs of people who now swarmed about like bees, buzzing and flitting. Suddenly, a hush fell upon the room as the gallery door opened. Alexandra, the lady of the evening, had arrived, much too fashionably late, looking like an impenetrable statue floating across the room, as though gossamer wings were attached to her perfectly chiseled shoulders.

Her new couture accentuated her finest and favorite attributes, the neckline of her Givenchy dropping so low that her faux boobs, helped along by a push-up bra, accosted all the eyeballs that had the good fortune to feast upon them. She looked so grand and sensual that Duncan, forgetting he was gay, produced an ever so slight erection when she undulated across the floor.

I took it all in, watching Alexandra work the room, plying air kisses and extending her hand without making contact. She was an ice sculpture that never melted, a cool beauty to whom every male responded. Her eyes darted as she looked for Blake, the man of the hour. Finding him over in a corner, she glided toward him.

His eyes caught hers, and a smile appeared on his face—a smile that was usually reserved for me but now was owned by her. The harsh smack of jealousy hit me. I recalled Alexandra's words at lunch: *He's wanted to fuck me forever.* I stood frozen in place, stunned and unable to move. If my mother and Alden hadn't closed in on me, I might be standing there still.

"Darling," Madeleine greeted me, "you look divine . . . a tad too heavy on the eyeliner, but for tonight, what the hell? Throw caution to the wind and be extravagant."

Alden, by her side, kissed me on the cheek. "Have you seen my son?"

"Not yet," I said. "Spencer said he might be late. He's coming straight from the hospital. Two back-to-back deliveries."

"Why is it women *always* choose the most inopportune times to give birth? And they're always late to boot," Alden mused. "I'm glad I've phased out of obstetrics."

"The nature of the beasts," my mother said. "Must be girls. They're never on time."

"Well, I'm going to get a drink. Maddie, can I bring you one?" Alden asked.

"Champagne would be lovely."

"Maddie now? My, aren't we cute," I said after Alden had walked away.

"I for one think it's adorable. Alden is filled with terms of endearment. The man is a charmer. Can't get enough of me. I haven't had a moment's rest since we started having sex. He said he's found his second coming."

"Third and fourth comings, too, I presume."

"I'm not complaining. So do you think I've overdone it with the purple?" My mother circled the floor in her latest ensemble.

"You might want to lose the headband, Mother. A bit over the top."

"Don't be silly. The headband pulls it all together." She kicked her leg out. "What do you have to say about these?" She flashed the most atrocious-looking pumps I had ever seen—in purple satin, no less, which matched her Alberta Ferretti purple silk chiffon dress. She resembled a perfectly proportioned, sleek, and satiny eggplant. "Am I making a statement or what? The perfect look for tonight's do. Speaking of which, where's my dowdy sister and her equally drab entourage? They said they were getting here early."

"I just arrived myself," I said. "Haven't seen them."

"And where's our famous artiste?"

"Becoming more famous by the minute. He's over there." I nodded to where Blake was standing.

"I see that Alexandra has already sunk her claws into him."

"She didn't waste a second."

"Samantha, don't just stand here making small talk. Go over and retrieve him before the woman eats him up alive."

"I don't want to crowd him, Mother. It's Blake's night, and he needs to do his thing. You know how these openings are. There's plenty of time to be with him later."

"I don't know. From the looks of Alexandra's bust line, those babies might pop out at any minute, and every man in the place will be after her, including *our* boy."

Madeleine pushed through the crowd, inching her way closer to Blake. I followed behind, using my mother as a protective shield against the enemy camp.

"Sweetheart," Madeleine greeted Alexandra. "You look divine. That dress. It does *everything* for you. My God, you must have grown an entire breast size overnight."

Alexandra swung around, taking her gaze off Blake for a moment. "Mrs. Krasner-Wolfe, hello."

"Let's drop the formalities. It's Madeleine. After all this time, I consider you a friend. And Blake, darling, aren't you the be-all and end-all?"

Blake leaned over and kissed my mother, giving me a most lecherous stare. "Samantha, wow. I can't even find the words. You look gorgeous."

Alexandra stiffened. "Our Samantha *is* gorgeous. Now, Blake, dear." Alexandra grabbed his arm, leading him away. "Let's dazzle the crowds."

They disappeared into a sea of waiting admirers, all of them eager to meet the artist and perform the predictable groveling. My mother and I found ourselves alone.

"You see what I mean? That woman is a snake. Always was. You'll be lucky if you see Blake again for the entire evening—the entire night, maybe."

"Stop it, Mother. Blake thinks Alexandra is a royal pain in the ass."

"Royal ass is exactly what she is—and *has*. That woman exudes sex. I could smell it on her."

"That's her Chanel. It's her signature fragrance. One whiff of it and you know Alexandra is in the room."

"Call it what you will. To me, she reeks of pheromones."

By eight thirty, the gallery was bursting at the seams, making conversation nearly impossible. Alexandra was right: All of Manhattan's elite was here, dressed to perfection and dropping names all over the place. I recognized a few critics and was impressed, though not entirely surprised, that even the most illustrious among them, Pritchard Howard, had come. One good review from him and an artist could become an overnight sensation. As I sipped my second glass of champagne, I felt a tap on my shoulder. I didn't expect what followed.

When I turned around, a slightly recognizable figure stood before me. "Oh my God, Samantha, don't you know who I am?"

I studied the lovely creature, hardly believing what I saw. "Celeste?"

"Yes. Do I look *that* different?"

"I'll say you do. What happened?"

"When I went back to Sarah Lawrence, I decided to change my image. Whether you know it or not, you gave me that push I needed. I decided to go on a diet, and since the end of August, I've lost thirty pounds on Weight Watchers. I went from a size fourteen to an eight and still going strong."

"You look *amazing*."

"It didn't stop there. After the pounds started dropping, I gained an entirely new self-image. Guys started noticing me, and I began dating. And I don't mean those dorks at school, but really cool studs from Columbia and NYU."

"Your face looks different," I said.

"I went to a plastic surgeon who did computer imaging on me, showing me how I could look. In October I had a nose job. The only ones who knew were Aunt Madeleine and, of course, my folks."

"My mother knew? She didn't say a word."

"I asked her not to tell anyone. I wanted it to be a surprise."

"Well, it worked. I'm completely wowed."

"I also had some liposuction on my thighs and buttocks, and I've been working out with a personal trainer. My parents were so excited about my turnaround, they paid for everything, including my teeth." She opened her mouth, revealing a complete set of perfectly aligned porcelain veneers.

Her nails had been manicured and painted with a deep inky-black red lacquer, accentuated against the golden glass of champagne. Even her skin looked softer and blemish-free. All traces of her acne were gone. She seemed to have been brushed in an antique-white coating, giving her a somewhat ethereal look.

Celeste had also made a giant fashion leap, looking like she just stepped out of *Vogue*. She wore a silk organza bustier and a sheath dress. Her hair, she said, had been styled by one of Fekkai's finest; her makeup was perfectly applied, making her ample mouth pouty and delicious. In short, Celeste Bleckner, pain in the butt that she was, had emerged from an Eliza Doolittle state into a sexy siren—so much so that one man nearly spilled his drink when he brushed by her undulating knockers.

Wait until Blake sees her, was all I could think. That thought unnerved me slightly.

Celeste had come with the rest of the family: Aunt Elaine and Uncle Phil. Even the disgruntled lesbian daughter, Fern, had decided to put in an appearance.

Aunt Elaine swooped in on us. "So what do you think of our newly refurbished Celeste?"

"I never would have believed it," I said.

"Neither did we, but obviously, her visit with you in July did it. You always were such a good role model, Samantha."

"I'm afraid I can't take the credit, Aunt Elaine," I said diplomatically. "Celeste's time had come, and she was ready to make a change."

"I think that living with you last summer inspired her. Men are calling her all the time, and her date book is full."

"I wouldn't doubt it," I said. "She's stunning."

"At least we have *one* daughter we can be proud of," Elaine whispered. "Fern has completely distanced herself from us. She and her butch friend Murray have given your uncle Phil colitis."

"Murray? That's her name?"

"Her real name is Mary Townsend, from the Philadelphia Townsends—very Main Line, but you know how these lesbians are, anything to be different and attract attention to their condition."

"It isn't a *condition*," said the submerged Fern, overhearing her mother. They were the first words I had heard her utter in years. "Get used to it," she said. "Murray and I are an item. We're planning to get married."

"Not at the Pierre, that's for sure," Elaine snapped back.

Fern skulked away, giving us all dirty looks. She grabbed two canapés from the tray—caviar and cream cheese on toast points—tossing them into her mouth, leaving crumbs on her pointy chin, looking very much like the wicked witch in "Hansel and Gretel."

"Now, *there's* a girl who messed up her life," Uncle Phil said, downing a double Scotch on the rocks. "Bleeding ulcers, that's what Fern has given me. I live on Metamucil and see my gastroenterologist as often as your aunt Elaine goes shopping."

I inched away from them, observing the scene. Everyone was there: familiar faces from the social register, a smattering of film stars, artists galore, the glitterati, and all the social climbers who thrived on such evenings. They arrived in droves, to leer, to rave, to banter and babble. Some even came to observe the art, but more important, they wanted to be able to say the next day: "Wasn't Blake Hamilton's opening the living end?"

The fashion parade was in full regalia. After all, attending an art opening meant knocking 'em dead with the duds. It wasn't only what was hanging on the walls but what people were wearing. Ann Chernow, just back from India, was bedecked in her sari. Carol Fitzgerald sported her stones from Singapore, while Wendy Sherman, literary agent extraordinaire, looked ravishing in her Mexican poncho, her wig of red curls cascading down her back. At the last opening she'd come as a blonde.

In the corner, sipping spritzers, were Lance and Len, looking divine in their pleated pants and carrying matching toy poodles, schmoozing with whoever crossed their paths, especially if they were gay. And oh, the excitement when Wanda "Big Tits" Scott appeared hanging on the arm of Dottie Dupont's third ex-husband, G. Alger Dupont. In recent weeks, they had been seen all around town, and it was said that "Ponty" would be tying the knot again. Word had it that Wanda was in her first trimester and that Ponty was definitely the dad, even though he was eighty-two and everyone wondered how he still got it up.

There was a momentary hush as everyone stared at the most famous art buyers in the city: Morgan and Agusta Phipps, standing next to the baked chutney Brie with their defanged boa constrictor adorned with a rhinestone collar. Those knowing how Agusta pampered her pets insisted the boa's collar was Bulgari all the way.

My job was to oversee everything and make sure there were no blips. I continued taking it all in, intermittently seeking out Blake, who was surrounded by a wall of well-wishers, Alexandra always by his side. I kept my eye on Mavis York and marveled at her staff's efficiency at getting the food out there and the wineglasses filled. Not a napkin was left on a table, not a toothpick in sight. This was a tough crowd, many of whom treated art openings as a culinary adventure. Next to Duncan's Tree of Flowers stood the well-known movie producer Montgomery Rosenblatt, aka "Monty the Moocher," and his date, Evangeline, his new rising starlet and most recent bed companion. Monty made it a practice of inviting all his potential one-night stands out to dinner, then brought them to openings instead, telling them to "dig in—dinner is on the house." A good show, after all, is judged not only by the quality of the art but by the food and drink. And tonight was a gourmet extravaganza.

All my hard work had paid off and was being executed to perfection.

Two more arrivals silenced the room when Christo and Jeanne-Claude exited from a limo and entered the gallery. They headed straight for Blake, whom they had met in London when they lectured on the Gates.

"Her hair colorist must be the same as Ronald McDonald's," a Paris Hilton look-alike whispered to her equally bimbo friend.

As the evening wore on, the gallery rocked. Skinny supermodels slinked about, serving as arm candy to the men who had brought them along as ornamental ego inflators. The biggies of the art world abounded, interspersed with young hopefuls like Norbert Ashe. The critic who had reviewed his show at the Cole had been less than kind, smearing his name across the tabloids, slaughtering his career in one fell swoop with a slash of his pen: "Norbert Ashe's work has as much talent and depth as that of a first-grader with a box of Crayolas."

Alexandra was less than pleased and dismissed Ashe as a has-been, never to exhibit at her gallery again.

I tried placating Alexandra. "These things happen." I had worked with him and liked him.

"Not to me they don't," she said. "That's how a gallery loses its reputation. Thank God for Blake Hamilton. He'll save my ass."

But I had to hand it to Norbert. He'd had the balls to show up tonight. When he saw me, he ran over to greet me, clearly hoping I would bridge the gap between him and Alexandra.

"Samantha, my love, you're a vision of loveliness."

"As are you, Norbert," I said. He looked younger than his fifty-six years. Madeleine, keeping her eye on all the attractive men, scurried over to us. "Mother, this is Norbert Ashe. His show just closed here two weeks ago."

"So sorry to have missed it," Madeleine said, "but I was out of town": her standard excuse for any event or opening she purposely wanted to avoid.

"Norbert is very prolific," I said.

"And handsome, too," Madeleine added. With that, she whisked him away, leaving a trail of purple behind her as she and Norbert disappeared among the masses.

Gyrating through the crowd, I made it over to the far end of the room, where Alexandra now held court, her arm still linked through Blake's as though he were a permanent appendage. I could hardly breathe. I stood in front of Blake's painting *Cornucopius* and was accosted by a woman who couldn't wait to vent her opinion.

"It's obvious what the artist has in mind here," she said, cocking her head into a thoughtful and deliberate pose. "This painting represents woman's inequality to man. Notice how the figure is slumped below him in a subservient position. The man is the dominant figure who controls the female."

Her equally uninformed friend, a woman of about seventy-five, joined us. She squinted. She blinked. She looked like she hadn't a clue. "It looks like a canvas splotched with paint," she said. "That's it. Nothing more."

"But don't the splotches *speak* to you, Renee?" her friend asked. "Figuratively as well as metaphorically."

"I don't know what the hell you're talking about, Sylvia," Renee said. "I'm going to get myself a plate of those Swedish meatballs. That's the only part of the show that I care about. Give me a still life—a bowl of fruit—that's my kind of art. I don't understand any of this abstract caca."

Her bluntness, crude and undeniably naive, was almost refreshingly laughable.

I meandered off for another drink, only to be stopped by a woman of about thirty in a black leather miniskirt, denim jacket, fishnet stockings, and five-inch stiletto heels. "You work with Alexandra, right?"

"I'm her partner."

"Alexandra Cole is a bitch. She refused to even look at my boyfriend's paintings. We came in together last January."

I vaguely remembered.

"I'm Marie Antoinette."

"Really?"

"Yes, that's what I call myself. She was the most fascinating woman in history."

I tried picturing her headless.

"Alexandra Cole took one look at Brian's slides and told him he should keep his day job. 'Painting *is* my day job,' he said. She was brutal—nearly destroyed his self-confidence. What a ball-buster."

"I'm sorry," I said.

"But you—you have a great aura."

"Really? I never noticed."

"Are you serious? There's a halo surrounding you, giving off sparks. You're a walking vision of phosphorescent perfection. May I touch your hair?"

Before I could answer, Marie Antoinette drew her silver enameled nails at me, combing them through my tresses.

"Ouch," she said, "you're electrifying. You have static."

It was Aurora aka Estelle Goldstein all over again.

By eight o'clock, with still no personal contact with Blake, I was growing weary of making small talk with the art snobs and idiots.

A voice came up behind me. "You look like you need to be rescued." It was Spencer.

"Thank God you're here. I was starting to fade into the woodwork."

"Sorry I'm late, but those deliveries moved slowly. One resulted in a C-section with some minor complications. Let me grab a drink and I'll return."

"Is Roger with you?" I asked.

"Hasn't he arrived? He was supposed to meet me here an hour ago."

"I haven't seen him, but with this crowd, it's hard to find anyone. I could use a pair of binoculars."

"That's odd. Roger was planning to be here early."

"I'm sure he'll come," I said.

"And Blake?"

"Wherever Alexandra is lurking, Blake can't be far behind."

"The infamous Alexandra Cole. I'm dying to meet her."

"Let's go and find her," I said.

"What about you? Aren't you as much a part of the show as Alexandra? You *are* her indispensable right-hand gal, aren't you?"

"I'm her invisible sidekick," I said. "She prefers micromanaging alone."

Moving through a wave of bodies that ebbed and flowed, Blake was holding court with none other than Pritchard Howard. They were both smiling—a good sign—while Pritchard studied one of Blake's favorite paintings, *Schizophrenetic,* taking copious notes in the little black book he brought along on such occasions. For the first time all evening, Alexandra had left Blake to fend for himself.

"Angel." The familiar voice descended upon us. "I'd say it's all going fabulously well, wouldn't you?"

Alexandra, never missing the chance to snag a new man, had swooped in like a bird of prey to meet Spencer. "My, but you always seem to have such a gay assortment of men on your arm," she said to me.

I blanched at the word "gay." "Alexandra Cole, this is Spencer Gould."

"Enchanted to meet you," she said, her champagne high evidenced by her slurred voice and overbearing gestures.

"Samantha speaks so highly of you," Spencer gushed. "I've passed your gallery many times and have enjoyed your shows."

"Are you in the business?" she asked.

"Hardly. But I do appreciate fine art."

"Spencer is an ob/gyn," I said.

"Then you absolutely *do* appreciate art. What can be more compelling and artistic than a woman's genitalia?"

Yes, Alexandra Cole was indeed drunk.

"Aptly put." Spencer shifted uncomfortably. "This show in particular has caught my eye."

"You *must* go over and speak with the artist." Alexandra took Spencer by the hand, leading him off while I followed them like a puppy dog, ready to nip at Alexandra's Marc Jacob high heels.

"I've already met him," Spencer said.

"Oh, you do get around," Alexandra cooed.

Blake had finished talking to Pritchard and was now fortifying himself with a skewer of teriyaki chicken in orange glaze. He waved us over.

"You poor darling," Alexandra said to him, ignoring Spencer and me. "You must be famished. All that schmoozing. So, tell me, what did Pritchard Howard have to say?"

"The usual. He asked questions and offered no comments. That's par for the course. I take these critics with a grain of arsenic. But more important, I haven't seen Spencer since Madeleine's last brunch. How the hell are you?"

The two men shook hands. Blake, clearly considering Spencer his main competition, tried playing it cool while I stood there, amused by it all.

"So, you're friends, then?" Alexandra said. "What a delicious ménage à trois this could be, but that's the wine talking. Samantha, watch Blake for me while I borrow Spencer for a moment and introduce him to anybody worth knowing."

It was the first time all evening that she'd been willing to relinquish Blake from her clutches. Finally, a chance for us to talk alone.

"I wasn't sure I'd even get near you," I said.

"I know. Alexandra can be very possessive. She assumes I can't hold my own without her."

"She enjoys flaunting you," I said, "not to mention crediting herself for having discovered you."

"I believe it was you who made all this happen," Blake said.

"Alexandra will never accept that."

"And how are you . . . and Spencer?"

"He just arrived," I said, knowing that it had been only a matter of time before Blake would get on to that subject.

"Just in time to take you home."

"The night is young," I said. "These things can go on for hours. Speaking of which, has Alexandra rented you out for the entire night?" Two could play the same game.

"That's the plan. But when I tell her I'm otherwise engaged, I expect a mild earthquake to occur."

"*Are* you otherwise engaged?"

"That depends on you," Blake said. "While Alexandra is trying to shag me, Spencer might be devising his own little scheme of bedding you down for the night."

"Perhaps he and Alexandra should get together," I said.

"The last I noticed, they were. Look at them. She's cornered him over by the bar, and it looks rather chummy. How do you feel about that?" he asked.

"It gives me more time with you," Blake said flirtatiously. "So, what are you doing after the show?"

"What did you have in mind?" I asked, flirting back.

"A late supper and then back to my apartment."

"Do you think Alexandra would approve?"

"We can ask her to join us, if you'd like," Blake said. "Apparently, she's into ménage à trois."

"I'm more of a ménage à deux gal myself. I don't like to share."

"A typical only-child syndrome," Blake said, leaning over and kissing me.

And for the first time all evening, silly though it was, a part of me basked in the glow of knowing I had put one over on Alexandra.

Just as that easy feeling began taking hold, Cousin Celeste was wending her way over to us.

"Gird your loins." I nudged Blake. "What you're about to see might surprise you."

"Blake Hamilton, we meet again," the sultry Celeste greeted him, sounding like she'd also had a voice transplant.

"Please excuse me, but have we met?" he asked.

"Yes, last summer. I was staying with Samantha."

Blake studied Celeste, trying to place her face. "You *do* look familiar, but I'd love you to help me out here."

"Celeste Bleckner, Samantha's cousin."

"Really?"

"Honest. It's me."

"You look different."

"I'll take that as a compliment."

"As it was meant," he said.

The main players were assembled as characters in a play, each one acting out his or her respective role. Alexandra, completely enamored with Spencer, made it a point of circulating him around like her latest acquisition. Madeleine and Alden edged their way uninvited into conversations and tried to meet Christo, not expecting his wife, aka his personal guard dog, Jeanne-Claude, to keep them at bay. Try as they might, they never even got close.

Blake wouldn't shut up about how fantastic Celeste looked as she tossed furtive looks his way. Celeste, in possession of the key to Madeleine's apartment, where she'd been invited to spend the night, played up her new persona to the hilt. She used up all her daily allotted Weight Watchers points on champagne, which she drank to excess until she became slightly wobbly in her new pair of Jean-Michel Cazabat shoes.

"Celeste looks like she's had one too many," Blake said. "Someone should see her home."

"Tonight, home is my mother's apartment," I said. "Madeleine is staying with Alden and offered her apartment to Celeste. Since Celeste's redo, the two of them have gotten quite close. Celeste has become her favorite new hobby. Anyway, she's not your responsibility."

Toward the end of the night, Celeste had met a man named Eddie Sloat, alias Eddie Sabarese, who owned a fleet of taxis in Lodi, New Jersey; dabbled in the arts, and, even though he knew zip, made it a point to attend all the hot exhibits. When he first laid his eyes on Celeste, he was captivated by her beauty. Even though Eddie was a bit rough around the edges, he had a macho charm and was handsome in a rugged mafioso kind of way. Celeste was taken in by the compliments he extolled upon her. From the moment he arrived, he followed her around the gallery with a lecherous leer as though she were the Lone Ranger and he, her faithful companion, Tonto. Eddie had a nose as sizable as his bank account but recently had it chiseled down from a giant-economy-size honker to straight and narrow. He wore a shoe-polish-black toupee that was slightly askew. His eyes were inky blue, he oozed sexiness, and he desired nothing more than a chance to get into Celeste's pants. Aunt Elaine and Uncle Phil, extremely uncomfortable, watched from afar as Eddie put his moves on their daughter.

"That man is up to no good," Phil told Elaine.

"Phil, darling, let Celeste have her fun. God knows she's earned it."

"She should have left her body alone," Phil said. "She was a nice Jewish girl. Now look: Every man in the room wants a piece of her."

"Be grateful she doesn't take after Fern," Elaine said.

"I don't know which is worse, Fern the Dyke or Celeste the Diva," Phil sneered in his typically judgmental and offensive way.

NINETEEN

I'm not a committed bachelor.
One of my favorite oxymorons is
"engagement party."

—*Scott Roeben*

B y eleven o'clock, a handful of people were still milling about. These hangers-on had come purely to be seen, to eat the lavish hors d'oeuvres, and to have an obligatory glance at Blake's work. Tomorrow it would be some other artist's show, and the routine would repeat itself. However, among the majority of those who couldn't care less was one interested buyer who had followed Blake from London to New York. His name was Max Girard, and he was one of the most eligible older bachelors in New York. Max lived in a twelve-room apartment on Park Avenue that he filled with some of the best art in the world. He had flown in just this evening from his bungalow at the Delano Hotel in South Beach.

Max was seriously studying Blake's largest and most prized work, *Exotica,* with a price tag of three hundred thousand dollars.

At the same time, Madeleine and Alden were saying their good nights. Madeleine took one look at Max Girard and begged Alden to hang out for just a few more minutes.

"I don't believe we've met." She extended her hand to Max. "I'm Madeleine Krasner-Wolfe."

Max, recognizing her name, asked if she was related to the late Grayson Wolfe, and once she acknowledged that, he became interested in knowing more. Alden, smelling trouble, stood by Madeleine's side, was introduced to Max, and then was dropped like a hot potato while Madeleine and Max became engrossed in conversation.

The talk came around to Blake's painting.

"So, what do *you* think I should do?" Max asked Madeleine, only half seriously.

"You'd be a wise man to buy it," Madeleine said. "Our Blake is a rising star."

"You know him personally?"

"Of course. He was also a favorite of Grayson's."

"Do you own a Blake Hamilton yourself?" Max inquired.

"I'm afraid not yet. My collection boasts some great art, but I haven't found a wall large enough to accommodate a Blake Hamilton."

"Poor excuse," Max teased. "But I just happen to have an empty wall that's aching to secure a painting, and this one just might be it." He led Madeleine over to *Exotica* while Alden, sensing flirtation in the air, kept tightly by her side, interjecting some erudite comments to show he was just as knowledgeable as either of them.

"Are you a collector, too?" Max asked Alden.

"By all means," Madeleine answered for him. "Alden's apartment is a mini-museum."

"My latest is a small Dalí I bought at Sotheby's two months ago for way too much money," Alden said.

"I think I know the piece," Max said. "Were I a Dalí devotee, I might have given you a run for your money."

"Who do you like?" Madeleine asked.

"Right now? Tonight? I'm fast turning into a Blake Hamilton fan, especially this painting."

"Then by all means, buy it," I stepped in and boldly interrupted. "Hello, I'm Samantha Krasner, partner in the Cole Gallery, and you're obviously a man of discriminating taste."

"And you're quite lovely," Max said.

"I wouldn't have anything *but* a lovely daughter," Madeleine said.

"I can see that," Max agreed. "Like mother, like daughter. So you think I'm correct in considering this painting?"

"Considering? No. I think you *must* buy it." I was surprised by my own assertiveness.

At that precise moment, Alexandra, with Spencer still draped on her arm, appeared as if by magic, just in time to woo Max and add her two cents. I recalled one afternoon when Alexandra had told me about Max Girard being one of her former suitors. At the time the name had meant nothing more than another wealthy New York bachelor whom Alexandra was trying to snag.

"Max and I had once had a little thingy," she had admitted, "but after two months, I lost interest and broke it off."

Truth was, after a few months, it was rumored that Alexandra was even more aggressive as a lover than a gallery owner, and Max Girard couldn't take it anymore. But tonight she was all sweetness and light, and with dollar signs practically cha-chinging in her eyes, she greeted Max with open arms. "Max. Darling. I didn't even see you come in."

"I arrived late, but Samantha here is taking very good care of me."

"I taught her well," Alexandra said, "but the person you really want to speak with is Blake. Let me go fetch him. Spencer, introduce yourself to Max Girard while I go and find our man."

"I see nothing has changed," Max said, and the five of us laughed knowingly.

While Madeleine, Alden, and Max chatted away, Spencer whispered in my ear. "Have you seen Roger?"

"Not all night," I said.

"I can't understand what happened. It's not like Roger not to show up or call. I'm getting concerned."

"Have you tried calling him?"

"A zillion times, but he's not picking up. I think his cell phone is off."

"That *is* strange," I said. "He must have a good reason. I see that Alexandra hasn't let you out of her sight."

"She's got the hots for me, I think," he said.

"You *think*? The woman is practically vibrating. Has she put the moves on you yet?"

"Aside from the fact that she's kept her hand on my ass all night, no."

"That's Alexandra for you," I said.

Blake appeared, wiping perspiration from his brow. "These openings can do a guy in," he said. "I'm beat."

"Well, before you expire, I'd like you to meet Max Girard," Alexandra said. "Max is one of your biggest fans."

"Yes, we've met before. In London, I believe."

"Good memory," Max said. "Now, as you see, I followed you to New York."

"I'm flattered. You're a collector I hold in highest esteem, with some of the best art around."

"I'm thinking of adding another piece to my collection," Max said.

"Anyone I know?" Blake asked.

"He's standing right in front of me."

"Precious"—Alexandra oozed saccharine—"Max has fallen for *Exotica*."

"Yes, *Exotica* and I are establishing a meaningful relationship as we speak," Max said.

"It *is* for sale," Blake said. "I'd be more than pleased to have you as its owner."

Celeste, after overhearing the conversation, jumped in. "Are you talking about *Exotica*? I absolutely *adore* that painting. I wish I could afford to buy it."

"Another party heard from," Alexandra said.

Eddie Sloat, by Celese's side, put on his sunglasses to appear innocuous and instead brought even more attention to himself.

"Hi, I'm Celeste," she twinkled, "niece of Madeleine Krasner-Wolfe."

"This must be a family reunion," said the ever quick-witted Max, shaking Celeste's and then Eddie's hand. "I'm Max Girard."

Celeste was in her glory. Her eyes danced as she spoke. "Are you thinking of buying one of Blake's paintings," she asked.

"You're standing in front of it," I said, hoping that Celeste would keep her mouth shut.

"Well, I for one think there's another painting you might also consider," she said.

"Which one?" Max asked, checking out Celeste's bulging breasts.

"The one over there." She pointed to the largest painting in the room. "That, to me, represents Blake's most exciting work."

Like you know, Celeste. I wanted to punch her in the mouth.

We moved over to the rear wall, where *Galaxy* hung.

"How recent is this?" Max asked.

"It's one of my earlier pieces," Blake said. "And my favorite."

"Why a favorite?"

"It's entirely experimental. I allowed myself free rein to try something new. This painting opened up unexplored vistas. I didn't hold back. By letting myself go in an entirely different direction, I accidentally fell upon an exciting technique. *Galaxy* is probably my gutsiest painting. After I did it, I felt liberated. It was the entry into what was to follow. In that sense, the painting launched me into abstract expressionism."

"It's immense," Max said.

"That's because it's the galaxy," Celeste said. "It would have to be. It's like being at the planetarium."

Pretend she didn't say that, I thought.

But Max Girard wasn't cringing like the rest of us. He paid attention. He stood back and studied the work.

"I even have the perfect spot for it," he said after a few minutes. "While *Exotica* is where I was headed, I'm willing to negotiate on *Galaxy*—a painting that is obviously part of Blake's heart and soul. I like that. I am as much interested in the artist himself as I am in his or her work."

No one uttered a word. Even Alexandra stopped her normal gushing, knowing enough to keep quiet and allow Max Girard to continue.

"Furthermore, because it is an older work—when you were a lesser-known quantity, if you will—it's a fresher, more naive painting."

"That it is." Blake smiled. "You zeroed right in on what makes it valuable to me."

"Can we negotiate a price?"

Galaxy was priced at a half million. Alexandra stopped fidgeting with her cuticles and spoke. "Max Girard, you're such a fox. What did you have in mind?"

"*Exotica* is priced at three hundred thousand. Sounds high. *Galaxy*, on the other hand, holds emotional appeal for me. Understanding that Alexandra needs to get a large chuck of the action and that you, Blake, would like to walk away with a little cash in your pocket, I'm offering three-seventy-five."

There was that silent cha-ching again as Alexandra's eyes darted. "Max, sweet Max, can't you do a teensy bit better?"

"Afraid not, my dear. I'm holding firm on the price."

"Done," Blake said.

"Don't be so quick to sell yourself short." Alexandra glared at Blake. "Let me handle this."

"There's nothing to handle," Blake said. "I want Max to have it."

Max Girard took out a check from his inside jacket pocket, and with a few waves of his Mont Blanc pen, he scribbled the number without blinking an eye.

Thanks to Cousin Celeste Bleckner, in the space of five minutes, *Galaxy* had found a home and Eddie Sloat, watching Celeste in action, nearly came in his pants.

Blake sought me out while I was gathering brochures. "Darling, the dirty deed is done. Max and I are running over to the Carlyle for a drink. I'll be back in an hour, and then it's you and me, baby, for the rest of the night."

"Go," I said. "I have cleaning to do and settling up with the caterer. I'll see you in a while."

The gallery emptied, and Alexandra, acclimating herself to the fact that she had lost control, tried blaming me for Celeste's actions. "Your cousin is an absolute beast. A real horror. She's a trouble-maker who stuck her nose in where it didn't belong."

"You made a giant sale," I said. "Better than you ever expected."

"*Galaxy* is worth the asking price." Alexandra was practically snorting. "Even Blake agreed it's his favorite painting."

"Do you realize that you're holding a check for three hundred seventy-five thousand dollars in your hot little hands?"

"Samantha, frankly, I'm shocked by your attitude. I thought you understood the business."

"I'd say you came out ahead. How many other paintings of Blake's did you sell?"

"None, but that's beside the point."

"It's very much the point." I held firm. "This isn't about business, is it? It's about you losing power."

"Whatever are you talking about, Samantha? Have you gone bonkers?"

"And that's not all." I was on a roll, heated up and not about to quit. "That little raise you've been promising me—"

"What about it?"

"You never got around to offering it to me."

"In case you haven't noticed, I've been busy with Blake's show."

"No, Alexandra," I said. "*I've* been busy with Blake's show. *I'm* the one who's been working my butt off making sure every minute detail was accounted for."

"Samantha, I've never seen you like this. Have you gone completely mad?"

"No, just pissed. I've been here for several years, and not once have I heard as much as a thank-you come out of your mouth. You act as though I'm your personal slave and you're entitled to treat people any way you want. Well, I've had it."

"What does *that* mean?"

"It means that unless I'm compensated for my efforts, you can find yourself another Samantha Krasner."

"Is this all about the fact that I haven't given you a raise?"

"Not entirely."

"Because I think I know what's really bugging you: You've got your eye on Blake Hamilton for yourself. You're jealous because he's fucking me."

"Blake Hamilton is fucking *you*?" I was dumbfounded.

"Yes."

"I don't believe you," I said, hardly able to breathe.

"Why don't you ask him yourself?"

"I wouldn't stoop that low, but you're a liar."

"Am I? If so, you might ask yourself why Blake is on his way to my room at the Carlyle as we speak."

"That's ridiculous. Blake left with Max and said he'd be back in an hour to take me to dinner."

"Darling, I have news for you. Blake and I have other plans. Your little intimate supper for two will just have to wait."

I could hardly believe what I was hearing. There must be a catch. Blake who had verbally bashed Alexandra, Blake who had invited me to London and had professed his undying love, was, according to Alexandra, preparing for a mad, passionate night of lovemaking with her.

"As I said, sweetie, you don't understand the biz. How do you think Blake got into my gallery in the first place?"

"Blake is one of the biggest artists who has emerged on the scene," I said. "Any gallery would die to show him."

"No. Blake is only one of *many* new artists," Alexandra said. "It was a toss-up between him and that other sensation of the moment, Franklin Donnenfeld. I made Blake an offer he wasn't likely to refuse, and that offer included moi. How do think Norbert Ashe made it to the Cole?"

"So you sleep with all your artists?"

"Not all of them. I didn't sleep with Libby Lewis, who showed here last year."

"Libby Lewis is a woman."

"That doesn't stop me. I've sampled some of the hottest women artists around. For a while everyone thought that Meredith Rodale and I were a couple."

"Meredith whose husband is the big department-store tycoon?"

"Ex-husband. After she and Todd split up, Meredith came crying to me with her canvases and begged me to give her a show. Her work stank to the hills, but her body was more than delicious, so I put her work up for a month. It was the least I could do."

"You and Meredith Rodale were lovers?"

"Yes, and the same goes for the no-show Roger Sutton whom poor Spencer was pining away for all evening. I know the whole story."

"You know Roger Sutton?"

"Know him? We're practically best friends."

"But—but—Roger Sutton is—"

"Gay? Not entirely. Roger is bisexual. I know that for a fact. I also know that he and Spencer are going at it hot and heavy. But there's something else I'll tell you if you promise to keep it to yourself: Roger has a boyfriend in Lenox who runs his B and B: Avery Fox. Does your friend Spencer Gould know that?"

"He knows that Roger owns a B and B, yes."

"Well, I suppose that other small detail isn't important. Yes, Roger Sutton is a real catch. Unfortunately, he spreads himself around rather liberally, but he always returns to his Lenox love."

I sat down at my desk, trying to assimilate it all.

"I'll tell you something else. When Roger told me he had met Spencer Gould, I knew the name rang a bell. Then I remembered: Bruno Wilding, of course."

"Attorney Bruno Wilding?"

"Is there any other? Bruno Wilding is my attorney, too. He handled my divorce and became one of my confidants. He would have been here tonight, but he's in Milan with his latest boy toy."

"Bruno Wilding is a friend of the Goulds," I said.

"I know that. He and Alden Gould were big pals."

"You know Alden Gould?" I said.

"Not personally. Tonight was the first time I ever met him or Spencer. Isn't it sweet that he and your mother are so cozy?" Alexandra asked.

My head was spinning and I needed another drink.

"Don't look so horrified. Manhattan is a small, incestuous island where everyone knows everyone else's dirty little secrets."

"What about Spencer?" I asked.

"Oh, Spencer—yes, he is adorable. I can see why Bruno was smitten back then and why Roger Sutton is now. But Roger was afraid to show up tonight for fear I'd get drunk and my tongue might wag. I do have a terrible habit of saying too much when I get boozy."

"Spencer has no idea about any of this."

"Of course he doesn't, and we need to keep it that way. I don't plan on telling him, and neither will you."

"Spencer has fallen hard for Roger."

"All the men fall hard for Roger. That's his claim to fame. Every man he meets falls in love with him. I warned him to stop being so naughty, but he never listens to me."

"These are people's lives we're talking about," I said.

"Samantha, honey, when are you going to grow up? This is the New York singles scene. All these beautiful people get themselves mixed up in all sorts of high jinks. The women want husbands, and the men want to remain bachelors. It's just the way it is—the nature of the beast."

"But Blake—I can't believe Blake."

"Blake adores you," Alexandra said. "I know that. I can smell it a mile away. He's even told me as much. But there's a price to pay for everything."

"That's so cynical."

"I am cynical. I'm exactly the bitch everyone says I am. That's why I'm so successful."

"Not only a bitch. You're unscrupulous."

"Yes. That's how I can afford to give you the raise I promised."

I sat there taking it all in, unable to speak. How could I even consider staying on with Alexandra Cole? Even worse, if what she was saying was true, Blake had betrayed me, and I wanted to die. A part of me couldn't believe any of it. I tried gaining my composure and not giving Alexandra the impression I was even buying in to any of this. Yet she had sufficiently raised my suspicions, as only she could.

"I'd love to sit here chatting with you, Samantha, but Blake is probably getting hungry . . . or horny . . . or both, so why don't we call it a night? A very fruitful night, too."

That was the final straw. I couldn't take it another minute. "Alexandra," I said, dropping the gallery key on her desk. "You'll have to lock up yourself. I'm leaving, and I won't be back, not tomorrow, not ever."

"Stop being such a drama queen, Samantha. If that's your decision, c'est la vie. I was going to offer you a handsome raise. It would have kept you at Barneys for days to come. Are you sure I can't tempt you? You've got a cushy job here at the gallery. Don't let a silly thing like indiscretion get in the way. You've really got to learn how to play hardball if you want to make it in this city."

I got up, swung my coat around me, and walked out into the cold December air, hailing the first cab I saw.

I tried sleeping but couldn't. I lay awake in the dark, simultane-ously crying and thinking of ways to do Blake in. Finally, after I fell asleep at three A.M., my mother's phone call awakened me at eight. She sounded hysterical and furious.

"Calm down, Mother. I can hardly understand a word you're saying."

"Alden and I are driving up to Westport today. I came home to shower and change and gather a few articles of clothing. Alden said he would pick me up in an hour."

"And?"

"When I came home, there was that dreadful man from last night."

"What dreadful man? What are you talking about?"

"Celeste's friend. The Italian."

"You mean Eddie Sloat?"

"Whatever his name is. There he was standing in my bedroom closet, naked, with his faux hair."

"Eddie Sloat was naked in *your* closet?"

"That's what I'm trying to tell you."

"Where was Celeste?"

"Sitting on *my* bed wrapped in *my* sheet. When she saw me, she nearly died. They didn't even have the decency to use the guest room."

It was all I could do to keep from laughing. "That's it?"

"No, that's not it. I told Celeste, 'I can't believe you stuffed that dirty man inside my closet with my couture. I have furs in that closet.' And you know what he said? He said: 'Thank God for that. I was so cold I threw your chinchilla around me to keep warm.' Can you imagine? *My* chinchilla around *his* naked body."

"What happened next?"

"Gilda came back from the movies, walked in, and witnessed the entire scene. She was horrified."

"I'm sure Gilda has seen a naked man or two in her day, Mother."

"Not in *my* closet, she hasn't. She took me aside and told me there was something about Celeste that had always bothered her. As for that disgusting man, she could tell by his shoes that he was a bad apple."

"So he wasn't completely naked, then?"

"No, he was wearing shoes. As if that matters."

"That's what she called him? A bad apple?"

"Gilda said you can tell a lot about a person by his shoes. She came in just as he was throwing on some clothes, and the first thing she noticed was his shoes. 'His shoes are scuffed and badly in need of a shine,' she said. 'My late husband, Rolfe, bless his soul, never left the house without polishing his shoes with beeswax and spittle. My Rolfe was a gentleman and a credit to his sex.' "

The truth was, Rolfe Kruell had died forty years ago with a woman in his bed, and it wasn't Gilda. Through the years, Gilda had conveniently tossed that memory aside and still held Rolfe in highest esteem.

"Did Celeste offer any explanation?"

"She broke down and confessed that she was afraid if I saw Eddie Sloat, I would call the police. So Eddie hid in the closet when he heard me enter the apartment."

"It all sounds like some dime-store novel. Really, Mother, what's the big deal?"

"Aside from the fact that he was wearing *my* fur and was probably going to steal my jewelry or a piece of art, I guess nothing."

"Don't be so dramatic. Celeste brought a man back to your apartment and you don't like it."

"If I find out they had sex on my Frette sheets, I'll kill her."

"They probably did."

"Your aunt Elaine would die if she knew about this."

"Don't tell her."

"You bet I'm going to tell her. She and Phil were right: The man looks like a drug dealer and probably is. I had better check the medicine cabinet to make sure he hasn't stolen my Valium."

"Are they still in your apartment?"

"No. The drug dealer split so fast he left skid marks. Celeste was still sitting on my bed crying. That's when I called you."

"What can *I* do?"

"I'm not sure. Did you know about any of this?"

"Of course not. I have my own problems, Mother."

"That may be true, but nobody naked is lurking inside *your* closet."

"I should only be so lucky," I said.

"To think: That dreadful man was wearing *my* chinchilla. I want the entire apartment fumigated."

TWENTY

It isn't premarital sex if you have no
intention of getting married.

—*Matt Barry*

While I tossed and turned in my bed, back at the
Carlyle Hotel in Bemelmans Bar, Max ordered a double Jack
Daniel's. Blake ordered a B&B on the rocks.

"How did it all begin for you?" Max asked the first probing question.

"You mean when did I know I wanted to become an
artist?"

"Why not? Let's start there."

"Since I was a child living in Liverpool, I've been slapping paint on paper. I owned my first set of watercolors
when I was four, and it took off from there. By the time I was

ten, I drove my mother wild, messing up the house with oil paints. I even finger-painted the walls."

"What does your mother have to say about you now?"

"Sadly, she died many years ago."

"And your father?"

"He left us when I was a tot. He worked in the mines and took up with some young waitress at the pub where he got sloshed every night. Knocked her up and left my mother to fend for herself and me. Mum raised me, took two jobs, and made enough money for me to study art."

"Any siblings?"

"A brother who died at birth."

"You've had a rough go of it."

"That was a long time ago. The wounds have healed over since then. I only wish Mum were still alive so she could reap the rewards of my hard work. Once I started art school, I moved to London."

"Were you always interested in abstraction?"

"Not at first. For a long time I admired Picasso and became interested in cubism. My earlier work emulated his."

"So you're a copycat?"

"I was for a bit. When I was in my early twenties, cubism became my raison d'être. I did many cubist-like paintings. I even attracted the attention of a small London gallery that gave me a show, but I never sold a thing, and the reviews were horrible. I grappled with failure for several years and licked my wounds. I was greatly influenced by Jean Fautrier, the French abstractionist of the fifties who was raised in London and later moved to Paris. I went there to see his work."

"How long did you stay?"

"For a summer I wandered the streets of Paris, hitting all the galleries and obscure spots. I was trying to discover what made me tick."

"What *does* make you tick?"

"I'm afraid it took me a while to find that out. I'm still not sure I have the answer. All I knew is I wasn't happy. Didn't know what the hell I wanted. I was blown away by the idea of what I wanted to do, but I was terrified to trust my instincts and let myself go. That is, until a few years ago when I moved in an entirely different direction. The result: *Galaxy*—my first attempt at abstraction. I sent my slides to several galleries around London. At first nothing happened, and then the Pugg agreed to take two of my pieces. That was when Alexandra Cole first noticed me."

"A day to go down in infamy, I'm sure," Max said.

"Alexandra was in London on her way to the airport, back to New York. She decided to stop off at the Pugg. When she saw my work, she handed me her card and asked me how many more paintings I had. 'Enough to fill a small museum,' I told her. She canceled her flight and came to my studio. The rest is history. I have Alexandra Cole to thank for leading me toward the path of success."

"What constitutes success?" Max asked.

"Showing my work and selling it."

"I'm glad I could play a part in that. Frankly, your style knocks me out. That's why I just diminished my bank account by that much. I know that Alexandra thinks it's worth more, and she might be right. But considering it was the first piece that allowed you to become you, I'd say I paid a fair price."

"I'm happy with the way it turned out," Blake said.

"What are you working on now?"

"I began a painting in London called *Cinematrix*. It deals with the film culture, concentrating mostly on noir, and its influence on movies today. The painting also incorporates the women's movement and how that affects cinema. All of this is represented through the abstract."

"How far along are you?"

"I started it a few months ago, rolled up the canvas, and brought it with me to New York, ready to be attacked."

"I'd like to see it."

"That can definitely be arranged."

"This should be an interesting time for you, Blake, and I'm sure you're already in great demand," Max said. "But I'd like to introduce you around—have you meet some of my crowd. Big spenders who don't blink an eye at dropping a bundle for what they consider kitsch. I throw lots of parties. You should come, meet the masses, and see my art."

"I'd be honored," Blake said.

Max paused. "I'd like to tell you something—between us."

"Of course."

"Be careful how much of your carcass you allow Alexandra to pick. She'll peck at you slowly and then eat you alive, and I'm not just talking sex. She's a sharp cookie and knows how to get exactly what she wants."

"Trust me, I'm on to Alexandra," Blake assured.

"She's easy to fall for. God knows I did. I'm just saying—"

At that moment, as if already planned, Alexandra entered the bar. "Whew, what a night. I'm glad it's over. What are you two up to?" she asked.

"Blake was just filling me in on how he became Blake Hamilton."

"Did he tell you that I had everything to do with it?" she asked.

"That's exactly what he said," Max acknowledged.

"Good. I like my artists to feel grateful. What are you having, man drinks? I think this evening calls for something festive."

"I've got to get going," Blake said. "I told Samantha I'd be back in an hour."

"Don't you worry your head about Samantha. She knows that you might be very late. I explained that we had lots to talk about."

"Even so, we should probably ask her to join us," Blake said.

"Darling, with all due respect, this night isn't about Samantha."

"She *is* your partner."

"That is her title, yes, but I prefer keeping it intimate and entre nous. Samantha handles the schedules. I handle the sales."

"I'm going to ring her up."

"Don't." Alexandra put her hand over Blake's cell. "Samantha said she was tired and was going home. She didn't want to be disturbed. Now let's get somebody to bring me a champagne cocktail."

As the evening progressed, the banter continued until around one thirty, when Max decided to call it a night.

"Oh, Max, don't be such a party pooper," Alexandra said.

"You kids stay on," he said. "I've had all the excitement I can handle for one night."

"All right, then. Anyway, Blake and I have lots to discuss."

Several kisses later, Max left. Alexandra had Blake entirely to herself. Not wasting a minute, she was on to the next business at hand: Blake caving in too quickly to Max's price.

"*Galaxy* could have sold for much more," she said. "We should have upped the price. Max might have taken the bait."

"I think we made a fair deal under the circumstances," Blake said.

"Well, I don't. But that's water under the bridge." She guzzled her champagne. "Blake, I'm feeling ever so gay. Let's end the evening on a real high. What do you say?"

"We *are* ending it on a high. I'd say both of us are pretty looped."

"If I asked you to do me a favor, would you?"

"That depends."

"You mean you might actually refuse me—like you once did before?"

"I did?"

"Yes, in London, when I came to the Pugg to see your work. You rejected me and broke my poor little heart." She nuzzled up to Blake. "Blake, darling, don't you find me at all attractive?"

"You know I do, Alexandra."

"Then prove it. I am, after all, making you a very successful man."

"I thought it was *I* who was making me successful."

"That's what I love about you: your naïveté. You don't honestly believe an artist can make it alone, do you? I'm the gatekeeper, angel, and don't you forget it." She took Blake's hand and placed it under her dress, brushing it across her thigh. "Ooh, doesn't that feel good?"

Blake pulled away quickly. "Stop it, Alexandra, and I mean it."

"Oh, don't be so serious. We're just having a little fun. You must be getting all the sex you need without me. So tell me, is Samantha good in the sack?"

"Okay, that's it," he said. "We need to call it a night."

"All right, I'll behave. It's just that you're so irresistibly sexy. I get horny looking at you."

"This is inappropriate."

"When did you become such a big prude? I know you think I'm hot. Most men do. I don't know any man who wouldn't want to jump my bones."

"That may be true, but this man isn't going to."

"Are you queer? Maybe that's your problem."

"No, I'm not queer."

"Then prove it. Show me just how unqueer you are."

Blake asked for the check while Alexandra, clearly drunk, was all over him, her breasts slipping out of her décolleté.

"Here," she said, taking his hand again. "Feel these breasts. I promise you, they're everything you think they are and more. I can do amazing things with these breasts."

"No doubt you can." Blake tried manipulating his credit card with one hand and controlling Alexandra with the other.

"You're so ambidextrous, darling, and so unavailable. That's what makes it even more exciting. Come on, take me to my room. I'm much too drunk to travel the elevator alone."

"I'll have the concierge escort you."

"Goodie. If I can't have you, maybe he'd like to tuck me into bed."

Blake managed to extricate himself from Alexandra's clutches and get her to the elevator. He pushed the twelfth-floor button and brought her to her room, where she tried manipulating the door key. Once inside, he navigated Alexandra past the foyer and into the bedroom.

"Fuck me," Alexandra pleaded. "Fuck me the way you do Samantha."

Blake placed Alexandra on the bed, where she instantly fell asleep. He tossed a blanket over her, turned out the light, and left, heaving a sigh of relief as he made it downstairs to the lobby and back to his apartment.

TWENTY-ONE

I like being single.
I'm always there when I need me.

—*Art Leo*

I had finally fallen into a fitful sleep awakening the
next morning, bleary-eyed and furious that Blake hadn't
called. With all the commotion between my mother and Celeste, I had gotten sidetracked. Dressing for work, I realized
I was no longer employed at the Cole Gallery. If what
Alexandra had said was true—that she and Blake had fucked
their brains out last night—then this was it. Yet, knowing
Alexandra, I would first confront Blake and give him the
chance to explain. He deserved at least that. Until then I
wasn't going believe a word she had said.

The phone rang a few minutes later, with Blake on the other end.

"Good morning, darling," he said. "Did you have a good night's sleep?"

"Not as good as you did, I'm sure." My tone was less than warm.

"I'm exhausted. I didn't get home until after two o'clock. We closed Bemelmans Bar. Max left, and Alexandra got drunk and started to cause a bit of a scene, as only she can do."

"So you *were* with Alexandra, then." I had nailed him.

"Of course we were all together. You knew that. I went over to the Carlyle with Max to talk art. Alexandra showed up a while later."

"You never called me."

"Alexandra said you were tired and decided to go home. That you didn't want to be disturbed."

"And you *believed* her?" I was nearly screaming and caught myself sounding like a shrew. But by this time I was furious.

"I did believe her."

"Then you're a bigger idiot than I thought."

"You're angry."

"Goddamn right I'm angry. We had a date, in case you forgot."

"Sweetheart, I honestly thought you had given up on me and gone home. That's what Alexandra told me. I swear it."

"Oh, I believe that's what she said. What I'm having trouble with is you going along with that bullshit. You might have at least asked me to join you." I was bordering on whiny.

"I suggested that, but Alexandra was intent on being alone with Max and me."

"I'm hanging up," I said.

"Why aren't you hearing me?" Blake protested.

"Oh, I hear you loud and clear. Did you and Alexandra have fun together?"

"Hardly. She ordered champagne and proceeded to get stinking drunk."

"And then I suppose she invited you to her room?"

"That's exactly what she did."

"And you went." I didn't want to believe what I was hearing. Blake was digging himself deeper into a hole every time he opened his mouth.

"I put her in the elevator—which wasn't easy—got her to her room, put her on the bed, and left. There you have it, the entire story just as it happened."

"You're so chivalrous."

"I *was,* in fact."

"I have a different version. Alexandra told me you two have been sleeping together. No, her exact words were: 'Blake Hamilton has been dying to fuck me forever.' "

"And you think that's true?"

"What do you expect me to think?"

"Obviously, you don't know Alexandra. She's crazy."

"I'm getting off the phone," I said without giving Blake the chance to continue.

"I'll call you later," he said. "Are you free for dinner?"

"You've got to be kidding," I said.

Didn't Blake understand the damage that Alexandra had tried to cause? As much as I wanted him to prove her wrong, dinner seemed almost laughable under the circumstances.

As furious as I was with Blake, I had another mission to attend to: Spencer Gould. My first reaction after Alexandra had so bluntly and brutally told me about Roger Sutton's infidelity was to protect Spencer, warn him about what he was getting himself into. Another part of me felt I was meddling—that I should stay out of it and let Spencer fend for himself, letting the pieces fall where they may. But in the end, what he didn't know could kill him. It ultimately made me call Spencer and ask if he was free for dinner.

When I had first asked Lily Ann what she thought I should do, she said, "You sound like a Jewish mother. Stay out of it."

But I didn't. Ready to act as Spencer's personal savior, I met him on Thursday over drinks at the Waverly Inn.

"You sounded weird on the phone," Spencer said. "What's up?"

"It's about Roger," I said, cutting to the chase. "I've come bearing news."

"What news?" He eyed me in a jaundiced way.

"I wasn't sure if I should say anything, but I'm your friend, and that's what friends do—I think."

"Is it about Roger not showing up at the show. Because if it is, we've been in touch, and everything is fine," Spencer said.

"Really?"

"Roger said he came down with that awful stomach flu that's been going around. He decided to stay in Lenox."

"And you believed him?"

"Of course. Why wouldn't I? Although I will say it was a bit strange that he hadn't called all night."

"Spencer"—I took a deep breath—"I'd be careful with Roger Sutton. He's not all he's cracked up to be."

"What are you talking about? This is the man I love, or at least think I love."

"I know that. That's what makes this all the more painful."

"Samantha, what the hell is this about?"

"It's Alexandra. She knows Roger."

"I know that. Roger told me he's known Alexandra for years, being in the arts and all."

"That's not the whole story," I blurted out. "The other night after the show, while Alexandra and I were engaged in major verbal combat, she told me that Roger Sutton, the love of your life, is otherwise involved. Not that I believe a word of it. I'm simply reporting."

"What?"

"In the middle of our heated discussion, where Alexandra's tongue was wagging out of control, she said that the guy who runs his B and B is, shall we say, doing more than tidying up the rooms. He and Roger are making merry behind your back. In other words, Roger isn't exactly Old Faithful."

Spencer put down his mojito and stared. "Why are you telling me this?"

"I thought you should know."

"Why?"

"So you won't get hurt."

"You just ruined everything, Samantha. Now I really *am* hurt."

"But don't you want to know that the man of your dreams is sleeping with another guy? They've been together for many years. Apparently, Roger plays around on the side."

"Will you stop—please. You're getting me very upset."

"I'm sorry, Spencer, but when I found out, I was upset, too. I was crazed."

"So you want me to be crazed, too?"

"Of course not, but I did feel you should be warned."

"That's not your job. Your job is to be my friend."

"That's what I'm trying to be."

"How do you know what Alexandra said is even true? According to you, the woman is mental."

"She is mental, but she sounded sincere. She said it so matter-of-factly."

Spencer took a large gulp of his drink. "You've just made a mockery of my romance."

"I didn't. Roger did. I'm your friend, and I want to protect you."

Spencer looked pale. "God, I wish you hadn't told me this, Samantha. Now I have to confront Roger, and it's gong to get messy."

"Aren't you angry? Assuming any of this might be true?"

"Yes, I'm angry—*if* it's true, which I don't believe it is. You should be very careful about spreading rumors."

"This isn't a rumor."

"How do you know?"

"I only know this: As mean and destructive as Alexandra is, she's usually right. I hate admitting that, but it's the truth. Alexandra has the goods on everyone she knows, and thinks nothing of passing it along."

"Just like you're doing now."

"I'm not." I was becoming teary. "I honestly have your best interests at heart."

I felt terrible that I had even broached the subject. I never realized how damaging those words were. I should have left well enough alone and stayed out of it. But Spencer was my friend, and wasn't this what friends did? Keep them from making huge mistakes?

"I'm going," Spencer said. "I lost my appetite, and I need to leave."

"But it's Thursday. Waverly Inn serves their macaroni and cheese with white truffles on Thursdays." I was tyring to interject a lighter note. "Please, Spencer, don't hate me."

"I don't hate you, but I'm clearly not in the mood for dinner." He was starting to perspire. "I need to be alone."

"Will you call me? I'm worried."

But Spencer said nothing. He dropped a twenty-dollar bill on the table, got up, and quickly exited the restaurant, leaving me alone and full of self-loathing for having opened my big mouth.

The waiter came over, inquiring if I needed anything.

"Another mojito," I said. "And the mac and cheese with the truffles."

If I was going to be miserable, at least let it be on a full stomach.

Spencer didn't call me that night or the next day. When I tried him, he refused to pick up his cell or return the messages I left with Cindy, his receptionist with the high-pitched voice and big boobs.

"Please tell Dr. Gould it's urgent that I speak with him," I told her the third time I called.

"Is this an emergency, Samantha?"

"Not a medical emergency, but an emergency nonetheless," I said, aware that I sounded somewhat cryptic.

"I'll remind the doctor that you phoned yet again," Cindy said.

I was convinced that Spencer would never speak to me again. When my phone rang that evening, I quickly grabbed it, expecting to find him on the other end. But it was Blake.

"I'm assuming that you've cooled down by now."

"Don't assume," I said, in no mood to make small talk.

"Can we discuss it over dinner tonight?" he asked, sounding like a puppy dog with its tail between its legs.

"Why? It's not going to make me feel better."

"Samantha, darling."

"Don't call me darling," I said, leery of any intimate gestures.

"Samantha Krasner. You would be doing me the greatest honor if you would please have dinner with me."

"You're a liar and a cheat," I said, though I still wasn't completely convinced that Alexandra was telling the truth. Most important, I wanted to give Blake the chance to defend himself.

"No, my love, you've got it all wrong. The liar is Alexandra Cole."

"Are you talking about the woman at whose gallery you're presently showing? Because if she is the liar you say she is, why don't you pull your paintings off the wall and tell her to go to hell?"

"I can't."

"Really, and why is that?"

"Have dinner with me, please. I'll make a reservation wherever you'd like—Babbo, for instance," knowing it was one of my favorites.

"Babbo?" I brightened, my edginess temporarily dissipating. The thought of their delicious pasta, even under these grim circumstances, made me weaken. Blake certainly knew how to push the right buttons. And I wanted desperately to believe him. A quiet dinner for two might prove that he wasn't the devious womanizer Alexandra had tried convincing me he was.

"I'll call them right now and see if we can get in." I could sense his gratitude at being given another chance.

"Use my mother's name," I said. "She and Grayson were regulars."

I couldn't quite believe that I had succumbed to Blake's charms, but he had sounded so sincere that I thought he might be telling the truth. That along with Spencer, who had pointed out that maybe Alexandra was lying about Roger.

As I had suggested, Madeleine's name got us in at eight o'clock. Blake, looking particularly handsome, was waiting at the bar, working on an apple martini.

Dammit, I thought, why does he have to look like the incredible, amazing hunk?

While we waited for our table, he ordered me a drink, telling me I looked particularly stunning. "You're absolutely ready for tasting," he said.

"Let's cut the sweet talk. I'm in no mood."

As I sipped my drink, my ire subsided even more and I started to melt slightly. By the time we were seated, and with the help of the liquor, I had lost my hostile edge and decided to let Blake prove he was telling the truth.

The grilled octopus appetizer helped my mood along. Blake had ordered the steamed cockles with red chiles and basil, reminiscent, he said, of old London town, where cockles were often a specialty.

He chose a lovely red wine from the Tuscany region to accompany the osso buco for two, prepared with saffron orzo, cavolo nero, and chestnut gremolata. A beet salad was a refreshing accompaniment to the meal.

Babbo seemed the perfect confessional where Blake could speak his mind. We went back and forth, rehashing the fateful evening. We were so engrossed in conversation that by the time we got to the goat cheese tortellini with dried orange and fennel powder, all was forgiven. I was convinced that Alexandra was the bitch I always knew her to be.

Over dessert, I granted him a pardon for the crime he swore he didn't commit.

It had been three days and still no word from Spencer. I was concerned that he wasn't returning my calls. Finally, against my better judgment, I asked my mother if Alden had mentioned where Spencer was.

"Wouldn't you know that better than I?" she asked. "After all, you and Spencer are very close. But since you asked, Alden did say that Spencer was going up to Lenox for the weekend."

"Oh, that's right," I pretended, "he did tell me about that. I forgot."

"I would think he would," my mother said. "Is everything all right? You sound peculiar."

"I'm getting my period."

"Speaking of which," my mother added, "periods don't last forever. Samantha, when in God's name are you going to take your body seriously?"

"Meaning what?"

"Meaning that before menopause sets in, you just might want to think seriously about where you're headed, matrimonially speaking."

"I'm not getting married just to give you a grandchild, Mother. I want you to bug off and not bring this up again. Get used to the idea that I very well may go through life childless."

"Why do you always have to attack me?" I could hear her voice begin to tremble. "What am I asking that's so terrible?"

"You're always on my case about marriage. Face it, I just might want to remain a bachelorette."

"Bachelorette? Is that the new word of the day? I just don't know why it is you have to be so mean to me when all I want is your happiness."

"I *am* happy."

"Happy now, maybe, but years from now, when you have no son or daughter to take care of you in your old age, what then?"

"Is that what this is all about?"

"Certainly it is. Husbands come and go, but children are forever. I know what I'm talking about, Samantha."

"Mother," I softened, "are you afraid you're going to be alone in your old age?"

"What are you talking about?"

"Because you know I'll always be here for you."

"Of course you will. Why wouldn't you be?"

"I would be."

"Good, then there's nothing more to say."

"Keep your eye on the clock," Madeleine said. "You know what I'm talking about."

And to think I had almost gotten away with having the last word.

My mother had given me the one piece of information I was after: Spencer's whereabouts. I felt personally responsible that he had gone up to Lenox to confront Roger, yet I was relieved that this matter would be brought to the forefront and possibly settled once and for all.

Whether or not Spencer would ever speak to me again was another story.

Max Girard had returned to the Cole Gallery several times since the opening to view *Galaxy*. He stared at it for a long time, studying it from each angle, from up close and from a distance.

"Maxie," Alexandra said when he appeared again on Tuesday afternoon, "stop salivating. I know you can't wait to get this painting into your apartment, but if you're going to have a hard-on every time you view it, I want to be the recipient of your enthusiasm, if you get what I'm saying?"

"You never change, do you?" Max said. "Actually, I'm here because there's a matter I'd like to discuss with you. How about dinner tonight?"

"I thought you'd never ask."

"Good. I'll make a reservation at Alain Ducasse."

"Wow, it must be a very serious matter, Max. It doesn't get much better than Ducasse."

"It *is* serious," Max said.

There was no word from Alexandra, even though I hadn't shown up to work in several days. She was obviously getting on just fine without me. Blake, with whom I had made up and who was back in my life and in my bed, did pass along one interesting piece of news. "Alexandra called me," he said.

"Naturally. Alexandra will never give up."

"She apologized for making a complete fool of herself the other night. She said she was very drunk and didn't know what she was doing."

"I guess that took care of that," I said. "So she's back in your good graces, then?"

"Alexandra Cole will never be back in my good graces. But I did find out something interesting."

"That she's really a man?"

"That's funny."

"Well, I figured she's got the balls."

"Alexandra told me she and Max Girard are having dinner tonight."

"That's big news?"

"Apparently, it is. She called to say that Max had something to discuss with her."

"Perhaps he wants to buy another painting."

"Don't think that thought hadn't crossed my mind."

"He did have his heart set on *Exotica.* Maybe he can't live without it."

"We'll know soon enough," Blake said. "In the meantime, I don't want to get too excited."

"Fingers crossed," I said.

"Of course, if he does buy that piece, I'm going to make it clear to Alexandra that it wouldn't have happened without you and that you should be compensated."

"Like she'll really go for that," I said.

"Hey, baby, I do get to call some of the shots," he said.

On the other side of town, Alexandra was preparing for dinner with Max Girard, wondering what was so pressing that he would invite her to Alain Ducasse, one of the finest dining experiences in the world with a price tag to go along with it. At twenty dollars for the least expensive glass of champagne, it was more of an extravagant happening than a meal.

She had dressed for the occasion and looked stunning in a simple Yohji Yamamoto black silk and wool dress and Giuseppe Zanotti python sandals befitting her reptile image. No one could say she wasn't able to knock 'em dead with the duds. She was always a vision and looked expensive and sexy. Max took one look at her and proceeded to order more champagne, along with some Osetra caviar to set the mood.

"Max, darling, it's been a while since we broke bread together. Is this simply business or have you missed me?"

"Always the latter," Max fell right in. "But since you brought up business, we can discuss that, too."

"Oh, how boring. Must you?"

"I must and I will," Max said. "What I want to present to you is rather sensitive material."

"I should have worn my asbestos suit," Alexandra said.

Max Girard studied the menu, ordering an appetizer of thin slices of bluefin tuna with asparagus in a swampy green aioli with balsamic wine vinegar and ginger. Alexandra chose a cocktail of fresh scallops with a comfit of tomatoes and extra-virgin olive oil. This got them off to a good start and set the stage for what was to follow.

"Okay, Max, I'm all ears," Alexandra said.

Max, pausing to sip his cabernet sauvignon, proceeded to rock Alexandra's boat as it had never been rocked before. They talked for hours through Alexandra's truffled chicken in a sweet onion marmalade and Max's squab stuffed with foie gras. By the time dessert rolled around, with she and Max dipping their spoons into a crunchy praline soufflé, Alexandra's head was spinning from what she had heard. She drank the last remaining drops of her wine. Brandy soon followed as the talk continued.

"I just can't believe it," she said. "What now?"

"That all depends," Max said.

"On what?"

"On how we can ultimately make this work in our favor. Let's sleep on it."

"I'd like to sleep on you, Max darling," Alexandra said, in her usual rare form. "Will you be coming home with me tonight?"

Tempting though it was, Max Girard kept his wits about him and declined Alexandra's provocative offer.

Too early on an early January morning, my phone rang. I sleepily picked up.

"Oh, hello, Max," I said after he introduced himself. I wondered why he was calling. "Yes, he's here. Let me get him."

I handed the telephone over to Blake, who, still drowsy with sleep from our late night at Babbo and with his eyes closed, mumbled a weak "Yeah?" He sat up, rubbing his eyes. "Yes, Max, I can meet you for lunch. Is everything all right? Yes . . . one o'clock. JoJo. Sounds great. See you then."

"What was that all about?" I asked.

"I have no idea. He said we'd talk at lunch. Damn, I hope he's not reneging on the painting."

"He loves the painting," I assured. "He probably wants to talk to you about buying *Exotica*. You said he was having dinner with Alexandra last night. They must have discussed it, and now he needs to ask you a few questions."

"I don't know. He sounded abrupt, as if something were wrong."

"Don't be such a worrywart," I said, planting kisses all over Blake's face.

After a night of kiss-and-make-up bliss, Blake was back in my good graces. He seemed pensive while he ate a light breakfast of an English muffin with marmalade and freshly brewed café au lait I had made with my new espresso machine.

"Darling, you're working yourself up over nothing. I'm sure Max has something exciting to discuss with you," I said.

"I'll bet he decided not to buy *Galaxy*. He thought it over and decided it wasn't worth the price," Blake said.

"And I'll bet it has nothing to do with that. You'll see. You'll call me later and tell me how silly you were to even give this a moment's thought."

"I wonder if Alexandra will be there," Blake wondered.

"Why would she be?"

"I don't know. I'm being paranoid, I guess."

"I can get dressed and go with you," I offered.

"No, I can handle Max on my own."

"I'll be right here waiting to hear all, so take careful notes."

"You bet I will," Blake said, planting a kiss on my mouth.

By noon Blake was casually dressed and on his way to JoJo on Sixty-fourth Street. The restaurant's plush appointments added a touch of quiet elegance. Crystal chandeliers hung over the room casting a warm glow, conducive to conversation, although today Blake expected the worst.

Arriving first, Blake was nervous. He wanted to order a drink but decided to pass until Max joined him. Max, running late, had made the wait seem unbearably long. Blake checked his watch at regular intervals without really registering the time. At one twenty, Max walked in, said his hellos to a table of businessmen he knew, and then joined Blake. He didn't look happy, and his tardiness seemed almost deliberate.

"A double Tanqueray martini, George," he told the waiter. "And for you, Blake?"

"The same."

"Smart move. We'll embrace inebriation together."

"Max, are you all right? You seem unusually tense."

"I am. But the gin will soothe the savage beast within."

As soon as the drinks appeared, Max took a slug and nearly depleted the glass as though he needed fortification for what was to follow. "No need to mince words. Let's bypass the small talk and jump right into bed with this. I had a most interesting dinner with Alexandra last evening at Ducasse."

"Ducasse? Not bad."

"Yes, you should try it sometime. Now that you're a rich artist, you can afford such pleasures."

"I'm afraid my tastes are a bit less grandiose. I don't usually indulge in such grand culinary diversions." Blake tried assuming an air of self-deprecation to quell his apprehensions.

"Whatever your desires. As for me, I enjoy the occasional fine meal, and Ducasse is certainly that."

"I'm sure that Alexandra enjoyed it, too."

"Oh, yes, Alexandra. She was having a fine time, drinking expensive bubbly and eating some of the finest French food probably in the world. Too bad I had to burst her bubble."

"Why was that?" Blake sensed hostility emanating from Max, enough to match the dread creeping through him.

"Blake Hamilton, I hate to say this—no, actually, I don't hate saying this. In fact, I find I've been waiting to say this since last night. Blake Hamilton," he repeated, "I always sensed you were a smooth son of a gun, but what I didn't know was that you were also a fraud."

"What?" Blake dug his fingernails into his palms.

"You heard me: a fraud. And I'll tell you how I know, but not before I get the waiter over here and order myself another one of those martoonies. Maybe you need to join me. I think you need to get a buzz on. It will take the edge off of what I'm about to tell you."

Blake felt the color drain from his face. He knew where Max was headed.

"You're a smooth one, Blake Hamilton. Almost had me fooled, too, which isn't an easy thing to do. I pride myself on being a pretty smart bastard. But I have to hand it to you: You almost got the best of Max Girard."

"What the hell are you talking about?" Blake tried keeping his guard up.

"I'm getting to that, but first I like watching you squirm."

"Who's squirming?"

"Oh, I forgot, pathological liars don't squirm. They believe their fabrications. The sad thing is, I liked you. I really did. I took one look at your work, and I said to myself, This fellow has the stuff. This guy is going to make it big in the art world. That is, until the other day."

"What happened the other day?" Blake dared to tread.

"I was looking at my latest acquisition, *Galaxy,* and I thought, This is one hell of a painting. It's smart. It's savvy. It's absolutely brilliant. Then I realized I had seen it somewhere before."

"That's impossible. I never showed this piece before."

"Oh, it's been out there. I saw it."

"Max, go easy on the booze."

"Don't tell me to go easy. Don't you damn well tell me anything, okay?"

"Okay."

"Because today I'm going to tell *you. You're* not going to tell me."

"I still don't know what you're talking about." Blake played dumb while trying to keep up a brave front.

"Allow me to refresh your memory. Let's travel back in time to another place," Max said. "Tell me, Blake, were you ever in Paris?"

"Of course. Everyone's been to Paris, haven't they? It's an artist's paradise."

"So it is. So it is." Max suddenly stopped the caustic banter. "Let's order. All this talk has raised an appetite." Max signaled to the waiter. "What looks good today?"

George, a favorite waiter of Max's, rattled off a list of specialties. "Mr. Girard, the chef is prepared to make for you his famous tuna tartare with chive oil and gaufrette potatoes."

"In that case, George, bring it on. And let me see the wine list. This occasion definitely calls for wine."

"I'd like the arugula ravioli," Blake said, his stomach churning at the thought of swallowing food.

"A perfect choice," the waiter acknowledged.

"So, tell me, Blake, are you a red or a white man?"

"I swing both ways."

"I'm not surprised. Philip, a bottle of your nicest Bordeaux. I'll leave the choice to you."

"What I meant was—"

"I know what you meant. Tell me again, I forgot. When was it that you got into abstractionism?"

"I told you the other night: I had an epiphany."

"Oh yes, your epiphany. I almost forgot. Gotta love those epiphanies."

Blake, agitated and hardly able to endure this torture another minute, interrupted Max. "Can we cut the bullshit? If you have something to say, just spit it out."

"Sit tight. I'm getting to it. It's about *Galaxy*. The one I just spent a hard day's work enabling me to afford."

"I doubt that."

"I've seen it before, Blake. Would you like to know where?"

"You obviously want to tell me," Blake said, trying desperately to save his ass but weakening each time Max spoke, knowing that he was trapped.

"In case you didn't know, I, too, am a Francophile, and where better to appreciate art than in the museums, galleries, and lofts of Paris?"

"I agree."

"Of course you do. Like you, I was once a bright-eyed explorer—a navigator of sorts on the prowl for artists who showed promise—and guess what? I found him."

"Who?"

"Not so fast. I need to do this my way." Max, on his martini high, was slurring slightly.

"By all means, Max. This is your show."

"No, it's actually *your* show I'm getting at. But I digress. As I was saying, I know talent when I see it, just as I did when you appeared in my line of vision. I took a look at your paintings, both in London and now in New York, and you know what I told myself?"

"What?"

"I told myself: This fucking kid has talent. I knew I needed to own a Blake Hamilton. You know why?"

"Because I'm so damn irresistible?" Blake said, trying hard to divert Max by resuming a droll demeanor.

"Shut up, I'm talking," Max said. "Because I admired you so much, that's why."

"Thank you."

"Hey, don't thank *me*. You're the artist. I'm just the buyer."

"Well, I'm glad you like my work."

"I've been spending a lot of time at the Cole Gallery," Max continued. "And not because I want to fuck the owner, 'cause I've already done that more times than you can imagine. No, my daily rounds at the Cole were for another reason: to examine my latest piece of art: *Galaxy*. I studied that damn piece every day for weeks, wondering why it looked so familiar, and that was when I was catapulted back to the eighties, when I was in Paris."

"It evoked a memory?" Blake asked, trying to substitute chattiness for the panic that was consuming him.

"Oh yes, it did. I recalled it all. I once met an artist just like you, although he was well into his sixties at the time. And like yours, his work bowled me over, one piece in particular that I wanted. It was different from anything I had ever seen—the forerunner of neoexpressionism. I knew I wanted to buy it, but I had to wait until I could afford it, which I just did a few weeks ago for the humble price of three hundred seventy-five thousand."

"I don't follow you," Blake pretended.

"Oh, you will. I'm just warming up."

"Is that what this is all about? Money?"

"If only it were that simple. No, this is about something more important than money. It's about character. It's about integrity. It's also about stolen identity. Do you get where I'm going here?"

"Sorry, Max, I'm confused," Blake said, playing along but understanding perfectly.

"Let me make it easier for you to grasp." Max's voice was bordering on conspicuously vocal. "The painting I'm referring to, the one I fell in love with as though it were a beautiful woman I couldn't have, wasn't for sale."

"Too bad."

"That's what I told the artist. I offered him a price that I thought would tempt him, but he turned me down. Said something about it being his favorite painting, and he was saving it, for what I don't know."

"Some artists are sentimental about their work."

"Oh, are they? Are you one of those sentimental schmucks, Blake?"

"I often become attached to a piece."

"How about *Galaxy*? Have any emotional attachment to that?"

"No, Max. That's pure commercial interest all the way. That's why I sold it to you."

"And that's why I'm about to make you an offer you won't be able to refuse."

"Is this about another painting?"

"No, it's about *Galaxy.*"

"But you already own it. Unless you handed me a bad check, it's all yours."

"Sure, I own it, and I intend to keep on owning it, but you, Blake Hamilton, are going to give me my money back."

"The hell I am."

"The hell you *are.*"

"Why would I?" Blake was perspiring profusely.

"Because, you sleazebag prick, you didn't *do* the goddamn painting. An artist named Hamille painted it."

"Are you completely daft, Max?" Blake feigned appropriate shock to cover up his extreme horror at being found out.

"No, but I'll bet when we go back into your past, as I have, you'll discover that the artist Hamille is long gone from this world. You're a fucking imposter, and this is no joke."

Blake was hardly amused.

"Dead," Max said. "Hamille is a dead man."

"You know all this as fact?" Blake felt a momentary sense of relief.

"I do. It was actually you who led me to it."

Blake sat still, not uttering a word, afraid to get in any deeper than he already was.

"Cat got your tongue, Blake? Or should I be calling you Bobby?"

"Okay, so I changed my name, big deal."

"It *is* a big deal. A very big deal. You *stole* a name."

"Borrowed it."

"You reinvented yourself. Assumed the persona of the old guy, then took his paintings and claimed them as your own. It was easy to paint Hamilton over Hamille. A few strokes of the brush, and voilà! Intent to steal, that's against the law, in case you didn't know. While I'll bet that you have a whole pile of paintings back in your studio. *Exotica,* for instance."

Blake slumped in his chair.

"I've got you by the balls, and you know it."

"How did you find all this out?"

"That was the easy part. I have a good friend who lives in Paris. I asked him to do some sleuthing. He went over to the Passage des Panoramas, where I saw that same painting back in the eighties. He spoke to a guy who keeps watch over the place."

"You're delusional, Max." Blake threw his napkin on the table and stood up, ready to bolt.

"Sit down, Bobby, and keep quiet. Let me ask you this: Do you happen to know a Rene Bateau?"

"Should I?"

"I would think so, since he remembered you. Even knew your name: Bobby Tisdale. Said he once knew a Tisdale years ago. That was why it stuck. He found you snooping around the deserted holes one afternoon about eight years ago."

"What of it? I was curious."

"I know all about that. Bateau said you were a good kid. Did him a big favor, actually. They were getting ready to tear down these rooms, and you agreed to take the paintings off his hands—two hundred or so of them.

"Yes, I did. I wanted to use the canvases, and some of the frames were still in good condition."

"They looked familiar, too, especially that gold one that's hanging in the Cole. Heard that the artist stole the frame from a back alley in Paris one night. Found it in the garbage. Can you believe it? You made a killing. Frames and all—a real package deal."

"Oh God, you discussed all of this with Alexandra?"

"Damn right I did. Last night at Ducasse. I thought she needed to know."

"So you're going to blackmail me? Make a mockery out of me and ruin my career?"

"*Your* career? Bobby Tisdale doesn't have a career. Hamille *might* have had a career, but he was too downtrodden to know it. He was a recluse, a man of, shall we say, hidden talents, until you put his name off the map and reaped the rewards that by all rights should have gone to him. The poor bloke died sick and penniless."

Blake sat motionless, overwhelmed and horrified by what Max was saying. He reached for the wine, poured himself another glass, and devoured it in one long swallow.

"But I'll tell you what I'm going to do."

"What's that?"

"I'm going to save your life, that's what. Make you famous."

Blake was in such a state he had trouble assimilating anything that Max threw at him. Guilty as he was, it was difficult to keep up a front and not lose the last bit of composure he had mustered up. "What about Bateau?" he asked.

"Oh, not to worry. There's something in it for him, too, if he agrees to keep quiet."

"Will he keep quiet?"

"That's a chance you'll have to take. But since he had no authority to even give you the paintings, I assume he will."

"What did Alexandra say?"

"Alexandra has you by the gonads, too, exactly where she wants you. She agreed to keep your paintings up and have you continue selling. And with me behind you, promoting you all the way, you'll be the toast of the town."

"What's the catch?"

"Only one: I control everything. You hand over the money from the sales, and we work out an arrangement."

"You expect me to go along with that?"

"You have an alternative? I don't think so. If we probed further, I'm sure we could get a forensic art expert to analyze pigment samples and lift Hamille's fingerprints right off those paintings, not to mention the old paint cans lying around the studio. I'll bet at least one of them will yield a print or two. It's the not the first time that's been done."

Blake was trembling.

"The good news," Max said, "is that Bateau is quite certain there's no provenance—no documentation of Hamille's paintings—so look on the bright side: At least you won't go to jail. Jail's not a pretty place for boys like you. You'll get eaten up alive."

"And what if I don't go along with this crazy scheme?"

"Hey, *I'm* calling the shots now. You have little to say about it. For every painting you sell, Alexandra gets a large piece of the transaction, as do I, and here's the real perk: I get to borrow paintings for my apartment whenever I want. As for Bateau, we'll offer him a handsome settlement. Together, we can make him a rich man. He'll be beholden to us."

"This is a conspiracy."

"No, this is what we call an agenda—a plan."

"What about me?"

"Your reputation will exceed your wildest dreams. We're prepared to cut you a break—if you cooperate, that is. If you do, you'll be living like a king, so you can keep impressing that pretty girlfriend of yours. After all, you need to keep up the image, and I'm prepared to provide you with a percentage of the works sold in exchange for allowing me to micromanage your life. I have clout, and when I put my mind to making things happen, they do. That's my forte. After all, we can't have you be a starving artist, can we? It doesn't go along with your persona."

"And if I refuse?"

"You won't. You're too smart for that."

"Are there other people who know about this?"

"We looked into that. According to Bateau, Hamille had no family. He was up in that dilapidated room, painting away. The only one who spoke to him was Bateau. The beauty of it is: No one even knows about this studio. It was hidden away among all the debris. My friend casually asked around. A few shop owners and restaurateurs recalled an artist up there—some old guy with no name. Most people never even knew he existed."

"But you met him. He must have other fans."

"I met him because, like you, I was a snoop. We're two of a kind, Blake. Tell you the truth, I didn't even know his name until I looked at the paintings and found it scrolled illegibly in the right-hand corner. But you know all about that."

"This is cruel," Blake said.

"No, it's brilliant."

"But he was there every day. Someone must have seen him."

"No one even cared," Max said.

"And Alexandra went for this?"

"*Went* for it? She's gaga over it. Alexandra is a shrewd woman. She'll stop at nothing to make a few bucks. We're going to market the hell out of you. You might have to sleep with a few hungry art dealers and collectors along the way, but hey, that's a small price to pay for being one of the most eligible artists and bachelors in town."

"So you're making me your prisoner?"

"Now you're getting it. That's exactly right: a prisoner with perks. But I'll be a kind warden, I promise you that. After all, you belong to me now."

"You can't do this. I can report you."

"Report me?" Max guffawed. "To whom: the New York PD? Scotland Yard? And then what? They'll throw the book at you. You'll be guilty on so many counts that even Bruno Wilding and his team of experts won't be able to get you off. Let's face it, Blake: You're fucked."

Blake turned to the wine as a buffer. Together, they polished off the rest of the bottle while Max gloated like cock of the walk.

"I'd hate for Samantha and Madeleine to hear about this," Blake finally said.

"That's up to you. I'm not going to tell them, if that's what you're worried about. This will be our dirty little secret."

But secrets, dirty or otherwise, often can't be kept under wraps. What Blake was not prepared for was the worst blow he would have to deliver—this time to the one person he wanted least to hurt.

TWENTY-TWO

I am always looking for
a meaningful one-night stand.

—*Dudley Moore*

At four o'clock, a very rattled Blake Hamilton was back at my apartment.

"Well, was I right? It was all positive news, wasn't it?" I asked.

"Right as always, darling," Blake said, trying to appear normal.

"What did the rich and powerful Max Girard want, anyway? Did he twist your arm to sell him *Exotica*?"

"Not exactly."

Even though Blake was already quite sloshed, he made

himself a Scotch. Fortifying himself with more alcohol seemed the only way to get through the rest of the day.

"I'd say you're already pretty smashed," I said.

"Not really. Just a couple of glasses of wine. Max insisted on ordering a bottle."

"What *did* Max want?"

"The usual nitty-gritty that follows a big sale. He wanted to discuss *Galaxy.*"

"Oh?"

"He said the more he knows about the painting, the better he can intelligently impress others."

"That's a load of crap."

"I know, but now that he owns it, he feels he has personal dibs on me," Blake said.

"What did you tell him?" I kept probing.

"You sound like a goddamn detective."

"My, aren't you snarly. I once worked for a gallery, remember? Anyway, a painting is always open to interpretation."

Blake, realizing he was sporting an attitude, quickly got himself back in gear. "I gave Max the usual bullshit: that *Galaxy* represents the universe, blah, blah, blah—a world undiscovered yet waiting to be explored. It invites the viewers in to examine and contemplate, as though they themselves are transported through time and space by the use of abstract placement of colors and design. What do you have to say about *that*, my love?"

"You're right. It *is* bullshit," I said.

"Shall I tell you more? Because I can go on for hours. Or are your eyes glazed over?"

I wanted to change the subject. Blake was noticeably uncomfortable, and I figured the timing wasn't right for an in-depth discussion. "What I'd like is for you to shut up and make love to me. Take *me* through time and space to find that hidden place I long to explore."

"What hidden place?" Blake asked.

"My G-spot," I said.

. . .

After two hours of glorious lovemaking, we slept soundly in each other's arms until Blake's cell phone rang the next morning at eight o'clock.

"I'll call you back," he said through the hazy afterglow.

"Who was that?" I asked sleepily.

"Two guesses."

"Alexandra? Doesn't she ever leave you alone? It's Saturday, for God's sake."

"She gets off on talking about my paintings."

"You belong to *her* now," I said, stretching my arms, never realizing how close I had come to the truth.

"I probably should shower and get back to my apartment," Blake said. "I need to feed the dog. He's probably peed all over everything by now. You continue napping, my love. I'll call you later."

"Love 'em and leave 'em," I teased, grabbing him just as he was about to spring from the bed. "How about one more round?"

"My God, but you're insatiable."

"One taste of Blake Hamilton, and the ladies are begging for more," I said.

And with that, Blake, rock hard and always ready to oblige, gave me my afternoon delight. Then he showered and dressed while I drifted in and out of sleep. Just before he left, he kissed me gently on my forehead. "Talk later," he said.

On the way back to his apartment, Blake returned Alexandra's call.

"Sorry to have interrupted your little sexcapade," she said, "but we *must* talk."

"Is it important?"

"Darling, surely you jest. It's essential that we get together to work out, shall we say, some of the finite details. Can you meet me at my apartment at five?"

"This is all very unpleasant."

"I know, sweetie. I'm sure lunch with Max wasn't what you were expecting, but now that the cat's out of the bag, so to speak, let's all be grown-ups and make this as painless as possible. I see a very rosy future for you."

"You've quite possibly ruined my life," Blake said.

"Or just made it the most sensational life you could ever imagine."

"You and Max are sick."

"Come on, that's no way to talk about your sponsors. Why, sweetheart, your little peccadillo might very well be the best thing that ever happened to you—to us. You'll stop by? We have so much to discuss."

"What about Max?"

"I prefer having you to myself this afternoon—a quiet setting, the two of us."

"Alexandra, don't start pulling any of that sexual crap like you did the other night. You got me in enough trouble with Samantha."

"Are you telling me how to behave? Because the tables have turned, babe."

"You don't own me."

Alexandra let out a diabolic laugh. "Blake, you devil. We're going to have such fun together, you'll see."

Blake felt as if he had stepped into a B film noir where unexpected horrors lurked at every turn. "I have plans tonight, so it will have to be brief," he said.

"I promise. Just a quickie," Alexandra said with lust in her voice.

"I'm not kidding, Alexandra," Blake said.

Alexandra's apartment on Eighty-third and Fifth was as outrageous and eclectic as she was. Art objects and funky wall hangings abounded. Each room was painted a different color and ran the gamut from a gaudy Crayola pastel motif to soothing earth tones in the bedrooms. Major art hung on the walls, representing many different periods and styles. Alexandra's tastes reflected her many moods: where a small impressionistic painting might hang in one room, a piece of modern art would emerge from another.

"I'm a woman of many cravings," she liked to boast. "A good painting or sculpture, like a good man, comes in all varieties and shapes. I prefer keeping my walls well hung."

Blake, arriving on this late-January afternoon, found Alexandra dressed in her at-home ensemble: a paisley Betsey Johnson caftan that left little to the imagination. Blake wondered if she was even wearing underwear beneath the flouncy facade and prayed he would not have to find out.

"What are you drinking?" She led Blake over to the oak bar in her study.

"Just Pellegrino," he said.

"How boring. With lemon or lime?"

"Whatever."

"Why the long face, darling?" she asked.

"Come on, Alexandra, let's get down to it. I don't have all day."

"Ooh, you're such a grouch, but I completely understand. It's not every day your cover is blown. In fact, when Maxie shared it all with me, I was flabbergasted."

"I don't believe that a woman like you can ever be flabbergasted," Blake said.

"Come on, sweetie, you know better than that. I have a soft side, if you'd ever let me show you."

"Getting back to business . . ."

"Yes, well, let's sit here and talk." She offered Blake half the love seat while she settled in, allowing her caftan to reveal a shapely leg right up to the thigh. "I won't bore you with all the minutiae, since Max already summed it up for you. I want only to reassure you that as far as I'm concerned, your secret is safe with me—Bobby."

"Let's stick with Blake. It's the name I prefer."

"As do I. What I'm saying, Blake, is that I can be quite under-standing and empathic. I know exactly what you must be feeling, poor baby."

"Right."

"I also know that you've gotten yourself into quite a mess, and you could—should—by all rights be in serious doo-doo if it weren't for Max and me. Each of our agendas is completely different. He wants to humiliate and control you, while all I want to do is love and protect you."

"Give me a fucking break."

"Whoa, don't be so quick to negate what I'm saying. As Max must have told you, you're in no position to fight us. If you do, you might as well start digging your grave, because that's the end of Blake Hamilton as you know him."

"Are you threatening me, Alexandra?"

"Not threatening, darling: elucidating. I'm your staunch supporter, but now that your work isn't exactly yours, that changes the plotline just a bit."

"You've got it all figured out, don't you?"

"We're all three of us in this together, dear. Stop playing the victim. Once you give up that role, we can all work together, and life can be beautiful."

"For whom? My life is going down the toilet as we speak."

"You're so naive, so misguided, which is what I want to discuss with you. I want to lay out the blueprint, which, once explained and understood, might make you feel on the top of the world. As you're aware, Max Girard knows the entire universe. His name pushes buttons, and once those buttons are pushed, anything is possible. Having a man like Max behind you can take you beyond the rainbow. All of us can benefit if we play this right."

"Meaning?"

"Meaning"—Alexandra crossed one leg over the other so that her caftan opened wider—"we can take you to places you've never been."

"So Max tells me."

"I'll keep representing you. You'll have shows every two years, and we'll push you so hard, you'll be reeling. People will be clamoring to see your work—and buy it."

"And what happens when all the work is sold?"

"Sweetheart, not to worry. We have enough of Hamille's work—I mean Hamilton's collection—to carry us into the next millennium. By then, angel, you'll be so damn successful you can create a new style, have another epiphany."

"Yeah, those epiphanies are a dime a dozen."

"By that time you could paint a straight line across the canvas and sell it for a million bucks."

"Now, there's an idea."

"Don't laugh. You'll have the entire art world falling at your feet. They'll be sucking up to you and begging to kiss your cute little behind no matter what you paint. Look at de Kooning's fans. They drooled over him. So, are you ready to play hardball?"

"What exactly are the terms that you and Max have up your sleeves? Max mentioned a percentage for me from every sale."

"That's only fair. How does twenty percent sound?"

"Terrible. I deserve more."

"You deserve *nothing*," Alexandra said. "Twenty percent and not a penny more, but there are other perks that go along with this."

"Namely?"

"A nice allowance to carry you along. And a free apartment anytime you'd like it."

"What apartment?"

"Max and I thought that after your six-month stint in New York was over, you should maintain places in both London and New York. My apartment is up for grabs, and don't say no."

"Live with you?"

"Is that so terrible? I want you to know you'll always have a roof over your head, and I can make a lovely studio out of my guest room."

"I don't think so."

"I'm just putting it out there for you to consider. Strictly business. But we're not there yet."

"Samantha would never go for it."

"Who needs to tell her?"

"I'd never do that." Blake stood firm.

"Oh my God, you are so pussy-whipped. I love it."

"Shut up, okay?"

"Oh, and in exchange for my hospitality, I'm sure you won't mind if I use your London flat every now and then, when the mood strikes. Transatlantic real estate is so in."

Blake got up from the love seat and walked over to the window overlooking Central Park. He picked up a silver letter opener that sat on Alexandra's desk and studied it.

"If you're entertaining the notion of stabbing me, darling, forget about it. I need to be very much alive in order for this to work."

"Don't worry. I'm already in enough trouble," Blake said. "I don't need a murder rap pinned on me along with everything else."

"Now you're making sense, precious. Sit back down here and let me make you a drink. It's happy hour all over Manhattan, and I'm very happy."

"I told you, I need to go."

"Well, *I* need another drinkie-poo," she said. "There's more I want to tell you."

"Scotch on the rocks, and make it a short one."

Alexandra jumped up, her garment flying open. All she had on underneath was a thong. Blake's eyes went straight to her crotch.

"This can come off in a flash," she said. "Just give me the word and it's history."

"Just a drink will be fine for now," he said.

Blake stayed for another hour, getting slightly looped on Scotch but never laying a hand on Alexandra, who, try as she might, couldn't get him to succumb to her sexual wiles. He listened intently as she painted her own picture of what glorious days lay ahead for them all.

"As soon as your show is over at the gallery, Max will bring *Galaxy* home to his apartment and throw a little do in its honor—a soiree with the moneyed of Manhattan. In the meantime, I need to convince our dear Samantha to come back to the gallery."

"It won't happen. Samantha has had it."

"Is that what she said?"

"It's exactly what she said. You can't expect her to work for you after what you told her about me."

"Oh, for Christ's sake, the girl has to get a life. I was just about to give her a raise, too."

"She heard that one before."

"Does she tell you absolutely everything I say?"

"Just the lies," Blake said. "Samantha has too much pride and ethics to work for you."

"Now you're being cruel. I'm not really as bad as they say."

"Alexandra, you are, without question, the ballsiest broad I've ever met."

"That's part of my charm—and sex appeal. If you'd only let me show you."

"Give it up, Alexandra. It's not going to happen."

"Never say never, darling. Some of New York's most fastidious men will tell you I'm the best lay around. God, you make me horny."

"That's because you can't have me."

"Is this a form of foreplay? Because it's working. I'd give anything to have my legs wrapped around you right now."

Blake put down his drink and walked to the foyer. "I've really got to go."

"But we have so much more to discuss."

"It will have to wait. I have a dinner date."

"With Samantha."

"Not that it's any concern of yours, but yes."

"Try and convince her to return to the Cole. I'm not planning to hire anyone else, in case she changes her mind."

"You can start putting ads in the paper tomorrow," Blake said. "Samantha's gone."

"Oh dear, another divorce," Alexandra said. "At least I don't have to pay her alimony."

Blake opened the door while Alexandra stood there, her fingers running along the rim of her thong. "You're really missing out on one of life's greatest treasures," she said. "But, as with everything else, I'm willing to wait. You have a lot to digest, and I don't want to rush you." She reached her index finger inside her panties, then to her mouth, sucking it, slowly, deliberately. "Later, darling," she said.

"What is it, sweetheart? You seem so far away," I asked that evening over hamburgers at P. J. Clarke's, sensing that Blake was preoccupied.

"Just pensive," he said.

"No, that's not it. You're visibly distressed. Is it us?" I asked.

"Not exactly."

"So it *is* us."

The moment had presented itself for him to do what needed to be done. In a flash, he made the decision. "Samantha, I've been thinking."

"Uh-oh."

"Thinking about how crazy I am about you. So much so—and I know this is premature—but when Charlie returns from Europe and reclaims his apartment, I'd love to stay here in New York for a while so I can see you."

"Are you thinking of getting a pied-à-terre?"

"Even better. I'm hoping we can live together."

"Are you propositioning me?" I was totally unprepared.

"Yes, that's exactly what I'm doing. Would you consider it?"

"What about your London flat?"

"I'd keep that, and you can consider it yours, too."

"Blake, really? This is so unexpected."

"You know I'm unpredictable."

"Yes, but . . . wow."

"I'd still be in London a lot of the time. But when I'm in New York, I thought that maybe I could camp out here with you."

"That's cute. We can buy sleeping bags and canteens."

"Samantha, I love you. I want us to be together," he said with slight desperation.

"This is so sudden." I sounded like a script out of an old black-and-white movie. "I really have to think about it."

"Good. That's what I want you to do. As for me, I know what I want, and what I want is you. I can bring Charlie's dog over here, too."

"I don't do dogs."

"Just think about it," he said.

I felt that Blake was raging out of control. I needed to hit my emergency brake fast. My instincts were telling me that something was very wrong. Not that the idea of living with him was repugnant. But the timing was premature, mainly because he knew I wasn't ready to take such a big step.

The subject was dropped for the night. We returned to my apartment, where Blake awakened several times during the night. The next morning I wanted to talk.

"I've been up all night thinking," I said.

Blake, barely awake, shaded his eyes with his hand. "What's up?"

"I've been mulling over this whole living-together thing," I said. "I want you to feel free to stay here when you're in New York, but let's not make it official."

"Official?"

"You know, engaged or anything formal like that."

"So, what you're saying is I can be your roommate?"

"Roommate with privileges."

"Isn't *that* romantic," he said sarcastically.

"We'll have to discuss the finances—the rent, electricity, all the mundane aspects."

"My God, Samantha. I really *am* a roommate. Maybe we should forget the whole idea."

"Maybe you need to understand that you're moving too quickly."

"I thought you were happy that I'm in New York."

"I am, but let's not rush things. This is the time to get to know each other."

"That's what I'm proposing: living together under one roof so we can get to know each other before we decide to move ahead."

"Move ahead?"

"To the next level," he said.

"I'm not sure I'm into the whole living-together scene," I said, feeling extremely uncomfortable with the conversation.

"What *are* you into?"

"I don't know, exactly. Marriage, I guess, when the time is right."

"I'm with you on that," Blake readily agreed.

"You are?"

"Yes, but I would never get married unless I lived with a woman first."

"We're not on the same page with this one. I have a different take. I've seen too many couples split up after living together. It's pure fantasy and has nothing to do with real life. It's an adult version of playing house."

"Since when have you become so fifties?"

"Whoa, there. Is that an insult?"

"Let's just forget it. This is ridiculous."

"Yes, forget it: I think that's a great idea," I said.

"Maybe I should go back to my apartment."

"Whatever."

"Is that what you want?"

"Stop manipulating, Blake. You're acting like a spoiled child who has a temper tantrum the minute he doesn't get his way."

"When did you get so high and mighty?"

"You're acting like an ass."

"You know, I think I *will* leave."

"Fine, if that's what you want," I said, wishing he would do exactly that.

"I don't want. I'm just feeling confused and out of sorts."

"Why? Everything was going along great with us until you decided to drop a bomb."

"Loving you and wanting to be with you is dropping a bomb?"

"It feels like a bomb. You sound angry."

"Good God, I do believe we're having our first fight," Blake said.

"I believe you're right. I hate it."

"So do I."

"Why don't we stop talking? I'll make us breakfast, and we can start all over again. Pretend this conversation never happened."

"That's what I love about you, Samantha: your wonderful sense of denial."

"Not denial. Switching gears until we're better equipped to handle all this." I had reached my saturation point and hoped he would stop. But, he was on a roll and wouldn't quit.

"Handle all this what?" Blake asked.

"Oh, no, I refuse to go there," I said. "I'm fed up with all this jockeying back and forth. Can we please change the subject?"

"Will you at least think about it?"

"How long are you planning to be in New York?" I sounded calculating even to myself.

"I don't know. It all depends."

"On what?"

"On how well I'm doing here with my work and all. Max Girard wants to make me his new project. Push me hard and introduce me to his friends."

"Really? That's not a bad thing. Max Girard knows a lot of people."

"So I hear."

"If he thinks you're hot, he can make you even hotter. That's actually good news. Alexandra will want to get in on the act. She'll take all the credit for having discovered you."

"Speaking of Alexandra—last I heard, she wants you back at the gallery. Says she can't live without you."

"Yeah, right. Is that what she told you?" I was amazed. It was so unlike Alexandra. Wanting me back was the supreme form of groveling. In some strange way, I felt flattered, though I would never entertain the idea.

"She told me she's not planning on hiring anyone new. It's you she wants. She even mentioned that raise."

"Why is she telling *you* this?" I asked, my suspicions raised once again.

"She's a blabbermouth, you know that. And she thinks I might convince you to come back."

"I'm not doing it, Blake. The less I see of Alexandra, the better off I'll be. How can you expect me to go back there after all that's happened? After the lies she spread about you and her?"

"Alexandra is . . . Alexandra. She'll never change. But you had a good job and liked it."

"Not that much. I liked it when she wasn't around. Since she returned from Europe, it's been a living hell. No, thanks, I'll look for other work—maybe another gallery. I'll find something."

"Just think about it. I'm going back to my apartment. I'll call you later," he said, throwing on his clothes and leaving me to wade through the emotional mess that his crazy antics had ignited.

A sense of uneasiness began creeping in. Blake was no longer amusingly enigmatic but was downright weird, as though covering up something. I began wondering what. His need for reassurance was of large proportion and weighed heavily on my mind. That, coupled with an abnormal need to interrogate me, seemed so out of character. "For God's sake, Blake," I had snapped over dinner at Le Boeuf à la Mode the other night. He continuously reached over with his fork to retrieve food from my plate, a romantic, playful gesture under normal circumstances, but it now seemed irritating and more of a vehicle to grab my attention—as though his desire was to consume something more than food: me.

"Stop it," I had urged when he pierced my chocolate soufflé as soon as it was placed before me. "You've got your own."

"But yours is so much tastier," he had countered, trying to sound adorably spirited as he ran a stream of chocolate across his tongue.

As the days went on, I found his behavior more offensive than charming.

· · ·

Needing a temporary fix, I once again turned to Aurora, who I thought might be able to shed light on the latest turn of events. Out came the bottle of Windex. She gave her crystal ball a spritz and sat down in her chintz-covered chair. Her recent acquisition, a blue-eyed parrot named Paul Newman, mumbled away in the background. If the bird could actually talk, he'd have some tales to tell.

She stared at the ball long and hard. "Oh my God."

"What? Is it bad?" I asked.

"I never do bad," Aurora said. "All I'll say is it's looking foggy."

"What's foggy?"

"Your future."

"I have a foggy future?"

"I see clouds. I see precipitation, and the static is so electric, I'm getting a buzz."

"What about your toe? Is it tingling?"

"Not yet, but I am experiencing some numbness in my left leg."

"Is that a sign?"

"It's probably nothing. Just mild sciatica, but I do sense turmoil. Has something in your life changed since I last saw you?"

"Yes, I left my job, and my boyfriend wants to live with me."

Aurora pushed her ball aside. "Really? *That's* good news. I can't even meet men, and here you have a guy who wants to move in."

"That wasn't exactly part of my plans."

Aurora studied the ball further. "Hmm."

"What?" I leaned across the table. "I don't see anything."

"It's not for you to see. I'm the psychic, remember? You don't have the same karma that I have."

"Sorry, I didn't mean to infringe on your space."

Aurora toyed with her crystals and rubbed her large turquoise ring. "Samantha, there's trouble brewing. I can feel it."

"Your tingling toe?"

"No, my nipples."

"Your nipples tingle?"

"They itch."

"Really?"

"Yes, another telltale sign for sure."

"Maybe you need to see a doctor."

"I don't need a doctor. What I'm saying is that when my nipples itch, it means there's carnal confusion. My crystal ball is getting congested. There are several images all interfering with one another. Samantha, I'd be very careful if I were you."

"I know. That's why I don't want to rush into anything too fast."

"Like the boyfriend?"

"Yes. He's coming on very strong, almost out of desperation."

"You don't need a clingy man to contend with."

"What do you suggest I do?"

"I never tell my clients what to do. I simply tell them what I see, then let them take that information and assimilate it."

"What about my job? My boss wants me back."

Aurora scratched her breasts. "Emphatically no. Your boss is trouble."

"I'll say she is. You're so perceptive."

"And one more thing—I'm getting another vibe."

"Your nipples again?"

"Yes. What you think to be one thing might very well turn out to be another."

"What does *that* mean?"

"I don't interpret," Aurora said. "I go by my ball's aura, and at this moment it's very hazy."

"Maybe it needs more Windex," I said.

In some strange and inexplicable way, Aurora had made me feel better. As silly as it sounded, if her crystal ball was showing interference, who was I to argue? I would put Blake off until I felt the time was right to discuss his moving in or not. The beauty of our relationship was enhanced by the fact that he had his own digs. It gave us both the separation we needed until the answers became clearer.

Perhaps in a few months Aurora's tingling toe and itchy nipples would be more forthcoming.

I decided to take it slow, be kinder to Blake, but not allow him to push me in any direction I didn't want to go. As for Spencer, he had called, asking me to dinner. Our friendship was back on track; he had let me off the hook for reporting to him what Alexandra had said. We met at Varietal on Wednesday.

"That bitch really had me going," I said. "I'm sorry. I should have known better than to believe a word she said or pass it on to you. I was only trying to protect you."

"I know you meant well," Spencer said. "You did exactly what Alexandra hoped you would. That woman could destroy an entire country if given the power and control."

"Which is why I quit my job," I said.

"Good for you. Now what?"

"I'm not sure. I'll take some time off and put out feelers."

"Roger has connections," Spencer said, "having been with the Museum of Fine Arts for so many years. He knows tons of gallery owners in New York and a few curators. He'd be happy to help."

"Thanks. That would be great. But I think I need a month or so to decompress."

"How's the boyfriend?" Spencer asked.

"Getting pushy," I confided. "He's talking about moving in."

"I thought he was already committed to another apartment."

"He is, but after the six months are over, he's thinking about staying in New York for a while. Max Girard is wooing the hell out of him. Sees real talent in Blake and wants to lead him toward the path of success."

"Nothing to sneeze at."

"That's what I told Blake, but in the meantime, he's latched on to me big-time. Enough of that. What happened between you and Roger?"

"We drove up to Lenox last weekend. I met his business manager, Avery Fox."

"The one Alexandra accused Roger of schtupping?"

"Yes, but it's not happening. Avery, though nice enough, is hardly Roger's type. He's much too California beach boy for Roger's tastes."

"So it's return to paradise?"

"Things couldn't be better. All of my concerns were unwarranted. Roger is coming down next weekend. Maybe the four of us can do dinner."

"If Blake is even talking to me. We had a fight—or rather, a heated discussion."

"Over his moving in?"

"You got it. I tried putting him off, but he kept on pushing. I told him he could stay with me when he's in town. But he seems out of sorts these past few days. Something feels wrong."

"Did you ask him?"

"Of course. He denied it. Maybe it's PMS." I laughed.

"Or male-menopause hysteria. Haven't you heard? It's going around."

"Spencer," I said, "you always manage to cheer me up."

"Dr. Gould, at your service," he said, giving me a bite of his sweet-pea flan with asparagus and shiitake mushrooms.

"I believe I just died and went to heaven," I said, tasting the magnificent appetizer.

"You're so easy," Spencer said, handing over another forkful.

Around ten o'clock that night, Blake called. "I need to come over. We need to talk."

"Please, Blake, if it's about the moving in, I'm not in the mood. We've exhausted that subject for the time being."

"It's not. It's something else, and it's important."

"Fine." I was less than enthusiastic. "If it's that crucial."

A half hour later, he arrived, looking nervous and tired.

"You look beat," I said.

"I haven't been sleeping well."

"Me, neither," I said.

We sat on the couch, separated by a row of pillows.

"Samantha, this isn't going to be easy."

I was caught off guard. "What's wrong?" My concern was genuine.

"I'm going to ask you to really listen and try hard to understand what I'm going to say. I want to transport us back six years. What were you doing then?"

"I thought this was about you."

"Just bear with me, please."

"I don't know. I was thirty-three, divorced for a year, and still trying to find myself. My father had died, and I missed him terribly. I was grappling with career decisions and looking for Mr. Right, who I was convinced didn't exist. Sounds banal, I know. New York was filled with eager hopefuls just like me, scouting the clubs and bars, hoping to find the answer to their dreams over Bellinis or sashimi at tony restaurants that attracted Manhattan's finest singles sets. I kept reminding myself to be careful, lest I turn into a cynic before forty. Where the hell are you going with this, Blake?"

"I want to focus you on the fact that back then we were all unsure about our futures. We were immature and scared, which made us do wild, crazy things."

"What kind of wild, crazy things?"

"Just let me talk, okay?"

"You've got the floor," I said, getting up and going over to the shelf for a bottle of Courvoisier. I poured the brandy into two glasses, offering one to Blake. He accepted it eagerly.

"I'd like to tell you a story, Samantha. A story about a boy named Bobby Hamille who lived far away, across the ocean. He was thirty-four, in Paris for the summer, and enjoyed roaming the streets of the city."

"Sounds lovely," I said.

"One day he came upon the Passage des Panoramas, situated in the boulevard Montmartre in a hundred-and-ninety-year-old mall that today is still a haven for window-shoppers and tourists."

"I know the place. Very historic."

"As you enter this lighted tunnel, without warning, the sidewalk suddenly becomes tiles, flanked by pots of lush plants. Looking up, you can see a skylight that filters natural light through a pebbled-glass facade. Shops and restaurants line the passageway, making a casual stroll a most pleasant way to pass an afternoon."

"I visited there years ago," I said.

"Above the shops on the second level, deserted spaces are barely visible and have long ago been abandoned. One steamy July afternoon in 1999, a man named Bobby Tisdale began to explore and, climbing up the winding stairs, came upon a most interesting sight: an old abandoned artist's garret."

Blake took a sip of the brandy while I sat back. "Go on," I said, my interest piqued.

"Bobby was in his element. He was in Paris for two months working as an artist's assistant, and during his free time, he was a tourist in the City of Lights. On this particular afternoon, the afternoon sun poured through a dusty skylight and cast its rays on a broken wood easel, where large framed and rolled paintings were propped up against the peeling, paint-stained walls."

"You seem to know it so well. As though you've been there many times."

Blake continued, caught up in his reverie, as though reliving that time. "Bobby was curious. Few bothered going up there anymore, enabling him to trespass to his heart's content without worry of being discovered. Moving farther into the room, he was at first drawn to an old painter's palette encrusted in a rainbow of colors that had been there for so long they were covered in mold, resembling chunks of blue cheese. Bobby gingerly poked at a blob of paint that felt cold and hard. He pulled his finger away as though he had just touched a dead animal."

"Is there a point to all of this?" I asked.

"Please, I need to tell this my way. The paintings intrigued him. He was taken in by their brilliant colors and their cutting-edge images. Whose were they? How long had they been here? He was curious. Moving toward the corner, he broke through a spiderweb, finding still more paintings. Most of them were intact, though as dusty as the room. Bobby removed a handkerchief from his pocket and gently wiped a canvas. A spray of dust particles entered his nostrils. He covered his face with the white cloth as he moved from one painting to another."

"You have amazing recall. How can you remember all these details, Blake? I'm impressed."

Blake was going strong. "Suddenly, Bobby heard a noise. The sound of heavy construction boots weighed down the wobbly stairs. Creaks abounded, and a deep voice, questioning and foreboding, searched out the uninvited guest. Bobby stood still as a large man stomped in, spewing out French phrases that Bobby could barely understand. He said nothing as the man approached, and then, as a big smile appeared across the stranger's face, Bobby relaxed and smiled back.

" 'Who are you?' the man asked, his French punctuated by fractured English.

" 'Bobby Tisdale,' came the reply.

" 'Where are you from?' the man asked.

" 'Liverpool, and in Paris for the summer.'

"The man introduced himself: 'I'm Rene Bateau.' He looked to be around fifty and spoke enough English to manage interrogating Bobby. Discovering that he was a student, Bateau became interested and sat down on an old orange crate to talk."

"Who was this man?" I asked.

"Rene Bateau, the watchman," Blake said. "He was paid to keep an eye on the Passage des Panoramas. After his wife died, he became more interested in 'the grape' than in overseeing the Passage. Regulars who knew him often slipped him money, which Bateau used to buy whiskey. By two o'clock in the afternoon, he was already feeling no pain."

"Whose garret was this?" My curiosity was building.

"This garret once belonged to an old artist named Hamille, who came there every day to paint—a man well into his eighties without friends or family, he paid the landlord with paintings, but that had been years ago. After the landlord died, the artist stayed on, and nobody said a word. He was a hermit, and except for Bateau, who checked in on him daily, he spoke to no one and lived a life of self-inflicted loneliness. He arrived at eight every morning and probably had no home, since he often slept on the floor of this little studio along with the pigeons that flew in from the broken skylight. As for the paintings, no one ever claimed them. They lay there abandoned or rested in large rolls like discarded rugs. 'When these rooms are torn apart for renovation, the paintings will go with them,' Bateau explained. 'In the meantime, they lay there to rot.' "

"Why is this story so important, and why are you telling me?" I asked.

"I'm getting there," Blake said. "Just be patient."

"Bateau offered Bobby a cigarette, which he readily accepted, though he didn't smoke. He held it between his fingers, regarding it as a welcoming gesture from Bateau, who engaged the boy in conversation for a while.

" 'So, you're a painter?' Bateau asked.

"Bobby laughed. 'Working on it. It's a shame that these paintings might be destroyed.'

" 'No one wanted them,' Bateau said. 'Aside from the frames, they're worth nothing and are simply the eccentric visions of an old man who lived a sad and meaningless life. Never even sold any of his work. He died two years ago.'

" 'I'll take them,' Bobby said in a moment of impulsive bravado.

"Bateau chuckled. 'Oh you will?' His pained attempt at speaking English caused drops of saliva to form around his lips. 'What the hell are you going to do with them?'

" 'I can use the canvases,' Bobby said.

"Bateau looked him up and down and shook his head. 'Take them, then.'

" 'How much for the lot?'

"Bateau let out a hearty laugh. 'I should be paying you to get them off my hands, but tell you what: You provide the transportation, and I'll help you load these into your truck. You're doing me a big favor, sonny.'

"Bobby thanked him and said he'd be back the next morning with a truck. They shook hands. Bateau pulled a small bottle of cheap gin from a paper bag in his hip pocket. 'Here, don't be shy. Have a swig before you go.' He handed Bobby the bottle.

"Not wanting to appear unfriendly, Bobby wiped the top of the bottle with his shirtsleeve and drank. The gin felt warm to his throat, though its aftereffect, slightly abrasive, made him cough.

" 'That's it, sonny, smokes and drink—that's all you need to get through the day.' "

I glanced at my watch. "And then what happened?" I stifled a yawn.

"The following morning Bobby rented a pickup truck. By noon he had retrieved all the paintings, along with the frames, most of them put together with scraps of wood except for one extravagant gold one. Rene Bateau assisted him as passersby stared momentarily and then moved on. The entire move took under two hours. Bobby depleted the entire studio, leaving with at least two hundred rolled paintings and fifty stretched canvases, the culmination of the poor artist's life's work."

"So Bobby took them all?" I asked.

Blake stopped talking. His eyes welled up.

"Blake, darling, what is it?" I reached over to him. "What's wrong?"

"Everything," Blake said.

"Tell me, please, I want to know."

"I can't. You'll never understand."

"Try me," I said, putting my arm around Blake's shoulder.

"I'm . . . I'm . . . I was . . . I am that artist, Samantha."

"What artist? What are you talking about?"

Blake cupped his hands over his face, trying to conceal himself from me.

"I don't understand. I'm sorry, Blake. I'm just not getting this."

Blake gripped my hand tightly. "I'm that artist who found those paintings—the one who removed them from the artist's studio."

"I thought you said Bobby Hamille took them."

"Sam, I . . . I am Bobby Hamille."

"What?"

"But it doesn't stop there. It gets much worse. I assumed an alias. I became the artist."

"Whatever are you saying?"

"I became him."

"Him who?"

"The artist. I took on the name Hamille—or Hamilton."

I sat back, stunned, as though Blake had splashed cold water over me.

"His paintings were signed, and I changed the name."

"What happened to them?" I asked.

"I'm showing them, Samantha."

"Oh my God, Blake, you mean those paintings at the Cole aren't yours?"

"No." His sobs became deeper. "They're Hamille's."

"Who else knows about this?"

"Max, for one. He's the one who found me out."

"How?"

"Max had visited that same studio years ago and stumbled upon Hamille's work. His canvases impressed him as much as they did me."

"I can't believe this."

"I know, but it's true, every ugly word of it."

"What about Alexandra?"

"Yes, she knows now, too. We're all in this together, and if I don't go along with their grand charade, they'll ruin me."

"You mean blackmail you." I took a long sip of the brandy and stared. "This is all so horrible, so incomprehensible. But why? You're a talented artist in your own right. You didn't need to assume a different persona. You were on your way. You were making it big in London. You said yourself that Stripley Hughes loved your work."

"It's a competitive world out there, Samantha. When I saw Hamille's work, I knew I had fallen upon genius. These paintings were different from anything I had ever seen. Hamille had a style all his own, so unique. I was awed. I knew he needed to be discovered, brought to life, if you will."

"So you were the one who was going to do it for him."

"It's crazy, I know, but yes. I figured that *his* life was over. He was a nobody, and I was an up-and-coming artist and could bring him to the forefront."

"You mean bring yourself to the forefront. Claim his fame without doing the work. That's disgusting, Blake."

"That's the worst part, Sam. That I lied to you."

"Oh, stop it, Blake, you're not upset about that. You're just sorry you got caught. If you hadn't, you never would have told me the truth."

"I wanted to. I swear it."

"But you didn't."

"I was scared. I knew you'd go ballistic."

"You got that right," I said. "Now what?"

"My life . . . it's over."

"Hardly. You're being touted all over the place. You're goddamn lucky that Max didn't report you."

"He still could."

"Don't be ridiculous. Max is a businessman. He knows a good thing when he sees it. He's probably deliriously happy that you've been exposed. He's going to milk this for all it's worth—capitalize on your fame and fortune. As for Alexandra, she'll milk it, too, for all *you're* worth. They must be having a field day. Just tell me: What's in it for you? I'm sure Max discussed that over lunch."

"If I don't go along with their plan, it will be all over for me."

"What do you get out of this, Blake? Or should I be calling you Hamille?"

"Samantha, please . . . don't you start. I need you to try and understand. I was weak, disillusioned."

"I don't understand—not a bit. I'm devastated, Blake. I really am."

"So am I—mostly about you. I told Max not to tell you, but I couldn't lie to you any longer."

"Oh, shut up. I can't stand your crocodile tears." I began trembling. I refilled my brandy glass and paced around my living room. "I want you to leave now, Blake. I need time to assimilate all of this."

"Can't you please find it in your heart to forgive me? Samantha, please—"

"I don't know. But I can tell you this: I will never trust you again."

"Don't say that." Blake wept.

"Please go."

And with that, Blake Hamilton, aka Bobby Hamille, put down his glass of brandy and left without saying another word.

TWENTY-THREE

Getting married for sex is like
buying a 747 for the free peanuts.

—Jeff Foxworthy

The next week a January snowstorm blanketed New York in silence. It was as though the city had stopped moving and come to a standstill, alleviating some of my internal demons. Blake had sucked the lifeblood out of me, and I was numb. He left numerous phone messages and e-mails, but I wouldn't respond. Finally, I picked up the phone and put him off with the excuse that I was busy looking for another job and was recovering from a bad flu. On Monday he appeared at my door with chicken soup from Zabar's. "Consider this forced entry," he said. "Chicken soup—guaranteed to cure whatever ails you."

I was taken by surprise and was not exactly thrilled, especially since I had made it clear that I needed time to think, and maybe it was best if we took a breather. I feigned a deep cough and told him I still had a fever.

"Okay," he said, "I can take a hint. I'll call you later."

"Later" always meant several more times a day. He was bordering on relationship stalking, a term I had made up to fit the occasion. I had confided in Lily Ann about how needy Blake had become. But I never told her the whole story. In some inexplicable way, I still wanted to protect Blake.

She said, "Sounds like you both need a time-out. He must be going nuts, though, especially since he came to New York primarily to be with you."

"No, Blake came to New York for Blake and the Cole Gallery," I said.

"What's happening with that, anyway?" Lily Ann asked.

"I've decided not to go back. Alexandra called me and even begged, in her way. She asked if I was still holding a grudge. 'This goes way beyond grudges,' I told her."

"She might have finally given you that raise."

"Yes, she said that if I returned, she would make it worth my while."

"That's tempting."

"She couldn't pay me enough. My days at the Cole are over."

"It's not easy finding employment."

"Bennett did."

"Yes, but he had an in with the publishing house. Even then they gave him the runaround for a while. He's damn lucky. He's leaving California for good and will be back in New York in a month."

"You see? Life works out for some of us."

"You sound so glum, Sam," Lily Ann said.

"That's why I need a job. The sooner, the better. Spencer said that Roger Sutton has major connections with the art gurus."

"How *is* dear Spencer?"

"Madly in love with Roger. For a while he was worried, but that matter was cleared up."

"And we heterosexuals think we have it rough," Lily Ann said. "I guess we all have our problems."

"Except for my cousin Celeste. Last I heard, she and Eddie Sloat were inseparable."

"Eddie the greasy Italian I met at Blake's opening?"

"Yes. Apparently, he popped Celeste's cherry, and now she feels indebted to him."

"Nothing like a fabulous fuck to put a gal back on track. I can't believe she was still a virgin."

"Celeste, shall we say, was a bit sexually retarded. But look at her now: new boobs, a nose job, and a tummy tuck. At Eddie's request, she even bleached her hair blond. The guy is crazy about her. Took her to Las Vegas last weekend, where she made a killing on the slot machines. She's thinking of leaving Sarah Lawrence and marrying him. Between Celeste and the lesbian daughter, Fern, Elaine and Phil are ready to commit double suicide."

"At least you got her off *your* back, and Blake's, though I'm sure she'd still jump Blake's bones, first chance she got," Lily Ann said.

"What a combo that would make," I said, loving the whole perverse idea of Blake and Celeste going through life together. That would definitely be his ultimate comeuppance. I chuckled at the thought.

And then the biggest bomb of all was dropped. Late Thursday afternoon, I received a frantic call from Gilda. She was crying hysterically, assuring me in between sobs that my mother was fine.

"*Who* isn't fine, Gilda?" I asked. "Just calm down and tell me."

"It's the doctor."

"What doctor?"

"Dr. Gould."

"The father or the son?" I waited frantically.

"Dr. Alden. He's had a heart attack."

"Is he alive?"

"We don't know."

"Where is he?"

"At the hospital."

"The one he works at?"

"Yes."

"All right, calm down, Gilda. Where is my mother?"

"Mrs. Krasner-Wolfe is on her way over there. Dr. Spencer called her."

"When did this happen?"

"Dr. Alden was at the office, complained of chest pains and dropped. That's the whole story."

I envisioned a patient on the table with a speculum still in her vagina. "I'm going to go over to the hospital," I said.

"They're in the emergency room. At least that's what Mrs. Krasner-Wolfe told me. Oh dear, the poor man. I liked him so much."

"He's not dead yet, Gilda."

"We don't know that," she said, going off on another tangent of tears.

I dropped everything and tried my mother's cell—she wasn't answering. I quickly threw on a coat, and within minutes, I was in a taxi en route to New York Presbyterian Hospital. I called Spencer on the way. He picked up on the first ring.

"Samantha."

"Gilda called me. Where are you?"

"Samantha."

"Yes?"

"Dad just died."

"What?"

"He suffered a massive heart attack. He died in the ambulance on the way to the hospital. We're in the emergency room."

"Oh my God, Spencer. I'm on my way. Should be there in a few minutes. I'm so sorry. Is my mother with you?"

"Yes. As soon as she heard the news, she lost it. She taxied over to the hospital, where she's being sedated."

My mind raced furiously. Alden Gould hadn't smoked a cigarette in all of his seventy-five years. He exercised regularly and seemed to be in perfect health. As for my mother, she had lost two husbands, and now, on the heels of mourning the loss of Grayson, Alden was gone. Five minutes later, I was in the emergency room cubicle, where Madeleine was spread out on a gurney with Spencer by her side. I hugged him and turned to Madeleine, who was consciously sedated but noticeably upset.

"This was all so sudden," Spencer said. "Dad was examining a patient. The next thing I knew, I heard a scream, walked into the examining room, and found him on the floor."

Spencer seemed relatively controlled under the circumstances. We stayed at the hospital until well into the evening, Spencer signing papers and making arrangements for the body to be kept in the morgue until funeral arrangements were finalized. Being on staff allowed him to push through the red tape and move the process along quickly. Word spread quickly. Members of the hospital staff, upon learning the news, came down to the emergency room to offer their condolences. Nurses who had worked with Alden in the OR broke down, asking if they could help in any way.

I stayed with my mother, who, after an IV Valium drip, was calmer than I had seen her in years. Her mellowness was a nice change. Perhaps she should come in at regular intervals and be hooked up, I thought.

"Spencer, can I bring you anything to eat? Something to drink?" I asked.

"I'm fine. I need to take care of all the details, and then we'll see. I'm concerned about Madeleine. She's taking this very badly."

"I know. She adored your father."

"This must be opening up some old wounds," he said. "She's been through a lot this past year."

Spencer left the room and phoned Roger. He relayed the news, and Roger said he was leaving Lenox and would be in the city in a few hours.

"Should I come directly to the hospital?" he asked.

"Call me when you get nearer to Manhattan, and I'll let you know. In the meantime, Madeleine and Samantha are with me."

By eleven o'clock, the nurse recommended that we all leave to get a bite to eat.

Madeleine, still slightly sedated, moved in and out of uncontrollable grief. "And to think: Alden had made reservations at Daniel for eight," she said.

I elbowed her in the ribs.

"I was just saying—"

"Please, Mother, this isn't the time to talk about restaurants."

"Each of us handles grief in our own way, darling," she said.

Roger made great time and met us at Madeleine's apartment, where Gilda whipped up her special cheddar-cheese-and-scrambled-egg concoction for us all. I cracked open two bottles of red wine.

"Who is Roger Sutton, and why is he here?" my mother took me aside and whispered.

"He's a good friend of Spencer's," I said.

"He looks a little light in the loafers."

"There you go, Mother, making judgments. Spencer wanted him here. He needs all the support he can get."

"Something smells rotten to me," she said.

After our supper, we lingered for a while, going over the events of the past several hours until around one A.M., when Madeleine suggested that Spencer spend the night at her place.

"Gilda can make up the guest room, dear," she said.

"Thank you. That's very kind, but I'd feel better being at home tonight. Roger will stay with me."

Madeleine shot me a look.

"We'll talk in the morning," Spencer said. "I think it's best that we try and get some sleep."

He and Roger left.

"As I said, I'm picking up vibes," Madeleine said.

"Enough with your vibes, Mother."

"Samantha, I'd like you to stay here tonight. Would you mind?"

"Of course. I'd be happy to. You shouldn't be alone." It was the least I could do.

"That seems to be my plight, darling. All the men I've ever loved seem to die on me."

"Mere coincidence," I said.

"And to think: Alden's erections were just starting to get really good," she said.

The next morning, even though I was still furious with Blake, I phoned to tell him the terrible news. That was the least I could do.

"You should have called me last night. I could have been with you."

"It was all happening so fast. I was with my mother and Spencer at the hospital until very late."

"All the more reason to have me there. I feel out of the loop."

"Let's not make this about you," I said. "I just wanted you to know. The funeral will be sometime this week."

"Samantha, I miss you. This is ridiculous. Why can't I see you?"

"I told you: I need some time to think. Right now I have Spencer to deal with. This was quite a blow, so sudden and unexpected."

"Was Alden Gould ill?"

"No, he was perfectly healthy, and then boom: gone. No warning. He just keeled over."

"Where was he?"

"In his office."

"Please pass along my condolences to Spencer, and let me know when the funeral will be."

"I will, I promise."

"If you see your way clear, Samantha, give me a call, and we'll work in a lunch."

"No time for lunches right now," I said, realizing how brutally cold I sounded.

"Samantha, I know you have every reason to hate me."

"I really can't do this right now."

"I'll call you," he said.

"No, *I'll* call *you*," I told him, hanging up.

The next week flew by as Dr. Alden Gould was laid to rest at Frank E. Campbell on Madison Avenue. Flowers studded the room as though this were a wedding instead of a funeral. Duncan, the flower maven, would have had an orgasm. Throngs of people turned out, most of them from the medical profession, saying their last good-byes through eulogies and other expressions of grief. Blake, a study in black, stood by my side like a faithful puppy.

Spencer was magnificent: resolute and strong at both the funeral and the lunch following, where, in true WASP fashion, he remained the perfect host, serving up an array of goyisha delicacies. This was a far cry from Jews, who had grand shivas with fish spreads and bagel varietals. The goyim, less concerned with food, zeroed in on the booze and delicate tea sandwiches, which went down more smoothly than oily white fish with bulging eyes and pickled herrings in cream sauce, smothered in onions. Madeleine, not exactly a widow but a significant player nonetheless, acted out her role as "very significant other" as though she were up for an Academy Award.

"We had even talked about marriage," she announced to all who were interested or would listen. "And now my darling Alden is gone." This set her off on a tirade of tears as though she were playing a part in some melodrama with a very unhappy ending.

"Mother, no one cares." I took her aside. "Let's not add to the already somber scene."

"Samantha, you have no idea what you're talking about. You never lost a husband."

"What about Daddy?"

"When you lose a spouse, that's entirely different." Madeleine poured more wine into her glass. "Between you and me, sweetheart"—she regained her composure—"I think the coffin that Spencer chose is too ornate. The Jews prefer understated pine boxes—sweet and simple. What the goys lack in food preparation, they make up for in death. Have you noticed they take death very seriously? The hereafter and all. It's quite comforting. When a Jew dies, that's it: finito, so long and, in some cases, good riddance. With the goys, it's: see ya later."

Roger Sutton stayed for a while and then left to go back to Lenox. He and Spencer said their good-byes. Later Spencer told me:

"I'm thinking of getting away for a couple of weeks after Avery Fox returns from his vacation." he said. "Roger and I might fly to Italy and drive down the Amalfi coast."

"Sounds like the perfect remedy," I said.

"I'm also thinking of bringing in a new partner. Dad and I had talked about it, and now I think it's a no-brainer. With Dad gone, I can't handle the patient load alone." Spencer became teary.

"Anyone specific in mind?"

"I've interviewed a few people and found someone who's extremely competent. He did his residency at Mass General and has credentials up the kazoo. His name is David Samuels. He's from the Boston area, went to Harvard undergrad and Tufts Medical. He's brilliant and personable and interested in partnering with me."

I wanted to ask if he was also gay, but unlike my mother, who got right to it, I was more diplomatic in my approach. "Is he married?"

"No, he's a bachelor and definitely heterosexual. He told me he dates a lot, but so far, no one special. That means he can devote more time to the practice."

"Sounds perfect," I said, the wheels turning. As soon as Madeleine discovered this nugget of information, she'd be off and running with the tick-tocks.

Blake walked over and expressed his sadness, sounding right out of the Bereavement Book of Good Etiquette. "I'm so sorry for your loss, but I am glad I met your father," he told Spencer. "He was obviously a dearly loved man who will be sorely missed. If there is anything I can do, please let me know."

"Thank you," Spencer said. "That's so kind."

"I, too, lost my father years ago. I know firsthand what it feels like."

"My condolences."

"Yes, it's never easy," Blake said, "but time does lessen the pain."

"I'll remember that," Spencer said, shifting his feet and clearly wishing Blake would cool it with the bereavement pitch.

I wanted to puke.

The weeks went by, and slowly, we hardened ourselves to Alden's death, but the sadness lingered on. My mother fell back into a state of mourning, constantly bringing up not only Alden's name but also that of my father, Henry, and Grayson Wolfe.

"I'm destined to face my old age with no one by my side," she repeated over and over again.

"Mother, you're hardly old, and who knows what the future will bring? Bachelor degree, remember? It's part of your lifetime ambition."

"It's so discouraging, Samantha, when they all drop like flies at my feet."

And off she went into a diatribe about how all the men she ever loved had abandoned her.

To add to the gloom, Blake kept calling, and I kept rejecting.

"I'm not ready to see you," I said. "When I said I needed time to think, I wasn't kidding."

In the meantime, Blake became the permanent property of Max and Alexandra, who treated him grandly as long as he played it their way. Often Alexandra invited him to dinner, and dare he decline, she reminded him that being evasive and coy was no longer an option.

"It's just dinner," she said. "A chance to go over business and talk about the little brunch Max wants to throw in your honor."

"Brunch?"

"Max is famous for his brunches. He's very excited about getting *Galaxy* home and inaugurating it. You're already making the news. Page Six of the *Post* glorified you. Now it's Max's turn to show you off."

Blake Hamilton was introduced to the world as the new rising star. *The New York Times* claimed *Galaxy* as the painting that marked the beginning of neoabstractionism. Blake was well on his way to becoming the hottest artist on the scene, and despite the "dirty little secret," the attention he received was intoxicating and hard to resist.

Madeleine ate it all up, giving her friends the daily scoop on Blake in order to impress them, thus, becoming important herself by association. She called me after reading another review. "What did I tell you? *Our* Blake is making headlines."

"You sound like *you* discovered him, Mother."

"I'm just being enthusiastic. I also understand through the grapevine that Max Girard is throwing him a little do. After Alden's death, we could all use a change of pace to get us out of the doldrums. I'm exhausted from all this grieving."

"That sounds positive."

"That's not to say I'm not devastated still, but this will be the perfect antidote. I'm thinking of getting a new hairstyle to perk me up."

A week later, the engraved Cartier invitations were in the mail:

Max Girard invites you to meet the artist

Blake Hamilton

Valentine's Day — noon to three o'clock

1790 Park Avenue

RSVP 212-555-0055

Madeleine was the first to respond.

. . .

Sunday mornings all over America, a grand ritual otherwise known as brunch, is played out. It is a time when the bleary-eyed, still sleepy from a late Saturday night or on a hangover lull, make their way to somebody's home for Bloody Marys and a chance to regroup before the crash of a new week.

Never is brunch more apparent than in Manhattan, where one goes all out to make the interlude between Saturday night and Monday morning a welcome hiatus at which guests can be gently eased back to reality. Conversations move slowly compared to the Saturday-night breezy banter, designed to impress. By Sunday, people are too tired from overeating and boozing the night before to even care. In that way, brunch is an occasion that brings us down rather than forcing us to rise to the occasion and keep up facades. Saturday night is bigger than life, all dressed up with diamond brooches and ribbons in the hair. Sunday is bags under the eyes, a worn-out-on-its-last-legs day when protocol doesn't count and no-frills is more the order of the day. Saturday night is showy and pushy. Sunday is casual. Show up on Sunday in a pair of jeans, and no one blinks. That is, unless the brunch is hosted by Max Girard and the guest of honor happens to be Blake Hamilton.

In February, after the show closed at the Cole, Max brought *Galaxy* home and hung it over his fireplace, the first thing you saw upon entering his living room. When word got around that Blake Hamilton, the sexy artist, was going to be the guest du jour, the New York art crowd went crazy. Everyone wanted to be invited.

"It will be small and intimate," Max assured Blake. "The idea is to pass you around like a choice hors d'oeuvre and show off your main attribute: *Galaxy*.

Blake cringed.

Over lunch, Alexandra reiterated: "Max is inviting just a few of his nearest and dearest. He does this whenever a hotshot emerges on the scene, and that's you, darling. All the art phonies and big spenders will be there. All you need to do is show up and let Max do his thing. Samantha received an invitation, as well as Madeleine and Spencer, so you'll feel right at home with your people."

"I don't want to see Alexandra ever again," I told my mother when Max's invitation arrived in the mail that week.

"Oh, stop it," she admonished. "Max is honoring Blake. You *have* to be there. I'm buying a new outfit for the occasion."

"It's only brunch, Mother, not one of your charity benefits. Whatever you wear will be fine."

"You still have so much to learn, sweetheart," Madeleine said.

"Hold on to your skivvies," Lily Ann said when I told her. "You ain't seen nothin' yet."

"It's going to be awkward as hell. I was hoping to never again lay eyes on Alexandra. The beauty of living in New York is its anonymity."

"Alexandra *is* New York," Lily Ann said. "You can't escape her."

Sunday arrived and with it fifty of Max's friends, who, usually fashionably late, appeared at the stroke of noon so as not to miss a minute of the festivities and to be the first to get their hands on Blake. New York's most attractive and elite—the women in their latest designer duds, the men in colorful ties and jackets—swarmed around Blake like bees ready to sample his nectar. Max's famous industrial-strength Bloody Marys sat in glass pitchers on the buffet table next to the mimosas. Max had hired Incredible Edibles, the tony catering company he used for such occasions. The food extended the entire length of the table, with enough selections to satisfy the most fastidious taste buds.

"This can't hold a candle to Gilda's brunches," Madeleine said, who'd shown up looking like a walking work of art in her new Emilio Pucci, with her new hair created by yet another of the trendy stylists who had recently emerged on the scene. "But leave it to Max: He puts it all out there. And Blake is eating it up. He certainly knows how to hold his own. Everyone's wild about him. Look at the guests: They're practically swooning at his feet."

That was the easy part. All Blake had to do was stand there looking gorgeous while the brunch contingent swooped down upon him, trying to sound erudite and hoping to learn all about what made him the singular sensation he was. I watched him and felt a wave of nausea creep through me as I mentally rewound the tape of Bobby Tisdale.

Finally, Blake stepped away and found me nibbling on a salmon mousse tart.

"How are *you* doing?" he asked, moving me outside to the terrace, where a blast of February air hit me in the face.

"Still breathing, I think. Alexandra and I haven't spoken a word."

"The hell with Alexandra. Just take her in stride and try and enjoy yourself. This is actually quite humorous, if you can see it that way."

"Yeah, very funny. How can you make light of this, Blake?"

"Come on, I meant Alexandra. Watching her work the room does have an element of comedy attached to it."

This was the first time in days since I had seen Blake. Surprisingly, under the circumstances, he looked well rested. I was also struck by the fact that after everything he had told me, I still missed him.

"I'm so glad you're here," he said. "I'm hoping we can put our differences aside and start over."

"I needed to sort through some of my feelings," I said.

"And have you?"

"Yes."

"Care to elaborate?"

"This isn't the time."

"May I be so bold as to invite you to dinner on Saturday?"

And in a moment of pure impulse, I agreed to have dinner with Blake.

A smile came over his face. "I was hoping you'd say that."

• • •

Blake couldn't have been happier, though on the inside, as far as his "contract" with Max and Alexandra was concerned, he knew he was trapped forever. Max's artsy brunch was just a prelude. Blake was being dangled like a carrot to lure people into buying his art. Alexandra and Max, beaming from ear to ear, watched their protégé strut his stuff. It bordered on revolting.

After the plates were cleared and the guests were sated, Max gathered everyone into the living room, where they congregated around *Galaxy*.

"For those of you who haven't had the chance to talk with the artist because you were too busy stuffing your mouths"—Max oozed charm—"now's your chance to pick his lively and most creative brain. Allow me to introduce our new star of the moment, Blake Hamilton."

Blake bowed. "I'd be glad to answer any questions," he said with his usual air of casual suaveness that seemed almost contrived.

Immediately, hands flew in the air, and Blake addressed each question one by one. As he waxed eloquent, he watched to see my reactions. I stood there listening as *Galaxy* was dissected in the most absurd ways. A tall strawberry blonde with a southern drawl inched her way through the crowd until she was standing in front of Blake, flaunting her ample breasts in his face and batting her eyes for even more effect.

"I just absolutely *adore* your work," she said. "Can you tell us how a style is developed, or is it simply something you're born with, like good teeth, for instance?"

Blake caught my eye. It was all I could do to keep from laughing.

More often than not, Blake and I were connected. With a mere glimmer of a glance, we were able to share in a moment. In that respect, we had a lot in common: We understood eachother's insights and reactions. But in the big picture, I couldn't deny that everything had changed. His confession had put a rift between us that could never be repaired. As I stood there watching him impress the crowd, I knew it was only a matter of time until I would tell Blake Hamilton I no longer wanted to see him.

TWENTY-FOUR

A bachelor is a selfish,
undeserving guy who has cheated
some woman out of a divorce.

—Don Quinn

Etiquette books don't stress proper protocol for ending relationships. There aren't always answers as to even why they *must* end, except in my case, it was obvious. But there comes a day—a morning, an evening—when you look at your mate and know it isn't working. Sometimes it takes nothing more than peering over the breakfast table when he asks you to pass the jam. In that fleeting nanosecond, something inside you goes flat, and you realize you never want to pass jam to him again.

Or when he takes your hand in a movie theater, or crossing the street, you are acutely aware of the gnawing feeling that tells you this isn't the hand you want to keep holding for-ever. Not that the person attached to it isn't good or kind, isn't a wonderful father, a fine lover, intelligent, funny, and eager to please but suddenly, the rhythm is off, the balance askew. You search your mind, asking yourself why, and, unable to find the answers, con-tinue on, pretending everything is fine. Then a time comes when you might be walking alone or are in bed in a dreamy, half-conscious state and you allow your mind to drift. And it is there, in the quiet, secret place of your unconscious that the answer becomes as clear and cold as ice. It comes from a place so deep inside where you never before trespassed—that uninhabited spot where self-reflection was off-limits, for fear that what you might find would be so confound-ing you might not survive it. And so, once again, you dismiss it.

Weeks, months, maybe years later, older now and less compla-cent, you at last see your way clear and find yourself asking the same question: What happened? When the fog dissipates, you take that first step, then another, and dare to explore the hidden recesses of your mind. Despite all the shoulds, coulds, and maybes, after all the con jobs you did on yourself, you arrive at the truth: You were never really in love. Or, perhaps the love that once sustained you has now died.

For me, that truth became apparent even before Blake had blown the lid off our relationship. While he and I had shared mag-nificent sex all these months, it seemed to be more about that and less about the basic, fundamental values of which he seemed to be so lacking. Since his arrival to New York, coupled now with his deceit, I felt depleted of emotion, as though something inside me had emp-tied. After careful and painful deliberation, I decided to make a clean break.

Yet it wasn't that easy. Severing ties with Alexandra and the Cole Gallery had been a piece of cake. Leaving Blake was another story. A part of me still wanted to hang on, to believe he was remorseful, that he could change. I wanted desperately to excuse the whole Paris fi-asco, but I knew I couldn't. Doing so would go against everything I believed, every ounce of integrity I held dear, all the teachings my father had passed on to me. By staying with Blake, I would be surrendering my soul.

I knew that he would try and convince me otherwise. Even the stunning ambience of Gilt restaurant couldn't change my mind. Up until now I had shared my decision with no one but Lily Ann.

"I can't believe it. Blake is such a catch," she said.

"I'm not after a catch. I'm after true love and as much as I wish it weren't so, Blake isn't the one."

"At least your mother will be happy. She's always had her eye on a guy like Spencer—better marriage material."

"My mother is starting to pick up vibes with Spencer. When Roger Sutton showed up after Alden's death, she was puzzled. When the two of them left her apartment together, she really got suspicious."

"You can't fool Madeleine Krasner-Wolfe," Lily Ann said. "Never could. Never will. She was always on to us. Did you tell her that Spencer was gay?"

"Never. She'd probably try and convert him," I said.

It was difficult to go to Gilt without the purpose of enjoying oneself. The decor alone instantly drew one in and could elevate the mood of even the most cynical and depressed. Chef Paul Liebrandt's food presentation resembled poetry on a plate, staged so beautifully it was worthy of exaltation. When I dipped my fork into my lobster seasoned with vanilla and set on a cauliflower puree, I actually gasped from sheer delight. Blake was equally impressed by his woodsy scented loin of lamb, slow-roasted with pine needles and surrounded by bits of veal sweetbreads. When the dessert arrived, our eyes popped. Our wasabi and green apple sorbets were accompanied by a treasure chest filled with chocolates that was unlatched by our server. But none of this could raise our spirits on an evening that was fraught with deep sadness and regret for something that might have been but could be no longer.

Blake listened while I tried explaining why I needed to break it off.

"It's really all about the lie, isn't it?"

"Not entirely," I said. "I've been feeling this way for a while."

"I won't even ask us to be friends," he said, "because I know we already are, aren't we? But the rest of it was so good, Samantha."

"I know it was—in many ways. But it isn't how I envision my future."

"What does that mean?"

"I'm not sure. I just know that you and I together are wrong."

He found the courage to ask the one crushing question: "Do you hate me?"

"No, I feel sorry for you."

"That's even worse. The thought of you pitying me is more than I can stand."

But, since it was by his own doing, what other choice was there?

After rehashing it over and over again, through unrelenting tears, I dared to give Blake the final piercing verbal blow. "I don't love you, Blake," I said.

He sat, silent for a few seconds, then caught his breath. "I *never* should have told you the truth."

"That's crazy. I would have found out eventually. You can't hide these things."

"That's what did it, isn't it? The fact that I'm an imposter—a liar?"

"That certainly didn't help. But it's not only that. This has been coming for a while."

"It's Spencer, isn't it?"

"Of course not. Spencer has nothing to do with it."

"Someone else?"

"No one. At least not for now. Who knows? I might never meet Mr. Right."

"Someone as beautiful as you? I doubt that."

"I thank you for that," I said. "This is hard, Blake. It really is. For us both, but if you dig deep down and are really honest with yourself, you'll see that we're both such different people."

Blake couldn't speak. He was more morose than I had ever seen him. But there seemed to be something else he wanted to ask me.

We made it through coffee in awkward silence, and then Blake finally said, "We can still see each other for the occasional dinner, can't we?"

"Let's give it some time," I said. "I think it's best to separate for a few months until the rough edges are smoothed over." I sounded frighteningly like Dear Abby.

"I'll never forget you, Samantha."

"Of course you won't, you dope," I said, feeling a sense of relief I hadn't felt in months.

Blake paid the bill and escorted me to the door. "Can I see you home?"

"I think I should grab a cab," I said.

And there we stood, in front of the Palace Hotel on a cold winter night, passersby pulling their collars up around their necks, with the noise of car horns and the chilly Manhattan wind encircling us as we hugged each other tightly and said our good-byes. Then, releasing myself, I got into the taxi and on toward my uncertain future, never once looking back.

EPILOGUE

It's a wonderful thing, as time goes by,
to be with someone who looks into your face
when you've gotten old and still sees what
you think you look like.

—*The Bachelor*

Two years later

The Delano Hotel and its elegant poolside bunga-
lows, with white interiors and custom-designed furnish-
ings and private patios and marble bathrooms, was the
jewel of South Beach. Max Girard kept a bungalow at his disposal for his frequent visits throughout the year.

Now, in December, he sat in the Rose Bar, waiting for
Madeleine to return from the Aqua Spa, relaxed and ready
for a drink.

The last few months in New York had been hectic, with
back-and-forth wedding arrangements, but now all the
pieces had come together. They were finally here, having

arrived a few days before their bicoastal guests, most of whom would be checking in on Friday.

When Spencer's partner, David Samuels, and I first met, our eyes locked, and it was love at first sight. We dated for nine months, and on my fortieth birthday, he presented me with a rock so large that Madeleine joked it might give me carpal tunnel syndrome.

"I'll take my chances," I said.

Madeleine's wish for a double wedding had come true. She and Max Girard and David and I were to be married on Saturday night in the Delano's Orchard, a lushly landscaped lawn just past the pool area, or the Water Salon, as it was called, where soothing underwater music lulled tired swimmers to languish lazily on their floats.

I called her cell. "Mother. Did you get ahold of Duncan? He promised to let me know about the gardenias by this afternoon." Max had flown Alexandra's very own Duncan down to Florida to orchestrate the wedding flowers.

"Darling, it's all arranged. I spoke with him an hour ago. The pool will have floating gardenias, I promise. Will you and David be joining us for dinner? Max made a din-din reservation for eight o'clock. Lily Ann is invited, too."

"David left New York an hour ago, so yes, if he gets here on time, we'd love to."

"Don't forget, we have our fittings with Raffaella on Thursday. She needs to check your gown one more time." Raffaella, Madeleine's dressmaker extraordinaire, was also on tap, flown in from Manhattan to handle any last-minute fashion disasters.

"It's only Tuesday, Mother."

"I know, but there's so much to do. And sweetie, you might want to skip the desserts between now and Saturday, just to be safe. Vera Wang doesn't plan on bulges. Are you frowning, Samantha? Because I can hear you frowning over the phone. You don't want wrinkles on your wedding day."

"I'm sure a shot of Botox will take care of that," I said.

"Kiss, kiss, and huggie love until later," Madeleine said, hanging up.

She turned to Max. "That girl is a bundle of nerves, darling."

"To be expected. She's a blushing bride," he said.

"Well, so am I." Madeleine snuggled in closer to Max. "And I'd absolutely adore a gin and tonic."

"Tanqueray and tonic with a twist, Simon," Max instructed the bartender.

"Coming right up, Mr. Girard," he said, passing a bowl of cashew nuts.

The guest list came to two hundred and fifty of our closest friends. The Delano went all out, promising to leave no hors d'oeuvre unheated, no bouquet left undone, and no sushi unaccompanied by chopsticks. They even assigned two personal wedding planners to go over each detail.

The dinner menu was created by Chef Claude Troisgros and directed by Jeffrey Chodorow, whose job it was to oversee everything. The modern French cuisine was paired with flavors of Brazil and would include such fabulous culinary items as fresh hearts-of-palm salad with grilled octopus and lime vinaigrette; roasted Atlantic salmon fillet wrapped in tomato and zucchini gratin; or caramelized rack of lamb with toasted Moroccan couscous, almonds and pearl onions, and a passion-fruit-mint glaze. As for the desserts, Madeleine and I were still racking our brains between the chocopistachio—melted bittersweet-chocolate cake with pistachio ice cream—or the strawberry and meringue symphony with lemon curd and liquor and chocolate swirls.

Sam-Sam, as David now called me (short for Samantha Samuels), had helped turn independent, feisty me into the biggest JAP-in-training on the East Coast. As much as I resisted, I had acclimated well to my new role. Having Madeleine around to guide me only perfected my technique. At least until the wedding was over, I would give myself over to my mother and bask in the glow of being utterly spoiled rotten.

Lily Ann, also staying at the Delano, had flown down with me to lend moral support, with Bennett arriving on Saturday morning in time for the wedding.

"I can't believe I'm actually wearing a white Vera Wang," I said. "I look like a marshmallow in tulle. The gown needed a seat of its own on the plane."

"Oh, just sit back and enjoy it," Lily Ann said. "You deserve to be completely pampered."

"David says this is just the beginning. That he was put on God's good earth to keep me living in the style to which I should be disgustingly accustomed."

"I always said that David had style."

"A girl can get used to this. And wait till you hear the rest: I'll be giving up my job at MoMA for a few months."

"Being an adjunct curator of drawings doesn't come around that often," Lily Ann said. "You're crazy."

"No, I'm pregnant—and I expect you to keep that entre nous. I'm planning on taking maternity leave in June. I'll go back three months after the baby is born. But we're not telling anyone until I start to show."

"Oh my God, Sam, what fantastic news. Was it planned?"

"I stopped using protection two months ago. I never expected it to happen so fast, but here I am, a blushing pregnant bride."

"Wait till Madeleine gets wind of this. You'll be maternity shopping for weeks to come. Oh, Sam, your life is turning into a fairy-tale ending."

"Please don't go getting all soppy on me. I was counting on you to help me maintain my caustic edge."

"All right, I'm going to tell you something: Bennett and I are pregnant, too."

"You mean you upstaged me again?"

"Yes, and our kids will be best friends and go to Brearley and Bennington together."

"This is a joke, right?"

"I swear it. I'm entering my third month." She lifted her T-shirt, displaying a slight bulge. "Can you stand it?"

"This is cause for celebration. Unfortunately, we'll have to settle for apple juice instead of champagne."

We went down to the beach and walked along the water's edge. Sitting in the oversize chairs, we stared out at the ocean, reviewing our lives and how far we had come in the past few years. The sun was lowering in the sky, and it seemed like we'd sat for hours when our conversation was interrupted by David's phone call.

"The plane just landed, honey. I'll grab my bag and taxi over to the hotel."

"Mom and Max want us to join them for dinner. Lily Ann is coming, too."

"In that case, how can I say no? You know how much I love flirting with Lily Ann."

"I'll tell her you said that."

"But I love flirting with you even more."

"Spoken like a true husband," I said.

The next few days were abuzz with wedding activities and last-minute details that needed attention. The entire Bleckner family, including Fern and her new lover, Chastity, had taken rooms at the hotel. Celeste, who had gained back all her weight after Eddie Sloat walked out on her for a manicurist/massage therapist/waitress, turned her attention to the only two men she could count on who would never let her down: Ben & Jerry.

On Friday morning Max had sent a car to the airport to pick up Alexandra and Blake. When Celeste saw Blake by the pool later in the afternoon, she practically went apoplectic. She extended her new breasts, which she referred to as her "body jewelry," and quickly adjusted her swimsuit to hide the cellulite that was starting to form on her upper thighs. She flirted away while Blake, completely oblivious, emerged from the pool in his black and very snug bikini swimsuit. Celeste, assuming the position of the femme fatale she longed to become, stretched herself out on the chaise, trying to engage Blake in small talk.

"Blake, I never knew you had *those* kinds of muscles hidden beneath your clothes. Even dripping wet, you look good enough to eat."

Blake picked up a towel and dried himself off.

"If you'd like, I can help you do that," she said.

He gave her his don't-even-think-about-it look and sauntered off, leaving Celeste to wallow in her misery. When he was out of sight, she headed straight to the poolside bistro and ordered a hot-fudge sundae in which to drown her hatred of men.

The past two years had been kind to Blake. His paintings were selling like hotcakes, and the Met had decided to take *Exotica* for their permanent collection. Dealers all over the world were making offers right and left. Thanks to Max, who kept Blake in the mainstream, he had made a small fortune, most of which he handed over to Max and Alexandra. He had become so famous that *Time* magazine had nominated him as a Man of the Year. He didn't make it but did appear on one of their covers. He became the most eligible bachelor in New York, getting into the panties of horny debutantes, rich widows, and supermodels, but never into Alexandra's. Try as she might to lure him in, he always reneged. On occasion, when he rejected her advances, she threatened to expose him as the fraud he was.

"Don't be stupid," Blake told her. "I've made you a very rich woman. Are you willing to give that up for one lousy fuck?"

But Alexandra never stopped trying. One night she got completely smashed after a party she had thrown in her apartment. Blake carried her off to bed, where she begged him to undress her and sketch her in the nude. "I'll pay you a thousand dollars if you do it," she said. Blake agreed. While Alexandra lay spread-eagle on the bed, her hands alternating between her nipples and her vagina, Blake sketched her. He later turned that charcoal sketch into a small abstract painting that bore no resemblance to Alexandra at all. A few months later, he sold it to a couple in Greenwich, Connecticut, who paid Blake twenty thousand dollars for it. He titled it *Alexandra in Heat*. He never told her or Max about it and kept every penny for himself.

As for Spencer, one night over beluga at Petrossian with Madeleine—who had called him up because she was in a caviar mood but really wanted to get the scoop—she asked him point-blank: "Spencer darling, are you gay?"

He hesitated for a moment and, realizing he could never fool Madeleine, admitted the truth: "Yes," he said. "Did Samantha tell you?"

"Samantha hasn't told me anything since the day she first started talking. Vibes, sweetie. I've got the vibes. I also have a man for you."

"I'm seeing someone," Spencer said.

"Who? That fairy from Lenox? You can do better than that."

The next day, independently wealthy Grant Parker, bon vivant, and Manhattan's most eligible gay catch among the forties set, called Spencer and invited him to dinner on his yacht, which he kept moored at the Seventy-ninth Street Boat Basin. He also gave Spencer the best blow job of his life. A month later, Spencer and Grant were an item.

"Roger took it surprisingly well," Spencer later told me.

"And you were worried," I said.

Madeleine took all the credit and prided herself on being a gay rights activist.

The wedding came off without a hitch. Everyone was high on love and endless bottles of champagne, which flowed until the wee hours. Accolades abounded over the food, the flowers, the gowns, the band. Madeleine, not wanting to upstage me, looked gorgeous and quietly sexy in her Oscar de la Renta that Oscar himself had designed exclusively for her.

"Oscar and I go back years," she told all those who commented on the dress. "He *begged* me to let him whip up a little something for the wedding. He and Grayson were big pals."

When Alexandra came up to me in the receiving line, a momentary rush of adrenaline hit me as I faced my enemy head-on.

"Oh, Samantha, darling," Alexandra said, "let's just pat our boo-boos and make up. We both have Blake's best interests at heart, and it should make you happy to know that Max and I are watching over him while he takes the world by storm."

With that, she hugged me tightly, her boobs undulating in her Christina Herrera red satin gown that clung to every curve and had every man in the place drooling.

"And just in case you were wondering, the sex between Blake and me is really hot."

On any occasion other than my wedding day, I would have punched her in the mouth.

Before dessert was served, Max rose from his chair, picked up his butter knife, and clinked it against his water glass. A hush fell over the room.

"I'd like to toast my beautiful bride," he said, looking at Madeleine, who, try as she might, couldn't so much as muster up a blush. "To happy endings, darling," he said, raising his champagne flute to hers. "And to *our* Blake Hamilton, artist extraordinaire, who brought us together."

Madeleine followed suit. With her own glass raised, she turned to me. "To bachelor degrees," she said, "with highest honors."

"What does that mean?" David leaned over and asked me.

"Inside joke," I said, smiling.

The loose ends of everyone's lives were starting to come together, except for Blake's. He moved through his days as though in a trance. He was never completely convinced that I wouldn't blow his cover, or that I wouldn't blab and have it all come out in the open. But I never would. That constant fear was the punishment he would have to endure for the rest of his life. In the meantime, Max and Alexandra pulled his strings and turned Blake into their marionette who flipped and flopped in any direction they wanted him to go.

On a Saturday afternoon in March, more than a year later, Blake—who had recently returned from London, where the buzz of the day was that the Tate Modern had picked up one of his pieces—called and asked if we could meet for drinks. I decided to put the past memories on hold and agreed to meet. "Three o'clock would work for me," I said.

David had taken the baby to the park. I left him a note telling him where I was. Blake and I met in the lobby of the Ritz-Carlton, where he was staying.

My first reaction upon seeing him was that he looked slightly older and tired, although his boyish charm was inescapable. He smiled widely when he greeted me, revealing a few crinkly lines around his eyes, which made him look even sexier than I had remembered.

"Samantha . . . or is it Sam-Sam now?"

"Please," I said, "I want to kill David every time he says that."

"Well, I think it's endearing. I like David."

"What's not to like?" I said. "He's wonderful."

"How's Victoria?"

"Growing like a beautiful little flower."

"Samantha, I'm so happy for you, I really am."

"And you, Blake?"

He paused, taking a sip of his Campari over chipped ice. "Oh, I'm doing okay."

"Okay? I can't pick up a magazine without reading about you. All the paparazzi have you linked on the arm of another beautiful woman. You're famous. How's the work going?"

He looked at me, trying to decipher a deeper meaning behind my question. "I'm toying around with another technique."

"Really? But you've been doing so well with your abstract paintings."

"I know, but I want to do something new—something that's all mine." He searched my face for a reaction but found none. "I suppose I'm becoming bored," he finally admitted. "I often entertain the idea of moving away."

"Really? Where?"

"To another place where I can be alone and not be constantly mauled by the madding crowds of art patrons, curators, docents, and galley owners."

"So how *is* Alexandra?" I asked.

"She keeps me hopping, plans on showing my work every two years, and tries to run my life. But Max and Madeleine seem happy."

"Madeleine knows how to show a man a good time. Yes, they're fine. She's thrilled to be a bride again. Max says he sees you regularly and that he and Mom and you and Alexandra had dinner together."

"We did. Alexandra has become annoyingly persistent. She latches on to me every chance she gets."

"So I understand. She said the sex between you is hot."

Blake threw back his head and laughed. "When did she tell you that?"

"On my wedding day."

"Oh, *that's* cool."

"Alexandra was never one for protocol," I said.

"That's Alexandra for you: always living in her fantasy world."

"Not that it matters anymore," I said, "because we've all moved beyond that, but *have* you slept with Alexandra?"

Blake picked up my hand and gazed at me with his sincere, puppy-dog look I had come to know over the many years.

"Of course not, Samantha," he said. "I may be many things, but a liar I'm not."

"Right," I said, almost wanting to cry.

Two hours later, I returned to David's and my apartment on East End Avenue. I walked into the living room and found him with Victoria asleep in his arms. A painting by Blake, given to us as a wedding gift, hung on the wall above them. It was titled *Megalomania,* which Blake had said represented delusion of greatness or wealth.

"Look at it and think of me," he had said.

A few months later, I took it down and replaced it with a landscape that David and I bought in Cape Cod. It was a painting of sand dunes and water views with rolling tumbleweeds in the background and a large blue sky overhead. It was serene and comforting, and whenever Victoria looked up at it with her big navy blue eyes, she pointed to a seashell and laughed her sweet baby laugh.

My mind wandered back to that time. The artist, a blond-haired girl with smiling eyes, told us she had painted it on a day when the sun was high in the sky and she found out she was pregnant with her first child.

"It's a happy painting, then," I said. "And we want to buy it."

David wrote out a check, and we carried it off, my pregnant belly extending in front of me like a giant balloon on that hot August day.

Suddenly, I was jolted back to the present. I looked at the clock. It was nearing five o'clock. David's eyes opened slightly, seeing me standing here, he smiled through a sleepy haze. Victoria stirred, yawned, and fell back asleep in the crook of her father's arm.

"When did you get back?" he whispered.

"A few minutes ago."

"How's Blake?"

"Blake is basking in the glow of being Blake," I said.

David nodded, his eyelids lowering once again.

The late afternoon sun poured through the window, spilling its warm rays upon my husband and child. Still in my coat, I lingered for a bit, watching them sleep. Winter was nearly over, and the scent of spring was in the air—a time of renewal for us all. I had finally come home.

JUDITH MARKS-WHITE joined the staff of the *Westport News* in Westport, Connecticut, in 1985, penning a humorous/reflective essay column about life, love, and family dynamics. She also worked for Time Inc. and has taught writing for many years. She has received numerous writing awards from the New England Press Association, the Connecticut Press Club, the National Federation of Press Women, and Matrix: Women in Communications. She is a member of the National Society of Newspaper Columnists, PEN America, and the National Association of PEN Women. She was an adjunct professor of English at Norwalk Community College for eleven years where she was awarded Teacher of the Year for 2005 and where she remains an instructor in the field of humor writing. Judith has contributed to many anthologies including the *Chicken Soup for the Soul* books, *I Killed June Cleaver, Pandemonium: Or Life With Kids,* and numerous publications on a variety of humor. She lectures frequently to wide audiences on the writing and marketing of humor and other related topics. In March 2003, Judith was honored as one of the Ruth Steinkrauss-Cohen Outstanding Women in Connecticut, celebrating her achievement and dedication to public service through the art of column writing. Her first novel, *Seducing Harry: An Epicurean Affair* was published in 2007. Judith lives in Westport, Connecticut, with her husband, Mark. Judith Marks-White can be reached on her website *www.judithmarks-white.com* for speaking engagements and book talks/signings.